T0049687

SONS OF THE EAST

Ifeoma Chinwuba

Published in 2023 by

Griots Lounge Publishing Canada
www.griotslounge.ca
Email: info@griotslounge.ca

SONS OF THE EAST
Copyright © 2023 IFEOMA CHINWUBA

All rights reserved. The use of any part of this publication reproduced, transmitted in any form or by any means, electronic, mechanical, photocopying, recording, or otherwise, or stored in a retrieval system, without the prior written consent of the publisher—or, in case of photocopying or other reprographic copying, a licence from the Canadian Copyright Licensing Agency—is an infringement of the copyright law.

This is a work of fiction. Any names or characters, businesses or places, events or incidents, are fictitious. Any resemblance to actual persons, living or dead, or actual events is purely coincidental.

Library and Archives Canada Cataloguing in Publication

ISBN: 978-1-7386993-0-8

Interior Design by Rachelle Painchaud-Nash

Printed and bound in Canada.

With the generous support of the Manitoba Arts Council.

...the man was the greatest of all the sons of the east.

Book of Job 1:3

Other books by the author

Merchants of Flesh

Fearless

Waiting for Maria

African Romance

Head Boy

The Pandemic And Me (ed.)

DEDICATION

To Nnewi, revered father

Oguta, nourishing mother

Onitsha Ado N'Idu, illustrious husband.

PROLOGUE

One of the women stared blankly, unbelieving, at the turn of events. It seemed just like yesterday that she had donned the black robes. A year had passed without her beloved, and the day to divest the mourning garments had dawned.

"Wear white," the women's leader advised.

"I like blue."

"White," Eliza repeated with a scintilla of impatience. "It is significant for the next step."

"What next step?"

"Just a little while, and you will know."

The widow gave in. As a widow, you became a child again. People told you what to do; you could no longer think for yourself. Her ankle-length lace gown made her look like a bride. In her mind's eye, she saw the cairn which hid her beloved. She sighed, jiggled her thighs, and fondled the chaplet in her hand. The other widow, Mary Jane, sat beside her, bright-eyed and eager.

She could hear someone rising to their feet. All eyes swivelled to him, including the widow's. He was the oldest man in the community. A murmur arose among those gathered, then subsided and died.

"Opaku, I greet you."

He lifted his palms in greeting, pivoting to the left and right to take in the assembly of townsfolk seated in a circumference of benches around him. He cleared his throat forcefully and removed his red felt cap, which he rotated in his hands. He turned to face the widows.

"Our wives, it is true that a big calamity befell you. Do not our people equate a husband to a woman's chewing stick, which suddenly snaps and breaks? Your chewing sticks have broken. But our brothers left behind many kinsmen who can assume a husband's role."

He turned to the menfolk. "Do I speak for you?"

"Ishienyi," they hailed. That was his title: Elephant Head.

Encouraged, the fellow faced the widows again.

"So, I ask you, Mary Jane, out of your late husband's kinsmen, who do you choose to take his place?"

"Ebuka," the woman replied without hesitation.

A murmuring rose among the community. Ebuka, the young and upcoming trader whose mother belonged to the same age group as Mary Jane.

A shrill voice rose from the women's corner. "Of all the men in our community, you target my son."

The elder ignored the emoting and continued. "You?" he asked the second widow.

All eyes returned to the woman. She was in her prime. Her skin, the colour of ripe papaya, was translucent. The men salivated. The married women in the audience fidgeted anxiously. Everyone held their breath.

The widow wrung her hands. So this was the next step. Distribution of the widows.

With operatic suddenness, she cried out, "Blood of Jesus! So it is true; I am a widow. A wido-ow-ow-ow!"

Her cry reverberated in the enclosure. It hit the walls, bounced back, and echoed in the air, "Widow-ow-ow-ow."

The brethren horripilated, shook their heads, and grieved anew.

CHAPTER 1

December 2013

Echezona Okonkwo, CEO of Zona Group, watched intently as Chief Igwilo went through the process of releasing Jasper from bondage. That was how Igbo people considered the end of an apprenticeship: the end of a person's period of bondage. Many people gathered in the Opaku village square, under a canopy of foliage of mango, almond, and oak trees, to witness this landmark event in the life of the community. A phalanx of apprentices would gain their "freedom" from their masters. Many interned in the motor parts sector, a few in fabric sales, and a couple graduated from the patent medicine business and second-hand goods sectors. A pair was trained in the building materials industry.

Business tycoons, tradespeople, kinsmen, and friends wandered about, but Zona was fixated on his brother, Jasper. He watched the proceedings hawk-eyed, unblinking. The significance of the ceremony was not lost on him. His brother would begin to hustle, make money, and aspire for social standing in the community. He could even acquire a title, a *nom de guerre* that oozed grandeur and inflicted dread on all around him. He punched the thought down.

Zona leaned forward, stomaching the hunger pangs that rattled his insides, intent on catching every word. Envy and trepidation roiled him as he listened to the words of praise tumbling from Igwilo's lips.

"… Jasper Okonkwo served me diligently, respectfully, and honestly these past seven years. Therefore, per our agreement, I release you to start your own business. I present this key to a shop in Lagos, rent of one year paid and stocked with assorted motor spares to the tune of five hundred thousand naira, all of which I offer you freely."

"Oke Nmanwu!" The crowd of onlookers hailed the master. It was the mogul's title, Great Masquerade.

Chief Igwilo paused to bask in the recognition, stroked his white goatee, and adjusted his shirt, fashioned from the local ishiagu fabric. Yellow images of a roaring lion's head dotted the red velvet material. A square of kerchief poked out of the lone breast pocket. The okra-coloured kerchief matched the tips of the crocodile-skin shoes that peeked out from under his black gabardine trousers. He was known to pass down his outfits to his apprentices after a few months of use. Jasper, kneeling in front of him, was decked in one of such hand-me-downs.

"Here is a cheque for five hundred thousand naira, seed money to launch you on your way." He waved the paper for all to see. "May heaven and our ancestors favour you."

"Amen!" the witnesses roared. Zona kept mute.

From all sides, people again saluted the master, "Oke Nmanwu!"

The so-hailed swivelled three-sixty degrees as he waved to the spectators. He had invited some of his business confreres to the event. One by one, they rose and offered something to Jasper to support their colleague. Some passed envelopes to the young man, and others released wads of notes over his body. The notes fluttered in the air and sailed to the ground. One mogul spoke their minds when he echoed Chief Igwilo's praises for this exemplary apprentice. The man revealed that the Chief never had any cause to complain about Jasper. He presented an envelope to the freedman and enjoined the other apprentices to emulate Jasper.

Chief Igwilo concluded with a popular Igbo proverb: "If a child washes his hands, he can dine with elders. Jasper has washed his hands. He can now ascend to the table of masters."

Zona cringed.

"His type is rare," a squat spectator affirmed as Jasper rose and bowed to the throng of people before bending down to gather the splayed notes. A motley orchestra struck up a number, and invitees stood up to dance and plaster Jasper with more notes.

"There are no two masters like Oke Mmanwu," one of the guests declared. "First, no quarrel with the apprentice, then to go over and above the statutory settlement expected from a master. One-year rent of a fully stocked shop. It is unparalleled."

No quarrel with the apprentice. Dishonest masters often picked a spurious fight with an apprentice on the cusp of liberty, accused him of vagrancy, insubordination, or theft, and threw him out, denying him his hard-earned compensation.

Zona flinched again. Many times, he had short-changed his apprentices in this manner. He knew that he should join the tycoons to "bless" Jasper. But he could not rouse himself. Animosity towards his brother enveloped him. He slunk deeper into the foam, his eyes darting from one corner of the square to another. Apprentices wove through the crowd, shaking hands here, embracing there. Young girls milled around as well, looking to catch the eye of the freedmen. It was general knowledge that once a man completed service to his master, he would think of starting a family.

Jasper was all smiles, revealing his finely chiselled teeth like corn on the cob. He was beside himself with excitement as he fondled the key, caressed the envelopes, and cradled the notes. The money would serve to register a company and rent an apartment. He weighed the cash gifts. Heavy. He already knew the name he would give his business. At twenty-seven years old, he was setting out late. Most apprentices started "Igba boi" when they were eleven or twelve. Before twenty, they gained their freedom. Twenty-seven, however, still cut it. As a popular saying goes, "When you arrive at the market, you begin your trading."

"Oke Nmanwu!" he gushed, bending and clasping his right ankle with his right hand in deference. He proceeded to kneel fully. All his life, he would defer to Chief Igwilo because all the knowledge he had acquired about the spare parts trade came from him, as well as many things about life in general, like peaceful co-existence and devotion to one's wife. *A man who loves his wife is only loving himself,* Oke Nmanwu used to tell his servants. Jasper's only regret was that his father was no longer alive to witness this milestone in his life. Henceforth, Oke Nmanwu would be his surrogate father.

"Chief, daalu," a woman shouted above the music and cacophony of sounds in the square. "Thank you." She flapped a plaited palm fan at him. It was Iyom Mgboye, the matriarch of the Okonkwo household. Jasper went to show her the key and gifts.

"I am happy you served your master well," Iyom beamed. She placed the fan on Jasper's shoulder. "Your father will be happy where he is. On his behalf, I bless you, my son. Go and prosper. Forward ever, backward never. Armed robbers will not see you. Amen. Fire incident, police trouble, flooding, no mishap will befall you. Profit, profit will be your portion, in Jesus' naaaame. Amen."

Zona burned at Iyom's words. It was the usual blessing conferred on a child setting out in life, yet it pained him. He was the first son. He did not want Jasper or any other upstart to upstage him or usurp his God-given position.

Jasper had the innate Igbos' can-do spirit, which propelled them to embrace challenges and soar beyond expectation. Zona surreptitiously flipped his thumbs against his middle fingers in a silent curse: *God forbid!* Jasper would never overtake him. He would make sure of that. He felt someone twiddle his shoulder. Before he turned, Zona caught the musty scent of their matriarch.

"Omeifeukwu," she greeted him by his title, Doer of Great Things.

"Iyom."

"Won't you join our kinsmen to support your brother?"

Before he could respond, she turned and sashayed into the crowd. Zona reset his cap, stood up slowly, and gestured for the mic.

"Oke Nmanwu, I thank you and congratulate all the apprentices being freed today. Jasper, I thank you. Our people say that the thing born of a serpent must resemble a string. Are you getting my point? The encomiums poured on you today show you have come from good stock. Iyom has already said that our late father, Agbisi, would be proud of you. You did not disappoint. To support you as you set out, I shall import goods for you from China using my supply chain. Pay when able. Thank you."

"Omeifeukwu!" The assembly acknowledged. The two brothers embraced.

"Omeifeukwu," Jasper echoed.

Zona waved his short staff briskly and then flumped into his chair. Sweat streaked his face.

Rapu, the youngest in the Okonkwo family, also witnessed the event. He was still an apprentice himself. He prayed that his master would be as generous as Oke Nmanwu when the time came for his freedom. He was raring to begin his hustle.

The yellow sun was gliding down in the firmament when the square began to empty. Someone mentioned that a friend was carrying wine to his future in-laws in a neighbouring town. The revellers boarded several cars and tail-gated there, WizKid blaring, horns shrieking. As guests mingled there, Jasper made the acquaintance of an attractive maiden, Amata.

CHAPTER 2

"Is Jasper in?"

"Who is looking for him?"

"Elder Okeke."

"Is he expecting you?"

The debonair gentleman frowned. He had an incendiary answer at the tip of his tongue, but he swallowed it. Aloud, he said, "It is only in Lagos that a visiting kinsman is asked if he is expected. But we are not in Lagos now, are we?"

"I am sorry, sir," the youngster remonstrated. "Jasper went to the backhouse. He will be here shortly." He pointed the old man to a seat. "There is a seat, sir."

"O-o, my child. What of Iyom?"

"She went to a meeting."

"Wonderful. Women and meeting!"

The elder leaned heavily on his walking stick and lowered himself into the sofa, one of several arranged around a wooden centre table that had seen better days. He glanced at the line of sepia-tone framed photos of the family on the wall. Beneath them, a dogeared almanac hung from a nail. *Opaku Women's League* screamed the headlines. Okeke had seen many such calendars. He knew it would be filled with pictures of women, one for each month of the year. All the church feasts would be denoted on it, as well as the Igbo market days: Eke, Orie, Afo, Nkwo. Above the entrance door was a crucifix. He could discern the smell of beer. Flies buzzed around the empty crates stacked in one corner of the room—the remnants of the previous day's revelry.

Jasper came in, wiping his hands. He was a tall man with strong, muscular shoulders sticking out squarely from his white singlet. His red-tinged lips were lush and full, the upper lip crowned by a copious handlebar moustache. He tipped the baseball cap.

"Morning, sir."

"Jasper."

Okeke extended his stick. Jasper hit it with the back of his arm three times and once with the inside arm. Then they clasped palms in a handshake and embraced like kinsmen.

"Congratulations, son, on your freedom."

"Thanks, sir."

"Wonderful. Your late father would be proud of you."

"Yes, sir. How are my siblings?" Jasper's elbows rested on his knees. He rubbed his hands together.

"Well, they have seen today. We are looking up to God."

A hen and its brood strolled into the room, clucking nonchalantly, picking breakfast scraps off the floor. Jasper shooed them out.

He shouted into the belly of the house for kola nut. A youngster soon materialized with a saucer, on which a lobe of kola nut wiggled. A handful of bitter kola nudged a strip of alligator pepper. Jasper presented the offering to his visitor.

"Kola nut has come, sir."

Okeke hesitated. "This early morning?"

"Yes, sir. It is small kola."

After another back and forth, Okeke accepted the plate. He cleared his throat, inclining slightly to show reverence for what he was about to do.

"He who brings kola brings life," he acknowledged, taking hold of the lobe and pointing to the sky. "We shall be."

"Ise." From your lips to God.

"We shall derive life from this kola."

"Ise."

"Progress and strong health."

"Ise."

"In Jesus name."

"Amen."

He pried the nut open, chose a piece, and flung it outside. "Ancestors of Opaku, this is for you."

"That is how it is."

Elder Okeke took another piece, cracked some pepper, and passed the dish to Jasper. They chewed in silence.

"Welcome, sir," Jasper said again. It was a cue to the visitor to state the purpose of this matinal visit. The day was setting out, and one could not spend it sitting idly.

Okeke cleared his throat again. "Thank you for the kola." He was looking down at the floor, his hands in a steeple, as if contemplating how to broach the purpose of his visit.

"I myself came with this bottle of schnapps." He fumbled in his copious robes and brought out a green bottle, which he deposited on the table.

"Ha. Is this big gift for me, sir?" When Jasper saw the bottle in his visitor's hands, he suspected what the visit was about, but not seeing anyone else around, he banished the thought.

"Wonderful. It is not even big enough. When are you going back to Lagos?"

"On tenth, sir."

"January 10. Wonderful." And then came the request. "Please, I want you to take my last born, Ebuka." He faced the open door and shouted, "Where is that boy? Ebuka!"

A lad appeared in the door frame. He was tall and lanky, his elbow muscles stringy.

"Good morning, sir," he said to Jasper. He smelled of sweat.

"Morning. Someone there, run and see if Omeifeukwu is in," Jasper shouted to the house.

"He's been out since morning," a female voice answered.

"What of Rapu?"

He pointed the boy to a chair, but Okeke signalled to him to remain standing. They waited till Rapu joined them. Jasper offered the kola to Rapu and Ebuka in turns. When the visitor saw that their company was complete, he spoke up.

"Jasper, I came because you have done your freedom. Forgive me if I came too early. A frog does not hop in the daytime for nothing; something must be after its life. I said to myself; Jasper is a good man. If I do not hurry, someone else will beat me to it. So, forgive my badgering you so early. When I knocked, someone asked if you were expecting me. I retorted that it is not our custom to ask a visiting kinsman if he is expected. Your house is my house. My house is yours." He looked to Jasper for agreement.

"That is how it is," Jasper nodded consensus.

"Agbisi, your father, and I were like two lobes of a kola nut."

"I am aware of that, sir."

Okeke lifted his stick lightly and hit the floor.

"Please take this boy and train him for me. If he remains in the village here with us, he will not amount to much. His mother dotes on him and will not let him be useful to himself. He is a good boy, very obedient, very hardworking."

He sat back and waited for Jasper's reaction. The room was quiet. The whistle of birds on the trees outside reached them. Somewhere, a vehicle backfired. A goat bleated. A rooster crowed. In his turn, the host cleared his throat.

"Elder, nno. Ebuka, nno. Welcome. Yes, I did gain my freedom yesterday. I am now free to start hustling for myself. And yes, I will need one or two apprentices to help me while I show them the nuts and bolts of the business, just as Oke Nmanwu showed me. It is a big thing for a man to entrust his child to another." He paused for the weight of his words to sink in.

"What can we do?" Okeke replied. "Government is not giving us opportunities. Otherwise, a young man like this should be in school. But where is the means?"

Jasper turned to his sibling. "Rapu, what do you think?"

"Igba-boi is the way of our people. I, myself, am I not apprenticed to Chief Nwoye?"

"Ebuka, are you willing to serve me for five years?" Jasper asked after a momentary silence.

The youngster shifted on his feet and looked to his father, who interjected, "Is it five or seven years?"

"I did seven years," Jasper said.

"Me too," Rapu contributed. "I am entering my seventh year now."

"I thought as much," Okeke acknowledged.

"Our people do seven years in the main," Jasper said confidently. "Some slash it to five. If an apprentice puts his mind to it, I think he should be ready in five years." He looked pointedly at Ebuka.

"Five years it is, then," Okeke said. "You are the one holding the yam; you also have the knife."

"Five years is good," Jasper reiterated. "You may sit down."

Ebuka, in two long strides, found a chair and sank into it. His knees reached his chest.

"Can you do elementary arithmetic?" Jasper asked.

"Yes, sir."

"O-oo, he finished Junior Secondary. It is money that we lack for him to continue," Okeke added to support his son's answer.

Jasper reflected for a bit, then turned to the lad, "If something, say a fan belt, is seven hundred and fifty naira and a customer wants five, how much will that be?"

Ebuka's eyes assumed a faraway look as he worked the math. He gesticulated with his finger, adding in the air and carrying over on an invisible abacus as he murmured numbers. Finally, he said, "Three thousand, seven fifty. But if there is no profit yet, I will collect four thousand naira minimum."

The adults were impressed. Okeke swelled with pride. He shook his head regretfully as if to say, *If things were the way they should be, my boy would be in school, aspiring to a civil service career.*

"Good. Very good," the master-to-be enthused. "You understand that we are in business for profit, not to go and answer present in the market. I will return to my base on January 10. Give me one month, then you can come."

They exchanged numbers.

"Thank you, sir."

"But before you come, go and learn how to drive a car. Any car. You cannot sell motor parts if you don't understand how a vehicle rolls."

"I can afford that," his father assured. "It will not be a problem."

"And how to cook," Jasper added. "Because it is what you concoct that we will be eating."

"As for that, no problem," the old man assured his host again. "Buzzing around his mother like a fly rubbed him off well in the kitchen department. He pounds the fufu I eat. Impeccable, no lumps." The elder brought the tips of his thumb and index finger together.

"Then, let us drink to that."

Rapu ran in and re-merged with tumblers. Jasper fiddled with the cork of the bottle. But the elder waved his stick for a halt.

"There is something that Oke Nmanwu and all the masters who freed their apprentices yesterday forgot to mention, which I think was an omission."

"What is the thing?" Jasper asked. Rapu leaned forward. Someone was pounding something out back, and the old man's voice was frail. One had to listen carefully to catch his words.

"It is the matter of afia ntu. Powder business. In all the advice that they gave the young men, no one said how slow and steady wins the race. No one advised them categorically not to dabble into drugs as the fastest means of making it. See, this kobo kobo that comes in every day, sometimes, not at all, is the way to go. I thought it should have featured in the advice given to the freedmen."

The two brothers exchanged knowing looks. Their mutual glances were not lost on the old man.

"Maybe they are not into the business of hypocrisy," Jasper said flatly.

A ewe with a distended abdomen sauntered into view, bleating plaintively as it contemplated the gathering while chewing something. It trotted to the door frame and rubbed its flank repeatedly against it before releasing some droppings and ambling away.

"So, Jasper, my son, I am confiding my son to you. It is to learn the spare parts trade, not to carry drugs or any contraband. At any point in time, if you feel that he cannot continue in this line, please, in the name of God, send him back to me. If anything happens to him, his mother will not survive it."

"You have nothing to fear, sir. It is only spares that Oke Nmanwu taught me. That trade you speak of, Jasper does not know about it."

"Wonderful. You may pour the drink now."

Jasper pried the cork open. He poured libation to his late father, Agbisi. Next, he spilled some drops on the ground to the forefathers of Opaku.

They drank to cement the deal.

Rapu announced that he had errands to run before the heat of the sun became unbearable and excused himself. This was the cue Okeke was waiting for. He sent Ebuka home ahead of him and rose. Okeke reached out to Jasper, and together, they took measured steps toward the exit. Jasper suspected arthritis or gout. The old man paused by the massive oak gate beside Agbisi's grave. He wrapped the carved head of the stick with his palms and leaned over it. A glance to the left and right assured him they were out of earshot of eavesdroppers. Still, he lowered his voice.

"Opaku has decided that Agbisi's two boys from Akwaeke should inherit from his estate." He looked up and held Jasper's eyes. "Are you hearing me?"

Jasper nodded. "Yes, sir." He kept the man's gaze.

"You know your brother would have none of it when he was approached."

Jasper was aware that the kinsmen had met with Zona on the issue, and the latter had bluntly refused to concede an inch of territory.

"You know the people I am talking about?"

Jasper nodded again. "Jideofor and Jidenma, born by Akwaeke."

"By the *widow* Akwaeke." Okeke was careful to emphasize this point. "Akwaeke had three sons, but it is only the two born as a widow that we are talking about."

"Tsk."

"Accommodate them," the old man repeated, lifting the stick and hitting the ground for emphasis. "When our kinsmen summon you as they plan to do, accept the proposal." He paused, summoned phlegm, and expectorated. "Agbisi left three landed properties, I believe?"

"Yes, sir. Apart from this one."

"This one is not in contention. It is Zona's by right as the first son. But out of the other three, concede one to Akwaeke's sons. Agbisi's blood runs in their veins. Do you hear?"

"Yes, sir."

"It is the right thing to do."

"Yes, sir."

"Wonderful."

With that, as if having gotten rid of a heavy burden and seeming energized, Okeke heaved himself erect and trundled out of the compound with a rhythmic swing of his stick.

Jasper turned. Agbisi's unkempt cairn lay beside him.

"Agbisi," he saluted, removing his cap. He bent down and straightened the stones that bordered the patriarch's final resting place. He uprooted some withering grasses, then repaired to a corner of the compound, causing a stampede among his mother's domestic animals.

Overhead, a flock of birds scurried back and forth, trilling as they tore fronds from one tree and flipped to another, weaving nests. Jasper tucked Elder Okeke's advice in one corner of his brain to chew later. He had a pressing matter in hand. He fished out his phone and squatted under the lone cocoa tree, whose mottled dry leaves provided a meagre shade.

He dialled the number. At the same time, his eyes noted the time: 8:05 a.m. Was it too early? If not for Okeke's impromptu visit, he would have called her earlier. As an apprentice, you were not allowed to date. Now that he was free, his loin stirred at the thought of feminine companionship. He bounced on his heels.

Girls were expensive and a distraction, especially Lagos girls. They could bankrupt a fellow. Better to marry as early as possible and concentrate on growing his business. Amata seemed to tick all the boxes. She was from a neighbouring village, fair-skinned, and had finished schooling. A frightful thought skipped into his head. Would she want him, a poor trader and an upstart at that?

"Hello?" a groggy voice murmured. It was barely audible. To Jasper, though, it was enough. He leapt to his feet.

"Hello. Amata. This is Jasper. We met yesterday at the Amichi wedding. You served our table." He waited. Would she remember? She must have many admirers.

"Oh. The energetic dancer."

He exhaled. Ah! She was approachable. He remembered his exaggerated dance steps and tittered. "I got my freedom from my master yesterday. I was dancing in celebration of that."

"Congrats."

"Daalu. I can hustle for myself now, make my money."

Silence.

"Are you there?"

"Ee."

"Kedu?"

"O di nma."

"As an apprentice, we were not allowed to dabble into girls—"

"Now you can dabble all you want."

He laughed. "Even now, I want to settle down and grow my business." His throat was suddenly parched. He cleared it.

"Good luck. I have to—"

"Don't cut, don't cut," Jasper panicked. Now was the time to deliver his manifesto. "I am from Opaku here. It is true that I did not finish my education due to family circumstances, but I know about Shakespeare and Chinua Achebe. I like you. If you want a serious guy that will hustle and provide for you—"

not allowed to date. Now that he was free, his skin [illegible] at the thought of [illegible] companionship. He bounced on his heels. [illegible] were expensive and [illegible] and [illegible]. They could be [illegible] a fellow [illegible] to marry as early as possible and concentrate on growing his business. Amaka seemed to tick all the boxes. She was from a neighbouring village, hardworking and had finished schooling. A fearful thought skipped into his head. Would she want him, a poor trader and no master yet?

"[illegible]" a [illegible] voice murmured. It was barely audible. "[illegible]

[illegible] was enough [illegible]."

"Hello Amaka. [illegible]" [illegible] Would she remember? She must have many admirers.

"Oh, the [illegible] dancer."

He [illegible]. "[illegible]" [illegible] his exaggerated [illegible]. "I got my [illegible] from my master yesterday. I was dancing in [illegible] of that."

"Congrats."

"Daalu. I can handle [illegible] myself now, make my money."

Silence.

"Are you there?"

[illegible]

"Nedu."

"[illegible]"

"As an apprentice, we were not allowed to dabble into girls."

"Now you can dabble [illegible]."

He laughed. "Right now, I want to settle down and grow my business." [illegible] He cleared it.

"[illegible]"

[illegible]

CHAPTER 3

December 2014

"Amata!"

"Ma-a!"

"Do not keep your husband's people waiting," Odoziaku admonished. She liked the taste of the word on her tongue: husband. Amata's husband. First daughter has married.

The bride was going about greeting folk. She was still wearing her festive purple Indian madras and fuchsia head scarf with spiky ends after changing from the white wedding gown with the off-the-shoulder style trending among brides. She embraced this sibling, hugged that cousin, and shook an outstretched hand. She was overwhelmed with happiness.

You are lucky, sha, her mates cooed. *To graduate and do NYSC and get a husband immediately. A businessman, for that matter, and from a neighbouring town.*

Amata ruminated on this in her heart. Yes, indeed, she was one of the lucky few. She and Jasper had not known each other for long. They had met at a wedding on the day of Jasper's release from his apprenticeship and had exchanged numbers. He had said he did not want to waste time girl-friending and boy-friending and wanted to settle down. True to his word, within a year, he had knocked on her father's door, and here they were. Many Igbo girls of marriageable age remained single because the grooms that should walk them down the aisle were languishing in foreign jails for a slew of crimes or were searching for gainful employment. Amata was lucky to have caught Jasper's eye. The snag: he was not a graduate.

Her clansmen and women stood by as she progressed to the idling vehicle like a gazelle, her gold ornaments glittering. She embraced her mother. Inside the minivan, a few of her in-laws were already seated. Shyly, she smiled at them and sidled into the middle pew. Jasper edged in after her. The new bride waved tearfully to her mother.

"I put your gifts in the boot, plus the pots and pans from the Umu Okpu."

The Nkwa Women's Association always gave brides noisy household crockery.

"...and the fowl," Odoziaku shouted as the bus rolled towards the exit.

Amata nodded. She wiped a tear and stared straight ahead.

"Wait!" Jasper called out to Rapu, who was behind the wheel. The vehicle screeched to a halt.

"What of Omeifeukwu and our kinsmen?"

Echezona had come in full force with members of his Elite Merchants Club of Nigeria, their trademark blue muffler around their necks, with the name of the club stitched into the seams. The canopy dedicated to them, to which a steady procession of food and drinks had flown, stood deserted now. Empty bottles and food remnants were strewn about the shed.

"They have left. You are the last to leave." It was Amata's father, whom they called Onwa out of respect. It was the diminutive of Onwanetiliora, The Moon That Shines For All. As the family patriarch, he had earned that title.

"All right, then. Rapu, let's go!"

"Bye-bye nu! Safe trip!"

At the gate, Onwa gestured for the vehicle to stop again. He leaned into the driver's window, locking eyes with Rapu. "You are carrying my jewel," he warned solemnly. "Please, drive carefully."

CHAPTER 4

A full moon was rising and shining bright when Jasper's wedding party cruised into Opaku. Villagers congregated to serenade and welcome their new wife to her new home. Young girls knocked stones on pans and sang Amata into the Okonkwo compound. They danced merrily around her and praised her beauty, her luxuriant hair, thick eyebrows, doe-like eyes, and her fair complexion, incandescent in the moonlight. They noticed her almost flat chest and slim lips and gossiped about the masculinity of her body. Her expensive jewels were not lost on them, either—the gold and coral beads around her neck, the matching bracelet strapped to her wrist. Earrings rounded out the set. Obviously, she was a car among rickshaws.

Members of Iyom's sorority uncovered several cauldrons that were sizzling on fire. The aroma of native fare floated into the air, tickling the nostrils of the newly arrived company, waking their hunger pangs. The men dragged a demijohn of gin and cartons of beer forward. Three nebuchadnezzars of the local brew were upended, and the marriage feast continued. At first, Zona's generator provided electricity and powered the music set. Sometime in the night, it ran out of fuel and breathed its last. The revellers sighed in relief when the overbearing noise died with it. Jasper dislodged his car battery, connected it to the music box, and the entertainment continued. Iyom lit bush lamps, but these were not needed. The full moon, directly above their heads, dispelled the darkness.

Amata sat tucked beside Jasper and observed her new home in bewilderment. The shadows of the houses looked ominous. The surrounding trees appeared like big-headed giants with outstretched arms ready to swoop on her. She averted her gaze to the young maidens dancing coquettishly, rolling their midriffs wildly and wiggling their buttocks. They pirouetted and flailed their arms, inviting the menfolk to the dance floor. The Omekagu, the young men of Jasper's age, bounded into the circle, holding their palms high and shimmying. The meat of their breasts twitched and jiggled. Their lower bodies shook. Everyone displayed their conquest dance steps, and hormones soaked in dopamine took the merriment far into the bacchanalian night.

Zona, laconic, sat slightly apart, drink in hand, watching the simcha. He scrutinized the new bride. Compared to Amata, his Charity resembled a washed-out rag, hung out to dry. He envied Jasper.

CHAPTER 5

The Southeast Trade winds rattled the wooden windows of the room and roused the new bride. Amata went outside to inspect her new home in daylight. She glanced at the other bungalow with its fancy bricks, modern roofing shingles, and bay windows. Then she took in the old structure where Iyom still lived with Jasper and Rapu, where she had spent the night. It looked tired and neglected. During her courtship with Jasper, he had brought her to the family house. Amata, afraid of sexual imposition, had cut the visit short. She stared at the bloated wall, noting the lightning cracks. The paintwork had peeled in patches, and water stains drew clouds on the walls. When the harmattan winds whistled, certain parts of the roof flapped as if they would fly away. Someone had placed several bald tires on the sheets to keep them down. She located the broom and swept the grounds of rusty leaves. Iyom smiled her approval.

"It was wise to do all the ceremonies in one day," the matriarch remarked. "Church wedding in the morning, traditional marriage in the evening, one reception for everyone. That way, you save money. Very astute. Look after my son o. He is not the troublesome type."

"Yes, Ma," Amata smiled like a compliant bride. She was raised in the lap of luxury. Her family house in Nkwa village was palatial, boasting different wings and luxury furniture. In contrast, her new home was a huge step down. Her spirit had dimmed when she beheld the old wooden bed with arthritic legs that squeaked with the slightest movement. The mattress was worn out, and the pillows were depressed and musty. *What! Could he not buy a new foam to welcome his bride? And new pillows and bedding?* Yet, Jasper appeared to have potential. *He is setting out,* she said to herself. *He will make it.* Her own father's beginnings were also humble. It had been a grass-to-grace trajectory.

The living room floor felt grainy under Amata's feet. She swept it out, but it remained sandy. In her home, floors were draped in luscious carpets that caressed the feet and ankles. Amata looked around while Jasper lay, inebriated from the previous night. A chockablock of boxes and portmanteaux competed for space on top of an old-style, rickety wardrobe with rusting hinges. Two disused Singer foot machines nestled each other in one corner.

"Agbisi's sewing machines," Jasper said, following her roving eyes.

The bride made better acquaintance with her mother-in-law, Iyom. Everyone called the old woman Nne—Mother. Amata also befriended Charity, Zona's wife. Two toddlers trailed Charity everywhere she went, like bodyguards. Two girls. No son yet. But Charity's stomach was swelling again. She saw that Jasper had no sisters, just two brothers, who all lived in the big compound. Their late patriarch's house, with a high gradient roof, squatted in the middle of the yard. Echezona, as the first son, would inherit it on Nne's passing. Until then, he had built a modest bungalow to one side of the compound. There was still ample space for his siblings to erect their dwellings if the first son permitted them.

The sun was still shining bright when Amata repaired to the backyard and called her mother. Odoziaku was perplexed. They were waiting to hear from Jasper how the night went. Instead, Amata was complaining about her new home.

"That is what a wife is for," Odoziaku reprimanded her, "To add value to a man's life. Whatever you see that is out of whack, amend it. Arrange things to your taste. Bye."

Bye? Then her mother called again. "We are waiting to hear from your husband."

"Mama, nothing has happened." She felt obliged to explain, though she did not comprehend. "The party continued here till late. We hardly slept."

"Just know that your father is waiting," Odoziaku repeated. After a moment of silence, she added, "We are sending your dowry. The driver is on the way."

Her father's truck duly arrived, laden with the gifts her parents bought to help her set up home.

"Go front," Jasper directed the fellow. "Use back to enter!"

When they threw open the hatch, the neighbourhood children gathered to watch. They soon spread the news. *Come and see our new wife's dowly: Bland new Flidge, fleezer, air-conditioner, miclowave, doubre bed, mattless and pirrows, gas cooker, sewing machine, and portmanteaux.*

Amata dismantled the grumpy bed and mattress and set up the new ones. From one portmanteau, she fished out a bedsheet and spread it over the fresh foam. There was no room for the other gifts. Jasper stacked some in available spots atop the already overfilled wardrobe; others he shoved under the bed or leaned against the wall.

When Iyom saw the electrical appliances, she chortled. "Where is the electricity for these?"

The dowry roiled Jasper's kinsmen. Such a bridal accompaniment had never been seen before. The men resented Jasper for marrying from a well-to-do family and asked themselves: *Why had they not looked for one such girl to marry? Why take a church rat as a wife?*

The women gave Amata the evil eye. *What is she trying to prove? That she is better than us?*

Envy gnawed at Zona's innards when he saw the stacked household furniture. He made a biting remark about one getting a spot on the ground before hustling for a mat. Here was Jasper with a huge mat but no place to spread it.

~

Jasper and Amata spent time in Opaku. Three market days after their marriage, Amata accompanied Jasper to the ceremony of Rapu's freedom from his master, who empowered the Okonkwo Benjamin to set up a motorbike and tricycle business. The motorbike, alias okada, and the tricycle, aka keke, were increasingly becoming the go-to means of transportation in Nigeria.

CHAPTER 6

In the new year, Amata watched the village quieten down as festivities petered out. Town dwellers returned to their stations. Already, she looked forward to the next December and the festivities it would bring because the traditional ruler had declared a mass return for all Opaku indigenes.

The new couple moved to Lagos and set up their home in Jasper's pad on Randle Avenue. It was not much better than the village house, but Amata reminded herself again that Jasper had potential and was self-driven. Things would get better.

As Iyom had said, her man proved easy to live with. The only trouble was that they were yet to consummate their marriage. All that time in the village after their marriage ceremony, they visited family and friends and went on outings. Jasper did not make any moves to possess his possession.

"Welcome your monthly visitor in my house first," he told his frustrated wife.

This stance surprised Amata, who thought that the first night after the wedding, a groom would be in a hurry to pounce on his bride and devour her. *As an apprentice, we were not allowed to dabble into girls,* she remembered him saying. Yet here they were. She tried a couple of times to seduce him, but he rebuffed her. The monthly first, he insisted.

He wants to make sure you will not slap him with another man's pregnancy, Amata reasoned. Remember David and Uriah.

Wait for your menses, girl. The problem was her menstrual cycle was not regular. It could disappear for months and reappear unexpectedly, like a guest from home.

They waited.

Two months after the wedding, the monthly visitor had still not knocked. Periodically, Jasper would ask about it.

She would shake her head.

"And you are not pregnant?"

"No."

He would palpate her belly, asking himself what bus he had boarded and to where. It negated the little biology he had learnt.

"Has it always been like this?"

"Yes, sir."

"And you didn't let me know?"

"It will come. It is just a matter of time."

"What shall we call this?"

One night, after a wash, Amata perfumed herself and slipped into a flimsy night half-dress. Perhaps with some loving, the menses could be coaxed to appear. She lay on her side of the bed, legs apart. From the room, she could hear Jasper talking on the phone. Tonight, she could tell it was Iyom he was talking to, checking on her welfare. An invisible umbilical cord still connected mother and son across the miles.

She waited. Jasper took a shower, summoning phlegm and spitting out loudly as he did just before he stepped out of the bathroom in the new towel she had given him to replace his old threadbare one. By the time he joined her in bed, he had donned his bogus Hawaiian shorts. He stretched out, his back to her, and in no time, began to snore. Amata was flummoxed. *Blood of Jesus,* she mumbled.

On Sundays, he took her to the National Stadium and taught her how to drive with his ageing Toyota Corolla.

"You must have an idea how a car works to be able to sell its parts," he said. "You are lucky that this vehicle is automatic. In our time, we had to contend with the accelerator, brake, and clutch. Imagine that in the early morning go-slow, as you join the

Eko Bridge from the ramp at Costain. With an automatic, you are either braking or accelerating. The car drives itself. Before you ignite, make sure your foot is pressing the brake. Otherwise, the car could jerk forward."

Amata nodded.

"This is the horn. In Lagos, one cannot drive a car with a faulty horn. You blast it to warn other drivers that you are in front, behind, or beside them, especially the taxi drivers. Use it to warn pedestrians and motorbike operators not to try it."

"Try what?"

"Whatever they contemplate doing."

They laughed.

"This whole thing is the dashboard. Tells you the speed you are doing, how much fuel is in your tank, and the time. Watch out for this sign. It means the car is overheating. It is an issue because of the Lagos traffic. A journey that, under normal circumstances, should take ten minutes can drag on for hours. That is why we leave home early. Five, ten minutes can make all the difference in the time you arrive at your destination and eventually on the wear and tear on the vehicle."

After the driving lesson, Jasper would sometimes return to the sports arena to play ball with the boys. Soccer and volleyball pleased him no end, though his favourite stars were in basketball—Shaquille, LeBron, and Kobe Bryant. Evenings, it was the Premier League and UFC. He was a Chelsea fan. He adulated the team and spoke of them in superlative terms, comparing players and teams whose names Amata could not retain.

The house where Jasper and Amata lived counted many flats. Their apartment was at the rear. During the day, the men would be away toiling, looking to earn a living for their families, while their women busied themselves with grocery shopping and domestic chores. Laundry flustered on lines. Different aromas wafted out of neighbouring pots. The most dominant and mouth-watering was the ogiri condiment, used in preparing a host of native soups. Also easily recognized were the smells of goat meat and stockfish. One salivated just walking through the yard at meal preparation times, as any slight breeze carried the fragrance and stirred the intestines.

Itinerant hawkers traversed the dwellings, proposing wares. Amata could hear negotiations and haggling going on. At times, the other housewives' humming of praise and vernacular songs reached her ears. The Nollywood channel droned in the background. Occasionally, a shouting match erupted between neighbours over dirt gathered on someone's threshold or the uncleared human manure of a toddler.

"It is a transit point," Jasper said when Amata narrated her daytime encounters with their neighbours. "Soon, we shall move to a bigger place. Let me gather some money."

One Sunday, after dinner, four months into this arrangement, Amata gingerly approached her husband. Jasper was sitting contented and genial in his easy chair on the veranda. She stooped before him on all fours, picking up pieces of the used toothpick.

"Will I sit at home all day?" she began in a velvety voice. "Find a job for me so I can bring in something, no matter how small."

Being a graduate, she was thinking of a civil service job, nine-to-five, Monday to Friday. Or would her certificate be left under the biblical bushel?

"Stay at home and be doing what?" her hubby growled, eyes arched. "Gossiping and quarrelling?"

Amata looked at him fondly, ogling his muscular biceps and hairy chest. She longed for him, but they were living like siblings.

"You will join me in the business. You will keep the books while Ebuka and I hustle for customers. Next week, you will start." Jasper paused, "What of your visitor?"

The playful mood ended. Amata fixed her stare on the foot of the chair and shook her head. "I have not seen it yet."

"What shall we call this?"

CHAPTER 7

The next day, Amata called her mother and confided in her about the lack of intimacy. Odoziaku was aghast.

"And you have waited all this while to tell me! When I have been crying here that Amata betrayed me, Amata betrayed me. Did your father not promise you girls a Jeep if you are found intact by your husbands? And I am counting the time to come for omugwo when I can come to take care of my daughter and my grandchild. Go, run, rather, to the nearest clinic immediately."

After Jasper left for the market the next morning, Amata knelt and prayed fervently for a miracle. *Blood of Jesus, let me see my menstrual flow,* she pleaded with the heavens. *Let me see it so we can consummate our marriage. I want a child, but there can be no child if my husband does not make love to me, and he has sworn not to until my period comes. Please, God, let this period come. Biko. Please.*

She headed down Randle Avenue, looking for any women's hospital. Clinics punctuated every street corner, sometimes two or three within shouting range of each other. She entered one on the third floor of a building at Bank Olemoh Street. *Okun Women's Clinic,* the sign said. After the usual protocols, a nurse led her to a bright consulting room. A mousey male doctor in a white lab coat and a stethoscope around his neck was peering into an iPad. His nose was a perfect equilateral triangle. He waved her to a seat without looking up, his goggles straddling his shiny forehead. The nameplate on his table identified him as Dr. Oworo.

"Yes?" he muttered, still engrossed in the iPad.

"I have not seen my menses for some time."

The room reeked of disinfectant. Posters of the human anatomy decorated the white walls.

"Are you pregnant?" The medico finally looked up. He poked the oversized spectacles down to sit on his nose and drew a folder closer.

"No."

"How do you know? Amenorrhoea is the first sign of pregnancy. Let's do a pregnancy test."

It came back negative.

"I told you," she said.

"And you are married?"

"Yes, sir."

"Having relations?"

"No, sir."

He recoiled like a serpent. His lips curled up in a way that made Amata think of the cloaca of a fowl. He was an ugly specimen of a man.

"Is your husband away?"

"He is very much around."

"Is he incapacitated in any way?"

Jasper was not. She had spied his eggplant those times she attempted to seduce him. "I don't think so. We are waiting for my menses to show first."

"Lie down. Let me check you."

Amata was reluctant, but her eagerness to normalize things with her husband propelled her to the examination table. She bunched her long gown above the abdomen before perching on the examination table. She dreaded the touch. Dr. Oworo approached and tipped her back. He pushed her frock up to her neck, lifted her brassiere at the same time and exposed Amata's puerile chest. He patted her stomach with cold fingers and listened ostensibly through the stethoscope. His hand palpated her chest, tapped here and there, and tweaked her nipples. In the cold room, they had stiffened to attention. *Is this usual?* Amata wondered, to twiddle a patient's teats? Where was the nurse? Should she not be present? The doctor proceeded to pull down her panties. Amata tensed and raised her head.

Relax, his left hand gesticulated. "Spread the legs. Now bend the knees."

He caressed the thick, silky hair, grabbed tufts, and combed them with his fingers. The next minute, he pried open the lips and poked for the eye. Surely, this was inappropriate. Amata heaved herself up. The lab coat was swollen at Oworo's groin.

"Lie back," Dr. Oworo whispered, breathing like a dog. He shoved her back on the foam, but Amata shouldered him aside, swung her legs down with extra energy, and slid from the bed. She patted herself down, grabbed her bag, and stormed out.

Out on the street, she remembered that Charity was again with child. She called her.

"Go to Dr. Ogedengbe's clinic," Charity advised after Amata told her about her experience with Dr. Oworo. "She is a woman like us. Just down the road, at Ayilara."

Amata turned back along the way she had come until she located the clinic. The waiting was long, but she persevered. Jasper usually returned around seven in the evening. She reckoned that she would be home way before then.

When she finally found herself before the renowned gynecologist, she exhaled. The doctor telegraphed friendliness.

"You say the preg test was negative?"

"Yes, Ma."

"Lie down on that bed. Remove your underwear."

Everyone wants to poke you down there, Amata thought, but she obeyed. The doctor donned gloves and wheeled the olive-green curtain for privacy. She parted the patient's thighs.

"Are you married?" She tried to slide two fingers into the body. It was difficult.

"Yes, Ma."

The physician lubricated the area and tried to insert one finger. No way.

"You may come down. Step on the stool." She cupped the patient's elbow and helped her down.

"Okay. Your periods are not regular. It is a hormonal issue. I will prescribe some drugs, and we will see you again in—" Dr. Ogedengbe tapped her lips with the pen. "Three months. Start these drugs as soon as possible and take your temperature regularly. Once there is a spike, it means you are ovulating. Welcome your husband then."

"He will want to see the blood first."

"If you see blood, that means the egg is wasted," the doctor said, a tad too tersely. "Pregnancy cannot occur then. But the chances of getting pregnant increase if you catch it when it is released."

"I understand, Ma, but he will not touch me until he first witnesses the flow."

Dr. Ogedengbe reflected for a while. She scanned her notes, trying to figure out what she was missing.

"On second thoughts, I will increase the dosage. Take the drugs continuously. After the first menses, we can begin to monitor your temperature, right? Conception can happen during the next ovulation. You do want to get pregnant, right?"

"Very much, Ma."

"All right. I'll see you again in July."

CHAPTER 8

Amata began accompanying her husband to his John Street stall in the Idumota area of the megacity. Jasper led the way on the first day, elbowing through people and carving a path for her. They jostled through the crowds going in all directions, hurrying like soldiers to war. In the middle of this rush of humanity, a beggar sat on the ground, arms stretched out for alms.

The shop was in the middle of a warren of stalls. Along the way, stragglers stood, beckoning customers, declaring, "Yes, I have it."

"Nde oso afia," Jasper explained.

"They have no shops but earn a commission on any customers they bring to retailers," Amata said, seeking confirmation.

"Exactly. Sometimes, we include a markup in the price for them."

Amata soon saw the flashing neon sign above the double doors: Jasper Gee's Trading Coy Ltd. General Auto Merchants. The boards of the open doors displayed auto symbols. Three of the signs were factory-made, while the others appeared to be the work of a local artist. She recognized the three circles of Toyota. The upstanding lion of the Peugeot model, front paws outstretched, had pride of place at eye level. Beside it sat the four overlapping rings of the Audi. Beneath that, a big silver "H" represented the Honda logo. The encircled three-pronged star of her father's Mercedes Benz was familiar. She ticked off several others as she let her eyes roam over the boards.

Jasper saw her looking at the signs. "I intend to diversify into every model that moves," he said. "As our people say, one does not stand in one spot to regard the masquerade."

Ebuka was leaning on the wooden chest-level counter along the entrance, barricading access to the shop. A glass showcase under the counter displayed assorted accessories: headlamps, rear-view mirrors, and wipers. Behind him, floor-to-ceiling shelves lined the three walls on which boxes of goods were neatly arranged. A floor-to-ceiling grid covered the stores to prevent pilfering.

"Step up," Jasper invited her, lending her a hand up the concrete elevation that set the store off from the walkways of the marketplace.

The market was already bustling with activity. Amata could see traders on the stoops of their holdings. A duo of latecomers were still sweeping their appurtenances while others were hanging stuff on hooks and displaying wares on their doorsteps. She noticed the same rubber hoops hanging from large hooks on the door of their shop.

"Fan belts," Ebuka said, following her gaze. He had an air of superiority, showing off his newly acquired knowledge of the spare parts business.

The news that Jasper's bride was around circulated quickly. Marketplace neighbours stampeded to welcome the new wife.

"Wife, welcome o!"

"Jasper Gee! Congrats, sir!"

"O-o. Daalu nu. Thank you, all," Jasper responded.

All day, trading associates trooped to the store to gosh at the new missus, inspecting and admiring her like she was a new vehicle. Jasper was all smiles at the attention. He knew that men competed with one another via their wives, comparing height, complexion, attributes, and even level of education. He laughed with glee, caressing his sides, confident that Amata ticked all the boxes.

The bride smiled shyly at the greeters. The way some looked at her, she could tell they were undressing her and imagining her and Jasper in bed. If only they knew.

At quiet interstices in the shop, Jasper educated his wife about their business.

"Toyota is the new Pijote."

Amata flinched at the misnomer, but she did not correct him.

"Observe, every other car on the road is a Toyota. It is very popular. Toyota sells itself and has second-hand value. This is good for us because most of the cars on our roads are from Belgium, used abroad and exported to Nigeria. Technically, we deal in all spare parts. Technically. By that, I mean that if a customer wants a part we don't market, do not let him go away. Rather, offer him a seat and a drink, then send Ebuka to find the part. Omeifeukwu deals with Mercedes Benz parts, and my master, Chief Igwilo, sells Toyota and Lexus—"

"Former master."

Jasper smacked his forehead. "I keep forgetting that I am a free man now." He grinned. "If they don't have the part, ask any of our neighbours, then you mark up the price. Hiace parts move fast because the brand is used to transport company personnel."

"And for commercial transport," Amata added. She had seen enough of them on the roads to know that.

"Yes, but commercial operators hardly buy brand new parts, if at all. That is why their vehicles are ramshackle. If the need arises, they patronize second-hand sellers at Ladipo and Alaba."

"Is Lexus the same as Toyota?" Amata asked.

"Toyota makes Lexus, yes. Lexus is Toyota's big brand, a luxury model that competes with Mercedes Benz and BMW. The other Toyota models usually compete with Honda and Nissan. We are also branching into Lexus because it is getting popular in Nigeria as a status symbol. That and Range Rover."

Jasper interrupted his exposition to wave to a passerby. "Yes, Master, check here. What part?" But the fellow moved on.

"Some parts are interchangeable among cars, but others are made specifically for each model. You will soon learn which manufacturers have their own special brands."

Jasper flitted through specific information on car parts and general sales techniques. Even though Amata was there to do the books, they needed every available hand to sell the goods.

"When a customer comes, ask them what brand of car, then what model or year. That is the starting point. But we do not wait for them to come to us; you must be ready to approach them outside while they are undecided and wondering what shop to enter. That is why I send Ebuka to the bus stop to ambush potential customers."

That first day, they bought breakfast of bean cakes and gruel. Hawkers of edible goods wandered up and down the narrow alley, stepping around the roadside sellers who traded on their haunches, trays, or hand carts rather than in stores. Moin-moin hawkers meandered by, leaving behind a delicious aroma. Sweet jollof rice followed, with the smell of roasted meat and fish. Vendors of Igbo delicacies like ugba, abacha, and nkwobi also perambulated the alleys. The air was redolent with food aromas.

At lunchtime, Jasper despatched Ebuka to a bush restaurant to buy "swallow" for the three of them. The apprentice's fare was meatless.

"I can cook better than this," Amata remarked, licking her crusted fingers.

"Will you compare this mass production with a meal you washed hands to cook?" Jasper riposted. "Even Ebuka cooks better than this market meal."

They helped themselves from a carton of pure water in the store. Amata made a mental note to wake early the next day to prepare the day's tiffin as carry-along.

"That will save us some money," she said when she told Jasper her plans.

"Oh, my wife!" Jasper gushed. "I am blessed."

The stench of garbage was strong. Discarded cartons, rags, and rotten food littered the paths. Mounds of oozing trash stood out like landmarks. There was constant traffic of pedestrians, hand carts, and wheelbarrows. The non-stop sound of buzzers rent the air, hawkers advertising their wares in yells. A newspaper vendor pumped a bike horn with gusto. Meat sellers displayed chunks of meat on trays and sharpened knives against knives. With a wave of the hand, they sent the fat flies that coated their wares scampering in all directions. Radios blared from kiosks. A peddler selling medicines from his car extolled the qualities of a super drug as he handed out free samples of it. He bamboozled the potential clients with claims of miracle diabetes and fibroid cures.

A vegetable monger with a baby strapped to her back, pushed a bunch into Amata's face. Three vertical tribal marks lined the forehead.

"Fresh greens, Mummy!"

"Buy plantain!" a bow-legged teenager counter proposed. A tray balanced on her head, hands-free, while she sipped from a coloured sachet.

"On this shelf are parts for Corolla, Camry, and RAV4," Jasper tried to steer the conversation back to business. "They are the most common Toyota vehicles out there. Over in that line, you have Honda parts. From exhausts to key starter kits, brake pads, ball joints, bearings, everything. You understand?"

Amata nodded.

"Here in the drawer are the invoice and receipt books. Sometimes, a customer will ask you to inflate the invoice or receipt. Oblige him, but note the real sum in this ledger. All right? At the end of the day, we want to balance our books, make sure we are making profits."

"At least if you lie to others, tell yourself the truth," Amata said.

"Exactly."

"Why don't we have a cash machine?" Amata asked. "Why the manual entering of sales?"

Jasper and Ebuka exchanged looks. At once, Jasper stepped out to the business machines store and returned with a cash register.

"It is good to marry an educated woman," he said to Ebuka when he returned. "She is equal to two men."

The next day, Amata made the acquaintance of some of the other wives who accompanied their husbands to the market. They were few and only had a minor role because the spare parts industry was mostly dominated by men. She also noticed some adolescent sons apprenticing for their fathers. *They should be in school,* she silent-screamed.

At noon, someone rang a bell, and a scattering of apprentices began to assemble. A leader emerged from their midst, clapping. He intoned a hymn, which the flock picked up and amplified. At the end of each chorus, the leader began another. The clapping and fervour intensified. More traders filed into the open space between stalls and swelled the number of the midday worshippers. The words rang out over the marketplace:

You are my Redeemer; You are my Comforter,
I have no other God, Father, hear me when I call;
When I ca-ll,
You are my Redeemer, You are my Comforter,
I have no other God, Father, hear me when I call.

At prayer time, no trading occurred. Those who feared stepping far from their shops stood on their stoops, head bowed. The act of praying in unity supposedly brought together all the traders on that line and made each their brother's keeper.

After the singing, the prayer warrior called out, "Prayer!" At once, a cacophony of murmurings and petitions rose from the congregation. Eyes closed, hands outstretched, they poured out their hearts to the Almighty. Some outbursts sounded like speaking in tongues. After a short while, the leader called out, "In Jesus name!"

"Amen!"

A closing hymn ended the devotion. The worshippers belted it out lustily as they regained their stalls:

Take glory, Father
Take glory, Son,

Take glory, Holy Ghost,
Now and forever more.

~

Just before sunset, the chairman of the Automobile Spares Traders Association (ASTRA) appeared at Jasper's shop, accompanied by his secretary. They congratulated the entrepreneur and welcomed his bride to the fold.

"We are family," the Chair said to Amata. "We trade far from home, so we are our brother's keeper. Our motto is *Onye aghala nwa nne ya*—Let none leave his sibling behind."

Depends on the sibling, Amata thought. Outwardly, she offered them a bashful smile, kept her eyes down and fixed on the Chair's sandals. In these parts, age was revered, and a youngster dared not lock eyes with an elder.

CHAPTER 9

Zona got tired of sitting in his shop, so he decided to stroll around the market to stretch his legs. As he approached his brother's shop, he beheld Jasper, Amata, and the apprentice standing behind the counter, gazing out. No customers, Zona noted. Good. When Jasper saw his brother, he ducked under the flap of the counter and rushed out to greet him. There they stood, chewing the fat. Onlookers would think that the Okonkwo brothers were united.

"I am thinking of expanding," Zona said, watching closely for Jasper's reaction. He wanted his younger brother to feel the gap between them. Jasper didn't show any emotion. He simply took the bait in his stride. Since his freedom over a year ago, he was yet to see the goods Zona had promised to import for him to help him establish his business. And yet, he thought, as he stood beside his brother, he was talking of expanding. It made sense to open branches within the city, in the neighbourhoods, to take the wares to the customers instead of waiting for them to brave the clogging traffic of the markets.

"To the south," Zona added. "Are you getting my point?"

This got Jasper's attention. "South? Is down south not saturated?"

Many car spare parts manufacturers were based in Nnewi, in the southeast. Major importers, too. But there were no functional ports in that part of the country. Importers ferried cargoes overland from Tin Can Island and Apapa ports to their Onitsha and Nnewi warehouses. It made sense to offload at Lagos and sell to Lagos-based distributors until the federal government saw it right to open the ports in the south. There were many viable ports, but most of them were virtually moribund, while the Lagos ports were overwhelmed and congested. Talk about dredging the River Niger at the Onitsha end to allow vessels remained mere talk, and it was loudest at election time.

"There appears to be more patronage here in Lagos due to its teeming population. And Lagos supplies goods to the whole of the West African Coast."

"But all of us cannot remain far from home," Zona said. He paused, waiting to hear Jasper's response before continuing. "Are you getting my point? Iyom is getting on. I am considering opening a store down south and on the West Coast. I hear there is a big market there."

"I have heard so, too," Jasper replied, "but my hand is not yet strong enough to expand outside Nigeria. Though I hear the Lebanese have cornered the West Coast."

"They have, but if one is strong, one can compete with them. Agric business is booming lucrative in Accra, Abidjan, and Guinea, but the locals do not command enough capital to venture into it big time. With increased democracy and economies stabilizing, foreign direct investment is streaming in. Opportunities abound. We should explore that side. Are you hearing me?"

Zona paused again, waiting for a response. There was none. "Many of our confreres are there already, plus nde ofe nmanu." "Nde ofe nmanu" was a pejorative term for the Yoruba. It literally meant people of oily soup.

Jasper balked at the slur but let it slide. "I'll go for it," he concluded. "Though by expansion, I thought you meant going into Ikeja, Victoria Island, Yaba, and other outskirts of Lagos."

"Every neighbourhood is congested as we speak," Zona posited. "Our people are everywhere now. Victoria Island has spilled into Lekki and Ajah. Are you getting my point?"

The comment hung in the air. They left the matter as abruptly as they broached it.

"We are ordering containers from China," Zona said.

"We?"

"Oke Mmanwu, Akajiaku, and myself. Ten containers. How do you re-stock? Have you established a supply chain yet?"

"I still collect from Oke Nmanwu, sell, then settle him," Jasper said.

"You should wean yourself from Oke Mmanwu. Are you getting my point? He empowered you adequately to stand on your own. Look around; there are ways and means."

"You are right, brother, but I am still trying to grow my customers. All the people I sold to before were Oke Nmanwu's customers. I cannot ambush them, poach them from him."

"Hmmm."

Zona tugged at his brother and dragged him out of earshot of the other traders.

"I see you have only one boy. For accountability, you need at least two apprentices. Some of us have three, four, even five. Nwachinemelu has eighteen! Think about it."

Zona was right, but it was expensive to keep an able-bodied young man with a healthy appetite that you fed three times a day, clothed and nurtured. Jasper could not afford another one, not to talk of two or three more.

"I'll bear it in mind," he replied.

They made their way back to the stall. Business was slow. Out of the blue, Zona said, "I want to redeem the pledge I made on your freedom day. So make a list of the spares you need. I will include it in my order. Pay when you sell."

"Ome-ife-ukwu!" Jasper hailed. He hopped on one foot and rotated on it, one arm raised in salute. He embraced Zona, a one-sided embrace.

"Thank you, Chief. I thank God for having a brother like you."

As Zona was leaving, Amata stood up. "How is my husband's wife?" she asked.

Charity was due any day now. Amata framed her words in the traditional Igbo way, referring to her brother-in-law as her husband. In Igboland, the women married into a family were co-wives.

"Call your mate," Zona flung his response at her. A putrid odour rose from the gunk underfoot. He summoned phlegm and spat it out beside him. "She put to bed at the weekend."

"Ah! Chief! A boy or girl?"

"Her usual."

"Ah, Chief! We thank God for safe delivery."

Zona was already walking away. He was clearly downcast. Every man wanted male children. As the first son, Zona was expected to produce the first grandson. Now that son number two has married, what if Jasper's wife delivered the first grandson of the family? Zona had peeped at Amata and was keen to note the flat stomach. Nothing there yet, he thought, but the countdown surely had started.

"Has her mother come?" Amata shouted after him.

"By weekend!" he yelled back without turning.

There and then, Amata sought Jasper's permission to visit Charity the next day.

"No objection," Jasper said, euphoric at the spares Zona would order for him. *Pay when you sell,* his brother had said.

"When you go, greet our senior wife. Ebuka, bring paper and biro."

CHAPTER 10

"Charlingo!" Amata shouted as she stepped onto Zona's porch in Alaka Estate.

"Amata, fine babe. Iyawo!" Charity used the Yoruba word for a newlywed. It was common for Igbo in Lagos to learn some Yoruba through their daily interactions.

Charity was still in her nightdress, hair unkempt. She was a pretty black woman, with a beauty spot on the right cheek. Her eyes darted about, and her plump lips uncurled a toothy smile. Her braless breasts rolled about, jostling for space under the flimsy muslin.

"After six months, am I still Iyawo? Am an old bride now."

"Until you give birth, you will still answer to a young bride."

"Congrats, Charity," Amata said enthusiastically. "Thank God for safe delivery."

"How did you hear?"

"Omeifeukwu came by our shop yesterday."

"My dear, I am in trouble." She sighed. "Come inside."

"Trouble?" Amata walked into the parlour, tastefully furnished in hues of blue. The smell of talc greeted her. The room was chilled, and a Nollywood movie played silently on the large screen while Charity listened to Christian music on her phone.

"Did you not see Zona's face? He is not happy that it's another girl."

"I saw it."

"He said I am doing myself no favours and will keep going to the labour room until I give him two boys."

"No wonder. When he came to the shop yesterday, he just threw out the information as he was leaving. I asked if the baby was a boy or a girl, and he said 'the usual.' Is it not what he put inside you that you will drop?"

"It is well. God will do it. At least, I am fertile. Many women have married and are still waiting on the Lord for the fruit of the womb."

Amata cringed.

The two women pushed the children's toys to one side and sat next to each other on the three-seater corduroy sofa.

Charity's eyes turned to Amata's stomach. "Why is your stomach still like a flat tyre?"

"My sister, leave matter for Matthias." Amata did not care to discuss her reproductive shenanigans. Many would not understand that she was still a virgin six months after marriage, and it was not like her husband travelled.

"Chief says your mother is coming at the weekend."

"Yes. For one month. Then his mother will take over."

"It is a fair arrangement. Since Nne did not produce any female child, she will be doing omugwo for her sons' wives."

"I get along with the two women, so anyone that comes, as long as I have company."

"How is the baby?"

"She is fine, sleeping now. How is the market?"

"I'm learning. You don't come at all?"

Charity grimaced. "Zona does not want that. Says to mind the home front. I have subtly appealed to him to open a shop for me. I could sell fabrics, trinkets, and baby wears. See all the women hustling at Tejuosho Market, Oke Arin, Balogun, and all I do is stay home."

She paused. "It is well."

Despite a life of luxury and provision, Charity was clearly unfulfilled.

"Do not say I told you, but I hear he is planning to expand to the East and across the border."

Charity was astonished. Her husband must be very rich. She shrugged. "It is still his boys that he will put in charge. Though, I wouldn't mind going down south."

"And leave all these high-class Lagos parties?"

"There are parties in the East, too."

"Not as star-studded as the Lagos ones, with all the Nollywood babes and famous socialites."

They made small talk. Charity palpated her belly. "Let me lie down, Amata, so you press me hot water."

"I have no idea about such things."

"I will show you. I need to do a hot press to expel clots of the after-birth."

Charity brought a face towel and a bowl of hot water. Amata performed the hot compress.

"Pour some into a basin. Add alum. I will sit on it. It soothes the birth canal and tightens the muscles down there."

In the bathroom, Charity winced as she lowered herself into the pan. "This baby tore me to pieces. I have sutures from my vagina to my backyard." She shook her head wistfully. "What we women go through—"

After attending to Charity, Amata helped bathe the newborn while the mother took a shower. Afterwards, when Charity stretched out her limbs on the ottoman and began nursing the baby, Amata headed for the kitchen. She picked up toys here and there and put away the chinaware.

"I passed by the fish market on my way. Pepper soup with utazi loading."

"Just what the doctor ordered." Charity was grateful. "Amata, i gadi. You will live long."

Amata scaled and gutted the fish. Then she located a pot and lit the burner. She raised her voice and continued chatting from the kitchen. "You can't manage alone, Char."

"My house-girl went to school. She will be back soon."

"That is the condition for getting help nowadays," Amata acknowledged. "One must send them to school."

"Do you blame them? Otherwise, who would give away their child at such a tender age?"

Amata thought of the young apprentices at Idumota, who were largely unschooled. She wondered whether to raise the issue. Would Charity understand? She took a chance.

"In the market, some apprentices are so young—too young to leave their mothers."

"It is a terrible system," Charity agreed. "No safety nets, no free education. At least up to high school. With rising school fees, how many can afford that?"

Charity's response gave Amata the confidence to continue.

"Some of the boys should really be in school. Some cannot parse a sentence in English or do simple arithmetic. They rely on the reckoner."

Amata's mind flew to her brother. At eighteen, Rex used to accompany their mother on errands. That way, he imbibed family values, acquired home training, and enjoyed a wide range of leisure activities. But what choices were open to his mates who were apprenticed to traders? What kind of future did they have, being raised in the market environment? She knew they could not be called street urchins, but were they much better?

At the table, they engaged in more small talks.

"How is Adaobi?"

"She is fine. She is five years old now. In kindergarten."

"And Alaoma is sleeping."

Amata let the names of the children linger in her head. Adaobi. First daughter of the compound. It was a fitting name. Charity had produced the female. But the male child, so important in Igboland, was still elusive.

Amata had scribbled some lovely names she would call her own children when they came. If they came. She suggested some to her sister-in-law.

"Hmm, Chimamanda. Chimkalifa. Nice, but we will wait and see," Charity said dismissively. "Names are not lacking in Igboland; it is the father's prerogative."

"What a deep sleep," Amata observed, gesturing at the sleeping toddler and changing the topic. "She's been lying there since I arrived."

"She cried herself to sleep. She stresses me a lot. I had to give her a cough mixture to make her sleep. That was the only way I could catch some rest."

"It's tough."

"Have you joined the Women's Meeting?"

"I have joined the Catholic Women's Organisation at our parish, St. Anthony's."

"Good. But I meant the Opaku Women's League. There are two—one for the daughters of Opaku and the other for wives of Opaku men. It is the second one that you must join. They meet on the last Sunday of the month. One p.m."

"Where?"

"At Twin Motors. The owner lets us use his facility for free."

"Okay, when you wean baby, we could go together."

"Wean, kwa? That's in one year. I am sure you know I can go out once we do the baby's outing service. Then we will attend. I'll introduce you."

"Sounds good."

"It is lucrative to join early, before you born. They have a rich maternity package."

"Ooo."

"It is now six months since your wedding, I think?"

"Exactly."

"Have you missed your period?"

It was a private matter, Amata felt, but in the traditional Igbo society, no topic was taboo. Everything was out in the open.

"The thing is, my period has never been regular. Even in school, I could go months without a flow."

"And you don't worry?"

"Then one day, I will feel it gliding down my thighs like escaped piss."

"So you could be pregnant."

"My dear, I have told you to leave that matter for Matthias."

Charity contemplated her visitor. Was Amata hiding her condition so that her in-laws would not use witchcraft to sabotage it? Some people believed in hiding their good fortune until ripe to avert dark forces.

"This one pass Matthias o!" she retorted with a side-eye. "People have started counting for you, if you don't know. Once you do the marriage ceremony, they start calculating."

"I know. Even the chairman at our wedding reception said as much. That after nine months, Jasper and I will invite the guests back, this time for a naming ceremony. Now it's past six months, and see how flat this tummy is." Amata patted her belly.

"It is well. If you ask me, I would say go for a check-up."

"I have gone. Remember? You gave me the name of the doctor to see."

"Of course." Charity smacked her forehead. "This child has taken my brain."

She switched the baby to the other breast, which had started leaking. In her previous visits, her mother had counselled her to empty the two gourds at each feeding. She gritted her teeth.

"Is it painful?"

"Very. Like slicing the scrotum with a knife."

"Charity!" Amata chuckled. "But they have no teeth."

"No teeth but sharp lacerated gums tearing the skin around the nipples. I'm sore all over."

"Ndo. Sorry."

"O-o. Your own is coming. Were you able to locate Prof. Ogedengbe?"

"Yes."

"She is the best. What did she say?"

The wall clock struck three p.m. *So people still had such things?* Amata marvelled. With the ubiquitous mobile phones, who needed clocks? Amata waited for the chimes to end before she answered. "We are on it. She gave me some drugs to bring on the flow."

Ah, to bring on the flow? Charity thought, *not to get pregnant.* They were in for the long haul here. It occurred to her that she could very well drop another baby before her fellow wife. She prayed for a male next time so she could exhale.

Aloud, she sighed, "It is well."

At four, after washing up, Amata rose to leave. "Let me go and prepare for Jasper's return." She pressed an envelope into Charity's hand. "There is not much inside, but one cannot come empty-handed to welcome a new arrival."

"Amata, you are too much!" Charity exclaimed, caressing the envelope. "After this expensive fish pepper soup and hot press? Thank you. I am happy to have you as a sister-in-law. You will never lack."

"Iseee. From your mouth to God's ears."

CHAPTER 11

When Amata got home, there was a power outage. The whole quarter was clothed in darkness. She hurriedly prepared bitter-leaf soup, Jasper's favourite, on the kerosene stove. She threw in plenty of stockfish, goat intestines, and smoked asa fish.

After dinner, the couple sat on the veranda, reviewing the day. The whirring of several generators disturbed the quiet of the night. The engines emitted fumes that mingled with the mephitic vapours rising from the debris-filled gutters and competed with the sweet aroma of various dinners in the neighbourhood.

In the distance, the Lagos traffic congestion continued unabated, heaving intermittently like a sleeping monster. Except Lagos never slept. Car horns, police sirens and screeching tyres serenaded the night. If you waited for the noise to die before turning in, you would be up all night.

Jasper waited for a lull in the traffic before he spoke. "It's good to be near Nne. All of us cannot be far away in Lagos and Abuja."

"Why are you talking like this? Why the sudden concern with Nne?"

"If there is an emergency, what do we do?" Jasper replied. "And she will not accept to come to Lagos permanently."

"What of Rapu?"

"Rapu has elected to base in the Federal Capital." Jasper let the thought sit for a bit before he asked, "Do you want to go live in the East?"

Amata eyed him in the dark. "Not without you. But why do you ask these things?"

Jasper's skin skittered. He caressed his bare chest. It felt good to be loved.

"I am thinking of going abroad sometimes." He paused. *Though not before consummating the union and dropping one or two babies.* "I want to know how abroad is. Importers always tell us stories about London, Paris, and Germany, how things work there—constant light and running water. Some have gone as far as Hong Kong and China. Me, I have not crossed the Seme border here."

"Well, you can go and return. But it is also good if you want me to relocate to the East to be close to Nne. Whatever you say, sir."

"This is one of the reasons I like you, Amata," Jasper said, scratching his elbows. A glowing feeling enveloped his body. He smiled at his wife. "I nwero nsogbu. You have no problem. I will think about it well. It will be good to travel abroad and be like one's peers, order goods, and ship them oneself. If you see the nonsense some of these manufacturers ship to us."

"True?"

Jasper was worked up now. "Dike ordered engines, full engines for Mack trucks and tippers. Paid cost insurance freight upfront. When he went to clear the goods, he called me to come and see the rubbish that the Chinese suppliers had packaged. And what about Mike Merchandise? He ordered jeans from Guangdong. He shed tears when he opened his container. That is why he sent one of his brothers to China. The guy lives there now and has even married a Chinese. He inspects every consignment before he ships them to Mike by himself."

Jasper took a sip of his Guinness stout. The best, Amata had commented once. Onwa is a major distributor of many brands, but he quaffs only Guinness. So it must be the best. Jasper took another sip as if to confirm that opinion. He was getting tired. It had been a long day. He yawned with his mouth closed.

"But is the visa easy to obtain?" Amata asked. "One hears all sorts of tales of woe about visas."

Jasper tried in vain to stifle a yawn before answering. "Not so easy. I will get a sponsor who will show me the way. But before then, I will go to Cotonou and maybe Ghana to disvirgin my passport."

In the darkness, Amata smirked. *You want to deflower the passport. What of your wife?* A chill enveloped her. She grabbed her elbows in her palms and looked absent-mindedly into the night. Over the noise of the city, she caught the end of something Jasper had said: "…apply for our passports this week."

"So soon?"

"The processing takes time. But if you mean so soon to travel overseas, the answer is no. We will move from here first. I saw a three-bedroom flat. We will need space to store merchandise if I go and procure some myself from foreign markets. No reason we cannot sell from home if need be."

"Are you thinking of investing in landed property at all? So we don't pay rent."

"Yes, I am thinking, but these people worry us a lot."

"Who?"

"The omo onile people. Those land touts make endless claims on Lagos landlords. I prefer to build in the East first, consolidate there in case of trouble."

"Trouble? In Lagos?"

Jasper nodded as he tipped his mug upside down to reach the last drops of beer. He tapped his right foot on the floor.

"You don't know what we see in this Lagos, how these people are hounding us, pushing us to vacate their land. Land that we bought with our hard-earned money. Were they sleeping when they sold us the land?"

"I wonder."

"The government recently sent a circular to our people at Ladipo Market to vacate the land because they want to rebuild the market."

"Where will they go?" Amata asked. "And only God knows how long that project will take."

"It's a trick to take away our stalls and allocate them to indigenes and all these politicians' friends. We know their plan."

"Will our people move?"

"Do they have a choice?" He bored his eyes into her and caressed her smooth cheeks. "Eventually, they will be forced to. Look at ASPAMDA—"

"ASPAMDA?"

"Auto Spare Parts and Machinery Dealers Association. At the Trade Fair Complex. Jakande pursued us from Jankara and ordered us to Alaba. Before, these areas were swamps. Our people sand-filled them, developed them. Now the government has eyes on the property, planning to edge us out."

"Government is a powerful force, a ruthless enemy. It can force people to relocate."

"Relocate to where, my wife?" Jasper yawned. This time, he did not try to stifle it. "They will not provide any alternative. Just move. Or the government will bring in caterpillars. Once that is done, people will scramble to save their wares and beg the tractors to give them a few hours to pack. I do not know what we Igbos have done. We are hustling, developing towns all over the country, all over the world. Yet people hate us."

"Our people should build at home, in the East. Let buyers come looking for them there. Customers can come to the East the way you want to go to Taiwan."

"Have you seen where money comes to find someone?" Jasper queried. His eyes would be bulging, lips parted, Amata knew, but in the dark of the night, she could only imagine it.

"You sit down and wait, and buyers come? You have to go in search of it, my dear. That is how our system works. Why does street trading thrive? We have developed our markets in Nnewi, Onitsha, and Aba. It is expanding that we are doing, going out like the Jews, to increase and multiply our holdings."

He stood up, and Amata followed suit. She advised him to look into the stock market. Igbo moguls constituted the major depositors in banks but did not invest in them. A portfolio there had merit.

"So?"

The blackout persisted. Jasper stretched, extending his arms above his head, crackling his bones, arching his back. They used the light from their mobile phones to navigate their way around the furniture.

CHAPTER 12

Not quite two weeks later, a more spacious flat on the first floor of their block became vacant. Jasper grabbed it. They painted the flat and changed the door locks.

"We have ample space for storage and for our family when the kids start coming," Jasper enthused.

Without climbing your wife, where will the kids come from? Amata scoffed.

Jasper adored the wraparound veranda that skirted their new home. He would sit outside in the evenings after dinner, listening to the night sounds while having a beer and watching one NBA match or European soccer on his phone.

"Ebuka!" he called from the verandah.

"Sir!" The young apprentice stuck his head outside.

"Come and clear these plates."

"Yes, sir."

The inverter he installed was a good idea. Fully charged, it provided six hours of electricity. If they were lucky, power would be restored by then.

Jasper shared his good fortune in the apprentice with Amata. Ebuka had turned out to be a hardworking and honest servant. For a master, these were the two most important qualities sought in an apprentice. The young lad treated Jasper's affairs as his and handed over the complete money they made in the market. He thought again about Zona's advice to engage more apprentices. Most of Jasper's market neighbours boasted of several interns, each watching the other closely. But Ebuka was honest and did not need other apprentices to shadow him. It was customary for a master to have more than one boy, but the cost was huge. Your profits could easily be swallowed up by housekeeping expenses. He pushed the thought aside, recalling an Igbo saying that "the wrapper that has not adequately covered the hips, you want to trail on the ground."

While Ebuka washed the dishes, Amata took a shower and lay in wait for her sweetheart. She liked being in his company. They conversed well and understood each other. Only intimacy was lacking, and it irked her. Her body ached, looking at him so near and yet unavailable. Perhaps tonight, after their chat, he would melt and extend the closeness to the bedroom.

Thoughts of their meeting at the Amichi wedding flapped through her mind. It was auspicious that he and his group sat at one of the two tables assigned to her. She had ensured they lacked none of the delicacies usually hoarded and reserved for the high table. He had noticed and expressed appreciation. The flirting had started there and then. She had watched, bemused, when the young men were called out to dance with the groom. Jasper had twisted and turned, displaying energetic and acrobatic moves and steps, peacocking.

They had exchanged numbers, and a telephone romance was ignited. It idled for a while, but they spent time in their neighbouring villages at Easter and the relationship took off. By August, when their respective towns celebrated the New Yam festival, Jasper had proposed.

Do you permit me to go knock on your father's door? Jasper had asked.

Permission granted yesterday, she had giggled.

It was not lost on Amata that some would consider their courtship too short, but by then, she was panicking. She had completed her national service and still had no boyfriend. True, she had had to sever budding friendships with fellow undergrads in the university when they sought her honeypot. Each time a guy toasted her, he expected to go the whole hog. One beau almost succeeded, but she remembered the SUV her father had promised his girls and left the young man to his own devices. That was when she decided it was best not to date at all.

You will die an old maid, her roommates derided. *Bedmatics is part of dating in the citadels of knowledge.*

Citadels of carnal knowledge, you mean, she had sneered back.

Her panic increased when her mother called her aside and asked, *Is there no one pricing your market?*

When Jasper started sniffing around her, she was more than ready. And now, here they were.

From the bedroom, Amata heard Jasper double-lock the entrance doors. She waited, decked out on the cool foam, refreshed after the wash. She drifted off but was awakened by the sound of him in the shower.

To stay awake, Amata dialled her sister. Louisa was two years younger and a student at Nnamdi Azikiwe University, Awka. No answer. Amata tried again. Still no reply.

She sent an SMS. *How is Na U?*

The reply, when it came, surprised Amata. *For shame.*

Blood of Jesus! Shame? What was going on? Amata's heart beat faster, piqued by her sibling's insult. Did she miss something? If there was an issue, was it not better to discuss it? Why resort to abuse?

Back to sender, she replied. She checked her Facebook page hoping to find an explanation for Lulu's outburst. Her sister had unfriended her.

Her phone jingled. Louisa.

Amata ignored it. As the first daughter of Onwa's household, her siblings owed her respect, reverence even. It was not only an exalted position. It was spiritual. Upset by the lack of deference, she let the call ring out. Her phone jingled again. And once more, Amata ignored it.

"Answer the call or shut it up!" Jasper snarled from the bathroom.

She swiped right.

"I am sorry," Louisa began. When Amata did not respond immediately, she continued. "It's because you did not collect the Jeep."

"Whatever it is, Louisa Umeh, you have no right to talk to me with disrespect. I am not only older than you but also occupy a revered position in Chief Umeh's household."

"I am sorry, sis. Truly."

Amata relented.

"So if everyone is railing against me, I cannot count on my one and only sister?"

"You know you can, Ama. It's just that Onwa is devastated. He told me to watch it and not to disappoint him like you did."

"You remember my problem?"

"The monthlies?"

"Yes."

"You mean you've not done someth—"

"I am seeing a doctor. One of these days, I will call Onwa and collect."

"Not you, your husband."

"Don't uproot your hair. Onwa will get the call."

"Hurry, because, I mean, how long does it take? I even thought I would be coming to Lagos next Christmas holiday to carry baby."

"God will do it. Jasper will soon call Onwa."

Amata heard the empty plastic bucket being upturned. She ended the conversation hurriedly and lay facing the ceiling, a Modigliani nude. Soon, Jasper strolled in with a cloth tied loosely around his waist. Sometimes, he did not wipe his body dry but left the water to cool him and soak into the bed. If he saw Amata spread-eagled on the bed, he did not let on. His wife watched as he sat down on his side of the bed, unravelled the wrapper, and then settled into the foam. He exhaled audibly as his head hit the pillow. Amata lay still, waiting. Then came the whirring. As he sank deeper into Orpheus's embrace, Jasper's snoring became louder, more regular, like the whine of an idling petrol engine.

Is this man's manhood defective? To lie beside a nude woman and not be moved. Is he gay? Why get a wife and ignore her night in, night out? What market is this that I have entered?

She pursed her lips. Under her pillow, she permanently placed a chaplet. She felt for it, cupped it in her palm, and fondled the beads. *Blood of Jesus,* she prayed, *let my period come. Because a woman in her prime, without the monthlies, is but a man.* She knew it was a matter of time before in-laws and busy-bodies would start asking Jasper what she-man he had brought home to be his wife and advise him to get rid of her and marry a proper lady.

Amata winced. She stroked the beads with increased frenzy. *Madonna, please, please,* she gasped as sleep nudged her. *I beg you, talk to your Son. Let my period appear. Biko.*

CHAPTER 13

Charity's newborn's dedication took place one sunny day. She was happy because the event also marked her outing ceremony. After that, the new mother could go out. Once the church service was over, guests proceeded to Zona's house for the socials.

For this occasion, Amata resurrected the purple Indian George fabric "up-and-down" that she had worn at her own traditional marriage. The wide-necked blouse showed a hint of cleavage. In some women, half of the breasts hung out of the blouse like loose headlamps. *These tailors really overdo it,* she thought, tugging at the neckline. That was when she felt a warm sensation in her pudenda, then of something drooling down her thighs. She hurried to the nearest table, deposited the tray she was carrying, and dashed to the washroom. A long line of guests was queueing to use it, so she sought out Charity for the key to her bedroom.

There, her suspicion was confirmed. She had never been as elated seeing her period. Twelve months absent! *Thank You, Lord. Thank you, Madonna. Thank you, Prof. Ogedengbe.* Finally, her husband would know her. Luckily, it had not stained her outfit. She helped herself to her co-wife's toiletries and re-joined the fanfare, all smiles and light-headed.

An orchestra was playing a highlife number when Amata emerged. She waved to the musicians and danced a few steps in passing. The rays of the setting sun were in her eyes. She glowed.

She glanced at her husband under the canopies. She watched as Zona's business partners and guests mingled, cracked jokes and shouted ribaldries at each other. Assorted hot drinks flowed endlessly. A special canopy was dedicated to the members of the Elite Merchants Club of Nigeria, Lagos Branch. Amata watched Zona go from the high table to the Merchants' canopy, greeting guests and swapping banter. One club member, the sole distributor of Yago Spanish wine, gave him ten cartons of wine as a gift. Zona exchanged arm greetings with him. The fellow was dressed in a long, white lace fabric. In his hand was a round leather fan with his title emblazoned on it. He waved it in greeting his cohorts. Later, it would serve to shoo away flies that circled his brew.

The zinger was the arrival of the leader of the Igbos in Lagos, Eze-Igbo, High Chief Donatus Ubanese. He was in full regalia, accompanied by a retinue of aides and praise singers. Amata could see a checked wrapper peeping out from under his ankle-length velvet ishiagu. His neck was bedecked with layers of orange and ivory coral beads and a chunky gilded chain. A white feather trembled on his red cap. He advanced in measured steps, heralded by a lad with inflated cheeks, blowing the oja. The High Chief extended one snakeskin mule after the other, struck his staff on the ground between them, paused and waved to onlookers in slow motion, basking in their adulation. A peacock, Zona thought as he hurried to meet the dignitary, jubilant at the honour the chief's presence bestowed on him.

"Anu anagba o na ata nni!" he hailed the High Chief by his full title, The game that continues to graze while hunters are on its trail. They exchanged arm greetings.

"Omeifeukwu," his chipmunk jowls bobbed.

"Agbalanze. I salute you, sir."

Zona led the guest of honour to a sofa overlaid with red velvet.

In one corner of the yard, a caterer, Nwanyi Nnewi, was conjuring local delicacies for the guests. She had mingled strips of locust beans and palm oil with bits of stockfish, garden-egg, and crayfish to summon up the pungent aroma of *ugba*. There was abacha made from fermented cassava and spicy nkwobi that made Amata's mouth long to taste the cow foot delicacy. She perceived the ngwongwo, a goat head delicacy spiced with pepper, onions, potash and herbs, and she could almost taste the delicious peppered oil running down the bronzed sides of the roasting chickens. A profusion of mouth-watering aromas filled the garden. A long line of guests formed in front of the giant cauldron of breadfruit porridge. Faced with all this lovely food, even the most ardent dieters among the guests jettisoned their resolutions and indulged. It was a lavish function. Clearly, Zona was a rich man. *Yet he could not give a face-lift to the family house to welcome a new bride,* Amata smirked as she turned away to find Charity.

She saw Charity walking towards Zona. Many guests had already stopped by Zona to drop envelopes for the baby, and she was on her way to collect them. "Baby money is for the missus," she heard Zona remark to those around him as his wife drew nearer. "It is money for hot compress."

Charity's mother, Odibeze, also overheard him, and her eyes lit up in expectation. She was sitting in the middle of the guests, carrying the newborn and marvelling at the expensive clothes and accoutrements on display. She wore a white lace blouse atop a local Ankara fabric. Charity had braided her mother's hair in a corn-row style, though the thick jacquard scarf sitting like a helmet on her head covered all but the fringes. Charity had asked her to tie a "george," the high-end trending Indian sari Igbo women donned at ceremonies. *Who does that?* Odibeze had asked in bafflement. Wear expensive cloth to carry a baby that pisses and pukes every hour? And she had settled for the inexpensive ersatz version.

Odibeze jiggled her knees to rock the baby, who was beginning to fidget and whimper. *I pray that Charity gives birth to a boy next pregnancy so she can safeguard her marriage. Three girls in a row?* That was stepping on a slippery slope. How long will my in-law's patience last? She also prayed that Zona would do her well at the end of this omugwo. The last time she had cared for her daughter's newborn, she had gone home with six high-quality wrappers and a weighty envelope. This time, she hoped it would be no less. However, the omugwo, which should have lasted three months and afforded her time to rest from farm work and women's unending meetings, was being cut by half so her in-law could come too. She recalled that her son-in-law had not wanted to celebrate the outing service because the child was a girl. *You must treat each child equally,* Odibeze had advised. Luckily, Zona had listened to her.

She could detect the onset of stiffness in the right knee. She passed the infant to the house girl and rose to de-cramp her legs, adjusting her wrappers to equalize their ends. This accomplished, she swanned with the music. It was a rhythmic number by the Oriental Brothers that one could not help but sway to. Charity rushed to her mother's side and showered her with crisp naira notes. The notes swirled in the air before flittering to the ground. Odibeze let them be because it was a cue for the guests. Many, dancing to the music, approached the matriarch. They exhibited a few jigs around her before flipping notes on her. Not to be outdone, Zona swaggered through the crowd and flung some high denomination wads his in-law's way.

Amata took in the scene, grabbed a grocery bag and began picking up the money. Odibeze, sweating, regained her seat after dancing to three numbers, which included the popular *Sweet Mother* by Nico Mbarga, a favourite among women because it extolled the virtues of mothers. Amata handed her the grocery bag.

The musician turned his attention to Zona.

"Omeifeukwu," he crooned into the microphone. "Omeifeukwu, able Chairman, CEO, Zona Group of Companies. Omeifeukwu, astute mogul. Everything you touch crafts money."

Zona strutted to the vocalist and plastered the singer's forehead with wads of N100 notes. He lifted one foot, stamped it on the ground, jerked this way, lifted the other, stamped it and oscillated his shoulders, then turned to regain his seat. But his confreres of the Elite Merchants Club would have none of it. They waylaid him halfway and surrounded him, dancing around him and unleashing paper money on him. Their tasselled red caps bobbed as they danced and sang his praises: *Echezona Okonkwo. CEO, Mr. Moneybag, Opaku Big Man in Lagos. Zona. Zona. Omeifeukwu, Omeifeukwu, with the Midas touch. Major importer. Your hand is money, your leg is money.* The circle around Zona was three-person thick. The moguls, unable to reach him from where they stood, flung inch-thick wads of naira at him.

"Daalu nu," Zona enthused, overwhelmed. He hailed each magnate by their title.

"Okosisi."

They exchanged the arm greeting, one with his leather fan, the other with his short staff made of ivory.

"Nnabuenyi."

"Ochendo Abiriba."

"Oga Dubai. Agu Opaku."

When the magnates finally vacated the dance floor, the ground was a carpet of notes. Zona's apprentices gathered the money in jute bags, hauled them into the house and handed them over to Charity. She locked the bags in the bedroom and slipped the key into her bra.

CHAPTER 14

The sun had lost its sting when Jasper and Amata extricated themselves from the merrymaking.

Once they settled in the car, Jasper turned to Amata. "I saw you run into the house. Hope no problem."

Sweat streamed down his face. He fiddled with the air conditioner knob and removed the black fez he'd worn all day.

"My period has come."

They drove on in silence.

At home, Amata wiggled out of her party clothes and dived into the washroom. Her husband followed immediately and watched as she removed her bloodied underwear. Before she could pour water on it to clean it, her husband took it from her and closely looked at it as if scrutinizing it to be certain it was really her menstrual blood. Amata quietly watched him till he dropped the underwear into the bucket of water she had prepared.

After the wash, Amata dug out a box of sanitary towels that had been gathering dust at the back of the medicine cabinet. She padded herself and jumped into bed. Her mind played back the day's naming ceremony. Eloduchi: As it pleases God. What a lovely name. It was an acceptance of the child's gender. Yes, the parents longed for a male child, but it pleased God to send another female. What would be the pet form? Elodie? Chichi? No, Chichi, the diminutive of so many Igbo names for boys and girls, was common. Elodie was rare.

"Are you awake?"

Through slits in her eyes, she saw Jasper standing beside her, but she feigned sleep. After a while, he strode to his side of the bed. The air conditioner purred intermittently, sending waves of cool air up the drapes. She could hear the frogs croaking in nearby gutters while the night crawlers braved the snarling traffic in the distance.

Amata heard his bedside drawer creak open. Jasper took something from it. She held her breath as he popped out some tablets, which he threw into his mouth. Then he unfurled his loin cloth and paralleled his wife.

Soon, Amata thought, they would consummate their marriage, Jasper could call Onwa, and the SUV would land. She smiled and relaxed. As a co-wife, she had been expected to attend to Zona's guests all day. Her legs ached.

"My shy wife," Jasper cooed. He rolled onto his side and faced her. Little by little, he untied the bow at the neck of her night dress and slipped the gown off. His hands shivered as he caressed her all over. Amata frowned. She hoped he was not about to mount her in this state. She locked her legs.

He tried to tease them open. She resisted.

"O gini?" What is it? He tugged at her bra, expectant. He had not anticipated this resistance. After all, was it not his merchandise? Fully paid for?

"With all this blood?"

"No matter," Jasper ruled.

"It matters, biko." She pulled the quilt over her.

"It does not." He tossed the cover aside. He knelt before her, braceleted her calves, and drew her down.

"It does." Amata fished for the duvet.

"Is it not my property? To collect when I want?"

She sat up and shifted away.

"Amata."

"Sir."

"What shall we call this?" He sounded beat. He had not envisaged this obstacle.

"Onwa said if our husbands find us intact, he will gift us a Jeep."

"So?"

"How will you prove it with all this blood?"

"So, as a man, I cannot know if my woman is a virgin?"

"I don't know."

"Amata."

"Sir."

"Open your legs!"

"No."

"Open your legs. I am your husband."

"After the visitor."

He looked left and right and exhaled loudly. "What shall we call this?"

He tried again to pry the legs apart. Amata resisted with all her might and rolled out of reach.

"For the last time, open your legs for me."

"After the blood."

He edged away and crawled to his side, his tumescent phallus disappointed. He was breathing heavily, wistfully, perhaps contemplating his options.

They lay beside each other in the half-light, each unsure of what would happen next. *What is an extra three days?* Amata thought. Her head flooded with questions. *Did he belong to some cult that demanded sex while a wife was having her period? What would he do? Would he be violent? Force her? Rape her? If one's husband "by-forced" it, was it rape? Was a wife allowed to say no? To dictate things?* If only she could reach out to Odoziaku now.

The rays of the moon and outside security lights projected into the room through slits in the drapes. The anti-burglar bars made weird cruciform shapes on the wall. She stole a glance at Jasper. His chest was heaving. This was their first quarrel. She needed someone to talk to. Her mother. But there was no way to call home. Slowly, Amata turned on her side, adjusted her scattered braids and wrapped her arms around her head.

"I will send you back to your father." Jasper's disembodied threat hung in the room.

"Blood of Jesus. On what grounds? What wrong have I done?"

"You don't know?"

"Because I said to wait till after my monthly?"

"Have I not waited long enough?"

"Then you can wait another day or two."

Silence descended on the room again. *How can a wife, fully paid for, rebuff her husband's advances?* Jasper thought. Some of his friends had warned him about university graduates wanting to wear the trousers at home. He should have listened. Eventually, he spoke.

"I waited for you to bleed in my house because I did not want another man's child. Now that your monthly is here, I am reassured. Allow me."

She had no more excuses. She remained silent, and her husband took it for acquiescence. He unsnapped her bra and swooned. For the first time, he allowed his eyes to feast on Amata's body. Afraid his body would outrun him, he engaged gear.

"Open your legs!"

"They are wide open."

When Jasper had spent himself, Amata got up to go to the washroom. Jasper pulled her back.

"Daalu, Stainless," he murmured in a solemn, husky voice. "Thank you."

There and then, in a raucous voice, he burst into a song, raising his hands and extolling Mighty Jehovah.

> *Take glory, Father, take glory, Son.*
> *Take glory, Holy Ghost, now forever more.*

Amata gathered her clothes and hastened to the washroom.

CHAPTER 15

Something changed in Jasper for the better that night. His feelings towards his wife held him in their thrall. He ensconced her in his arms.

"I did not know that it was possible to go through the university and emerge untouched," he said as they lay side by side. "All the stories we hear about life on campus, parties and bashes. You escaped that."

"I was tempted. But Odoziaku got Papa to promise us girls a brand-new SUV if we remained intact till marriage. It was a huge incentive. Everyone on campus longed to drive a Jeep. I faced my books and scorned boys."

He rubbed his chest in contentment. He was a lucky man indeed! The only one in his wife's life, past and present. And the future, surely. It was rare in present-day Nigeria, where girls rollicked full-time.

"Please call Onwa in the morning," she said, yawning. "When you came to knock, I reminded him of the deal. Please call him. I want my ride."

Jasper was alive now. The sleep that used to knock him out once his head kissed the pillow left on a long-distance journey. He cleared his throat forcefully. Not quite satisfied, he emitted a fusillade of coughs.

"Listen, my dear, and listen well. I have been thinking. We cannot drive a Jeep now because I am just starting out. If we do, we would send the wrong signal that I have made it, not quite two years after my freedom. What of Oke Nmanwu, my master? He will think I defrauded him during my service to him. What will Zona think? How can he import—?"

"Tell them it is a wedding gift from your in-law."

"You do not understand human nature. They will punish me in their jealousy."

They faced each other in silence. After a while, Amata had an idea. "At least, call Onwa. Let me redeem my image, collect my reward. Afterward, we can sell it, buy a smaller car and invest the surplus into our business."

It was a reasonable compromise.

"It is your due. I cannot stand in the way of something coming to you."

The next day, when his father-in-law's voice boomed in his ears, Jasper hailed him, "The moon that shines for all. Only one Moon in the whole world. Onwa!" he exclaimed.

"My son."

"Onwa, I thank you, sir, for gifting me this rare gem of a wife. You are a great in-law."

"My son, between two men, I have been waiting for this call. I have been wondering, what is keeping my in-law? I asked Odoziaku, but she assured me everything was fine."

"Good news has no expiry date, sir. In fact, it is good to delay it to extend the happy feelings it generates."

"I am happy my jewel did not disappoint me. I have a wedding gift for her. My boy will bring it tomorrow."

"Ha. Another gift, sir? More than what you have gifted us already?"

"It is a pre-nuptial agreement with my jewels. I am duty-bound to honour it."

"Onwa!"

"My son."

"We are greeting Odoziaku."

"She will hear."

Odoziaku was grinning when Onwa put the phone down. He had put the phone on speaker, so she had followed the gist.

She beamed at the news, for it meant that she had succeeded in raising a well-behaved daughter.

She heaved a sigh of relief and said a new prayer. *Now, may the monthly disappear so Ama can get pregnant. Please, Jehovah, let me also undertake the omugwo visit like my peers. As our people say, when you long for what is rightfully yours, it is not greed.*

CHAPTER 16

The "tear rubber" Toyota Prado arrived in Lagos the following day. It was laden with assorted foodstuff—yams, plantains, pineapples, garri, and snails. The bearer of the gifts was awestruck.

Turning to Amata, he said, "Congrats! It is no mean feat. Nowadays, men prey on young girls and do not allow them to face their studies. They use all types of ruses to ensnare them, especially in our universities where there is no parental supervision. Do you know politicians ship female students from tertiary institutions to provide entertainment at their parties? Madam, you have done well." To Jasper, he said, "You are a lucky man, sir."

That night, sleep eluded Amata. She turned and twisted, too excited to relax and shut down. She imagined herself in the shiny black vehicle, cruising around Lagos and lording it over lesser cars, Beyoncé blaring, the air conditioner chilling in the tropical heat. It would be sweet to drive the SUV in the village, too, so that her mates would see and "jealous her."

The next day, when a lone rooster was croaking its wake-up service and the muezzin was calling Moslems to prayer, Amata crept out of bed. Her heart pounded as she let her hand glide over the shiny black paint. She pressed the electronic fob key and climbed into the driver's seat.

Jasper startled her when he tapped the window. She turned on the ignition and rolled down the glass.

"Okwu oto ekene eze."

She smiled at his description of the SUV as "One who stands upright to greet the king." Had he also been excited? Might they keep the car?

Amata ran her fingers across the dashboard, turned on the radio, and opened the pigeonhole. She rapped the steering to the beat of the music and inhaled the distinctive new car smell. She posed in front of it, and Jasper took a picture of her, trying in vain to suppress a smile. Amata was like a child with a new toy. She immediately sent the photo to her sister and brother via WhatsApp. "I have collected my Prado o! Luz, Lulu, Louisa, whatever, it's over to you now," she texted.

"Remember that we cannot keep it," Jasper warned. "It will cause a lot of bad blood if we do. Don't get attached to it." He taped a FOR SALE on the front and rear windscreens.

"But why not drive it around the neighbourhood for a bit? After all, it is by parading a goat around that it gets sold."

Neighbours oohed and ah-ed over the vehicle as it reflected in the morning sunlight. It was like an elephant in the modest yard. *Amata is very humble, they said to each other. To come from a rich home and submit to a struggling young man like Jasper.* In private, some gave her the side-eye. Envy gnawed at their intestines. Some housewives berated their husbands: *If you know what your fellow man did to make it, go and do the same.* And the men pinched themselves, regretting that they married from poor and needy homes. *I was looking for something in the pocket of someone looking for something,* they admonished themselves. *Why did I not think of marrying rich?* They sighed and ground their teeth.

During the day, Jasper parked the car out front. Soon, many buyers came calling. However, Jasper declined all their offers.

"Too low, Stainless," he said to Amata. "It still wears the factory cellophane it came with! It is brand new, not tokunbo, not Belgium."

"Whatever you say, di m." My husband.

"Drive it around some more."

Amata was only too happy to oblige.

On the last Sunday of the month, she drove it to the Opaku Wives Meeting, where she met Charity, who, as previously agreed, introduced her to the association.

The meeting went well, but Amata became the talk of the Opaku Diaspora. *Jasper has bought a brand-new Jeep for his wife. Imagine. How did he swing that? He must be into afia ntu,* some said. Others postulated that he must be into the "Yahoo Yahoo" internet fraud or had shortchanged his former master. Many wives pestered their husbands for a new ride for themselves.

On returning home from the women's meeting, Charity mentioned the car to Zona, trying to elicit envy.

"I'm corralling three children and moving about in an old Golf. Open a shop for me so that I can make money and buy myself what I want."

"It is Onwa who bought the car for his daughter," Zona fired back in an icy voice. "What dowry did your parents gift you apart from a Butterfly sewing machine and some aluminum pans? Empty vessels making noise, much like their owner."

Just as Jasper had predicted, the Prado brewed bad blood between him and his brothers and fellow traders, the way Joseph's coat of many colours had strewn strife among Jacob's sons. He prayed for a credible buyer so they could get rid of the vehicle from their lives.

One happy day, a politician's wife came calling. Jasper was expectant because everyone knew politicians' pockets were filled with oil money.

"It is brand new, Ma," he forewarned the socialite as she circled the vehicle. "Tear-rubber. You do not need to look at the engine. It is first class. The mileage on it was to drive it from the East to Lagos. The battery, brand new; factory-fitted AC, in top condition, ideal for this humid heat of Lagos. See? Alloy wheels, with spare tyre and jack and emergency kit. There's a sunroof and central locking. Full options. And black is an executive colour. It's perfect for you. Give me twelve million, carry go."

The politician's wife tried to haggle for a discount, but Jasper was a seasoned negotiator. "Let me tell you, Alhaja, some people already offered me fourteen. I don't know why I did not collect their money. Maybe I should just allow my wife to drive it. After all, is she not a human being? How can I forbid her a good thing?"

He bore his eyes into the dowager, leaving the silent codicil of his pitch unspoken: *I am selling this car to you because my people are not in government and do not have a hand in the government till. Your people are ruling, so you can intercept the good things of life from us.*

Alhaja, already salivating, paid up.

Well after the Prado had left Jasper's household, it was still the subject of talk in the homes and shops of his associates. When Jasper explained that it was a gift from Onwa to his daughter, his associates became jealous of him for astutely marrying into a wealthy family that would not make incessant demands on him. Several of his mates were obligated to provide for their wives' families. By marrying into wealth, Jasper had pre-emptively plugged those stressful leakages.

To make up for selling the vehicle, Jasper bought his wife a second-hand Camry and invested the rest of the money. When Amata attended the next women's meeting in the Camry, envy towards her ballooned threefold. *Last time, it was Prado,* they commented. *This time, a Camry. O-o-o, some women are just lucky. And she has not even "born." We, with broods lining up from here to the bus stop, depend on keke for school runs.*

Jasper did not tell anyone the proviso that resulted in the gift. But secrets, by their nature, hardly remain so for long.

CHAPTER 17

With the seed money from his master, the Benjamin of the Okonkwo family planned his autorickshaw business. Rapu favoured the several satellite towns of the Federal Capital Territory that allowed tricycles and motorbikes to be used for commercial transportation. He scouted far and wide for a suitable stall, one that was secure, visible, and accessible. He was lucky. A plaza was sprouting along the Abuja-Keffi highway. He made a down payment for a stall on the ground floor. As soon as the decking was done, he put an iron gate on the store and got an electrician to wire it. A visit to the Abuja Electricity Distribution Board connected electricity to his shop. He was in business.

Stanley, an Opaku indigene, signed up as his apprentice. He spent nights in the store while Rapu lived in a rented mini-flat nearby. Occasionally, Rapu travelled to Nnewi to buy a few knocked-down tricycles and bikes and bought spares from Innoson Group, which shipped the parts to his store. Business was so good that within a year, Rapu envisioned opening a second shop. He reckoned he could enlist Zona's help to import directly from Taiwan, and if all went according to plan, he would be an importer himself within five years, supplying retailers from Onitsha to Owerri to Aba and the Federal Capital Territory. He'd leave Lagos alone. Lagos already had its full share of importers. It was better to expand outside it. *When the business and the expansions stabilize,* he thought, *I will think of starting a family.*

One morning, Rapu found a series of bloody XXX marks on the graffitied walls outside his stall and an angry warning: STOP WORK BY ORDER OF KLG. He confronted the builder.

"What is happening? Why has the Karu Local Government ordered you to stop work?"

"I don't know. Better ask the developer."

Rapu shuddered. He had paid two years' rent upfront on the store, and he needed to sort the trouble out before he lost his money. "I will settle them," the fellow said when Rapu challenged him about the order.

He showed his development permit to Rapu and Dan, another tenant who sold plastics. This eased Rapu's concerns. Clearly, the developer knew how to deal with the officials because work resumed on the plaza the next day, and Rapu was open for business again. There were no more closures like that, and in no time, the building grew another floor and another wing.

One day, Dan invited Rapu to meet his sister, visiting from home. Oluchi was a pretty young girl who was a final-year student at the Nekede Polytechnic, Owerri. They exchanged phone numbers, and Rapu's thoughts of starting a family were stirred again. He found himself thinking that if he met someone suitable, he could work towards marriage within a year and then focus on his business.

Later, Rapu was in his stall with his head full of revised plans for developing his business when his phone rang. The name on the display said "Oluchi." He answered.

"It's Oluchi Igbokwe, Dan's sister," the mellifluous voice said. When he didn't respond immediately, she specified, "the plastics seller."

A smile formed on Rapu's lips. "Oho, Kedu? You will live long. I was just about to call you."

"Not true."

"True to God."

"Anyway, I called to say hello and to thank you for how you and my brother cooperate with each other at the plaza. Please keep it up," Oluchi's voice rose an octave. It must have taken a lot of courage for her to make the first move.

"No problem in that department, my dear. We are one." Rapu's heart skipped a beat. *She fancies me,* he thought. Maybe he should ask her out.

"Are you around for long?"

"Unfortunately, not. I head back East tomorrow to start my final year."

"Oluchi, Oluchi, what a fine name," he sweet-talked as he formed a plan. "Want to meet for a drink before you leave?"

They agreed to meet at a local eatery at sundown. Rapu spent the rest of the day dreaming of his future. Oluchi was set to graduate in a year and then do her National Youth Service. Could she be posted to the FCT? One year was a good period to court and plan a wedding.

He called Iyom.

"Nne, kedu?" he said when she answered.

"We have seen today," his mother replied cheerily. He knew that she would be listening to his voice to detect his mood. "How is market? Are you selling?"

"We are pushing it."

"What of Abuja people?"

Before he could answer, his mother continued, "Be vigilant," she cautioned. "That is enemy territory. You are a stranger there, so keep your eyes and ears open. You understand?"

Old people are easily xenophobic, Rapu thought, but replied, "Yes, Ma."

"I hope that your apprentice is serving you well?"

"Stanley is trying, Ma."

"You have reached marrying age, my son, so keep an eye open for a good candidate."

"There is a girl from Owerri that—"

Iyom did not let him finish. "Owerri? Have girls finished in Anambra?"

"Owerri is Igbo, Nne."

"Did I say that they are not Igbo? My question is: Are brides scarce in Anambra? Your older brothers married from outside Opaku. Zona went to Lilu. Jasper to Nkwa. Are we osu to be marrying from outside our town? Biko, my son, marry from Opaku."

"O-o-o Nne."

"When you are ready, we will look for a good wife for you from around here. You understand?"

"Ee."

"Do you hear what our in-law gifted Amata? Tear-rubber Jeep. Look for somebody from such a home, son. They do not have two heads."

Rapu had heard about the SUV. Jasper was lucky, marrying from a wealthy home. Iyom had a point. He should get a girl from such a background, not this Oluchi type whose school fees were probably paid by a struggling brother, a neophyte in business.

Despite his ambivalence after the conversation with Iyom, Rapu went on the date with Oluchi. The initial excitement he usually felt when he toasted a girl evaporated, stifled by Iyom's antagonism and bigotry. He spent half of the time scrolling his phone and watching videos on Instagram. When Oluchi complained, he retorted that they were important business matters. Instead of discussing their future, they endured the awkward silence.

Oluchi had been hopeful. Rapu looked ready for marriage; the signs were there. He had served out his Igba-boi and was growing a business. That was usually the first step. The next in the life of an adult male was family. What could have happened between setting up the date and the event itself? She had no inkling of his mother's admonition, but she mentioned to her brother that there was no thoroughfare on this route, contrary to what they had thought.

CHAPTER 18

The goods that Zona and his associates ordered duly arrived and were cleared from Apapa Wharf. Zona sent word to his brother to come and pick up his order. COD.

Jasper and Amata were in the shop, behind the counter, sitting on two high stools, watching out for customers, when the message arrived.

"What is the meaning of this COD, cash-on-delivery?" Amata asked, frazzled. "Did your brother not say you could take them on credit and pay after selling?"

"I thought so," Jasper answered. An imperceptible chill washed over him. He put a call to Zona.

"My dear, if you can drive a tear-rubber Jeep, you can pay cash," Zona's bland voice roared over the phone. "Are you getting my point?"

Amata heard it loud and clear and shuddered.

"This is what I feared," Jasper said to her after ending the call. "Our market is dog-eat-dog. Everyone is going about with a hidden dagger; one moment of inattention, they stab you in the back and twist the handle. That is why I said we would not drive that SUV."

He put the phone down, crossed his arms in front of him and reflected for a while. Some things were not clear. He called his brother again.

"Omeifeukwu, how much are the goods?"

"Two point two twelve."

Two million, two hundred and twelve thousand. "I thought we agreed on two million."

"Plus the freight and customs clearing, palm-greasing and all, two point two twelve."

"Okay, I am coming, sir."

He ended the call and looked at Amata, crestfallen. "He has included freight and clearing charges, which he said he would bear himself."

Jasper rose slowly. He felt weak in the legs. Shame washed over his face. For a brother to treat a junior like this in the full glare of outsiders was wrong. Where, he wondered, did this rain start to beat the Okonkwo family?

Ebuka approached with a customer he had engaged at the bus stop, who was clutching a faulty part.

"Front wheel bearings. Honda Accord, 2009."

He held out the part for Jasper to see. Ebuka took the part from him. There was a power outage in the market, and the air inside the shop was stale and humid. Jasper watched his apprentice disappear into the darkened interior. With a heavy heart, he wiped his brow and sat down again. He looked at the empty spaces on the shelves and on the floor. They needed to re-stock desperately. What was a trader with no wares to sell?

Jasper spruced himself up, donned his Shaquille baseball cap and dipped out. As he crossed the market to his brother's store, he sensed that envy had entered their family by his marriage to Amata and the SUV gift. When he met Amata at Amichi, he had no inkling of her family wealth. When he proposed to her, he did not know there was a prize on her hymen. Expecting to marry a virgin these days was like looking for a brand-new car in a used-car dealership. He had just been lucky. But his peers did not see things from that angle.

"Omeifeukwu!" he greeted as he entered Zona's inner office.

"Jasper Gee!" Zona acknowledged. "Come o, what is your praise name?"

"I am still a small fish, sir. I have no hailing name yet."

"I hear you, small fish driving tear-rubber Prado."

"Omeifeukwu, that car was Onwa's wedding gift to his daughter."

"Go round this market and ask all the married men how many of them got a spoke from their in-laws, starting with me. Are you getting my point?"

"I did not know about the SUV when I proposed," he said defensively. "But on to more important matters, Sir. What of madam and the children?"

"They are there. The person of your house, kwan?"

"We thank God, sir."

"Where are these boys?" Zona shouted into the air. "Bring cold water here!"

Unlike Jasper's store, Zona's shop was cool. It boasted a large, noiseless generator that was strong enough to run the AC. With the doors closed, the noise from neighbouring generators was almost inaudible, and the brothers could talk easily.

"It's about the goods you so kindly imported for me, sir."

In reply, Zona called one of his boys to bring the invoice.

"Show him!"

Jasper peered over the list of goods on the bill of lading. His eyes ticked the items. Everything was there. Finally, they darted to the total at the bottom: N2,212,000.

"They are in my warehouse. As soon as I get notification of payment, you take delivery. Are you getting my point?" Zona picked up the copy of the *Daily Sun* that was lying on his desk. "If you don't mind," he said, "I want to finish reading this article on the Apo Six. Such a tragedy."

Jasper's legs quivered. He had trouble breathing. The amount on the invoice twirled in his head: Two point two one two, remove nothing. Two point two one two, twopointtwoonetwo.

Zona shook his head and pretended to spit on the floor beside him. "Impunity! No law enforcement in this country. No value for human life."

He turned to Jasper, "How can the police kill six young people simply because a girl in their party rejected his advances?" He spat out again. "Tufia! And no justice for them?"

"Is it in the papers? It happened several years ago."

"In June 2005. The matter is in court—came up for hearing."

"It was horrible. Those lads traded here, in this market."

Zona's eyes went back to the paper as he read the names. "Ifeanyi Ozor, Chinedu Meniru, Augustina Arebu, Anthony Nwokike, Paulinus Ogbonna, Ekene Isaac Mgbe."

"Igbo folk. Does the government care?"

"Because the Augustina girl rejected the love advances of the policeman in the disco hall. Are you getting my point? If a girl rejects your love advances, you look elsewhere. There are many fishes in the market, or is it the sea?"

"Yoruba people have it that the girl who rejects your love advances is saving you from bankruptcy."

After reading some more lines, Zona folded the paper and flung it away. He stared at his brother. You could tell his spirit had chilled.

"I'm listening," he said.

"My wedding set me back some," Jasper explained, aiming to ask for time and to collect the goods on credit and settle in instalments.

However, Zona would not concede an inch.

"These Customs people are rogues, daylight robbers," he blurted out with operatic suddenness. "They collected all the cash I had on me. It was my turn to clear the containers. Akaji-aku cleared for us the last time. Are you getting my point? That is why I cannot give on credit. I am owed left, right and centre."

What happened to our brotherhood? Jasper wondered. When did the water soil? His stock was depleting. He needed wares to remain relevant. He advanced another proposal. "Suppose I collect the merchandise, then you give me two weeks to run around and see."

Zona was already shaking his head. "It seems you do not understand what I am saying. Have I done like this before to you?"

"That is why I am at a loss. You said I could collect on credit, sell and—"

"It is the market. Are you getting my point? Run around and see how much you can get between now and the weekend. Otherwise, I will sell the wares, and you will have to wait for our next order."

Jasper was taken aback. Zona's abruptness was not fraternal in the least.

"My shop is depleted. I need these goods," he pleaded.

Before Zona could answer, they were interrupted by a sales boy who came in wielding a muffler. A bulky customer was at his heels.

"He is pricing seventeen thousand, sir. I told him twenty last."

The customer waved to Zona. "Omeifeukwu."

"Ah, Chief? Na you?"

"Yes, sir. I told your boy I buy all my parts here and asked him to give me a discount."

"Ah, Chief, how much did we buy it now? Chief does not want us to remain in business."

"No. You will remain in business, Omeifeukwu."

"Amen. Sunday, shave five hundred off for Chief. He is a long-standing customer. Look at him well so you can give him the best price next time. All right? Chief, sit down now; let us bring you cold water."

"Next time, Omeifeukwu. My mechanic is waiting."

Jasper pinched himself. He sold the same part for less.

"Market is good in this part of Idumota," he observed when the fellow was out of earshot. "We sold that same part for fifteen thousand naira in our shop."

"It is all psychology," Zona replied, happy with himself. "And salesmanship." He realized that he was relaxing and changed tack abruptly. "So, as we were saying—"

"I sold the Prado. I explained to my woman that we are not yet at the level of gathering such items."

"If you sold it, you must be rolling in cash then. Are you getting my point? A brand new Prado can't fetch anything less than ten million."

Jasper flinched. He should not have mentioned the vehicle sale. The two brothers locked eyes.

"Two point two one two. Before the weekend." Zona stood up. The conversation was over.

Jasper felt an invisible noose tightening around his neck as he stepped out of his brother's stall. He was certain he would lose the goods if he did not pay upfront as demanded. Maybe he should go to his former master to borrow the money, he thought, but decided against it. He could not continue running to Oke Nmanwu for everything after he had been weaned. Or he could ask Oke Nmanwu's matronly wife, who had been like a mother to all her husband's apprentices. But going to her, Jasper knew, was tantamount to going to her husband. There were no secrets between the couple.

One last option reared its head in Jasper's mind: he could borrow from Amata. He had placed the Prado money in a fixed deposit. If they touched it now, before maturity, they would lose the interest. He was lost in thought, contemplating a way out, when someone shouted his name.

It was Cy, his erstwhile fellow apprentice. They had been freed on the same day by Chief Igwilo. Cy was a trader but liked to dress in two-piece suits, complete with a bow tie and fedora.

"Jasper Gee! Nwoke m." My man.

"Cy Mukeke!" They knocked arms the traditional way. Jasper studied Cy's clothes and compared them to his own modest appearance. He really needed to take more care with the way he dressed. *Fake it till you make it,* Amata had said when he told her they could not afford to cruise around in a Prado.

"What are you thinking about that your face is twisted like a screw?" Cy asked.

"Nna. Many things are competing for attention in a man's mind."

"Take it easy. Life no get duplicate."

"How market?" Jasper asked.

"Good, good, good."

"Triple good?"

"Nna, I've branched out o. Motor parts business is too congested. I'm now international. Voilà."

"In this business, we pick the kobo one by one. Slow and steady."

"Nna, I'm not in that slow and steady business," Cy said. "See all the chicks out there? None of them understands that language. It's money for hand, back for ground. Voilà."

"You are right; it's money that woman knows."

"How is madam?"

"She dey. It's our daily bread that we are pursuing."

"I hear you got a Jeep. Nna, you are not slow and steady o. You are a firebrand. Nna, show me the way o."

The way Cy teased Jasper was amusing, and it lifted the latter's spirit. *Show him the way, when I'm in hot soup and cannot boast of two point two million naira.* He forgot his predicament for a while.

"Cy Mukeke!"

They slapped their palms again.

"It's you that will show me the way," Jasper told his friend. "You are the international one, wearing the correct suit and tie and looking corporate. I was thinking of exploring across the border myself."

At the mention of tie and suit, Cy adjusted his tie and dusted his lapels. "My dear, this suit and tie na camouflage. Things are tough."

"Just to break even is daunting," Jasper agreed.

"There is space all over the West Coast. I'm in Cotonou for now but may move to Ghana. Voilà."

"No, Cy, not Ghana. Those people are not friendly at all to our people."

"It is envy. Voilà."

"What of ECOWAS?" Jasper asked. He had heard of the Protocol on Free Movement of Persons in the Community. "Does it not cover us?"

"My brother, ECOWAS is on paper. Instead of the Ghanaians apprenticing to us and learning, they want to use their government to push us out. Even some of our boys married their women to safeguard their investments. Yet, that one is paining them too."

"Just like in South Africa."

"Voilà. Their women prefer us. We spend on them, man. That is why, once in a while, they attack us and destroy the fruit of our sweat. So, shine your eyes. Do not just up and go. Francophone countries have law and order, so they are better. You can operate in peace once you pay your tax and contribute to their economy."

"I hear you."

"Let us keep in touch," Cy said by way of conclusion. He tweaked his tie and gave Jasper his number. "It is not easy to don a suit in this heat," he cracked. He lifted the fedora, fanned himself briskly with it, and pressed it back on his head.

Jasper saved the number and gave Cy his. "I have applied for a passport. Once it is in my possession, you will hear from me."

"Voilà. Jasper Gee!"

"Cy Mukeke!"

The chance encounter with Cy confirmed that news of the SUV had reached the whole market and beyond. Jasper realized that he was in a quagmire. Who would lend him the money if everyone had heard about the vehicle?

CHAPTER 19

When Jasper returned to the store, Amata was in the middle of another sale.

"I just want to service my RAV4," the beefy man wheezed at her. "I need this fuel filter and oil filter."

Amata took the samples from him and looked at the brands.

"We have these, Chief. Ebuka, bring them for customer."

"Come inside, have a seat," Amata said affectionately. "It looks like you could do with a rest. I'll get you some water while you wait."

The fellow stepped in and slid into a stool.

"You probably need some fresh oil, too, Chief. For the RAV4, we recommend Mile Master 5w-20 or 5w-30. And do you need some brake fluid?"

The fellow smiled. "Bring one gallon of the 5w-30 and a bottle of brake fluid."

"You should get two gallons of oil, Chief. RAV4 is heavy engine. If you have leftover, you can use it to top up later."

Over her shoulder, Amata shouted to the apprentice, "Add two gallons of Mile Master 5w-30 and some brake fluid to the customer's order!"

Amata handed the customer a sachet of fresh water. The gentleman tore it open and squeezed some spurts onto his face. Then he sucked vigorously from the tear. It was hot outside. He was happy to rest his legs and cool down.

"Actually, I also need the front right fender. One okada rider crashed into me at Palmgrove."

"Front right fender for RAV4. What year, sir?"

"2008."

Amata took the filters and fluids from Ebuka, who had just emerged from the shelves. "Ebuka, run to our warehouse and bring right front fender. RAV4 2008. That's the old shape, remember. Run! Do not keep Chief waiting."

She turned back to the customer, "These motorcycle riders spoil Lagos. Hope you were not hurt, sir."

"No, thank God." He sucked on the sachet. "How much is it?"

Amata had no idea of the price. It would depend on the cost called by the owner.

"Let us get the part first, sir. Price will not be a problem. What of the side mirror? Was it affected?"

"How did you know? Yes, I will need a side mirror."

Ebuka was already on the stoop, so Amata shouted, "Ebuka! Get a right-side mirror too! Quickly!"

As Ebuka slipped into his flip-flops, Jasper whispered to him to check with Zona and Akajiaku in that order. His stock of fenders was exhausted. It was in the inventory in Zona's warehouse.

Within five minutes, the apprentice returned with the spares under his arm. "Fifty-five thousand," he whispered in Igbo as he handed the items to his master's wife.

"Prepare the invoice for our customer," Amata told Ebuka. "Charge him the cost price. You heard that a motorbike ran into him. And insurance being what it is—"

"Exactly," the customer concurred. He reached out, wiped the back of his neck, and then exhaled loudly.

The bill came to seventy-nine thousand naira. The fender was sold for sixty thousand.

"Ebuka, leave what you are doing and carry these goods to the car for our customer."

When Ebuka returned from helping the customer, Jasper counted out fifty-five thousand. "Go and pay the people you got the fender from."

Amata marvelled at the vibrancy and dynamism of the market. "Everything is possible once you have the idea," she said.

"Yes," Jasper accepted.

"That was a good sale," Amata remarked. "It has justified our day at the market."

Jasper nodded absent-mindedly. "Business is turnover."

Amata could see he was more fidgety than usual. "How did it go with Zona?"

"He has backpedalled. Won't budge. Says when he gets the bank alert, I can take delivery of the goods, not before. And I have till the weekend or—"

"Or he will sell it to another? Blood of Jesus! And we are running short. That fender, we sold our last piece last week. We need to re-stock."

"I know."

Amata and Jasper retreated into their own thoughts. A young girl stopped in front of the shop.

"Pedicure, manicure?" she asked, nipping a scissors. "I will do it well for you, Mummy." She stooped down and caressed Amata's toes, then looked expectantly at Jasper.

"Why are you looking at my husband for permission? Is it not my foot you want to pamper?"

"It is from master's pocket."

Amata thought about it. She did not have much time outside market hours for personal grooming. "Why not?" she said, thrusting her legs to the girl.

Jasper sank into a seat.

"Just a change of polish, I want, not a complete pedicure."

Turning to her husband, she said, "Stop worrying; it will be well."

The itinerant beautician deftly wiped the crusted nail polish. Jasper's gaze followed the pedestrian traffic scurrying past the shop.

By the time the pedicure was over, the sun had gone down. A gentle breeze blew in from the lagoon. Smells of different foods filled the air. Iya Kazim, who sold bean cakes and chicken legs in the evenings, was busy setting up shop.

"Let's pack up," Jasper said and stood up.

"Ubanwa said his car was broken into last week and a laptop stolen," Amata said as they walked to the rented parking stall.

"When he likes to park by the roadside, why won't he suffer losses? He is too stingy to cough out two thousand naira per month for secure parking. You don't want to spend two thousand, and then you lose something worth fifty times that."

The traffic was heavy but moving as the Corolla rolled into Carter Bridge. Jasper planned to join the Eko Bridge from the Iddo Terminus Road. Amata bought grocery from the hawkers that lined the route. Within an hour, they were at the Stadium T-junction where Masha Road abutted Western Avenue. Many commuters appeared to be stranded, scrambling for the few available buses. Traffic ground to a halt.

"Wind up!" Jasper fidgeted with the dials, and the air conditioning kicked in. Osita Osadebe's melancholic voice filled the car with strains of *Onuigbo.*

When they got home, Amata prepared white soup with fresh fish. It was one of Jasper's favourites. She was out to spoil him and get his mind off the money his older brother was demanding. After dinner, they cuddled on the couch, but the money issue hung between them.

"What of the Prado money?"

Jasper took a while to respond. "I fixed it. If I withdraw it now, we will be penalized."

"I could get a loan from my father," Amata responded. "We can pay it back once the deposit matures."

Again, there was a long silence. "I did rollover."

"You can always cancel it. Re-negotiate another term."'

Jasper said nothing.

"What is the time now? Nine-thirty. Let me call Odoziaku. She will talk to Onwa."

Jasper shook his head vigorously. "I feel reluctant to borrow from my in-law. He gave you the SUV, and now I turn around and ask for a loan. Mba!" He patted Amata tenderly. "No, Stainless, do not worry. I will sort it out. By the time I meet one or two kinsmen—"

CHAPTER 20

Jasper was in a bind. Time was running out to find the money. He was standing in the showroom of Okosisi, a kinsman in the building industry.

"What is a Jeep owner doing looking for ordinary two million two?" Okosisi deadpanned. Jeep was general term for all SUVs. He seemed nervous, but Jasper couldn't think why he would be. After all, he was the one asking for money, not the other way round.

"I sold the vehicle, sir." Jasper felt like a penitent in a confessional.

"You sold the vehicle!" The response seemed to increase Okosisi's nervousness. His hands went under his armpits. His trousers were shaking visibly as he continued. "And where is the money?"

Jasper hesitated. If he said he spent it on other things, his kinsman might think him frivolous and that he had squandered his resources. If he told him he invested it, Okosisi might think he was a smartass. In the end, he decided to be honest.

"I placed it, sir."

The tycoon threw back his head and had a good laugh.

"O-o-o-o! You placed it. In a bag?"

"No, sir. In..."

"Of course, in a bank. For interest. And now you have come to collect Okosisi's own money that he uses to trade. Have you not heard that the wisest man in the whole world is still a fool in Nnewi? I am from Nnewi, if you have forgotten." He beat his chest several times with an open palm. "My friend, go and break the deposit and trade with it. Don't talk ajanbene here. I don't have time for cock and bull."

On his way out, Jasper called Rapu. He had lent Rapu some money to help him set up shop. He'd heard the tricycle business was moving fast in Abuja. Perhaps Rapu was in a position to pay back.

"Please give me another month or two," his brother pleaded. "I just ordered some goods, and I am empty as we speak."

Another month or two he did not have. He realized he was just walking à la Fela's song, perambulating without any destination. He crossed Nnamdi Azikiwe Street, heading towards Docemo Street. Should he turn around and head to Hiuna? Chief Hilary Unachukwu could lend him the sum effortlessly. Or he could trek all the way to Idoluwo Street. He had no one in mind to see, but maybe he would meet someone there that he knew. Many Igbo tycoons operated from Idumota Market.

Jasper was still mulling his options when he found himself near the Iga-Idugaran Palace of the Oba of Lagos. He had wandered too far. Smacking his forehead with his palm to jar himself back to reality, he retraced his steps, navigating the narrow and broken lanes in between stalls, awnings, and lean-tos. In this part of Isale-Eko, dwellings and shops co-existed. Laundry hung on lines, and dirty, skimpily-clad toddlers gadded about. The overhead plastic coverings blocked out the sun. Jasper was moving on autopilot again, deep in thought and unaware of his surroundings. He stopped to gauge where he was. A pedestrian bumped into him.

"Why do you stop like that without warning?" the stranger fumed, unleashing a slew of abuses.

"Are we going to the same place?" Jasper queried, mouth agape, eyebrows arched.

"Everyone is walking fast; some people are just layabouts," the fellow hissed. He sidestepped Jasper and continued on his way, mouthing expletives and looking over his shoulder.

Okosisi's rejection had knocked Jasper off balance. He had not expected an outright rejection. At the worst, he had hoped that Okosisi would give him part of the money, leaving him to scout for the rest elsewhere. But it had been an absolute no. He should not be surprised, he thought. Why would a third party come to his aid when his own brother, who had suckled the same breasts he had, would not help him? And who would lend money to someone who was said to have an SUV tucked away somewhere?

But why did the man bear the title of Okosisi, Great Tree (that supposedly gives shade to the weary traveller) when he lacked those qualities? He had proven himself to be a tree with brown foliage, offering no respite, no fruit. A withered fig tree. It was best to return to his shop to reflect on the next line of action. He burst out on Nnamdi Azikiwe Street again, this time in the direction of Tinubu Square. He could see the minaret of the Central Mosque ahead. It was almost time for Jumaat. If he did not hurry, the road would be closed, and the human traffic, already thick, would double with worshippers. On a lark, he veered to the right to take a shortcut behind the Mandilas Building onto Abibu Oki, then Martin Street, bypassing Broad Street and its throng.

At this time, though, everywhere was congested. There was hardly standing space. Traders extended their stalls by annexing the pavement in front meant for pedestrians. They displayed their goods on makeshift shelves and tables. Every available space was snapped up by table-top retailers sitting on low stools under wide-rimmed beach umbrellas. They beckoned to passers-by for patronage. Itinerant hawkers occupied the remaining spots. They stood dangling their wares in their hands or lined them up on their arms and wheelbarrows: underwear, toys, baby clothes, and phone accessories.

The whole market was awash with trash. Overnight, shopkeepers swept out dirt onto the streets and lanes and left the garbage there for the Town Council to evacuate. City Hall rarely showed up. Each day, more rubbish was heaped onto old garbage. Sprouting small hillocks of debris like anthills on the uneven walkway. The market decayed and oozed.

Music blared from loudspeakers mounted on the roofs of some shops. Tiwa Savage moaned from one, and Phyno serenaded from another. Into this cacophony, the muezzin megaphoned his plaintive chant. Jasper shook his head vigorously to clear it and trudged on aimlessly.

He was level with the Oluwole fake documents market when, from nowhere, a lass hawking tangerines approached and plastered a dirty slap on a groundnut seller's face. Her pan trembled from the blow and a few nuts jiggled and rolled down the sides of the pyramid to the ground. The tray would have toppled had Jasper not caught it in time and steadied it.

"Thank you, sir," the young hawker said, making eye contact with her benefactor. Jasper could see the three tribal marks etched on her cheeks.

"Adidas!" her aggressor mocked her scarification marks.

The girl put the tray down by the roadside.

"E-e, not in front of my shop!" the store owner warned.

The Adidas girl ignored the warning and tied her wrapper firmly around her waist, turned and pounced on her aggressor like a bulldozer. Bright orange tangerines scattered in all directions, gathering dirt along the way. A few tumbled into the slimy gutter.

"Oloshi! Oniranu!" she yelled. They hurtled into someone's wares and were shoved out.

"Were! Oloriburuku! Alakori!" the hapless merchant shouted as the two youngsters orbited each other, trading punches as they went. Other sellers surrounded the warriors, hailing one and booing the other. Jasper thought of breaking the fight, but time was not on his side. Today, the deadline to pay Zona was already far spent. He sidestepped them and continued on his way.

He was crossing Martin Street towards Balogun Market when he remembered one of the patrons of the market association. Chief Rufus Onyeje, Orimili Nnewi, had been good friends with the Okonkwo patriarch. The two men had belonged to the same men's organization in the church, the Knights of St. Mulumba. Chief and his wife were witnesses and sponsors when

Jasper married Amata. Why had he not thought of him earlier? Orimili was his best chance. His megastore was just ahead, at the UTC Roundabout. He and his brother operated a successful, rancour-free joint partnership, a rare feat. The blinking neon lights of the sign board beckoned Jasper. He speeded his pace.

Orimili's boys were in the middle of midday worship. Jasper joined them.

Jesus na You be Oga
Every other god, na so-so yeye
Every other god, na so-so wayo.

The ageing mogul appeared pleased to see Jasper. He asked after his business and his new wife. When Jasper mentioned the reason for his visit, Orimili's smile disappeared, and a twitch took its place. He opened his mouth, then closed it without uttering a sound.

Jasper's heart pounded as he waited for the old man to gain control of his stutter. Would he be turned down again? Or perhaps be given part of the money? He breathed in, bidding his chest to calm down. He tried to read the expression on the magnate's face but quickly averted his gaze. A youth dared not look an elder in the eye.

"It is—" Orimili said after ruminating on the matter. He looked intently at the young entrepreneur. "It is inexperience to put all your eggs in one basket. In business, we do not fi-x all our money. You keep a-a rolling fund to trade with. You divide your resources i-into different parts to give you room to manoeuvre. There is nothing a-s humiliating as a well-to-do man go-going cap in hand to a peer. So, learn from this. You have done your freedom, b-but an apprentice cannot learn everything from his master."

"Yes, sir."

"Oke Nmanwu w-as full of praise for you. You served him well."

"I tried my best, sir. For seven whole years. I removed nothing."

"Have you approached him for help?"

"No, sir. I reckoned that since he had freed me—"

"You have a point. B-but he remains your father. If you find yourself in a b-bind anytime, you can go to him. That is how it is. He is your father, and Obidie is your mo-ther," Orimili said, his efforts to hide his stutter failing on the last words.

"Yes, sir. It was he and my brother who jointly ordered the goods. That is why I did not go to him."

The chief sighed loudly.

"I heard they ordered ten containers."

"Yes, sir."

"I am surprised Zona would i-insist on money before releasing the, the goods, knowing you are still a novice in business."

Jasper did not answer. The magnate had not finished what he wanted to say to the young man.

"After all, do our people not s-say that if your sibling is in heaven, hell is foreclosed to you."

"Yes, sir, that is so," he replied. But to himself, he thought, *Not all siblings. On reaching heaven, some will shut the gate and ensure you do not enter.*

Jasper was impressed by Orimili's gentle demeanour. This was how one carried real wealth. See composure. See stately carriage. He was not like Okosisi, who was full of himself even as his trousers shook. He should have come to Orimili first instead of the merry-go-round he had embarked upon. One of life's worst feelings must be to ask for a favour from one capable of helping you and be denied.

"In business, sometimes there i-s cutthroat competition," Orimili said. "Traders forget that they are brothers and kinsmen when m-money is involved. R-remember that."

"Yes, sir. I will never forget that."

Jasper trained his eyes on the wall behind Orimili. Paraphernalia of the Arsenal Football Club hung from the wall. There was a woollen scarf, a pennant and a mug. Even the clock on the wall had ARSENAL splashed across its face.

Orimili saw Jasper staring at the football paraphernalia. "It is just like the Premier League. Those ahead want to remain on top and do not welcome competition or threat of relegation."

"Yes, sir."

Orimili pressed a button. His wife popped her head around the door.

"Come inside, Ocheze."

"Ocheze," Jasper repeated in greeting. *The Throne.* She acknowledged him, entered Orimili's office, and closed the door.

"Count t-wo million from the safe and give to Jasper. He is experiencing a cash flow problem. He will repay us when he is able." He looked at Jasper. "Ocheze is in charge of the money in th-is business."

Ocheze fumbled for a key around her waist and went to a corner cabinet.

"Orimili Nnewi," Jasper hailed again, overwhelmed.

"It is me."

"Orimili, I don't know how to thank you, sir."

"J-just pay us back."

He asked after Amata again.

"She is in the shop, sir."

"Oh, she comes to the market with you?"

"Yes, sir."

"For a graduate, she appears humble."

"Yes, sir, o nwero nsogbu. She does not have issues."

Ocheze presented the money to her husband, who pointed to Jasper. Jasper counted the pile of notes—two million. From his desk drawer, Orimili added two slim wads.

Ocheze slid a piece of paper before him. It was an IOU for the sum. Jasper signed willingly.

"Thank you, sir. Orimili atata," he beamed. Sea never dry. "God will not take bribe against you."

"Amen."

"Ocheze," he said again, inclining slightly towards the missus.

Jasper went straight to Zona's store. When he saw Jasper, Zona's first thought was that his brother had come to plead for an extension or a reconsideration. But here he was, holding the money. He had surreptitiously discouraged his peers from lending Jasper money, yet here he was with the full amount for the goods.

Jasper relished seeing his shelves once again bulging with merchandise. The rest of the day, he pecked at his calculator, deciding sales prices and profit margins. Ebuka nailed the poster of new Hyundai vehicles that came with the order on the wall. Elantra: Amata thought it would be a lovely name for a female child.

CHAPTER 21

Christmas 2015

When Jasper and Amata went home for Christmas a year after their wedding, Amata was on everyone's lips. *Exactly one year after her wedding,* they said, *her stomach is like a tubeless tyre.* One in-law teased, *Are you doing family planning? You university girls like to copy white people.*

It did not help that Charity was pregnant again. She was still in her first trimester, but already her stomach protruded, and she had to bend back and walk about in sluggish steps. It felt to Amata that Charity was trying to make a point about being fertile and reminding her that they were in an undeclared race to produce the first grandson.

Amata found time to visit her village. She and her friends sat in an orchard of palms, mango trees, and citrus. Beyond the orchard, the patch of farmland where they usually planted yam and cocoyam lay waste, the ridges losing height and growing dusty. The harvest season was long over, and the harmattan wind raised bronze leaves that flew short distances and re-settled elsewhere.

It did not take long for her friends to start teasing her, just like Jasper's family did in Opaku.

"We thought you would be inviting us for a naming ceremony," one mocked.

"She is rather busy cruising in the Jeep," another added.

When the friends left, Amata's mother drew her aside. Odoziaku had tried hard to hide her worry. As a mother of daughters, she worried if her daughters would get married and well. Now, she worried about Amata having children and whether the child would be male, which is reified in Igboland.

"*O gini,* Ama? Is anything the matter?"

"I don't know, Mama."

"Have you seen the doctor?"

"Yes, Mama."

"What did he say?"

"It's a she. She gave me some drugs. I am to see her next month when we return to Lagos. Odoziaku?"

"My child."

"How do you make your husband sleep with you? When I am ovulating, Jasper is not in the mood."

"Perhaps his brother has done something to turn him against you?"

"I don't think so."

"I hear his wife is delivering females. As the first son, he would like to produce the first grandson of the compound."

Amata reflected on her mother's words. She had not eaten any food whose source was in doubt, nor had she accepted any drink from a third party. She had served herself at Eloduchi's naming ceremony and didn't think anyone had tampered with her food. Could she have stepped on something? She could not remember.

"I don't think so," she repeated.

"What of the wife? She could block you until she has produced the first male child. It has been known to happen."

Amata had no answer to that, but she did not suspect Charity of any fetish practice.

"What of personal hygiene?"

"I do that, Mama."

"You wash well before bed? Powder, perfume?"

"Yes, Mama."

"And his thing, does it rise?"

"Mamaa!"

Odoziaku smiled. Children.

"At night, let him wash before you. When he is in bed, take your bath with a sweet-smelling soap. Perfume yourself, then walk naked to the room. Go and sit by his side and place your hand on the nozzle, you know what I mean?" She grabbed the branch of a nearby plantain tree and stripped its fan-like blades. "Like this. You see?"

Amata nodded.

"Then straddle him. Tell him I am waiting to carry my grandchild. Some men think only of business, money, and profit. Onwa was like that. I wanted to fill our home with children, seven or eight. But I ended up with three. Every time, money, warehouse, bottles, and crates are on his mind. That is how our men are."

"Charity is expecting again, and her last baby is not even one year."

"They are anxious for an heir. Persevere. You are young."

"Thank you, Mama."

"Jehovah, the God I serve, will give you children."

"Amen."

~

Rapu also came home for Christmas for the Opaku Town mass return. All the Opaku indigenes trading and doing civil service abroad touched base. Many were hustling in Onitsha and Awka. A lot were based in Lagos and Abuja. A few of them lived outside Nigeria. Associations of Opaku Indigenes in South Africa, Ghana, and Côte d'Ivoire thrived. Groups of Opaku residents were also in the process of establishing meeting platforms in the US, Canada, and Malaysia.

One evening, when the sun's merciless heat had subsided, Iyom called her youngest son to join her in the shade of the cocoa tree near her late husband's grave. From experience, Rapu suspected that she had something on her mind. He looked as Iyom bit off a bitter kola and held it between her lips. Her short hair was turning grey, but it was still full. Since it was shaved at Agbisi's death, she did not bother to plait it, preferring it fallow and trim. Her eyes had grown dull, and age spots dotted her neck, but she still carried herself with authority.

"Nne."

"Keep your eyes open for a good Opaku girl," the matriarch said. She crunched on the nut. "As you know, we have mass return this year. It may be up to five years before we have another. Find a girl. Do not let me hear that you want to marry outside our community. Look at my legs, crooked in the best of times, now weakened with age. I cannot trek far to see my in-laws."

Rapu stared at her blankly.

Iyom bit off another piece of the nut and tucked in her wrapper, which almost unravelled from a gentle breeze. Red broken plate: that was the name of the cloth. It was old and fading now. In its heydays, she wore it for special occasions.

"There is a woman," she continued, "Oduenyi. She finds partners for our people. I will enlist her support. Whatever specification you want, whether black or yellow, fat or slim, teacher, graduate, tell her. She will propose girls for you."

"I am not ready yet."

"Are you not the one who told me about some Imo girl?"

"I had a rethink, Nne. I want to wait and gather some coins first."

"Still, it is on Eke market day that we start preparing for Nkwo market."

Rapu understood. There were four market days in the Igbo week, and Nkwo drew the biggest crowd. You needed three full days to prepare for it.

"You should opt for a tall bride, seeing that you are not gifted with height."

"O-o, Nne."

The next day, Iyom summoned Oduenyi and introduced her to Rapu. The matchmaker was well put together. She wore a blonde wig with straight hair falling to her shoulders. Her eyebrows were scraped and lined with kohl, and her lashes curled like an arc. Rapu knew immediately that they were false. Maybe to make up for the tiny eyes. But she smelled nice. She had a catalogue under each arm.

"I find good wives for our young men looking to settle down."

Iyom excused herself. "I have cocoyam on the fire."

Oduenyi sat beside Rapu and opened the ring-bound folder of transparent plastic sheets.

"This is Nneka. She is a graduate, about to commence her National Service. Beside her, her sister, Nonso. She is in her final year at Okoh Polytechnic." She turned the page. "This is Chidera, their cousin."

She stopped and looked at Rapu. "Why don't you tell me what you are looking for? Let's start with complexion: black beauty or yellow beauty?"

"Black," Rapu answered without hesitation. "Black is low maintenance. Yellow girls spend a guy's money on creams and ointments and—"

"If it is natural, a woman does not need creams," Oduenyi quipped. "I know because, as you can see, I am light-skinned. Anyway, you say black." She made a note.

"Tall, short, slim?"

"Tall, fat, ugly."

Oduenyi clenched herself. Most men wanted attractive ladies, yellow, tall, slim, big-hipped, and busty. Here was one who desired a dark skin and ugly lady. She did not understand. Finally, she asked. "May I ask why?"

"I want a wife who will belong to me alone, not one that other men will contend for with me."

Oduenyi nodded. She flipped through the ledger and marked a page. Then she asked, "Do you want a girl with an English or a native name?"

"Does not matter."

"Good. This is Ezinma. And here is Kosiso. Ezinma is a medical doctor. Kosi is doing postgraduate at Na U, Awka, here."

Nnamdi Azikiwe University, he knew it. Rapu looked at the two pictures. Both women wore frilly wigs and were heavily made up with eye shadow and lipstick like the bottom of a baboon. He shook his head.

"O gini?"

"I don't like false hair. I like a natural hair person. I don't mind braids, but no wigs."

Oduenyi was exasperated. False hair was fashionable, and finding a young someone who didn't wear it would be tricky. She was currently sporting Indian hair but was considering changing to Brazilian hair, which had sheen, or Vietnamese rumoured to have bounce. Italian falsies were odour-free. Whenever she braided, she bought Mongolian because it proved easy to twist. False hair was in.

She went through her album again but found no one to meet Rapu's specifications. "I will update my inventory and get back to you. With this mass return, I expect more candidates to register. Many young girls are reaching adulthood and will be looking for partners." She started gathering her stuff. "You did not tell me the ideal age."

"I am in my late twenties now. If I get someone between twenty-two and twenty-five, it should be fine."

"Noted. Rest assured, I will get you someone from a good family. I check them out very well before I accept. No osu, no fast fingers, and no mental issues. My clients are vouched for."

"I shall be waiting."

As Oduenyi walked to the gate, Rapu kept thinking about her last remarks about no osu. The government had abolished the Osu Caste System, but everyone knew it was on paper only. In practice, the freeborn still avoided mingling with those who had been sacrificed to ancient gods. Most osus he knew had married outside Igboland because if they waited to marry Igbo, they would wait forever.

What of fast fingers? Some families had thieving blood in their veins. Some father-and-son gangs used to terrorize whole villages, zapping chickens and goats and money. If you married from such a home, it would be tantamount to fetching water in a basket. Your pockets would leak money faster than you could make it.

As for mental cases, you needed a strong character who would not succumb to the daily hardships people faced: no running water, no electricity, broken roads. What of insecurity? Extortion at police checkpoints? No health care? Kidnapping? You were on your own in this country. There was a saying among his friends: *May Nigeria not happen to you!* A featherbrain would be a liability.

The marriage facilitator was returning. "You have not given me anything."

At Rapu's questioning stare, she replied, "Five thousand to look at our profiles. Another five thousand to have your image in my album, so the damsels can check you out, too."

"Is five not too high to look at pictures? If I go online—"

"That's the fee, sir. You won't pay anything again until you get your choice. I have over one hundred clients that are vouched for. Online, you don't know who is who. With me, you have assurance. No stress."

Rapu stood up and pulled his wallet from his back pocket.

"Sit down. I need your picture," the matchmaker said.

Rapu sat down again and combed out his luscious beard with his fingers.

"You are too serious," Oduenyi teased. "You have your mother's full lips; use them to frame your teeth. Show off your smile! That's better! Hold it like that!"

This time, Rapu accompanied Oduenyi to the gate. When they were out of earshot of the house, he stopped and looked over his shoulders before he said softly, "Look for someone whose parents are rich, who can gift her a Jeep as a wedding present."

"You mean like Onwa gave Jasper's wife?"

He nodded.

"Do you know why Onwa gifted his daughter the Jeep?" She did not wait for an answer. "It is not part of the dowry. It is because she was a virgin."

"How?"

"I tell you. This is my business. I know the ins and outs of marriages in this vicinity. Onwa promised an SUV to any of his daughters deflowered on her wedding night."

"Seriously?"

"Quote me."

"Eh-eh! I think she has a sister."

"I will make enquiries. It is not unheard of for siblings to marry two siblings. Leave it to me."

~

Oduenyi curled and stapled her lips. What was the tenth commandment again? *Thou shalt not covet thy neighbour's wife.* This was more than a neighbour; this was a brother, a blood brother. She thought of educating Rapu about "ikughari nkwu nwanyi" in Opaku, the custom by which a man could transfer his wife to a brother if the latter was in love with her or if the bride preferred her brother-in-law. It was a practice that predated Christianity and had supposedly died out. The phrase literally meant "reversal of the bridal wine." It happened back when arranged marriages were the order of the day, when the head of the household summoned his daughter and told her that a family would be coming to ask for her hand. If it was a family with many male siblings, the maiden would start wondering which of the brothers would be hers. The groom's identity was only revealed on the day of the ceremony, and the woman had little choice but to play along.

Sometimes, if her lot fell on the "wrong" member of the groom's family, her admirer had the right to go to the groom and ask for a transfer of the bride. A day would be scheduled, and the preferred groom would provide drinks for the bride's village to signal a change in the betrothal. In those days, love and courtship had no place in the equation.

But if we can practise ikwuchi, Oduenyi thought, *surely ikughari nkwu nwanyi stands a chance. Would Jasper consent to transfer Amata? And would Amata agree to be passed down like a used car?*

~

It was a sober Rapu who walked back to the canopy of the cocoa tree. He realized what he had asked Oduenyi to do, but he wanted what Jasper had and what Iyom had asked him to look for—a graduate from a wealthy family. He thought about his time in the brothels at Mararaba and how the clients queued up outside each door. Once, when his turn came, he found a young undergraduate behind the door. On another occasion, he saw a book pile on the table. Law books. The girl was a student and a part-time call girl to pay for her studies. And here was Oduenyi, brandishing albums and catalogues as if these girls were cherubs and angels come down from heaven. Lawyer this, doctor that. He knew the truth, which made him want what Jasper had even more.

Iyom emerged from the house. Her appearance jolted Rapu out of his reverie.

"Bring the food here!"

Amata and the maid materialized and set up lunch.

"Rapu, sit down. Let us eat," his mother urged.

Rapu's stomach was rumbling, but not from hunger. What he had heard now about his brother stirred him in a bad way. Not only was Jasper's business blossoming, but he also got to marry a wealthy virgin. *Where does one get a virgin, let alone a virgin graduate, these days?* Envy, like acid, consumed his entrails.

And Rapu coveted Amata.

He also had other reasons for not wanting to eat with Iyom and Amata. He was ashamed that he did not contribute to the family budget. When he returned for Christmas, he gave his mother five thousand naira. A miserable sum. That was all he could afford. His excuse to her was that he restocked his store for the Christmas period, but sales had been unusually slow.

Jasper arrived the next day, his Camry bursting at the seams with assorted foodstuff. Rapu was in his room when he overheard Iyom gushing over some Dutch wrappers her son and his wife had given her for the Yuletide.

I will be the talk of the town. Jasper Gee! Thank you, my children. Amata. May God replenish your pockets a million-fold.

Rapu could not match that generosity and recused himself from Iyom's kitchen. But he knew that his stinginess was not from lack of money. He was tight-fisted and did not like to give. He wanted others to look after his mother while he hid behind the excuse of just starting out. *Where did I get this clenched fist from?* He wondered as Iyom dished out lunch. *Agbisi was a generous man, perhaps too generous, to the detriment of his own family. And Iyom shares freely. Why am I stingy and un-giving?*

He fled indoors. There was a meeting of townsfolk at sundown. He would eat there. When he came out later, Jasper and Iyom were picking their teeth; then, they recited the Catholic prayer to return thanks for the meal. Rapu's intestines twisted as he watched their mother pray and bless Jasper again, asking God to replenish his pocket for all the stuff he had brought.

"Bring a mat here!; let me take a short nap," Jasper called out.

Amata dashed in and re-emerged with a mat and some pillows. She made to clear the dishes, but Iyom stopped her. "You have worked enough, my child. Sit down and take a rest. Let Omenma do the clearing."

Omenma was ten and lived with Nne, who put her through school. While Omenma cleared the dishes, Jasper and Amata lay in the shade to enjoy the caressing breeze. Before long, the cool harmattan breeze lulled them to sleep. They woke to the aroma of soup wafting in from neighbouring kitchens.

"Someone is cooking stockfish," Amata observed, directing her statement at her mother-in-law, who was sifting through a tray of crayfish to remove dirt.

"Must be Mama Adaobi. They came in while you were asleep," her mother-in-law answered. "I have not seen anyone who loves stockfish as much as my Zona's wife."

"It goes well with ogbono soup."

"Sit up," Iyom nudged Jasper. "There is something I have been meaning to discuss with you."

Jasper raised himself on an elbow.

"I heard Zona imported goods for you as promised and demanded cash before delivery."

"You heard right."

"Are you people living in peace? Is something the matter?"

"You should ask him, Nne. He demanded cash before releasing the goods."

"Have you paid?"

"Ee. In fact, if you chance on Orimili Nnewi, thank him. He bailed me out. His name should be Oz' Igbo ndu, the One who saves the Igbo nation."

"What of Rapu?"

"What about him?"

"Could he not have bailed you out?"

"In fact, I loaned him some money. When I asked for it to sort myself out, he said he did not have it. Yet, I heard he ordered goods afterwards."

"Next time, ask me. I may not have cash, but we have one or two plots of land we can sell and convert to cash."

"Daalu, Nne." He inclined towards her. "But it has not come to that."

Jasper's heart fluttered at this show of love from his mother. He was happy he had not scrimped on buying her the latest Dutch Wax wrapper. Next Mothering Sunday, he would repeat the gesture and do likewise for his mother-in-law.

"You brothers must live in peace and harmony," Iyom began. Her heart was heavy within her. "An adult cannot be present while a she-goat gives birth on the leash. That is what your father said before he sucked his last breath. That is what he would have wanted. Money, success, no matter how big, cannot take the place of a sibling."

"Nne, Jasper has no problem in that regard," Amata cut in. It was unsolicited and unwelcome.

Jasper elbowed her. It was to stop her from going further. *Do not concern yourself about this matter,* the nudge communicated. He did not want to alarm or frighten her that she married into a family with squabbles and rivalry. She should understand it was a matter between him and his brothers and desist from interfering.

~

Iyom and Jasper, engrossed in their confab, were unaware that Zona had re-surfaced. He stood on the stoop of his house and observed the people relaxing under the trees. Jasper and his wife sat on their hams, facing Iyom on the bench, arms stretched out in supplication. Zona's face scrunched up. *Is it prayer that Nne is doing over Jasper and his wife, or what? Is she blessing them? What of her other sons? What is this? Favouritism? Conferring blessing on one was tantamount to withholding it from others.* Distrust and disgust towards his mother formed like smoke under the bonnet of an overheated car. He had intended to stop at the shade on his way out to exchange banter with his family. Instead, he strolled to the back of his bungalow and contemplated his property.

CHAPTER 22

One morning, with the harmattan winds howling outside and swaying trees, Amata struggled to leave Jasper's side. As the junior wife, it behooved her to sweep the compound's carpet of dry leaves. She prayed her rosary before casting the comforter off herself and tucking it around her snoring husband.

When the leaves and litter had been gathered, she entered the kitchen to prepare breakfast. She longed for their own apartment, like Charity and Zona had. She knew that in time, Zona would inherit the main house and that Jasper and Rapu would have to build their apartments elsewhere in the compound. They had ample space, but she knew it would be long before Jasper could begin such a project. He was still trying to build the business. She rued the items of her dowry scattered about the house, still boxed and unused, gathering dust.

After a breakfast of glutinous pap and akara, she approached Iyom to ask about lunch.

"I have palm fruits, fresh palm fruits, and some smoked asa fish in the rafters. Let us prepare ofe akwu."

Palm fruit soup was easily Nne's favourite. She could make soup for the "swallow" that accompanied it and stew for rice and yam. Opaku had palms in abundance, both the oil type and the kind that produced heady wine. For the night meal, they usually ate the leftovers from lunch.

Jasper was hardly home. He left after breakfast and moved from one meeting to another, from one function to another:

Opaku Development Union, the Age Grades, and the Men's Guild of the local parish. There were also marriages, funerals, and freedom ceremonies for apprentices. You had to attend other families' functions if you wanted them to come to yours, so he endeavoured to dip into as many gatherings as possible. Sometimes, the Okonkwo brothers would split themselves up for wider representation. As the eldest son, Zona decided who would go where, but he left Iyom to choose the events she wanted to attend.

If Jasper did not hurry out in the mornings, needy kinsmen cornered him at home, and he coughed out money for medical assistance, school fees and sundries. That was how village folks got by. They begged from their kinsmen. Some who had family abroad received handouts. As a result, Jasper rushed out after breakfast, only popping in briefly for lunch before dashing out again.

One evening, when Jasper was home at dinner time, Amata made his favourite oha soup. After he had eaten, he departed for another function, and the women retired to their rooms. A while later, Charity called on Amata. Amata found her sister-in-law sucking on a cocoa fruit, which appeared to be her craved food this pregnancy. She broke it into two and brandished one in front of her co-wife.

"What does this resemble, eh?"

The halved fruit bore a perfect resemblance to the female genitalia, complete with its embedded seeds. Amata laughed and elbowed Charity. "Onye ara. Crazy girl. Did you call me here just to play the games of young maidens?"

"No, I did not. Let us go and greet our husbands' umunna," Charity said, mouth full. "They are our husbands, too. Let them get to know you, and you, them."

Charity left her three daughters in Iyom's care. The youngest, Eloduchi, was crawling all over the place and playing with dirt.

Iyom grimaced and rubbed her knees. "I no longer have the legs to run after active toddlers," she complained. Charity called to her babysitter, "Chisom, leave what you are doing; mind the children."

The young wives pounded the dusty path out of the compound. The first home they visited was next door. Charity did the introductions.

"This is Amata, Jasper's wife, Zona's younger brother."

"Our wife, nno. Welcome."

"Thanks, sir."

"Amata, this is Paul Nwagbo, Paulinco. His mother and Agbisi were siblings."

"Yes," the host concurred in a raspy voice, "Your husband's father and my mother were osol' onye n'onye, siblings. My mother was the first daughter of the Okonkwo family. She married in this village too. If my mother was male, I would be answering Okonkwo like you. Have you taken her to Eliza?" He freed a cigarette from behind his ear.

"Not yet. It is our next port of call."

"Take her to Eliza," Paul urged Charity. "Eliza is from your mother's village," he said to Amata, "but married here. So, when you go, address her as Nne Ochie. Both of you being married to Opaku kinsmen makes you co-wives."

Locals never tired of explaining relationships and customs.

"Thank you, sir."

Nwagbo shouted into his house for kola. A young girl appeared with garden eggs, which the host passed on to the women. Kola nut was served to men and garden eggs to women. They took the offering, as was the custom, and then took their leave.

"Why are you walking like that?" Amata asked her sister-in-law outside Nwagbo's gate. Charity was slacking, and her body arched backward more than usual.

"Because I am expecting."

"So soon?"

"Yes, o. As if you don't know that the thing is sweet."

"Onye ara."

"Pray, let this one be a boy so I can rest. This every year visit to the labour room tires me."

"But why the rush? You are young. Space your children. You need to recover from one pregnancy before you carry another."

"Do these men hear that? I hear Zona is befriending one University of Lagos student."

"Blood of Jesus."

"Just pray let this one be male." She touched her stomach.

"Amen."

"It is well."

They continued along the dirt road, which was little more than a bush path. Charity cleared her throat and spat out the last of the cocoa seeds.

"What of you?" she asked, pointing to Amata's stomach.

"I am on it. Nothing yet. The visitor that first refused to come finally came and now has refused to go."

"The devil is a liar. Add prayer and fasting. My dear, the world is *immirimious* now. You don't know who is a friend or an enemy. Pray and fast. You understand?"

"Ee."

"This is Eliza's house."

They stepped through the rickety wooden gate.

"Eliza is a nurse at the Maternity Home," Charity whispered. "Her husband is into curtains. She is from Utu, like your mum."

"Utu," Amata laughed. "You make it sound like scrotum the way you pronounced it."

"I was joking. That's how Yoruba people murder our names in Lagos. I heard one calling Otolo. The way it came out, it sounded like dysentery."

"It is because Igbo is a tonal language. One word, same spelling, but different pronunciations, different meanings."

Charity clapped. "Greetings here o!" She clapped again. "After here, we go home. I am tired. Another day, we can visit other homes."

"Nne m ochie!" Amata greeted into the air. It meant grandmother. A middle-aged woman was sitting in a plastic chair on the veranda of the modest bungalow, stripping leaves off the bitter-leaf stems. The house appeared completed, but the walls were unpainted and looked drab and miserable.

"Nwadi," the hostess answered automatically, unsure who she was greeting. She peered at the visitors through thick glasses. Eventually, she recognized Charity and put two and two together. She bounced up, toppling her chair.

"My co-wife! You must be Jasper's new wife, Onwa's daughter! Your mother is my sister."

She threw her arms around her two co-wives, clearly elated by their visit.

"Old woman," she addressed Charity, seeing her pot belly. "The way you drop babies every year, Charlingo, it's like the labour room is sweet. Every year."

"Zona is anxious for a male child."

"God will do it."

"Amen," came the chorus.

The women shared news and told stories until Charity insisted on going home to sleep.

CHAPTER 23

The following morning, Jasper overslept, felled by Amata's dinner of heavy "swallow" and finger-licking oha soup. The town hall meeting of the Opaku Improvement Union was already in session when he arrived. Some of the elected officers were at the gate registering attendance and collecting fines from latecomers. Jasper paid.

It was hot, swelteringly so, and humid. Able-bodied men sat on plastic chairs around plastic tables. Many wore tops made with the local ishiagu velvet fabric. Others donned ensembles sewn with the local Ankara cloth. Different scents warred with each other, but the smell of sweat remained overpowering. It hung low and heady, circulating through the room with the assistance of the dry harmattan air.

Up at the high table, a gaggle of men sat. A dish of kola nuts and alligator pepper nestled against a heap of garden eggs and several bowls of fried peanuts. A dozen sachets of pure water stood by to slake their thirst.

Jasper slid into an empty chair at the back. A quick glance told him that there were easily a hundred men present, fanning themselves, chatting in a low buzz.

"Nna, when will government supply constant electricity to this town?" a bulky fellow asked of no one in particular. His red T-shirt, stained with perspiration, clung to him. "Every day, no light."

"Igbo people have suffered," his neighbour replied. "Since the war ended, we have never had it so bad."

"Which war has ended?" another person quipped. "Look at you, the war is still on. Otherwise, why should Ala Igbo not get its fair share of infrastructure? Military installations? Roads, bridges, institutions? Appointments? The war is still ongoing, if you don't know."

"Ssssh," the provost warned.

The chairman was speaking. "So, each man will pay five thousand naira—"

"Why each man?" a voice protested. "Let it be by family, by household."

"Allow the chairman to land!" other attendees protested.

"While each woman will pay three thousand naira."

Many voices spoke at once in response to the chairman's words.

"Let it be by family," the protesting fellow persisted.

"How much do you hope to collect with the pittance?" a baritone queried. "How many are we?"

"First, what is the budget for the project?" another countered. "We start with donations. After that, we know how much is left before we tax ourselves."

"That is the thing with these civil servants. They don't know about money, yet they want to be in charge just because they went to school. But when it is time to contribute to projects, they will donate moral support."

"Water will find its level," someone shouted.

"One house!" the provost admonished.

The chairman raised his voice above the din. "The contractor's budget is twenty million for the road from the Main Market to the palace."

"I donate one million," a voice hurled out. It was Zona.

Hands clapped. Shouts of "Omeifeukwu, Omeifeukwu!" reverberated through the hall.

"Did I not say so? That is how to do it. Bia, financial secretary, are you taking notes?"

"Any more donations? Oke Nmanwu? Odenigbo? Ishienyi? Oga Dubai?" He reeled out the titles of members. "Kpakpando? Agu Opaku? Akunetigbuilo?"

"One hundred bags of cement," Chief Agwu shouted.

"Akuenwebe!" the gathering hailed him. Chief Agwu's praise name meant "Wealth has no fixed address," and he had just been true to his name. One hundred bags of cement, at three thousand five hundred naira a bag, translated to three hundred and fifty thousand naira. It seemed like a modest contribution to the ignorant, but it was laudable to those in the know. Chief Agwu was in the second-hand business, and the government harassed dealers in that sector.

"Write one million against my name," Odenigbo, a building materials supplier with a warehouse at Ogidi, yelled from his corner. People murmured that one million naira was too small from the magnate.

"Is this child's play?" Agu Opaku asked the hall, feigning anger. "Is it one hundred bags of cement that will build the road? I donate five million. Let's move forward. We must build this road."

"Two tippers of sharp sand," Omekannaya yelled.

"How many tyres?" the scribe asked. He waited for an answer before noting the contribution. Sand was sold in tippers of different sizes. A ten-ton tipper had ten tyres, half-ton, eight. It made a big difference to the materials calculations.

"Ten tyres," the donor replied.

Some commentators might have considered Omekannaya's donation paltry, but his kinsmen were sympathetic. His warehouses were damaged in the most recent fire caused by a fuel tanker accident that destroyed Ochanja Market at Onitsha. Rumour had it that his losses ran into a hundred million naira. And like most of his peers, he was not comprehensively insured.

Jasper knew that many donors pledged out of pride, just for the accolades from their kinsmen. But when it came time to redeem their pledges, some would find it hard. It would take the persistence of the committee members to pry the money and materials out of their hands. He was a free man now and expected to donate to community projects. He raised his cap.

"One hundred thousand!" he shouted.

"What is your praise name?" the scribe asked him.

"Just write Jasper Okonkwo."

"Jasper Gee!" his neighbours hailed. "Jasper Gee!"

The Chair, impressed that a young entrepreneur, who had only recently been freed, saw it fit to rally to the cause, bestowed a praise name on Jasper there and then. "By the powers vested in me, I confer on you the title Ochinanwata. Boy King."

Zona frowned. *Who is he leading?* he muttered.

"Where are the other youth?" the Chair addressed the young lads. "Learn from Jasper. Nothing is too small. When we urinate together, it foams."

As donations were shouted back and forth and compiled, Oke Nmanwu wrote a cheque and silently slipped it to the financial secretary through the bearer of the tray of kola nut and alligator pepper.

Three middle-aged men at a table beside Jasper derided the proceedings. "After we build this road, will we tax ourselves again to build a railway and a hospital for our community?" one enquired. "And a bridge over the lake? And will we buy a transformer? Meanwhile, we produce petrol in this state."

"It is oppression, pure and simple," his cohort affirmed.

"If you do not want to give us our due, allow us to go. Is it by force?"

"On IPOB, we stand!"

"Who is IPOB-ing there?" the provost asked, keening over the men concerned. "This is not an IPOB meeting, please."

When the provost left their side, Jasper tapped the fellow on the shoulder. "Bros," he whispered, "What does IPOB mean?"

"Indigenous Peoples of Biafra," the man answered.

A bespectacled man, slightly past middle age, sat hunched in his chair. He was a senior civil servant and director of research in a government agency. The eyes of the Chair oscillated from one end of the room to the other, ascertaining who had pledged something for the project. His glance came to rest on the director.

"Pass the mic to Dr. Ofoma," he said to the provost, who was perambulating among the tables with a microphone. As soon as the provost handed over the microphone, all eyes swivelled to the gentleman. He grabbed the gadget enthusiastically.

"My Chair, Nwachinemelu, my kinsmen, I salute you. I thank all those business moguls who are chipping into this noble cause. We in government see how projects, infrastructures, and government presence that should accrue to us are diverted from here with the stroke of the pen and sited elsewhere, if not embezzled entirely."

"How much?" someone interjected. "A long homily is unnecessary at evening Mass. How much?"

"Long story short," Dr. Ofoma said, adjusting his glasses, "I pledge my moral and intellectual support to the project."

The gathering erupted. Everyone spoke at the same time. Some scoffed, and others exclaimed expletives.

"How much is that?" a heckler yelled.

"I have a doctorate in the metallurgical fusion of—"

The rest of his sentence was drowned in the melee that broke out. The provost came for the microphone, but the doctor had not quite finished, intent on concluding his statement.

"I shall supervise the quality and—"

"I ask again: How much is that worth?" the heckler shouted.

"Thank you, thank you, doc," the provost said as he yanked the microphone out of Dr. Ofoma's hand, jangled the bell and called for calm. The Chair banged down hard with his gavel and sprang up.

"We are now on item four of the agenda, Aku lue uno." He nibbled at the piece of kola nut in his hand. Bits of the snack lined his lips, giving them a red tinge. He licked the stray bits off his lips and continued. "I now invite the secretary to address us on that."

"Where is the kola nut tray?" someone brayed. "We have not seen it here."

The secretary pushed back his chair and rose to speak.

Cries of "Nnanyelugo! Nnanyelugo!" filled the air.

"Daalu nu." He acknowledged the salutation with a brisk wave of his hands. When the room had quietened down, he began. "Aku lue uno is familiar to most, if not all of us. It means "Invest at home." Most of us have property outside Igboland—in Lagos, the former federal capital, and in Abuja, the new capital. Many have hotels, schools, real estate, factories, and industries all over Nigeria, from Sokoto to Calabar and Jos, you name it. I will not spend time counting them for you. I will say only this: You know yourselves." He pulled his ears.

"Do not forget the issue of abandoned property. Do not forget how our people lost all their sweat after the war, their hard-earned assets and possessions when they fled for their dear lives from other parts of Nigeria back to Igboland. If they had invested all that money in the East, not only would they have developed our land, but their wealth would also have remained intact."

The abandoned property issue was a sore point for many Igbos hustling in different parts of Nigeria when the war broke out. Jasper had not been born yet, but he remembered Agbisi telling him he lost a property in Port Harcourt, where he had begun his tailoring business, clothing the expatriate community there. When the war broke out in 1967, Agbisi fled back to his homestead, just like many other Igbos from all over Nigeria. A good number were massacred at their stations and en route. The lucky ones who made it home had just the clothes on their back. They took refuge in their hometowns, often in schools converted to refugee camps. Agbisi waited out the war in Opaku.

At the end of the war, when some returned to their erstwhile stations to claim their houses and businesses, the Igbos were met by new owners. *You tried to secede, and you were defeated. You abandoned your property. It does not belong to you anymore,* they were told. All attempts to recover their property failed. *What happened to the "No victor, No vanquished" mantra of the federal government?* the returnees asked. *Go ask Gowon,* they were told. Gowon was the then head of state.

"Therefore, build up your towns and villages. Invest at home. It is clear that the returns will not be the same, but with time, people will come from all over the world to Igboland to look for our wares. Look at Innoson. Look at Ibeto. Look at Cutix. Invest in the Eastern Region. Let your wealth reach home," Nnanyelugo said.

The Chairman consulted with other members of the high table. This interlude gave rise to a buzz of exchanges in the gathering. The Chair tapped the signet ring on his pinkie against a glass for quiet.

"Silence!" the provost blared, patrolling the length of the hall. "One house!"

The Chair cleared his throat again. "Another matter that is troubling, and of which we are hearing plenty now, is brother reporting brother to police, getting brother arrested and put behind bars for a matter that could be settled amicably."

His eyes roamed over the audience. "I ask you, brethren, what happened to our fraternity? Have you tabled the matter before your kinsmen? Have they met and deliberated over the issue before you rushed to call the police on a kinsman? Let us have no hand in a death we shall be required to mourn. The Executive met and decided that henceforth, any kinsman that summons the police for a brother before mediation by the kinsmen will, in the first instance, pay a fine of—"

"One million naira!" someone shouted. One could tell that he was vehemently opposed to the practice.

"That is too high," a voice admonished. It was Zona.

"Look at you. Do you know how much they bribe the police to lock up a kinsman?"

"Hundred thousand naira!"

"Too small!"

Shouts of different sums crisscrossed the room. The Chair waved for calm.

"We understand how you feel about it," he said. His fingers were drumming on the table frenziedly like they had a life of their own. "As I said, the committee met and decided on a one hundred thousand naira fine for the offender. If the kinsman is tortured or injured or dies in custody, the fine rises to two fifty thousand, two he-goats and a cleansing ceremony. You know what that entails. Failure to obey will result in ostracism and banishment. Are you with me?"

"Yes!" It was a resounding answer. "Nwachinemelu!"

The discussion turned to instances of aggrieved persons, not necessarily of Opaku, who brought in the police in business disagreements with their fellow townsmen.

"It has not happened here," the Chair concluded, "at least, not to my knowledge. But it has happened in our neighbouring communities, which is why we decided to bail out the water while it is yet ankle-deep."

"My landlord's son died at the SARS detention centre at Awkuzu," a scruffy fellow told his neighbours. He leaned over a pot belly and stammered out his phrases with short thrusts of a clenched fist. He shook his head, remembering. "Over a land matter."

"It's usually a land matter," a listener volunteered. "Instead of going to court, paying a lawyer and enduring endless adjournments, they buy the Special Anti-Robbery Squad. Your rival is picked up, and that's the end of him."

The Chair cut further conversation short. "Now to the matter of Ohaneze Ndigbo inviting us to the regional meeting. We need two volunteers to attend the proceedings of this umbrella organization of the Igbo-speaking people. The plebeians and kings of the Igbo need our support."

By the time the meeting ended, the sun had long gone to sleep. Jasper shuddered as he made for the exit. The Chair's admonition about kinsmen reporting each other reminded him of Remigius, Zona's erstwhile apprentice. Zona had him locked up and tortured by the dreaded police squad. It was something Jasper did not care to recall. He had been learning the motor parts trade under Zona. Remigius, a native of Abia State, had been the head apprentice. One day, Zona went to Umuahia for a funeral. At the end, he decided to pay a courtesy call on the parents of his head apprentice. He went back and forth but could not locate the ramshackle hut where they lived. Unsure whether his mind was playing tricks on him, he accosted a passerby and asked for directions. *Their hut used to be on this spot. Now I see a storey building and corner shops.*

It is their son, Remi, the fellow answered. *He is a trader in Lagos. He raised the structure for them. Aren't they lucky?*

Zona had put two and two together and realized that his apprentice was robbing him blind. On returning to Lagos, he had handed Remi over to the dreaded SARS. Remi was never to be seen again. Zona had sent Jasper away. *You were there, you good-for-nothing boy,* he had screamed at his brother. Jasper was only nineteen then.

All entreaties from their mother to let Jasper complete his training fell on deaf ears. *He did not steal from you,* Iyom had protested.

But he was there. He should have detected the stealing.

Jasper had spent a year idling at home, tinkering with various trades, until their mother took him to Chief Igwilo, prostrated before the mogul, and begged him to make something out of a widow's son.

CHAPTER 24

Before Rapu returned to the FCT, Oduenyi called to brief him about Amata's sister. "Her name is Louisa Awele Umeh. They call her Luz or Lulu, for short. She is in her final year at Na U, studying Civil Engineering. She asked if you were a graduate."

The matchmaker was of these parts. She knew Agbisi's story. She knew he had neglected his family while fooling around with the widow, Akwaeke, and how he did not train his boys.

"You know that Agbisi died before I could complete senior secondary," Rapu replied. "We, my brothers and I, could not further."

"So?"

"Yes."

She knew Rapu was playing dumb but decided to play along. "You are a graduate?"

"No."

"I had to make sure," Oduenyi said. "There are many online courses these days. People who never smelled the four walls of a university are now answering to Doctor This and Doctor That. Long story short, with Louisa, we have met a roadblock. She is adamant that she will only consider a graduate."

Rapu did not hesitate to retort, "But Jasper is not a graduate, and her sister married him."

"Each to his own. But not to worry," Oduenyi reassured him over the phone. "I will get another suitable girl for you. Just be honest about your past and who you are."

Interiorly, she feared for Jasper, who was oblivious of the envy he was generating, ignorant of the snake lurking in the rafters. *Abel, Abel, beware of thy brother, Cain,* she thought as she ended the call.

The motor spare parts business experienced a spurt during December and January because of the mass hysteria of travel. Many non-indigenes skipped Lagos and hopscotched home. They serviced their vehicles, changed faulty parts, and panel-beat any dents. When they returned, vehicle owners had to deal with the problems that had arisen in their hometowns or damages from accidents on the commute back. Jasper had a good reason to return to his shop as early as possible in the new year.

In the first week of January, he and Amata set out for Lagos. "Take note of the models you see on the road," he said as they approached Onitsha. "If we know what cars are on the road, we can anticipate our customers and make sure we have spares available."

Amata started to note the makes of the vehicles. Jasper saw her looking back to catch the make of a commercial bus that whizzed by.

"Disregard the commercial drivers. They are more likely to patronize the second-hand spares market. They are our greatest enemies. They and the mechanics."

"Mechanics, kwa?"

"Don't you know that mechanics charge the car owner for a brand-new part but buy the tokunbo version instead?"

Understanding hit Amata. "No wonder car owners accompany their mechanics to buy the spares."

"Yes, and they stay until the part is fixed."

Jasper swerved to avoid a cow that had strayed onto the road. "It does not end there," he continued when he'd steadied the vehicle. "The customer must leave with the faulty part; otherwise, the mechanic will recycle it for the next unsuspecting client."

In the stretches of silence that accompanied them along the highway, Jasper's mind wandered to his future plans. He hoped to sell out his goods and repay Orimili. In due course, he wanted to use part of his profit to finance a trip abroad to evaluate whether it was worth importing directly from the manufacturers. It occurred to him that Ebuka might even relocate to source and ship goods to him. He recalled that Amata suggested they use part of the SUV funds to build their own house. He liked that idea. But build where? In the family compound? Beside Zona? Agbisi left some landed property. Perhaps it was time to ask for his share.

It seemed all the officials along the way were asking for *their* share. As they entered Okpanam, Jasper had to slow down for another roadblock. He was infuriated at having to do so again soon after the last checkpoint, where he had parted with two hundred naira.

"I didn't know we lived in a police state," he burst out as he released the throttle. His stash of notes with which to grease the palms of the patrolmen was depleting rapidly.

"It's for security," his wife said tenderly to soothe him.

"This is a highway, for goodness sake," he snapped, hitting the steering repeatedly with a clenched fist. "You have barely accelerated to one hundred kilometres per hour when you have to brake again and shuffle."

At the outskirts of Agbor, another roadblock loomed. Jasper hit the head of the gear stick. "*Choo* two hundred naira in the pigeonhole."

Amata checked. The supply of notes was exhausted. "I have a five hundred naira note in my purse."

"No, too high." He coasted to a stop in front of the uniform.

"Officer." He tapped his baseball cap in a weak gesture of salute.

"Wetin you carry?"

"Officer, just personal stuff." His voice was playful.

"Happy New Year," the fellow saluted sharply. "Something for your boys, sir?"

Jasper was expecting it.

"So sorry, Officer, I have no change on me." He patted his breast pockets. Amata adjusted the chaplet that dangled from the rear-view mirror.

"We have POS," the sergeant answered. "Or do you prefer transfer? I'll give you my account details?"

Jasper was shocked. These people were so brazen that they even had Point-of-Sales technology and mobile transfer. Did they not care that these methods were traceable?

"You have change?" he asked the agent. He did not want to risk using a card, in case they could clone it. He looked across the highway. The same scenario was playing out for oncoming vehicles.

"Yes. Any amount."

Eventually, Amata's five-hundred naira note rescued them. "Safe trip!" the uniform said as he handed them the change.

By the time they reached Berger, traffic had built up, and they crawled all the way home. Amata checked her temperature. It seemed like she was ovulating. She recalled Odoziaku's advice. Tonight might be a good opportunity to see if it worked.

After dinner, Jasper began to get ready for bed while Amata did the dishes. She waited for him to settle in bed before she took a wash. She powdered herself, scented her body, per her mother's advice and walked naked into the room.

Jasper was already snoring.

What kind of husband is this? She thought of waking him, but a yawn overtook her. The gynecologist had said to use all means necessary to be intimate so as not to waste an ovulation. Odoziaku had advised her to grab his gear stick and straddle him because, after all, it was also her property. She yawned again. It would be inconsiderate of her to wake him after a long day at the wheels and expect him to perform, so she let him be. She spooned into him and, in no time, dozed off.

It was not yet dawn when Amata felt the urge to relieve herself. A rooster was repeatedly crowing, perhaps to express gratitude for surviving the season's festivities. It had competition from the muezzin calling Moslems to prayer. It was funny how the Imam called his adherents by name. *Baba Sikiru, leave your bed; time for prayers. Pa Akande, your mates are already here; where are you?* Clearly, the tactic worked, for she could hear men shuffling along the streets, not wanting their names broadcast over the loudspeaker as latecomers to prayers or, worse, absentees.

Before returning to bed, Amata remembered to dab her Youth Dew perfume all over her body. As she stretched out on the bed, Jasper got up and stumbled to the washroom. This was her chance. She flung the sheets away and spread herself in the middle of the bed.

It seemed Jasper had the same idea. He let his boxers slip to the floor, sat on Amata's side of the bed, and bent toward his wife. His hands gathered her breasts. "Stainless." He plastered her with kisses.

Amata arched forward, her entire body tingling with desire. She purred, throbbing all over. They made love until hunger drove them to the kitchen for breakfast.

CHAPTER 25

On her next visit to the doctor, Amata complained that her monthly visitor had stopped coming. Again.

"I have not bled since Christmas," she said. "And now April has dawned. So here I am."

"Well," the gynae joked, "We don't want it to come, do we? It is an unwanted guest." She chuckled. "Much like the proverbial mother-in-law."

"True," Amata assented, playing along. "One never knows what evils accompany a visit."

She told the gynae how Iyom had looked with disdain at her discarded sanitary napkins. "She gathered them with a stick and called me. 'Be careful how you dispose of your used sanitary napkins. Gather them in a safe place and burn them. If they get into the wrong hands. You know, envious people, enemies.'"

Her gynae laughed and shook her head.

Amata continued. "Ee, I joke about it, but Iyom Mgboye does not exhibit any traits of the legendary wicked mother-in-law. Not yet. But I don't know how long her patience with a flat-bellied daughter-in-law will last. How long before Opaku tongues start wagging and they tell my husband to get rid of the she-man he married? I am worried about this visitor playing hide-and-seek with me, Doctor."

Dr. Ogedengbe took a urine sample, drew blood, and ran some tests.

"Well," said the doctor when her lab assistant brought back the test results. "I don't think you need to worry anymore. Congratulations! You are pregnant!"

Amata opened her eyes wide in disbelief. She looked down at her belly and patted it. "I am pregnant! It has happened! Thank you, Ma."

"I am always happy when we record a success story," Dr. Ogedengbe replied. "But dear, this is just the beginning of the journey. Until we get a healthy baby with a hale and hearty mother, we are just starting. You understand?"

Amata nodded.

"You must come back regularly for antenatal care. I would like to monitor you right up to delivery."

Amata stood up to leave, then, on impulse, walked over to the doctor and embraced her. She floated home on a cloud of happiness.

When Jasper got home that evening, she was waiting.

"You have scored a goal."

"Goal? Who scored?" She was sure his mind went to a football match, but before he got more confused and wondered about her sudden interest in furnishing him with details of a football match, she pointed to her stomach.

He grinned like a tipper grille, lifted her off her feet and spun around. "Amata! Amata!" He kissed her all over her neck. "You are sure? Amata!"

~

Despite Jasper's protestations, Amata continued to accompany him to the shop. Some days, they made quick sales. Before the banks closed, Ebuka would escort Amata to deposit the day's earnings into their account. They did not have far to walk. Many branches of banks stood smack in the middle of the market. Still, Jasper insisted that Ebuka accompanied her.

"There are so many street urchins, my dear. We must tread with caution."

One day, a customer strolled into the shop.

"Yes, Oga, e dey. What do you need, sir?" Amata asked.

The fellow showed her the stretched fan belt. "Honda Accord," he said as she took the item from him.

"Please have a seat, sir. I will bring it."

As she stood in front of the array of belts that hung from the doors, she called back to the customer, "Uncle, we have foot mats, too. The latest from the factory. Upgrade the car's look to the next level."

The fellow shook his head. "My mats are still okay. End of Discussion."

But Amata persisted. "What about steering cover? Dior. Alloy wheels? Big boys club. Uncle, Lagos girls notice these things."

The fellow was about to shake his head again but had a rethink. "All right, let me look at the alloy wheels."

Amata was finishing up with her customer when Ebuka breezed in with a tastefully dressed society lady. On her heels followed a rough-looking guy, clearly her mechanic.

"Ismaila, wait for me outside," the socialite said, taking charge of the situation. She had a list of items she needed for her car. First, tie rod.

"I came myself because these mechanics are rogues," she went on, like an actor on stage. "They inflate everything. Oh, this country! Honesty has decamped from Nigeria, let me tell you. Everyone cheats and marks up at random."

The Honda owner was piqued. "I got a contractor to build a small bungalow for me at FESTAC Estate. My dear, he used my money and materials to raise his own building. Imagine."

"It is terrible," Amata agreed. She pushed a seat over to the lady, who slumped into it gratefully.

"That is why I came by myself. I said to the mechanic, 'Write down all you need; we will go and price them.'"

"That is the way to do it, Auntie. And after buying the parts, you must sit with the mechanic to ensure they use the parts on your vehicle. Otherwise!" Amata shook her head knowingly.

"You telling me? I took off from work today because of this! I will sit with him in his workshop and drive my car home. Can you believe that the last time I sent my car for servicing, I was standing by the road waiting for a taxi when my mechanic cruised past in my car with his wife, dressed to the nines? They were going to a wedding ceremony. In my car! While I stood by the roadside, waiting for a cab."

"Some use their customer's car for illicit taxi runs for hours before they return it," Mr. Honda said. "Meanwhile, you call and ask how far? And they say they are almost done." He shook his head and stepped out.

"Honestly, this country." She shook her head.

"Auntie, what shall we offer you to cool down? We have Malta, pure water, coke."

"Malta, o jare."

It was a good sign. Once a customer accepted an expensive drink, she was morally bound to patronize you. Amata made sure to cross-sell as many items as she could. By the time she added up the total, the lady had spent over one hundred thousand naira at Jasper Gee's.

As she was attending to the woman, Amata had another idea for streamlining the business. "If you want anything, call us," she said. "Here is our card. Our boy will bring it to you. You do not need to suffer this Lagos traffic again."

"Oh, thank you, my dear. So thoughtful of you."

She made a note of the customer's name, address, the car, and the parts she had ordered. When the lady left, Amata created a database to keep track of all their customers' details. That was how Jasper Gee's home delivery service debuted.

CHAPTER 26

The pregnancies of the two co-wives progressed smoothly. Charity's, clearly more advanced, resembled the bonnet of a Kia Soul. Amata's was like its boot. Their paths crossed once at the ante-natal clinic.

"At last!" Charity hailed.

"Yes o," Amata replied and smiled.

They teased each other, calling each other "old woman," as expectant mothers are known. After that, Charity worried about the gender of the fetuses and prayed more fervently for a male child. She had gone for a scan but was told the embryo's presentation hid the gender.

When Amata was five months gone, the obstetrician thought she heard double heartbeats.

"Any history of multiple births in your family?"

Amata shook her head.

"Your husband's?"

"No, Ma."

"You should go for a scan."

Amata mentioned it to Jasper. But her husband, still struggling and anxious about the extra responsibility looming, waved her off. "Don't mind her," he said. "That is a business gimmick doctors use. You complain of headache. Before you leave the clinic, your appendix has been removed. We do not have twins in our families."

And they let it be.

Zona had vivid dreams of a male child. Was the long-awaited heir about to be born? On one occasion, he dreamt that he was present at the circumcision of a newborn. Another night, he saw himself cooing and bouncing a fractious boy on his laps. He love-bombed Charity, became solicitous, and enquired about her well-being, palpating her stomach, feeling the fetal kicks and the changing topography of his wife's belly at every opportunity. A footballer, he joked. He bought vegetables, fruits, and snacks for her and their girls and took them out for hamburgers and ice cream. Charity prayed frenziedly for a boy, even engaging pastors and prayer warriors.

Zona chanced on Amata during one of his perambulations in the market and was surprised to see that she was pregnant as well. His heart skipped a beat. What if? What if she brought forth a male as well? But Charity's belly was bigger; his son would precede Jasper's child.

One wet night in June, Charity went into labour. Zona drove her to the clinic and followed her into the labour room, all gowned up and wigged. It was his first time going into the room for the birth of a child. He prodded his wife to "Push, push, push, and get my son out. Are you getting my point?"

His eyes darted from one piece of equipment to another and back to the labouring woman, lying legs splayed, feet in stirrups.

"Cooperate with the nurse and release my son."

"Claim it!" the midwife urged the wailing woman. "Claim it!" She turned to the man. "Sir, your word will be made flesh."

Baby Number Four slipped out. Zona peered between its legs for the cone. When he beheld a swollen cowrie shell instead, his face scrunched up. The excitement that had lit up his eyes evaporated. He squeezed his nose and dimmed his gaze. He gave the women the side-eye, turned and stomped out of the hospital without looking back. The scrub and cap he discarded along the corridors.

Zona remained distraught and dumb about a name for the newest member of the Okonkwo family. The only name he had prepared was Ikenna. A girl who would leave her father's house and marry could not be named "Father's strength," so his fourth daughter grew up to be called Baby.

~

After her husband abandoned her in the ward, Charity was too ashamed to ask her kinswomen for help, so she took her newborn home in a taxi. From how Zona related with her, she knew she would have to find a son for him if she still wanted to enjoy her marriage. The next time she became pregnant, she would arrange with the nurse on duty to go home with a male child. She had heard that it was possible. Maybe she should change to Nurse Eliza's clinic. She was a kinswoman and would be able to organize it for her. Or she would resort to abortion. In her next pregnancy, she would do a scan. If the fetus presented as female, she would abort it. She couldn't afford another daughter. The matter had become critical. If she failed in having a boy, that UNILAG girl Zona was dating might upstage her.

"Come and name your child," she told her husband several times as he crossed the sitting room, eyes riveted on his mobile phone.

"You name her yourself," he countered. "She is a woman like you."

On one of such spiteful outbursts, Charity heard her mother-in-law, who had come to Lagos for the omugwo, admonish her son. "It is God that gives children. You should be grateful. Many do not have even one and will do anything to—"

"I saw you praying for my younger brother at Christmas," Zona interrupted. "Were you trying to pass my blessings to him? Is that why I am bearing females?"

"What a horrible thing to say," Nne rebuked him, recoiling from the venom in his accusation. "I pray for all my children. You are siblings. I heard that you made him pay cash for the goods you ordered for him, and I asked if it was true. What happened?"

"Who paid for my goods?" he fired back. His eyes blazed, his arms flailing in all directions. "Does a fowl peck into a goat's stomach? Are you getting my point? I pulled myself up by my bootstrings and heaved myself up. Let everyone do likewise."

"He loaned money to Rapu to grow his business. You could—"

"And I hear you plan to sell off our lands to support him. For your info, if you do that, I shall go to court. I shall sue you and any buyer."

"I cannot sell any land without your knowledge."

"Were you not there when he gave out our land to those bastards?"

"I had no hand in it. The kinsmen—"

"You have been warned!"

Charity could see Iyom flinch as her son wagged his dirty finger at her. What insolence! What a show of disrespect! She wanted to accost Zona and tell him he was wrong, but she did not want to add fuel to the raging fire, so she let it pass. If further aggravated, Zona could easily throw them out into the dark night. He was capable of that. So querulous and hard of heart.

"I want you three to live in peace and love and harmony. Squabbles do not pay and do not profit anybody. Agbisi would want it so," Iyom pleaded with her son.

"I am the first son. No one can take that from me." He was still angry.

Charity looked at her mother-in-law and, with eyes, silently indicated to her not to respond anymore. This was not a hill to die on.

After that encounter, Iyom's spirit was subdued. Something appeared to have entered their family. She did not know exactly what, but whenever she woke at night to ease herself, her mind would remember the exchange with Zona, and her skin would horripilate. Then she would wrap her arms about her and tuck into the cloth. Something was stalking the Okonkwo family, a sharp scythe that was ready to sever the connection between them. The phantom's scythe must be blunt. Perhaps that was why the thread had not given way. Maybe, even now, it was sawing away persistently at the connection, and the thread would soon snap. Or had it cut, and they were unaware? Had the goat already escaped the stable while the owners locked the doors at night, oblivious, trying to guard what was no longer there?

Zona put his foot down this time. No naming ceremony. "I invite my fellow men to welcome a female child each time. I must be the laughingstock of my friends. My father, Agbisi, gave birth to only males. Why is my wife giving me only females? Is it a result of your so-called prayers, Nne? To ridicule and diminish me? You have blessed Jasper and diverted all the blessings due to me to my junior."

Before she left on completion of the omugwo, Iyom named her granddaughter Makuachi—embrace God. She had vacillated between that name and Nkiruka—the future is greater. But did Nkiruka not mean one was dissatisfied with one's present situation and was optimistic for a better deal? Did it not indicate ingratitude? Shouldn't one rely on God no matter the circumstances? And so, Makuachi prevailed, Makua for short.

For the first time since Iyom had been coming to Zona's house for omugwo, she went home empty-handed. It was Charity, who, out of her stock, gave her one Aba n'anya wrapper, an ersatz version of the bespoke Dutch wax that her second son and wife had gifted her at Christmas. The envelope from her daughter-in-law was just enough to transport her back to Opaku. She refused to despair. With Amata finally expecting, another omugwo was around the corner. Jasper would treat her better, she knew.

CHAPTER 27

30 September 2016

At midnight, Amata felt a tsunami inside her. She called Odoziaku.

"Mama, how does labour feel?"

Her mother advised her to hurry to the hospital and let the doctors decide. Jasper drove like a Formula One racer.

Doctor Ogedengbe examined Amata and admitted her. "You have not dilated, but we prefer to keep you overnight."

Personnel in white uniforms streamed in to check on her. One after the other, they scrolled through her medical records.

"Did you do a scan?" the midwife asked. Amata shook her head.

Jasper, hunkering down on the couch, became anxious. "Anything the matter?"

The nurse had seen where the doctor suspected double heartbeats. She circled it and drifted away.

"Just deliver in peace, my dear," the husband implored. "Mother and child fine. Please, my dear."

Amata gave him the side-eye and pushed him away, "Ka m fu uzo," she hissed. Clear out of my sight. All the hassle for intimacy, her amenorrhoea and then the monthlies that resurfaced, the ovulation medication—all for this pain that had no equal. Amata howled and squirmed.

"Go away!" she shrieked at Jasper. He turned towards the door and took a few steps. Anything to please her.

"Come back here! Come and see what your penis—"

The nurses shushed her. "Bear it o, or you will keep howling in subsequent visits to the labour room."

"Eh! Subsequent gini? To where?" She opened her mouth all the way to her lungs and bawled to her heart's content, embarrassing Jasper.

In the morning, as the National Day parade was showing on the telly and the Head of State's broadcast was booming over the radio, Amata and Jasper's first child slid into the world. A boy.

"That's O'Neal!" the new father gushed in his hospital gown, beside himself with joy. His five o'clock shadow glistened like the grille of a Lexus. He received the wailing infant in his huge palms and raised him high like a chalice before releasing him to the nurse. The doctor was still fidgeting around the new mother, murmuring something about a scan or lack thereof. Ten minutes later, Dr. Ogedengbe introduced a hand into the birth canal and eased O'Neal's brother out.

"Two! Amata! Two!" Jasper screamed.

He stood, hands akimbo, in a daze, hammocks under his eyes. The doctor led him to a chair and lowered him into it. Jasper sat there, stunned and grinning like a goat that had licked salt. He called his mother-in-law, then Iyom. "Amata has delivered. Twin boys!"

"Odoziaku is on the way," the newly-minted father said to his bewildered wife. He turned and embraced Dr. Ogedengbe.

The doctor wiggled out of his arms. "It is your wife you should embrace," she said. "She did all the work."

CHAPTER 28

"What you could not do, your co-wife has done double," Zona hissed at his wife when news of the twins' birth reached him. "My peers' wives are delivering males. You, you fill my house with females. God forbid."

Charity wept bitterly. What she feared most had befallen her. What fate was this? Why this cross of bearing only females? Her younger sister, Obiananma, married to a pastor and living in Port Harcourt, already had a son and a daughter. Why not her? She went to her room and flung herself on the bed. *Not just one. Not one but two sons. Amata, who could not get pregnant, has overtaken me. Woe is me in my husband's house. Woe is me.*

Makuachi, asleep in the cot beside her, cried from hunger and discomfort. Charity ignored her. She knelt by her side of the matrimonial bed and buried her head in a pillow. When Chisom, confounded at the non-stop wailing, went to enquire, Charity let her in to take Baby.

"I must have fallen asleep," she lied.

Chisom took in Charity's red eyes and tear-stained face. Without showing any emotion, she lifted Makua out of the cot, took her to the children's room and cared for her.

Zona's sulk soared another notch. He came home late and locked himself in the spare room, only coming out for meals. He was always on the phone. Sunday, after church service, he would dash off.

"Where to?" Charity would venture to ask as she rocked a colicky baby.

"To a meeting," he would reply if he bothered to answer. Most times, he ignored her, threw away his face and breezed out.

It was to Helen's that Zona repaired. He had met her one evening when she was looking for a lift out of downtown. He had chatted her up, and they had gone straight to a bush bar at Surulere and had some bottles before he dropped her off at the University. She would be his girl, he told himself. He needed to strategize for a son. No law said he could not have sons outside the home. No law. And if Helen insisted, he would marry her. He just had to have male offspring for his lineage. If only one could consult the oracle to know which woman would bear sons before committing oneself.

Helen was a native of Umuahia. Her trap for a sugar daddy had netted a big catch in Zona, CEO of a spare parts dealership. He would take care of her. She came from a very modest home and could not expect any support from her indigent parents. If anything, they were looking to her to extricate them from grinding poverty, the type that denied sleep to the eyes. Funke, her roommate, invited her to parties where they cavorted with wealthy men who lavished cash on the university girls. Recently, Helen had grown tired of these parties. She longed for a permanent arrangement, for an ATM sugar daddy. Zona fit the bill. The way he was fawning over her, she knew that God had answered her prayers.

They arranged to meet at a short-stay hotel on Iwaya Road.

"I will take care of you," Zona had sweet-talked, with imploring doggy eyes and cradling her Tina Turner-wigged head in his hands.

Zona knew how fickle these undergraduates were and that they juggled several men at a time. He begged Helen to date only him, telling her she would not regret it.

Shortly after they started dating, Helen told him she had missed her period. He was not sure he was responsible for it, so he insisted on an abortion, coughing out a princely sum for the procedure. He told her again to discard any sidekicks and concentrate on him. When she graduated from Theatre Arts, Zona used his influence to lobby the National Youth Service Corps to redeploy her to Lagos. He could not afford to let her out of his sight or travel to Nassarawa State, where she had been originally deployed.

He rented a self-contained flat for her on Forsythe Street, near the Sandgrouse market, far from the family house in Alaka Estate. He furnished it with all the comforts and now spent most of his spare time there. He retired there after the day's hustle. As they enjoyed local delicacies for dinner, Helen salved his bruised ego and disappointment at the elusive heir. Once in a while, he would lie to Charity that he was travelling on business and would be gone for days and weeks.

~

Charity did not need anyone to tell her that her husband had another love interest. He was spending more time away from home on business trips. Once, when he claimed to have gone to Opaku, Charity called for him to bring back a parcel from her mother, only for him to claim that he had already left. Yet, he never missed seeing his in-laws whenever he was in the East. Also, they were hardly intimate now. At first, Zona's excuse was that he was giving her time to recover from her visit to the labour room. Later, when she made advances on those rare nights he was home, he claimed fatigue and headache.

"I thought it was only women who have headaches," she told her friend, Hannah, who was visiting. "I did not know that men now also develop headaches at night."

"He has another woman," Hannah said blandly. "And it does not look like a fling." She bored her eyes into Charity's. "Shine your eyes and possess your possession, Mother of Adaobi. Do not let another collect sleep from your eyes and sleep on your behalf. After four children. *Where you go go?*"

"I wonder. It is well."

The next time Zona returned after midnight, Charity locked him out and refused to open the front door. She peered at him through the window. Sweat broke out on his forehead, but she turned a deaf ear to the frenetic banging on the door, which woke the apprentices and neighbours. The housemaid hurried to the door, but Charity waved her back. Zona spent an hour shaking the house on its hinges before she relented and turned the key.

"Sorry," she said, rubbing her eyes. "We were afraid of armed robbers."

He locked the door behind him. He had never hit her before, so when the first slap landed on her cheek, Charity was aghast and thrown off balance. She heard a ringing in her ear, followed by a queer silence akin to deafness. The frustration that welled up inside her for months burst forth, and she pounced on him like a bulldog, gathering his shirt lapels tightly around the neck.

She dragged him around the room and jerked him roughly up and down.

"You will know me today," she screamed. "Run-away! Who is keeping you away from your home?"

Chisom pleaded with her to release Master. Charity sent her to get the pestle.

"I will pound you today. Who are you deceiving? Open a shop for me, no. You impregnate me four times back-to-back, then abandon me at home while you pursue rats."

"Let go!" Zona yelled.

Charity tightened her grip.

"Haaa m!" he bellowed. Instead, Charity twisted her wrists.

Zona staggered to the sofa, heaving Charity along. He tried to chuck her onto it. She did not let go. They collapsed into the chair together, her engorged breasts smothering him. He turned his head away to get some air.

"Leave me!" he shouted. "Haaa m, wild animal."

Charity would not relent. She heard some buttons pop as she crumbled the fabric of his shirt. In a swift move, she shoved his head between her legs. A whiff of her rival's perfume reached her. She coiled the lapels further and pulled. Zona tore blindly at her night dress, searing it to pieces.

The apprentices who lodged in the backhouse were pounding the door now. "Master, Madam?"

Zona ignored their cries and bade the house girl extinguish the lights. He was in a bad place. He was tired. Helen had sapped his strength. He needed sleep. It was past midnight. In his wildest imagination, he had never expected this confrontation. He was a titled man; what would his fellow chiefs say? The Elite Merchants Club? Already, his apprentices were privy to his shaming. He had to end this madness and salvage his image. He punched his wife on the sides with strong, short jabs, putting all the power he had left into his pudgy fists. Charity could not avoid the blows. Her body contorted with every strike.

"Release me now, or I kill you," Zona threatened.

"Kill me."

"Let go of my shirt! Leave it!"

He pummelled blindly, anywhere he could reach—her rib cage, navel, breasts, head, and lunged his head into her. Charity winced as each punch landed but held on.

"Prostitute specialist," she spat out. "You have a wife, but your feet are stuck outside. Ome ife ashawo." Patron of prostitutes.

Zona flinched at the insult to his title. This harridan had no boundaries. It hurt his pride knowing his apprentices could overhear the derisive remarks. He twisted like a contortionist and bit into the flesh in front of him. He tasted blood.

"My leg o!" Charity let go as the pain lanced through her body. Zona, freed, retaliated. He hit her head repeatedly against the wooden armrest of the sofa. Blood rushed to Charity's eyes.

"My head o!"

The children, awakened now, scrambled to the sitting room. They burst into tears at the sight of their parents engaged in fisticuffs. Charity went limp. Chisom shepherded the children out of the room. Zona kicked her to the floor and stood over her. "This will be the first and last time you lock me out of my house or fight me! Are you getting my point?"

"Your house?" she spat back. "Do you still live here? Fugitive! Ogboso One of Opaku!" Sprinter the First of Opaku.

"I have told you. You cannot hoard me. Unless I am not Echezona Okonkwo. You cannot give me a son! Should I sit here like your houseboy? Me?" He poked his chest. "Omeifeukwu, Agbisi's son? Did Agbisi not play away match? Did my mother kill him for it? Witch."

"Look who's calling someone a witch," Charity hissed. "Someone who operates at night when his mates are home. You are the wizard, a vagabond of no substance!" She was still screaming when he walked away, leaving Charity naked and crumpled like a cracked engine block.

After that tiff, Zona seldom came home. Once in a while, he would stop by to drop some money on the table, pack a bag, and disappear.

One day, a member of the Opaku Wives Association saw Zona going into a flat with a pregnant woman and told Charity.

The next Saturday, when Zona was busy in the shop, Charity appeared at the Forsythe Street flat. She knocked on the door. When an unsuspecting Helen opened, Charity immediately swooped on her. She yanked off Helen's expensive blond Dolly Parton wig and tossed it out the window. A fierce fight ensued. Helen, frightened out of her wits, screamed for help, covering her swelling belly and her spotless face.

"Husband snatcher! So you are the lunatic that locked the father of four in your stinking thing?"

Helen tried to extricate herself from the intruder's pummelling, but Charity pursued her around the flat, walloped her, and rained abuses on her.

Prostitute!

Homewrecker!

Round and round the flat they went, with Helen running, dodging, ducking, whimpering, Charity following, hitting. When she recognized Zona's shoes on the landing, she grabbed the shoe and struck out. Helen, overpowered, crumpled to a heap.

It was neighbours who saved her. They subdued Charity and coaxed her to leave the premises.

"Leave my penis alone!" she hurled at Helen. "Go get your own!"

Two days later, when Zona came home to pack a new bag, Charity told him, "Next time, I will come to your shop. And next time you travel on business, I know where to find you. Shameless vagabond!"

CHAPTER 29

It was a Saturday evening. Iyom and her maid, Omenma, were peeling yams for dinner and discussing the latter's progress in school when a vehicle horned feverishly at the gate. Omenma dropped her knife and made to go open it, but Iyom rebuked her and signalled her to halt. Nne walked to the entrance, clutching the knife in her hand.

"Who is it?" she called out into the twilight. She heard the vehicle door squeak open. She held the knife tighter.

"Nne, it is Charity," came the voice.

"Charlingo," Iyom called out. "Hope nothing?"

"Nne."

"How is your husband? Omenma, *wete* key now we know who it is."

The vehicle heaved into the compound and stopped at Zona's bungalow. Adaobi, Alaoma, and Eloduchi tumbled out. Charity cradled the baby.

"O gini?" Iyom asked as they trudged over to her. She flung the kitchen knife away. "Is it for Christmas? In April?"

"It is well," Charity said, forcing a weak smile, aware the kids were listening and had witnessed the run-up to this shanghaiing. Iyom turned around and walked back to the table where the yams were still waiting to be peeled. She waited for Charity to speak.

"Mummy and Daddy fought," Adaobi volunteered. "Daddy sent us away."

"Your son sent us packing. Actually, he sent me to my parents, but I came here instead. Zona has sent us out of his house." Charity's voice quavered.

"What happened that I did not hear?" Iyom was short of words but thankful that no one had died. Her shoulders were hunched as she spoke. "Whatever it is, welcome. The devil is a liar."

"Like this," Adaobi continued, punching Alaoma and pinning the latter's head in her armpit. Iyom separated them and embraced her granddaughters. They surrounded her, tugged at her wrapper, and inhaled her comforting old smell. Iyom always indulged them.

"You youngsters will 'naked' me." She secured her wrapper more firmly around her waist.

"Omenma, bring the bungalow's key." Turning to Charity, she said, "If you had given me notice, we would have at least dusted it. This is a surprise."

"Did I know, Nne? Did I know? I said he told me this morning to go back to my parents' house. He hired a truck and threw our things inside waja waja. Throughout the journey, I tried calling you."

"My phone is dead. No light since last Nkwo," the old woman hissed.

"It was at Niger Bridge that I said, how can I return to my father with four children? Is Nne aware? That is why I directed the driver to Opaku."

"You did well, my daughter. You all must be tired. Let us offload your stuff and release the driver. Omenma, bring one more yam from the barn. Put water on the fire so the children can bathe." At close range, the older woman noticed the bruises and the scab on Charity's face. She rubbed them gently. Charity flinched and pulled up her skirt, revealing the bite marks.

"He did this to you?" She flipped her thumb and middle finger of two hands. She remembered the youngsters. "We will discuss later."

She turned to her granddaughters. "Adaobi, you tall like obelisk! Alaoma. Eloduchi, you two pursuing your big sister. What do you Lagos people eat?"

"Nne," Charity said in a low voice. "Nne, I can stay anywhere but do not leave me empty-handed. Open a shop for me; let me also earn. I can stay anywhere as long as I am not idle. You cannot send me away empty-handed after four children. That is maltreatment. He will come and meet me here."

That is how Zona banished his wife and daughters to the village. The night they returned, when the kids were in bed, Charity lay awake and wept bitter tears at the direction her life had taken. She, who had thought she had a secure marriage. All because of bringing forth female children. *Oh, Jehovah Nissi. Jehovah Jireh. Jehovah El Shaddai,* she prayed silently. She was still sniffing and sighing, with Makua at her breast, when sleep tracked her down.

In her quarters that night, Iyom sighed. She had seen this coming. The birth of four daughters in a row had put Zona in a fiendish mood. The arrival of Jasper's twin boys had roiled him to no end. He picked quarrels with everyone. Now this. She had overheard Charity complaining to Amata that Zona had a mistress. *Well, he knows what to do,* she had thought. *He can get sons outside.* But he did not have to send his wife packing. She sighed again, massaged her aching knee, and stretched.

The day Charity left, Zona got the apprentices to clean up the house and move Charity's and her children's things into the warehouse. He brought Helen to live with him. That would teach Charity a lesson. She had gone overboard. Not content with fighting him, she had attacked his mistress. And was not remorseful, threatening to do worse. She had become the proverbial talisman that became overbearing: he had shown it the tree from which it was carved.

It was the best decision. Charity had begun to intimidate him with her incessant heckling. Tata-tata-tatata, non-stop. He had resorted to avoiding his house. His reputation was at stake. He, a high chief and an executive of the Elite Merchants Club.

Zona used his contacts in government to obtain employment for Helen at an organization caring for disadvantaged children. She began a one-year probation as a children's advocate, meeting government agencies and pitching programs for street children. She enjoyed her work, travelling all over Lagos State. But her boss, a woman from Mbano, would not let her drink water and put down the cup in peace. She complained about Helen's attitude, talked down to her and made life miserable for her. Every night, Helen would return to Zona in tears. *She is a feminazi. She is frustrated. She is this, she is that.*

Zona advised her to quit, telling her he would open a business for her. Anything she wanted. He was smitten and hated to see her tears.

"Let me give it a year. If Aruodo does not change, I will leave the job. Let her eat it. Can you imagine? A fellow woman, a fellow Igbo sister, is the one making life difficult for me. A Yoruba person helps me get a job, and my countrywoman will snuff it out. Can you believe that?"

"Na who know person dey kill am," Zona quoted. "If you expect your detractors to be strangers, you misfire. A man's enemies will be members of his household. Are you getting my point? So the Holy Book said."

She had miscarried after the scuffle with Charity and had spent a few nights in the hospital for a D&C procedure. After giving her a few days to recuperate, Zona resumed mounting her. He was that anxious for an heir.

The CEO kept waiting for Helen to announce that she had missed her period again, but the news was not forthcoming. Instead, she started demanding to know when he would go and meet her people.

"Soon," he said. "We will plan a convenient time. It is best towards the end of the year."

Truth be told, he had no intention of doing that unless she gave him a male child. Get pregnant and give birth to an heir. If not, he was willing to chuck her out and look elsewhere. But the thought of having a son outside of wedlock ate at his mind. As a Catholic, was it not better to have the heir via a mistress than to take in a second wife and risk excommunication? But as a first son, could you produce an heir out of wedlock? Would the lad have the same rights? His mind went to the two lads Agbisi had sired outside and how they were going about looking for relevance in Opaku. Would Jasper's sons lord it over his son for being born outside marriage? Thinking of Jasper unnerved him. His younger brother was progressing in business, and his home was secure now with not one but two male children. Bile gathered in Zona's mouth. He spat out and hissed.

CHAPTER 30

Feeding Charity and her brood proved daunting for Iyom. She watched helplessly as her yam barn dwindled fast. Before the Lagosians swooped down on her, she and Omenma managed on one tuber of yam every three to four days. Now, each day, two yams barely sufficed.

"What of bread and tea that you Lagosians eat for breakfast?" she asked Charity when she saw another empty column in the barn.

"Nne, where is the money for two or three loaves of bread?" her daughter-in-law queried. "Plus tea, sugar, milk? Yam is cheaper and can hold the children till lunchtime better than ordinary bread. Or should we opt for bean balls and pap? Look at the price of beans in the market. Yam is more affordable."

"How can a man leave his wife and children empty-handed like this?" the old woman asked dubiously. "What did you do to my son to merit this treatment?"

Iyom called Zona. When the line connected, she launched her tirade. "Charity is here with my granddaughters. What is the matter that you sent her home? Without food money? What work do I do that will enable me to feed all these mouths? When I complain now, you will accuse me of what I do not know."

She was thinking of the last argument between them. She waited. There was silence at the other end. She was about to hang up when a voice answered, "Master is with a customer now, Nne. He will call you back."

She waited in vain.

Iyom mentioned the matter to Jasper when he called another night. "Charity and her household are eating from my barn. I have difficulty feeding everyone."

"Maybe Zona is having cash flow problems," Jasper replied. "It happens in business. I will see what I can do."

~

The next week, Jasper heard that Zona bought a Lexus and a minibus for ferrying his apprentices to and from the market. He told the old woman. It dawned on Nne that Zona was deliberately punishing his wife. *What kind of man will leave his wife and children begging for food and turn around and buy new cars for his business?* But she knew. Zona had no heart. Blood did not flow in his veins.

She mapped out a portion of her farm for Charity to cultivate minor crops.

~

Zona wondered why Charity's people had not contacted him since she left his house. When Iyom called him, he understood. His wife had sought refuge in Opaku. He tried to avoid his mother's calls, but she was insistent and tenacious. One arbitrary weekend, he decided to go home. His intention was to see to the children's welfare and weigh a business opportunity. The *Aku lue uno* gospel struck a chord in him. He would explore investment opportunities nearer home.

When he reached Opaku, he was surprised to see his estranged wife thriving. She exuded freshness and joy and transmitted contentment. He learnt that she braided hair for clients in her free time and that Adaobi attended the local school.

"Open a business for her," Iyom advised him. "It is God that determines the gender of His children."

Zona listened to his mother's admonishments. The words entered through one ear and exited through the other. When she had finished speaking, he answered simply, "Nne, I have heard. Are you getting my point? I will look into it."

When his mother yawned without opening her mouth, Zona checked the time. It was later than he'd thought. He got up. A smiling moon shone down on the land, barely dispelling the thick darkness. From beyond Iyom's compound, he could hear tardy housewives pounding in the night. The sound of a grinding machine serrated the pastoral stillness. His stomach grumbled. He had not eaten since Lagos. He dreaded asking Charity for food.

He settled back into the seat. "What did you cook?"

Zona waited while Iyom conjured up her famous palm nut soup. Since the banishment, he and Charity had not exchanged words. He minded his business, still hurting from her wildcat attacks at him and his mistress. As much as possible, he had slept outside his home but had to contend with his apprentices. He was sure he was the talk of the town. Houseboys knew how to gossip and belittle their masters while making an exaggerated show of respect in their presence. At the moment, he was sure he was not worth a kobo in their estimation. He, Echezona, Omeifeukwu, Doer of Great Things! A woman would lock him out of his home? Make him less of a man in his own house? He had come up with the idea of sending her to her people until the alcohol she imbibed cleared from her brain.

No, it was too risky to eat his wife's food. She was capable of anything, that girl. As the house help set the table before Zona, Iyom bent down and stirred the soup with her index finger. She carved out a lump of the yam fufu, dipped it into the sauce, and swallowed.

"Good. Omenma did not over-salt it."

Zona knew Iyom did not need to taste Omenma's cooking. She had trained the girl well. He knew she did it to remove any doubt of poisoning, but he was too hungry to raise the issue with her. Famished from the long journey, he ate like a hungry bulldog. He crooked his index finger and wiped the dish clean.

Feeling fortified, he rose. Time of reckoning. He approached his bungalow. *Charity must have heard that Helen has moved in.* Fear niggled him and unsettled his stomach. He entered the kitchen and made sure to hide the pestle behind a drum.

CHAPTER 31

Charity waited up for her husband. When she had arrived in Opaku, she was ready to let all hell loose on Zona, but Iyom had calmed her down and drummed sense into her head.

I appreciate that you did not go to your parents' house, she had said. *You did well to come here. Secure your position. You have four kids. Do all you can to train them; that should be your preoccupation now. I will talk to my son. He will open a business for you. This is not the time that women stay idle.*

I'm all for it, Nne, Charity acquiesced.

Go to the market and see how women are hustling, toiling, and counting cash. Cool down. Men sometimes behave like children. Any woman who wants to survive her marriage must see her husband as her first child.

Charity had sobered up.

You remember Jonas Okunna?

Near the school?

Exactly.

Iyom summoned phlegm and spat it out. She looked up to read the sky. The clouds were congregating. Charity followed the old woman's eyes.

That is how they gather, Nne. They will blow away. Maybe go and rain at Nkwa or Lilu. You were saying—?

Jonas died. You see those last two boys that his wife delivered after his passing? Who do you think was impregnating his widow? Iyom did not wait for an answer. *Agbisi.*

Iyom noted the incredulity on Charity's face.

Yes, the father of my children was the one dipping his pestle into the widow's wide mortar. Did I run away? Did I make trouble? Am I not the one still here? Calm down. Where are the two who were pounding away behind my back? Dead and buried. Iyom is still here. Make peace with your husband. A wise woman keeps her home and her husband. I won't say more than this.

~

Zona stiffened when he saw Charity curtsy.

"Omeifeukwu. I am sorry," she said simply.

Zona stared straight ahead, suddenly remorseful at the way he had treated her. What woman would stand by and watch her husband sniffing around another woman like a mongrel, setting up home with another Eve and not do anything to protect her interest and her children? He conceded that he had not managed the situation expertly. But his pride stood in the way, and he could not vocalize his regret.

"Shall I serve you dinner?"

"Don't worry," he said curtly. "I have eaten."

Adaobi was still awake. She stumbled in, sleepy-eyed, and climbed onto her daddy's knee. As his first child, she occupied a special place in his heart. He cradled her, planted a kiss on her head and nestled it in the crook of his neck. In Lagos, the kid's hair was usually braided, with a weekly trip to the salon to attach bright, colourful rings and ribbons to it. He noticed the short, cropped hair.

"How are you managing with the children?"

"I drive Nne's keke while she minds the children. We share the proceeds."

"Nne has a keke?"

"Yes, did you not see it?"

Indeed, he had seen one yellow autorickshaw with a brown leather covering but thought the owner had parked it in their gated compound for security.

"Jasper bought it for her. To make some money for running the compound."

"Jasper or Rapu?" Rapu, he knew, dealt with tricycles and motorbikes.

"Jasper," Charity reiterated. "Rapu owed him some money. He said Rapu should pay with a tricycle. That is what I drive, and we use the money to take care of our needs. We are managing well."

He felt hollow in his stomach. He swallowed hard to keep his dinner down. Jasper bought a keke for Nne! His wife was driving it to support his family. Jasper! Everywhere he turned, he saw Jasper. His business was prospering. His marriage was stable. He had two sons already. And now he was caring for their aged mother. And providing for his estranged wife. Was he trying to usurp his God-given position? Sweat sprouted on his forehead.

Words failed him. Lodged on his mind was an image of him dressed in the traditional ishiagu outfit, walking down a slippery and smooth slope. *Better to nip this thing in the bud,* he thought. *Better to bail the water out when it is still at ankle level.*

His legs quivered. He realized his hat was still on his head. He lifted it and dropped it beside him on the sofa. Charity was still standing there. He had to say something.

"I leave early. Lagos is far."

"Will you be needing breakfast?"

"No, no. Too early. I shall eat on the way, probably at Benin."

"Shall I put out water for a bath now?"

There was no running water. They had to fetch from the water tank outside.

"Thank you." He yawned.

She set the bath things out, searched for a clean towel, and hung it on the overhead bar.

When Zona returned to the living room, Adaobi had finally succumbed to sleep. As Charity bent down to gather the child up, Zona waved her away. He lifted his daughter and adjusted her head on his shoulder. Their Lagos home used to reek of baby powder and urine. It was the smell of children. He missed it. He carried the sleeping child in to the king-size mattress. All the children slept there. Tenderly, he lowered himself to one knee and placed her beside her siblings. He tugged at the bunched-up quilt, making sure it covered all the sleepers.

A whiff of the piss reached him. He straightened up. Girls. Girls. All girls. The nostalgia he felt slowly gave way to nausea and regret. If only he had a son. What would it take to have a son? What? Yes, he was wealthy, but he could never be fulfilled without a male child. Never. He sighed. In his mind, he blamed Charity for the situation, for birthing only females. *I have done my part to provide for my family. Is it too much to ask for a son? Even one?*

He went back to the lounge. This temporary bungalow contained only two bedrooms. One room was for the children and their nanny. The other, he used to share with Charity. He was there when the power outage occurred. He swore at the distribution company.

"Should I switch on the generator?" Charity asked. Its noise might jar the sleepers awake and disturb the eerie silence of the village.

"No. I can find my way. Are you getting me? Is it not my house?"

Charity lay on the three-seater sofa he had vacated, covered with a blanket. A bush lamp stood on the floor, making ominous shapes of the furniture. Zona stretched out, tired to the bones. The windows were open, and he relished the cool breeze on his naked body. The darkness was impenetrable, the silence deafening. Stark opposite of Lagos. Even the housewives notorious for pounding late into the night were silent. Only the crickets chirped lustily. He scratched the thicket of hair below his belly and expelled a fusillade of farts.

The long drive from Lagos took its toll on him. He felt like a thief caught and beaten by a mob. He needed to sleep, but he could not ignore the powerful stirring, no, throbbing, of his engine. It stretched up, veering a little to the right, a little to the left. In the dark, it looked like a cobra head seeking a warm hole to crawl into. *I have a right,* he told himself. *As long as my in-laws have not returned the bride price, it is my right.* When he could bear it no more, he stood up.

Charity saw his silhouette in the doorway and tensed. *What is he going to do to me? Strangulate me? Finish me off to bring UNILAG prostitute in?* She watched as he advanced, arms extended like a zombie, avoiding the furniture. He stepped on a toy. It let out a loud squeak. She feigned sleep, tossing in a mild snore for effect as she quietly reached under the pillow and clutched the concrete roller of her grinding stone. He was beside her now, his erect penis swaying inches from her face in the low glow of the lamp. She lay still. Without a word, he flung aside the quilt and fished for her wrist.

Having stayed three months without a man, Charity was hungry for intimacy, but she resisted. She pulled back her hand.

"Come," he said sotto voce, so as not to wake the children.

"No."

"Biko."

She covered herself again and snuggled into the blanket.

Zona was in a tizzy. He bent down and discarded the cover. "Bia, o. Charchar."

"Open a shop for me."

"I will. Tomorrow. Just come, doh." Please.

Reluctantly, Charity allowed herself to be persuaded. She knew that some men, to punish their wives for wrong-doing, denied them intimacy, sometimes for years, while they themselves played around. A wife, ignored by her man, was left to stew in her misdeed and die in silence. She was lucky Zona still wanted her.

She remembered Nne's advice and followed meekly. He tried to tip her onto the foam, but she stood firm.

"You promise?"

"Ee. Tomorrow. Lie down."

She sat down. He divested her of the night dress and pushed her down, tingling all over. Her smell was heady, the abundant brush between her legs always maddening.

~

Charity's fragrance infused the room. Zona inhaled copiously. He lifted her arm and breathed in her armpit. He would recognize that smell anywhere. It was the smell of native soap, the type his mother made from plantain skin and palm. He exhaled and breathed the aroma again. Palm kernel oil. He and his siblings grew up with the palm fruit, eating it, bathing with its soap, and rubbing its oil. He lay back and relished it.

The scent took him back to his youth, to the many occasions when he would stand naked before the steel tubular bucket, shivering in the harmattan cold, teeth clattering like scissors, unable to splash the icy water on his body. Iyom would sneak behind and rub the ball of soap on his head in circles. *There, let me see you walk away without a wash,* she seemed to say. If you delayed, the soap would cake on your head and become harder to rinse out. The only way to get rid of it was to summon up courage and dump the bowl of water on your head. With frisky scrubbing, the suds melted, foamed and formed bubbles, and trickled at first, down his shoulders, to his chest, finally gliding to the distended stomach. A bout of more rigorous scouring chased away the cold and spread the lather southward to the thighs, legs, and feet. Another bowl and the water would cascade down, forming a lacy pool around his feet.

He inhaled Charity's scent again. It was all over her body, even her hair. In Lagos, she used to favour weave-on and braids and foreign wigs that lasted weeks on end. Unwashed, they emitted an unpleasant odour, which she tried to dispel with sprays. Here, her hair was natural and soft to the touch, washed with that heady native soap and rubbed with palm kernel oil. In Charity's arms, he was home. He squeezed her chunky cheeks and drew her closer. Kneeling between her thighs, he parted the thistles, and tunnelled in.

I'm at the threshold. Why hurry? He tried to slow down. But he had not reckoned with the long absence of her body. He increased the tempo. The floodgates burst open and scattered his mind.

"He... He....! He....! Helen-ey!" he roared.

Their bodies stiffened. The night stood still. Even the frogs paused their mating cries. Only the crickets chirruped nonchalantly, unaware of the hurricane washing over the humans.

His wife squirmed under him. She pushed him away, but he resisted and drew her closer.

"I'm sorry. I forgot myself. Forgive me." They lay side by side; she, in the crook of his arm.

As his seed trickled down their laps, he said, "You wanted to start a business."

It was an attempt at reconciliation. She ignored him. He nudged her.

"Yes," she said bloodlessly.

"What kind?"

"Fashion. I want to sell women's stuff."

She tried again to wriggle away from him. His midriff weighed on her, but he wedged her in with his thigh. "Are you not used to my stomach? It is evidence of good living."

She smirked. "Good living while we starve here."

"I repent. Look for a shop in town. I will pay the rent and stock it."

"I know people in Lagos that can sell to me and—"

"Lagos is out of the question," he cut her short firmly. "For now, you have to remain here. Are you getting my point?"

Charity wanted to rebel. Why was Lagos out of bounds to her? Was she to remain in the village while Helen took over as Zona's wife in the city? She remembered Iyom's advice and let it be. For now.

CHAPTER 32

Zona did not leave early in the morning as he had planned. After his blunder the previous night, he had no choice but to find a solution to his domestic problem. It was Sunday. There was little he could do. He went around to inspect the family's plots and paid outstanding condolence visits to bereaved families. At sundown, he sat outside with Iyom and watched the children play their clapping game, throwing legs apart like dancers, jumping shakily on the hopscotch board, and screaming gleefully when they won.

Makuachi cried frantically when he tried to carry her. He had become a stranger to her. To calm the frazzled infant, Adaobi patted her on the back. She pointed to him.

"It's Daddy," she said repeatedly. But Makuachi would have none of it. She strained her whole body away from Zona, gave him the side-eye and a pout as if to say, *You renegade! Are you not the fellow who refused to name me?*

Zona found a shop for Charity at Awka. He paid two years' rent in advance and gave her a lump sum to go to Onitsha to buy start-up stock. It hurt him to spend the money this way, money he could have ploughed into his business. But he had no choice if he wanted peace.

When he checked his phone, there were three missed calls from Helen. He had ignored all her calls while he was in Opaku. He dialled her now.

"Aruodo Eneh did not recommend to keep me at my end-of-probation interview," she said before he got a chance to explain his silence.

Zona's face dropped. Helen, his hope for a male heir, had joined the throngs of the unemployed. That means a shop for her, he reasoned. She clamoured for a make-up bar at Tejuosho Market to retail wigs and other make-me-fine accessories.

Before he left Opaku, he called his head apprentice.

"We made thirty-five thousand naira yesterday."

Thirty-five thousand naira in one day. That was small for motor spares. They were not selling cosmetics or pepper. Even condiment sellers raked in more than that a day. He hissed. The market was congested now. Motor spares dealers sprang up at every corner. Apprentices were freed every year; they grabbed every space, some setting up atop gutters and drainage routes. Some days, it seemed that sellers outnumbered buyers. He did not need more problems.

On the way back to Lagos, Zona stopped at the boisterous Iyaro station in Benin City for a bathroom break. Needing sustenance to keep awake on the long drive, he bought pastries and energy drinks from the kiosk. He noticed a woman standing by the roadside with a ratty travel bag. When she saw Zona sizing her up, she approached.

"Are you going as far as Lagos, sir?" Her voice was baritone. She smiled, showing off perfect teeth.

It would cost nothing to have company, but he was careful about giving strangers a ride. She could be fronting for carjackers.

"I could be," he said ambiguously. "Arc you alone?"

"Yes, sir."

She was tall for a woman, easily six feet plus. He observed her features: long limbs, dark skin, eggplant figure. Her hair was tucked inside a turban, and she had a tribal mark etched on each cheek. She wore a loose blouse with elbow-length cone sleeves and a wrap-around cloth at the waist.

"Okay. Jump in."

The lady seemed to be relieved at having passed the eye test. She lifted her luggage to put it in the back seat. Zona shook his head vehemently and pointed her to the trunk.

"Your handbag too, Miss," he said, nodding to the beach bag dangling by her side.

The lady sidled into the passenger seat. Zona extended a hand to her. "Chief Echezona Okonkwo, MD/CEO Zona Group of Companies, Lagos. Omeifeukwu."

"Modupe Simpson," the woman replied. "Gold digger."

CHAPTER 33

With a boutique set up, Charity decided to teach her mother-in-law how to operate the tricycle.

"It is not hard, Nne. You have been to Lagos. Your mates are doing it. They are even driving taxis and motorbikes. And the roads are busier there."

Iyom shook her head. She flipped her fingers, jutted out her lower lip, and looked away.

"What of my grandchildren?" she enquired, pointing to Adaobi and her sisters playing hide and seek in the cocoyam farm. "How do we manage them?"

Charity suspected edging on the old woman's part, an excuse not to handle the three-wheeler.

"Do not worry, Nne. We will drop Adaobi and Alaoma in school. The other two will follow me to the shop." She waved her mother-in-law into the vehicle.

"Get in! Chisom, open the gate."

But Iyom dragged her feet. "With my white hair, to start learning a machine." She grimaced again.

They were standing between the two houses in the compound. A ewe bleated, and her kid responded and trotted to catch up with its mother. Iyom shooed them away.

"Chisom, have you fed the goats?"

"Yes, Ma."

"Nne, you can do it," Charity said again.

"E-o! One does not learn left hand in old age."

The noise of a passing tricycle drowned their voices. The engine was clearly in distress. As it rattled towards them, it emitted little squeaks and bobbed up and down the broken road. At the level of the women, it tooted. A lithe hand emerged and fluttered a greeting. "Nne, Mama Adaobi!"

The women waved back. Iyom raised her eyebrows at her daughter-in-law. She pointed at the receding vehicle.

"Nwunye Moses?"

"Not the wife, Nne, the mother."

"Whose son is hustling in Pe— Pa—?"

"In Pakistan, Peshawar, the same."

"She is now driving a vehicle and tooting for me?"

The older woman needed no more persuasion. She mounted the tricycle. "Enter, my daughter; show me how to operate this."

On the way, Iyom filled Charity in on Jonas's widow and Agbisi.

"So Nne, you knew, and you did not mind?" Charity asked. She spoke with an air of recrimination as if to say, *You elders did not advance the cause of future generations of women. You took shit. Now, we must accept as much; otherwise, the men will condemn us. Did your mothers not bear as much? Why are you complaining?*

"It is not that I did not mind. It is our custom that when a kinsman is no more, instead of the widow to lie idle, a fellow kinsman can be elected to appropriate her."

"So, the Umunna chose Agbisi?"

"That is where my quarrel lay," Iyom exclaimed, clapping her hands. "The widow herself chose Agbisi."

"Is it the Umunna that should decide, then?"

"No one can shave your hair in your absence. She has to consent."

"So the widow's last two boys are Zona's half-brothers?"

Charity paused. They were at the level of the Opaku Central School. The school field was the favoured spot of driving schools.

"By tradition, they are Okunna's sons."

"There is something the white man calls DNA, Nne. By blood, they are Agbisi's children."

"Do not let Zona hear that," Iyom warned. "When Agbisi died, the boys asked for a share of his estate because Agbisi was their father. 'Who told you that Agbisi is your father?' Zona had barked. His eyes were flashing like this light here. I know my son has a terrible temper, but that day, it was like touching a tiger by the tail. 'Our mother,' they answered timidly. 'Our mother told us.' 'Did Agbisi pay the bride price on your mother?' your husband fired back. Silence. 'Did my father pay the bride price on Akwaeke?'

"Poor boys."

"They went to Jonas's first son and asked for a share of Jonas's estate. 'Did Jonas Okunna father you?' that one asked them with a smirk. 'Yes,' they answered. 'From the grave? My father died in 1995. You were born in 1996 and 1997.'"

"It is youth," Charity observed, swerving to avoid an erring fowl. "A child must have a cutlass firmly in his hand before interrogating the circumstances of his father's death."

"Or his estate. Jonas paid the bride price on Akwaeke. Any child she has under Jonas's roof belongs to Jonas, dead or alive."

Charity was subdued. All these shibboleths. If male children were treated like this, what would become of daughters? Would they have any rights at all? If gold rusts, what becomes of iron? In a strangled voice, she muttered, "The boys should have gone to the Umunna to decide."

"How did you know? That is what they did. Umunna saw how they were being dribbled left and right, how Jonas Junior sent them out of his father's house when their mother died. The kinsmen met and asked Zona to release one of Agbisi's lands to them. Zona would have none of it. It was Jasper who saved the situation. He came forward, and *Umunna* slaughtered a goat, spilled its blood on the land and transferred ownership to the boys so they could have something. Zona has not forgiven Jasper for that."

"Where are they now?" Charity asked.

"Jideofor was an apprentice in South Africa to one Ozubulu man. Jidenma graduated from the university and is still looking for a job."

"He should look for handwork to do," Charity said. "The government does not employ our people as before."

"He puts his hand here and there, scouts for customers for traders in the market and is paid a commission."

"That is the way. He has outgrown igba-boi."

Kro-kro-kro crowed the village blackbirds, flapping their wings as they perched on the fruiting mango trees. *Kro-kro-kro.* Below the tree's canopy, goats squatted, chewing the cud nonchalantly and bleating intermittently. A gentle breeze brought a whiff of their droppings to the women.

"Okay, Nne, I've shown you how to drive the tricycle. Now to the business end. Do not carry more than three passengers. Do not overload the vehicle. Before they dismount, collect your fare; if not, they could abscond if they reach their destination."

"And where are the legs to chase them with?"

"Exactly. Collect the fare before you reach their destination."

Charity made the old woman drive them home.

CHAPTER 34

After the birth of his twins, Jasper ruled that Amata's days in the market were over. "Look after my boys now," he said, bending over the sleeping bodies in the conjoined cots he had ordered for the twins. "That is your full-time job now."

Amata had really, really surprised him. Until the last moment, he was unaware she was expecting twins. Amata, who found it hard to conceive, was the mother of twins. It was a wonder. He praised God for the singular blessing.

His mother-in-law arrived first, for the post-natal visit. It was Odoziaku's first omugwo. She came loaded with condiments and groceries. Jasper saw how she relished it, how elated she was to join the club of grandmothers. She hummed lullabies in the vernacular as she went about the chores, bathing the babies, dressing them, and only handing them to her daughter to nurse.

"We shall need formula," Jasper overheard her counsel Amata. "Boys eat a lot. They can milk their mother dry."

Sometimes, when the babies cried from hunger, Odoziaku would position them with pillows, and Amata would nurse them simultaneously. To give their father a breather, the women relocated to the guest room, which had become the nursery. Even so, whenever Jasper was home, he spent most of his time there, cooing over the tots. He bought a television for the nursery and tuned it permanently to the basketball channel. Chicago Bulls and LA Lakers pranced around the screen.

"See your namesakes," he said to the babies, pointing to Shaquille and Bryant. "Next one will be LeBron," he said to his wife and dodged the cushion Amata lobbed at him.

"And Antetokounmpo," she teased.

As soon as he turned his back, the women switched to the Nollywood network. "Put that handsome man," Odoziaku would urge Amata, referring to Richard Mofe-Damijo or Ramsey Nouah.

After a month had passed, Amata's father called to enquire about Odoziaku's return. "Is omugwo no longer one month? Who will do your duties here?"

Amata burst into tears and pleaded with her father for an extension. "One baby, one month omugwo," she reasoned. "Two babies, two months. Papa, biko. Onwa!"

After much weeping and sniffing from his jewel, Onwa acquiesced.

"We shall find a babysitter for you," Odoziaku assured Amata. "One cannot manage twins all alone."

There was an avalanche of middle names for the babies. To the first twin, O'Neal, Jasper gave the middle name of Okpara, First Son, and to the second, Kobe, he added Okemefuna, My Own Will Endure. The grandmothers took turns to name the twins. Iyom bestowed on one, Chinecherem, God Thinks of Me and on the other, Nnanna, Paternal Grandfather. Odoziaku christened the one Chizaram, God Answered Me, and the other, Lotanna, Remember your Father.

There was no outing ceremony. Despite Amata's pleas, Jasper declined to have a public event. One Sunday, when the boys were about six weeks old, he went to their parish and asked the padre to baptize them.

The priest was not impressed. "No ceremony?" he asked. "Why? Why? Twin boys and no outing?"

Jasper could not resist a giggle. The church liked big occasions. Big occasions meant more guests and heavier collection boxes.

When Odoziaku sought a reason for the low-key non-event, Jasper explained that Echezona, as the older son, should have produced the first grandson. He did not want to give the impression of showing off or rubbing in his good luck. It was all by divine providence, he acknowledged with humility.

~

Later in the night, in those few minutes between lying down and falling asleep, Amata confided in her mother. "That is why he preferred to sell the Jeep that Onwa gave me. He said he did not want to rouse the jealousy of his siblings and peers."

"My dear, they are our husbands. We may not see the rationale in their thinking, but God has placed them over us. We defer to them." She yawned.

"But, Mama, is it not my property? Don't I have the right to use it as I choose?"

"Hear! Hear! You have sold the car, now you are complaining. Is it not medicine after death?"

"Because I had not consolidated, Mama. I was having issues with my monthlies, remember? Now that I have dropped not one, but two boys, I will insist on my voice being heard."

Odoziaku winced. She did not know what to make of Amata's ideas. Luz was yet to marry, and her prospects depended to an extent on Amata's behaviour in her husband's homestead.

"My dear, in a happy home," she said slowly, sculpting the words with care, "The wife defers to her husband. You bear his name; he hustles for you. It counts for something. When an issue arises between you two, bring it up for discussion. If he accepts your views, all well and good. If he overrules, you fall in line. That is how I have been doing with Onwa. And it has served me well."

She swaddled O'Neal and rocked him.

"It is because your father was poor, Mama."

"So you want to take your father's wealth to your husband's home? Amata, Amata. You want your father's money to swell your head in another man's home? When I married Onwa, what did he have? He was just a petty trader of soft drinks. Nothing more. Sold from a tiny cinder box kiosk. Why is my title

Odoziaku? One who hones wealth? Is it not because of supporting my husband? Is it from stubbornness? From having my way?"

"That was in your time, Mama. This is now. Why did I go to school? Is it to put my certificate in a drawer?"

Baby O'Neal was fidgeting, flailing his small arms and legs. He let out a whimper that incrementally advanced to a full-blown cry.

Odoziaku handed him to Amata. That effectively brought the discussion to an end. Amata latched the baby on her side, and soon, his contented gurgles filled the nursery.

"O'Neal," Amata crooned. The boys' grandmother glanced at Kobe, sleeping soundly. She prayed he would remain so until his brother finished nursing. His skin felt cold, so she tried to cover him with a blanket. He stirred and opened his eyes. Odoziaku lifted him and left the room, shaking her head.

Odoziaku stood by the kitchen window, rocking him to get him back to sleep. The baby writhed. He contorted his face and shook its head from side to side, sucking his knuckles. Odoziaku crooned her favourite Igbo lullabies:

Who beat the crying child?
Hawk beat the crying child
Bring some uziza, bring some pepper
Let the birds lick them up
O hawk, O hawk.

Her voice calmed Kobe. He stared at his grandmother intently. Odoziaku envied her daughter. She knew what she had seen in Amata's eyes: determination. She had had dreams too, dreams to excel, to be something more than her own mother. But she had lacked the courage and the wherewithal to actualize them. When Elias Umeh (he had not taken the Onwa title then) came for her hand in marriage, she had hesitated. She wanted to be a nurse, but her mother had convinced her to accept the offer of marriage.

Amata, in one go, and after only two years of marriage, had consolidated her place in her husband's household and now wanted to resurrect her own dreams to make something of her life, something more noble than buying and selling and rearing babies.

Onwa, inadvertently, had encouraged his daughter. By giving her the Prado, he had empowered her to pursue her dreams, something Odoziaku could not have done because her own father's means were pretty modest. "That fire in your mother's eyes, it comes from me," she whispered to the tot. "It is no good hiding it. It would be like lighting a lamp and hiding it from view."

The baby calmed down. His tiny fists twitched and punched the air like a shadow boxer. His eyes fluttered and then closed again. Odoziaku kept rocking him, her mind not on her daughter now but on the man Amata married.

Why did you marry a non-graduate then? She had asked her daughter on another occasion when the subject of Amata's dreams had come up yet again. They had just bathed the boys, and Amata was nursing one of them. Jasper had not returned from the store. Congo music was blaring from the telly, and an over-dressed dancer was contorting his body like a spineless creature.

Mama, look at our government. The Vice-president has a Ph.D. What does the President have?

How will you be free to express yourself without running the risk of being termed proud and insubordinate? Any time you have an opposing view, will he not ascribe it to too much education? Aha, you want to wear the trousers in this house because you went to university? Is that it?

But, Mama, he proposed to me. He knew I was a graduate.

"It is happening all around us," Odoziaku conceded. *Men who did not go beyond secondary school marrying university girls.*

The baby in Odoziaku's arms whimpered and twisted, upset at being ignored. She patted him tenderly, willing him back to sleep. She joined Amata in the room. Kobe turned fully to look at his mother, then opened his mouth toward Amata's breast.

"The baby goat already knows the way to the yam barn." She passed him to his mother.

What he needs is to get her a job outside the home, Odoziaku reasoned as she took the other twin and laid him on his belly to burp. *No woman can stay home like this, idling the grey matter. Either Jasper gets her an office job, or he opens a business for her. This mental idleness can dull the mind.*

CHAPTER 35

Six months after delivery, Amata attended the Opaku Wives meeting. On return, she called her co-wife.

"Charlingo! Long time." Amata kept it breezy and lively.

"So you no hear that I was sent packing from Zona's house?"

Amata almost dropped the infant in her arm. "Blood of Jesus! Sent packing? Since when?"

"Going on four months now."

"What happened?"

"It is because I have only given him girls. When I mentioned that to you a while ago, you thought I was delirious."

"Just like that?"

As the saying goes, no one is ever the asshole in his or her story. Charity left much unsaid, like her tantrums, her visit to the outside woman, and how she had locked her husband out and been aggressive towards him in his own house. That was a taboo in Igboland.

"So, where are you now?"

"At Opaku. I refused to go back to my parents. If Zona wants to send me back, let him restore my chassis to how it was before he married me."

"Exactly."

"We are here with Nne."

"We?"

"My daughters and I."

"I'm so sorry. I've been so busy with the twins and house-work. Does Jasper know?"

"Your husband sent a tricycle to Iyom. It helps keep hunger at bay. Zona has opened a shop here for me. It is not profitable yet, but we trust God."

"You run a shop now? You are a tough woman, Charity."

"Make I die? We all dey hustle. At least we have food to eat, and Adaobi and Alaoma get to go to school."

"So, is Zona here alone?"

"Alone. In Lagos? With all those Lagos girls? That UNILAG girl has taken over. I told you all this. Maybe you forgot."

"No wonder Nne is sending her house girl to me. Both of you will make do with one."

"Yes, Omenma is on her way to you. Chisom can manage. Nne and I eat from one pot."

The bawl of a baby interrupted their chat.

"I will keep in touch, Charity. Greet Nne. Believe me, I didn't know. I will mention it to Jasper. He could probably intervene."

CHAPTER 36

"I tried to intervene," Jasper said when he returned from the store after Amata mentioned Char's defenestration. "He said I should mind my business."

"What shall we call this?" she mimicked her husband.

"Well, as our people say, wisdom is a bag; each man carries his own and runs his life as he deems fit." He was excited. The NBA Eastern Conference was on. Toronto Raptors versus Boston Celtics.

"How is the market?"

"Congested. Everybody is selling the same things. The profits are no longer impressive and steady. Some days we sell nothing. And every day, more and more apprentices are freed and joining the hustle."

"What do we do? Change hand?"

"And start igba-boi again in a new line?" He shook his head.

"I think if one knows the supply chain and maybe gets someone to show one the way..."

"You must serve the master for some time before he can reveal the secrets of the trade to you. No one welcomes competition. Serving him is the only condition to show you the ropes. That is the thing. And me, married now, I cannot serve two masters."

"Who is the second?"

"A man's wife is his master, Amata, whether he likes it or not," he laughed.

"I'm not your master o," Amata said, rolling her eyes. "That is how you men deceive women, making us think we are the ones calling the shots. Who decided to sell my Prado? Who decided not to have a naming ceremony?"

"Don't let those minor issues pluck your hair, my dear. The world is not as you think."

"God will make a way," Amata relented after a short pause. Her ears were alert for baby cries. It was rare to have the boys asleep at the same time. She seized on such moments to put her feet up. She felt happy and fulfilled, without a care in the world.

To encourage Jasper in the face of dwindling sales, she narrated her father's fledgling start in commerce. "Growing up, business was slow, very slow for Onwa. He struggled. My mom and all the children took turns packing empties, counting bottles, off-loading, and taking inventory until the business stabilized and grew, and he was able to build a depot."

"Beverage business is unbeatable. Do you know how many bottles we consume in Nigeria daily? Not to talk of during ceremonies? Weddings, parties, funerals?"

"I hear that building materials move well, too," Amata said. Her bridesmaid had married a man in that line of business. They were affluent.

"Yes, very much so. But it is capital-intensive. You need a warehouse for the goods, though it depends on the line of materials you deal in. As long as people build houses, building material merchants have no worries."

"Maybe you should consider what Zona said. If this place is congested, one could look abroad."

"You talk of going abroad when our town union is preaching to invest at home."

"They have a point, Nigeria being what it is."

"Before now, we sold well. People came from all over West Africa to Idumota to shop. Now, our people have decentralized. They have spread to Ladipo, Alaba, Mile Two, Ikeja, and Idi Oro. Now, you need a presence in two or three different locations to have an impact or be a major importer, supplying to retailers."

He paused to crack his knuckles. "We shall see. I will think of something. It is my responsibility."

He tore off a piece of a carrot and popped it in his mouth. He nudged it to one side of his mouth. With a grating sound, he crunched on the vegetable.

"That reminds me. I need to call Zona. Our stock has depleted again. I hear they are ordering several containers. This time, I have the cash for the parts."

Amata sat still while Jasper dialled his brother.

"You are late," Zona's voice boomed from the device. "The containers are full. To the brim. No space."

"Blood of Jesus," Amata whispered, shaking her head.

"I will try Akajiaku," Jasper said. He forgot about the NBA game, overwhelmed by Zona's animosity.

The next day, Jasper went to Akajiaku to see if the mogul could accommodate his order. The businessman shook his head regretfully.

"You know we import jointly, Zona and I. He got orders from many traders. I don't know why he could not include his own brother's needs."

Jasper was in a bind. He approached other big importers, but they all said it was too late and told him to wait for the next round of importations.

He met with other upcoming entrepreneurs, traders who were freed at the same time as him, to see whether they could pool their resources and import a container or two. There, too, he met a roadblock. Their orders had all been subsumed by the major importers. Many proffered different solutions. One pointedly advised him against importing solo.

"There is a learning curve in importing," the fellow warned. "A supply chain. If newcomers dabble into it without learning the ropes, catastrophe. The supplier can package nonsense and send or withhold your money outright. What about clearing the goods? Do you have a reliable clearing agent? Have you been to Apapa Wharf? Tin Can? It's better to wait for the next round and approach your former master. He will not refuse you."

Jasper took the advice and waited. He was constrained to buy from fellow retailers to restock his shop. The profit margin was slim, but he widened his customer base.

One Sunday, Jasper took his family to the Murtala Mohammed International Airport. They mounted the viewing gallery and watched, awestruck, as planes taxied, took off, and landed. A Boeing 737 stood on the tarmac, unmoving, like a big fish. AIR PEACE was written on its flank. Technicians in blue overalls busied themselves around it, walking up and down like penguins, some at ground level, others up the stairway into its belly, dragging trolleys and equipment. Omenma closed the ears of the twins when a humongous noise emanated from one aircraft that was about to lift off. RUF-THA-NSA, she read.

"It's so big," Omenma observed. "It used to be tiny in the air."

Jasper bought drinks for everyone. The aeroplanes fascinated him, too. He longed to be carried off to Shanghai, Dubai, and Guangdong.

The airport experience seemed to have raised a red flag in Amata and brought Jasper's travel plans to the forefront. On the way back, she asked if he was still thinking of jetting off to far-away places.

"Yes," he replied curtly. He kept his eyes on the road but felt Amata's gaze boring into him.

That week, he went to the passport office at Alausa.

Soon, he was told. *You will get a notification.*

In preparation for the proposed trip, he called Cy Mukeke.

"Jasper Gee!"

"Cy Mukeke! Nna, I dey come Cotonou o!" he cooed into the phone.

"Nna, I no dey there again," Cy said. The smile on Jasper's lips vanished.

"Since when?"

"Three months now. Voilà. I dey Abidjan now. Come here. Come to where it is happening."

Cy explained that Jasper could take the luxury bus, De Young Shall Grow, which plied the West Coast from Lagos through

Cotonou, Lomé, Accra to Abidjan. "Take it at Maza-Maza. Voilà. I will meet you at Treichville, their terminus in Quartier Biafra."

"I want to deflower my passport," Jasper explained to his wife later that night. "So I will not appear like a novice when I go for the Chinese visa."

"I can manage alone for a couple of days," Amata said.

"Couple of days! That's what it will take me to get there. Another couple for the return journey. We are looking at one week, minimum."

They exchanged defiant looks. Amata rolled her eyes before looking down at the baby she was trying to lull to sleep in her arms. She was not enthusiastic about a prolonged absence.

"I do not understand this obsession with travelling out," she snapped. "I suppose it is in your blood, and unless and until you satisfy it, you will not be free. Normally, people get the wander-lust out of their system before they settle down. You, you have a wife and two soldiers on the ground, and you want to embark on a journey. God forbid something happens. What do I do? What becomes of us? And while you are at it, please transfer the Jeep money to my account."

After hearing this, and to please his wife, Jasper shelved his travel plans. Even though he understood his wife's anxiety, his spirit withered a little. When the financial transaction matured, he moved the proceeds from the vehicle's sale to Amata's account and rolled it over. He also knew that if he kept the funds in his account and something happened to him, she would be hard put to claim it. Still, his angst did not subside. The popular Igbo proverb came to his mind: one cannot stay in one spot to watch a masquerade. Was Cy Mukeke, his apprenticeship mate, not married? And was he not the one moving from one country to another, searching for the elusive currency? Was Cy's wife holding him back?

He wanted to hustle and make money. Yet, here was Amata, constituting a stumbling block in his quest for financial independence. If he hung around to admire his wife and sons, who would feed them?

They lay side by side in the dark, silent.

"We can use the Jeep money to build," Amata said after a while. "But not for travel."

"You have a point. It is better to devote it to a project. Fixed deposit is sleeping money, lazy money. If we invest it well, it can multiply a million-fold. I will look into it."

"Or for expanding the business. Don't wait for the stock to deplete before ordering." She eased her nipple out from between Kobe's lips and placed him on her belly to burp.

"I'm on it," he said simply, an eye on his phone. The NBA playoffs had started. "Someone said I should join the Elite Merchants Club, that they prioritize their members when ordering goods."

"That should be easy. Zona is in the Exco. He, whose brother makes heaven, has hell foreclosed to him."

He cleared his throat loudly and groped around the bedstead for his lager. "Under normal circumstances," he replied. The codicil of his answer, he kept to himself; this brother, once in heaven, will bar the gates, double-lock and barricade it against his kinsmen.

CHAPTER 37

Rapu stopped going to the Geopolitical Zone shack after he ran into his apprentice, who had also come to relieve stress. The shack was sectioned into six parts, each harbouring queens from that part of Nigeria. He had already patronized the service providers of the Northeast and North Central Zones. His next stop: the North West chic. Lo and behold, Stanley! In line for the same woman. Astounded, he had turned 360 degrees despite the apprentice's readiness to cede his spot on the queue to his master.

Astounded was too mild to describe his feelings. He was disgusted and scandalized. His apprentice! Patronizing brothel queens! With what money? He had wanted to confront him but thought better of it. Bystanders would accuse him of callousness and selfishness. He had absconded from there and stumbled on another joint at Mararaba. The Highlife Bush Bar specialized in undergraduates. The first time, he came across a law book and thought it was a chance encounter. The second time he strayed there, he saw accounting books for the ICAN exam on the grubby table: Institute of Chartered Accountants of Nigeria, read the logo on the cover. It was a prestigious body. On another occasion, a huge anatomy book peeped out of a raffia bag that hung from the shoulder of a chair. He could not resist the urge to ask the teenage hustler her occupation. She was a student at Prime University. All the way from Edo State.

It's not far, she had the pluck to add. *Only four hours by road.*

Don't you have lectures?

I support myself in school, was her answer, as if that justified her involvement in the slimy trade. A woman carried currency between her legs, he realized, which she used to acquire any object she liked, from a certificate to a car to a house.

His mind went to the matchmaker and her catalogue of brides. These ones will graduate and find themselves in the matchmaker's books, not knowing they were ex-brothel dwellers. And Luz had the arrogance to reject him because she preferred a graduate.

Rapu hissed. Jasper had the best deal of all in Amata.

He became a regular at the bush bar. The serene ambience and the highlife music they played there stirred something in him. Sometimes, he would go directly to the joint from work, leaving Stanley to close the shop. So far, he had not crossed paths with his apprentice at his new favoured hangout. Occasionally, he flinched when he remembered their chance meeting at the geopolitical joint. He felt disturbed but was unsure how to handle it; dismiss Stanley so he could womanize to his heart's content? Rapu was almost sure the apprentice was stealing from the shop to finance his escapades. He had blocked all loopholes, or so he thought, but an apprentice determined to shortchange his master found ingenious ways to siphon money out. He thought again of inviting Stanley to share his living quarters with him to keep an eagle eye on him but jettisoned the idea. (Rapu seemed to have forgotten that some apprentices bedded down on passages and verandas of their masters' dwellings. Some passed the night in parked vehicles. The hardship was part of the intern's training. He also had slept on rough patches during his years of igba-boi).

One serene evening, Rapu was at the joint when a "big boy" breezed in with a retinue of hangers-on. Or were they his business associates? They did not look like his equals. The leader was clearly in control, directing his followers where to sit. Rapu had satiated his urge and had a front-seat view. He eavesdropped on the group's conversation as he sipped his goat pepper soup and quaffed his lager.

The leader was a Johannesburg-based businessman. "Come to South Africa," he enthused to Rapu when he found out that the tricycle dealer was a son of the East. "Opportunities abound there. Their girls prefer us, correct girls." His hands formed figure eight in the air. "Not these local girls with hips like a bicycle spoke, making oversize demands."

He rummaged for his phone and summoned a picture of a middle-aged woman with a slim waist but endowed with humongous hips. When she walked in the video clip, her rear cheeks rolled in all directions like a misaligned Austin 911 truck on a dirt track. Rapu licked his lips. He was won over. They exchanged numbers.

"I'll certainly reflect on it," he vowed.

He was thinking of opening another shop in the FCT. But a second shop would mean another apprentice. Could he afford to feed and clothe two able-bodied adolescents with the appetite of elephants? He could look into getting contracts from government agencies. He had heard that a contract of, say, twenty million could be done with one-fifth of the sum, leaving you with a cool net profit of over fifteen million. If he did two or three jobs like that, he could put up a small dwelling akin to Zona's bungalow and think of marriage. He could not bring a wife into the hovel that the Opaku homestead had become and squat with her and Iyom as Jasper was doing. And with Jasper's two kids, they would resemble an over-loaded Tata truck, bursting at the seams.

CHAPTER 38

Chief Igwilo, Jasper's erstwhile master, woke up one morning clutching his chest. His wife raised an alarm, and the apprentices rallied to her aid. They bundled their master to the hospital. One of the chief's boys called Jasper to inform him of the situation, and he rushed to the hospital, abandoning the newspaper he had just started to read. Chief's family was gathered there, shooting the breeze and praying. Unfortunately, Chief Igwilo succumbed to an infarction at the entrance to the theatre. He was just sixty-seven years old.

Chief Igwilo's wife, Obidie, was a solidly built local woman. Her husband's wealth had allowed her to dress like a society lady and reduced her uncouthness. When she was led out, Jasper hastened to her side.

In her grief, her primitiveness resurfaced, and she looked pathetic in her lacklustre clothes and crimson eyes. She loosened one end of her cloth and sobbed into it. Her shoulders quaked.

"Bear up, Obidie. Biko," her entourage urged.

Jasper collapsed on his knees when he realized what had just happened. Tears careened down his cheeks. He remembered how she had mothered him during his apprenticeship, preparing food for the apprentices and encouraging them to give their best, that Oke Nmanwu would repay them in due course. Jasper had been a favoured beneficiary of the couple's largesse.

He followed them home. "Mummy, what happened?"

She sniffed. "Since he was duped by that Chinese company, he never recovered."

"Eh! Duped?" Jasper had not heard.

"He ordered goods of almost fifty thousand dollars. Sniff sniff. Trusted the manufacturer. Paid up-front. Send the Bill of Lading." Obidie held Jasper's hand. "Stories. Send Bill of Lading, nothing. Eventually, the fellow sent one, but it was in the name of another importer. Sniff sniff. Oke Nmanwu disputed it with the chap. Their association mediated and advised them to clear the goods and share; maybe they could at least make their money back. When the container was cleared and opened, it contained rags and worthless stuff. It affected Oke Nmanwu badly. Many nights, he would pace the room and not sleep. I begged my husband to forget, that we would make the money back. Now see. Oh, Oke Nmanwu. Oke Nmanwu."

Obidie got up, and before anyone could stop her, she threw herself on the ground, wailing. "Oke Nmanwu, is this how you left this world? Oke Nmanwu, good man, fine husband. God o! The stick I leaned on is broken."

Sympathizers hurried to her, lifted her up and cajoled her back to the mat, pleading with her to endure it.

"Obidie, biko."

Jasper, always reluctant about physical contact with his master's wife, placed a quivering palm on her shoulder. "Mummy, please, I beg you, take heart. Firm your heart. Please, Mummy, please." On his way out, he embraced Chief's children, who were sprawled around the lounge, weeping.

Jasper barely touched the okro soup and fufu dinner his wife placed before him. He sighed repeatedly. Fortunately, there was power. He stretched out on the couch and flipped on the TV. The New York Knicks versus Milwaukee Bucks. He remembered the newspaper he was perusing before rushing to the hospital.

> *The Federal Government has launched Operation Python Dance in the southeastern part of the country. The Army spokesman, General Banshi, said the operation would*

flush out the secessionist elements hell-bent on dividing the country. He, therefore, warned IPOB adherents to desist from gathering and disturbing the peace of the nation. Commenting further, the General said the operation would last for three months and cover the whole South East Geo-political Zone. He reiterated that the unity of the country was non-negotiable.

Jasper turned back to the match.

~

The Igwilo clan came together to plan a funeral befitting their father. As was the custom, they approached the palace of the traditional ruler for an available date for the funeral. They obtained one, four weeks down the line.

A massive renovation of Chief Igwilo's village home ensued. The perimeter walls were re-plastered and painted as was the storey building he had erected but only enjoyed at Yuletide and on his occasional visits home. A series of obituaries appeared in the major newspapers. One was placed by his family, another by his business associates, and another by the Opaku Town Development Union.

Amata was reading the latest edition of the *Daily Sun,* intermittently folding it over to fan herself. There was a blackout again, and the kids were fractious. The day was hot. Stale air floated in with the mosquitoes. The inverter was down. She lacked the energy to refuel the generator and switch it on. She led the children to the sit-out, hoping to catch a slight breeze. She leaned against the railing and read the obituary:

Home Call
The Igwilo family of Umueri, Opaku, regret to announce the sudden and untimely home call of their son, husband, father, grandfather, uncle, and great philanthropist, Chief Silas Madumere Igwilo, alias Oke Nmanwu, Chairman,

Managing Director, SIMIG Group of companies and Patron of the Elite Merchants Club, which sad event occurred after a brief illness, on Tuesday, 29 May 2017, in Lagos.

Death is always untimely, Amata noted. She chewed on a piece of yam. No death is ever on time. She leaned back against the railing again and continued reading.

Burial arrangements:
6 July 2017: Wake-keep at his Lagos Residence, Yaba
7 July: Requiem Mass at St. Dominic Catholic Church, Yaba
13 July: All-night wake-keep at his country home, Opaku
14 July: Requiem Mass: St. Silas's Cath Church, Opaku, followed by interment and reception
15 July: Condolence visits
16 July: Outing Service: St. Silas' Catholic Church

Left to mourn him:
Chief (Mrs.) Lydia Nkechi Igwilo, alias Obidie
Silas Ugonna Igwilo (Son) – Lagos
Michael Osita Igwilo (Son) – Abuja
Fidelma Ngozi Obi, née Igwilo (Daughter) – London
Chief Jeremiah Tagbo Igwilo, alias Akunne (Brother)

Signed: Silas Ugonna Igwilo
Ogbu Ebunu Opaku
For the family

Amata thought about the late Chief and his influence on her husband and the Opaku community. Chief Igwilo had underwritten many projects for his people. The town hall had his imprimatur, as did the local dispensary and the parsonage. He had single-handedly renovated the village church, formerly St. David's, and renamed it after himself. He had also sponsored some indigent students at university.

She heard the whirring of the refrigerator. The blackout was over. She sighed, tucked the paper under her arm, and herded the twins back inside.

~

When Igwilo's corpse was transported to Opaku, the funeral party paused at the main market and was met by sympathizers at home. In a convoy led by the town crier, the Otinkpu, they drove to the mortụary where the remains would lie till the burial.

The Otinkpu's clear voice carried far and wide. He rang a bell and spoke solemnly into a megaphone: "These are the remains of Chief Silas Madumere Igwilo, Oke Nmanwu, of Umueri village, Opaku Autonomous Community. He went to Lagos to hustle like his peers, but death struck him down. It is his remains that we are repatriating from Lagos, his place of hustle, to lay to rest. Chief Silas Madumere Igwilo, Oke Nmanwu, Umueri village, Chairman, Managing Director, SIMIG Group of Companies, patron, Elite Merchants Club of Nigeria, a philanthropist, master entrepreneur, based in Lagos, is returning to Opaku, his ancestral home, to be laid to rest after a meritorious life in commerce and industry. Chief Silas Igwilo. Oke Nmanwu of Umueri village. Opaku Autonomous Community."

Due to Oke Nmanwu's exalted position in society and affinity to the Okonkwo family, the three Okonkwo sons travelled home for the obsequies. Jasper organized his master's apprentices, current and past, to take charge of various aspects of the rituals. Some erected canopies and hung up banners while another group controlled vehicular traffic, and others ushered guests to their assigned seats.

Back at the family house for a moment of rest, Jasper went behind the dwelling to survey the land. He gauged where a portable bungalow could fit in. With two toddlers and a babysitter, Nne's quarters had become a tad too small. It was time for him to start putting up his own dwelling place. What if Rapu got married, considering that the matchmaker was scouting for a bride for him?

"I am thinking of constructing a modest home in that corner," he said when Nne joined him. He pointed to the farthest part of the cocoyam farm.

"Your family is growing. It is time."

"Or perhaps I could add two rooms to the existing structure?"

"Don't try it," Zona said, emerging from the back door. He had watched as Jasper inspected the yard. "I intend to pull down this ramshackle thing Agbisi knocked together and put up a more imposing mansion that will occupy all this space." He spread his arms to indicate the whole property. "Are you getting my point?"

CHAPTER 39

Jasper assigned himself the duty of manning the cold truck from which all the drinks would issue. He did not think twice about sourcing the drinks: his father-in-law was a major distributor of all brands and was the obvious choice. He drove to Onwa's warehouse and stocked up.

As usual, when he drove past Agbisi's plots, he cast a quick look to ascertain their integrity. Jideofor and Jidenma, he noticed, had cleared the plot given them on Umunna's intervention. He saw a modest structure sprouting on it.

Jasper cruised on a low gear, assessing the state of development in the layout. He sped up and headed towards the other two plots that Agbisi had left farther afield. He was stunned to see that a building project was going on in one of the lands. Carriers were hurrying in all directions like soldiers. He parked, crossed the motorway, and accosted a labourer bearing a head pan from a whirring cement mixer.

"What is going on here?" he shouted above the din. "What are you doing?"

"It is Zona Group," the fellow revealed. "He is building a hotel."

"Which Zona?"

Jasper walked to the board, which had the client's name and other information. To his utmost surprise, the client was Echezona Okonkwo. Jasper could not believe it. Zona was building on their inheritance. Without any discussion with his brothers?

He was tempted to order that work stop, but he held himself in check out of respect for his father's first son.

Once home, he raised the matter with Iyom.

~

At sundown, the matriarch steered the tricycle behind the house. It was a signal that she had closed for the day. It had been a good day. On each trip, the tricycle had been full to capacity. As she stepped out of the vehicle, she observed her granddaughters and Chisom playing a clapping game in a corner.

Kuolu nu nwa ngwele aka
Elente
Nwa ngwele ejeghi ije, ma o gbala oso
Elente

They applauded the baby lizard that ran immediately after birth without passing through the stage of walking. A mother hen trotted by with her newly hatched brood, fearlessly pecking at victuals invisible to the human eye. At one point, the hen stopped, waiting for her chicks to catch up. She looked to the left, then to the right, and scratched the ground furiously while clucking tirelessly, alert for danger, then marched away like a businessman.

Iyom was delighted now to be able to stretch her long legs, which had been cramped under the steering of the tricycle. Seeing that her three sons were in, she decided, on the spur of the moment, to call a meeting. The family needed to thrash out the land matter. Zona had taken liberties with a communal asset. His excesses had triggered an alarm.

"Where is Zona?" Iyom called out when her two youngest sons were seated.

"He went to piss," Charity answered from beside the bungalow, where she was washing bitter leaves.

"Do not over-wash the leaves," Iyom shouted across the yard. "Leave some bitterness in."

"Ooo, Nne."

"Nne, that breadfruit," Jasper said, pointing to the tree with his chin. He was looking for something to say to dispel the awkward silence. His heart was racing. As usual, tension was high when a family meeting was called. "...is ripe. We should bring it down before it falls on somebody."

Would the meeting go calmly? Jasper wondered. Or would someone go ballistic? Resort to name-calling? Rapu was staring into space, crossing and uncrossing his legs. Across the yard, the children clapped:

Kuolu nu nwa ngwele aka, elente.

It was a soporific evening. The adults, waiting for Zona, were watching the children, smiling, no doubt remembering their youth.

"Is it only the baby lizard that ran at birth?" Iyom asked. "What of nwa okuko and nwa osa?"

Adaobi paused. "What is nwa okuko?"

Her father, emerging from his quarters, pointed to the chicks nearby. "Nwa okuko."

"Daddy, what of osa?"

Zona did not know. He looked to his wife. "Squirrel," Charity whispered.

"Osa is squirrel," Zona amplified. His spirits lifted, knowing that his kids were speaking Igbo. He was right to have sent them home. In Lagos, Igbo kids were learning Yoruba and were strangers to their mother tongue. He joined Iyom on the bench.

"Echezona," Iyom began. Whenever she called him by his full name and not his pet sobriquet, she was establishing her authority. "What am I hearing? That you are building a hotel on one of our lands? Eh, Echezona?"

Jasper took over from there to corroborate the allegation. "I drove by the property and saw a structure rising on it. When I confronted the foreman, he told me it was my brother's business, Zona Group, that was building, and I saw your name on the board too as the client. I came home and enquired from Nne and Rapu. They said they were not aware."

Iyom frowned. Jasper should not have spoken. There was a pecking order in the family established by order of birth.

All eyes turned to Zona for an explanation. He adjusted himself on the bench, floundering for an answer. His short, stumpy legs were shaking. He shoved his hands under his armpits and looked up at the evening sky through the foliage of the udala tree. He lowered his gaze and cleared his throat. Jasper's impertinence unsettled him.

"First and foremost, there is a pecking order here. Respect it. Two, who gave away one of our lands to Jideofor and his brother?" He snarled at Jasper, who glowered back at him, a grimace of distaste on his lips. "Agbisi owned three plots of land plus this family home." His fat index pointed to the ground. "He had three sons. Are you getting my point? Some riffraff comes and tells you stories, and you go and slaughter a goat on one of the lands and transfer ownership to them. Your father's land. Now, you have the audacity to ask me why I am building on my father's land. On whose land should I build?"

"By custom, this compound belongs to you as the first son," Iyom acknowledged. "Jasper wanted to put up something small in a corner, but you refused. Where will your brothers build?"

"That is the question he should have asked himself before giving away a plot. You can ask him now; perhaps he will answer. Are you getting my point? After all, Umunna approached me, and I said no! But Jasper went behind me and accepted, and now he is asking me where he will build. Come and build on my back."

"I am asking for equity," Jasper said in a trembling voice, ignoring the insult. He licked his dehydrated lips. He felt pained by the cavalier attitude of his older sibling. It was aggressive, belligerent, abrasive. When the Jeep arrived, Zona's behaviour toward him had changed drastically. With the birth of his male twins, it had worsened and bordered on hatred. This usurpation of their commonwealth was an outright provocation. Everyone knew the paternity of late Jonas's sons, knew that they were fathered by Agbisi.

He turned to Rapu to enlist his support. Rapu was the youngest, but he was already a man and had a say in family matters. Yes, he was busy establishing his fledgling business, but was the matchmaker not on the lookout for a suitable bride for him? Once he married, he would think of a dwelling, too. This was a good time to broach the matter. The children's excited songs and shrieks interspersed the serious conclave of the adults.

Kuo lu nu nwa okuku aka
Elente.

"Nobody said not to build," Jasper said calmly, turning back to Zona. "But something owned by many people cannot be converted to one person's property. Our father left three parcels of land. One parcel was a double plot, two plots that happened to be side by side. You are building on the two."

"As the first son, I pick first when there is something to share. That is the pecking order. Are you getting my point?" He fidgeted with his legs as if he wanted to be elsewhere and was raring to take off.

"By right, you already have this compound—"

"Can I build a hotel on this land?" Zona snapped. "On this ancestral, interior land?" He stood up.

"Where are you going?" Iyom asked, stricken. Was he going to turn his back on them? End the meeting without a sane conclusion about going forward?

Zona ignored her, fumbling with his drawstrings as he shuffled to the edge of the cocoyam farm. He inclined forward and unbundled his privates. After jiggling his manhood free of droplets and making sure his trousers were well tied to his waist, he rejoined the meeting, stamping his feet vigorously to shake off vestiges of urine and sand. He brought out a dirty handkerchief and wiped his hands. As he regained his spot on the bench, he glanced at his mobile. It was nearing time for the next ceremony at Oke Nmanwu's. All eyes dwelt on him as if he were a magician, and they were waiting to see what surprise would spring from his repertory.

Jasper was the first to look away in distaste. His eyes were dark and bloodshot. Iyom could tell that he was boiling.

"All of you, one by one, one after the other, suckled these breasts." She weighed her chest. "Let the eagle perch, and let the hawk perch, the one who—"

Zona cut her off. "No one is telling the other not to perch. Agbisi left three plots of land for his three sons. I have chosen one. Rapu, the remaining one is yours. Are you getting my point? Jasper already gave away his own. Next time, use your tongue to count your teeth before taking action." He rose and dusted his pants. "I am going."

Jasper sprang up.

"And I am saying there was enough for us, even after giving one piece to the Okunna brothers, as requested by Umunna. I shall go to court. My wife is a lawyer."

Zona was a few feet away when he heard the words *court, lawyer.* He stopped. He appeared about to turn back but seemed to think better of it and ambled on. His brothers watched his retreating back. His daughters saw him. They left their clapping game and competed to see who would reach him first. They crashed into his thighs, and their arms, like octopuses, encircled his waist. He extricated himself from their hold and entered his house. Charity was chatting on her phone, hands covered by foamy bits of the bitter leaves.

"No wonder," Iyom said, turning to her younger sons. "No wonder he comes home more often. I thought it was because of Charity and the children. It is because of his hotel project."

Jasper did not like the undercurrent of the meeting and its indecisive outcome. Perhaps they would each reflect and meet again. This was unfinished business. He wavered, momentarily losing balance.

They could hear music blaring from Chief Igwilo's compound. Around them, the orange trees were blooming, filling the air with a citrusy smell.

"It is time to go supervise the bar," Jasper announced. He felt pained at Zona's disrespect for their mother, ending the family meeting unceremoniously and strong-arming everyone. What had the meeting achieved? Nothing. He felt sorry for Iyom, a person traditionally venerated, who was being treated openly with scorn and contempt by her own son.

"Do not worry," the matriarch said to Jasper and Rapu. She rose on unsteady legs. She did not like Zona's attitude. Since her last omugwo visit and his unfounded and callous accusation of favouritism, she was walking on hot coals with him, dreading another tirade. Something, clearly, was eating him. "People fling plots of land all the time. I will be on the lookout for one in a good location. Do not go to court. Remember Umunna's admonition."

Rapu cleared his throat. He had been listening to his brothers speak, watching their body language and following their arguments. It was news to him that Jasper had wanted to build a structure in one corner of the family house and that Zona had rebuffed him. Jasper must be prospering. Everything was going well for him. Sure, it would have been easier if Agbisi had left more than three plots. Iyom's three sons would take one each and toss the extra one to Akwaeke's sons. But the plots numbered only three. True, one parcel contained two plots that could easily be split, but a hotel project needed space. True, Echezona should have consulted his siblings or bought them out. However, things being the way they were, he had to speak up. He gave his scraggly beard a quick scratch and pulled at its ends.

"This remaining plot, as Zona said, is mine," he said, looking straight ahead. "Zona has taken one. You, Jasper, have donated your own. This last one left is my own. Let there be no doubt about it." He turned his neck slowly, like one with a neck brace and looked defiantly at his brother.

Iyom's legs wobbled. She sank back onto the bench. "Rapu."

"What shall we call this?" Jasper asked. His brother ignored him. "I am your senior," he continued. "I gave you a four-year gap. Zona can open his mouth and yap as he likes, but you must accord me the respect that is due me."

"He is right," Iyom said.

"I knew you would side with him."

"I side with the truth," Iyom replied squarely. "A senior deserves res—"

"Everyone knows he is your favourite. What kind of mother are you? You bless him, pray for his success at the expense of your other children."

"Rapu! Did you eat palm fruit? What dirt is this emanating from your mouth!"

"Is it Nne you are talking to like that, Rapu? Are you out of your senses?"

"What will you do? Beat me?"

Contempt contorted the younger man's face. He was losing it, spiralling. He inflated his chest and clenched his fists.

Jasper stepped forward menacingly and shoved Rapu backward. Rapu toppled over the tree stump on which he was sitting, turned, grabbed a handful of sand and scrambled hurriedly to his feet. He lunged at Jasper, lobbed the sand in his face and grabbed him by the lapels. Jasper gripped his attacker's wrists, trying to unlock the choke hold. Rapu held tight and dragged his older brother a few feet like a goat. Iyom threw herself between them, prizing the younger boy from his sibling. She held them apart. Rapu, still smarting from the fall, lowered himself like a boxer to assail Jasper from under their mother's outstretched arm. Iyom saw it and tried to parry it, but she was too late. The punch landed on her shoulder.

"Ewooo!"

She crumpled to the ground. Charity rushed to her.

CHAPTER 40

The three Okonkwo brothers attended the all-night wake for Oke Nmanwu. The throng was immense. Every parking spot near the deceased's home was taken. Spill-over vehicles were directed to neighbouring compounds, the Opaku Central School, and the church premises, from where the guests trekked to the venue.

Three live bands graced the occasion, plus a motley group of budding musicians whose main instruments were the local oja, the ogene, and the ekwe. They took turns to entertain the revellers, invoking genealogies and praise names, angling for tips.

Opaku indigenes at the wake sat according to their age grades and societies. Zona alternated between his Oduagu age group and the Elite Merchants Club, which had the widest canopy reserved for them. Jasper and Rapu belonged to the same age group, Omekagu. They were the Tiger imitators. Jasper split his time between their awning and the bar-on-wheels. As the night wore on, he was irked by the amount of alcohol Rapu was consuming, and rebuked him.

"Hey, is it because you see free alcohol that you are quaffing it like there is no tomorrow?"

Rapu assured his brother that he could handle it. "When I reach my limit, no one will tell me to stop," he replied baldly, still sulking from their tiff. But inside, he was full of remorse. He looked to the liquor to drown his chagrin. What could have propelled him to challenge his benefactor like that? Jasper, who bailed him out and loaned him money now and again to grow his business? And Nne too? From where did his accusation of favouritism that he had levelled against her emanate? Surely, all fingers were not equal. He could not assume to be at the level of his brothers who, having started cooking long before him, were expected to boast of more pots and pans. From where did the bad blood that flowed through his veins come? His mind returned to the meeting and the showdown with Jasper. It weighed on him.

"Miss, another beer!"

Jasper is Nne's favourite, his restless mind asserted. *Jasper is Nne's favourite. He is. He is. And why should he not be? He buys her clothes and foodstuff. He gifted her a tricycle to feed herself with. What have I, Rapu, bought? What have I given her?* He took another swig of beer. *So, why should she not be partial toward him? Why? Why? It's log—*

"Another beer, Miss!"

Why am I stingy? he asked himself, unable to hide from the fact. *Nne raised us virtually single-handedly when Agbisi was immersed in the throes of his affair with Akwaeke. And yet, come Christmas, I cannot afford a decent gift for her. Mothering Sunday, nothing. But Jasper showers her with gifts. And now I turn around and accuse her of favouritism. If you were in her shoes?*

"Usher, hiccup, some Hennessy here." With each drink, Rapu sank deeper into his sorrows.

He spied Oduenyi making the rounds with her ledgers, accosting young men and women. It was past midnight when she gravitated to him. She slumped into the empty seat beside him, let out a loud sigh of relief and nudged her feet out of the shiny stilettoes. The air was festive, the music deafening. It made conversation hard.

"Any... hiccup for me?" he slurped, putting out a shaky hand for the books.

"I did not expect you to come to the funeral," the matchmaker said. She wiped her cakey face with a paper serviette, staining it. "By Christmas, I will line up some nice damsels for you." She pursed her lips and kissed her fingertips. "Some to die for." She looked at him coquettishly from under her blond bangs and fake eyelashes.

"All right-io!" He could feel the alcohol making him groggy. His words were starting to slur. "Do not f-forget m-my hiccup s-specifications."

"I won't: dark-skinned, natural hair, fat. Am I missing anything?" She noticed that he had difficulty focusing. She made a mental note: *Drink problem.*

"And ugly," Rapu added. "Very important. I d-don't w-want t-t-o com-pete with other me-en for her."

"Got it." She made to rise.

Rapu restrained her. "A-nd take full photo of the body, front and back, n-not just the face. L-let us see the whole mer-merchandise."

"Ooo."

Oduenyi loosened his grip and melted into the crowd.

~

Crowds kept surging into the compound. The night appeared enchanted. Floodlights beamed into the grounds. Smoke from the women's cooking tripods and cauldrons floated overhead. Moths and locusts had a field day. Wall geckos clambered on the poles, preying on the insects orbiting the light. Frogs croaked from the brushes, providing unsolicited bass vocals to the official bands.

At midnight, the sky prepared to rain. The indigo clouds eclipsed the full moon. Jasper consulted with the widow.

"Though we have canopies, rainfall would degrade the event," he warned.

Obidie assured him that the rainmakers had been contracted to hold the rain. Satisfied, Jasper returned to the cooling truck. Soon enough, the clouds swam away.

The Okonkwo middle child scoured his mind to make sense of the tempestuous family meeting and the altercation with Rapu. *Maybe I was wrong to give away a land to my half-brothers. But Umunna, in their collective wisdom, willed it so. An individual could not face off with his kinsmen; otherwise, in your time of need, you would stand alone. The best thing, as Nne suggested, would be to source a plot from the open market and run away from trouble. Land scuffles could decimate families, and my sons could be the enemy's target. But with what money would he buy land? Would Amata release her Jeep money for a plot? She had said to use the funds to build on the premise that land was available. Even if she agreed and we bought a parcel, what would be left for the edifice proper? And I cannot use my trading money to build. No one would bail me out again.*

With a shrug of the shoulders, he tossed the matter aside like a filthy fuel filter and called for a bowl of stewed drumsticks. Waiters meandered through the guests with plates heaped with assorted delicacies. The weather was as temperamental as the moods of those attending. Clouds would gather, dark and indigo. Faces creased with worry. Then the sky would alter itself, the moon would shine brighter, and drinks would flow. The creases he had seen on people's faces eased.

Many age groups entertained in their regalia. There was no dull moment. Oke Nmanwu had been a boss of bosses. He had trained and empowered many, including those unrelated to him by blood. They had all donated towards his funeral and had come to pay their final respects. Jasper found it amusing to see how the eating and drinking had transformed the wake into a merriment.

Sometime in the night, a young man strolled by to ask for a drink. The youth's resemblance to Agbisi was striking. He had the same lanky frame and wide-set eyes, the hawk-like nose, the bowtie of a mouth, and scanty moustache. Jasper froze. He blinked a few times in quick succession at the spectre. For a moment, he thought his father had, as so often happened, come to escort Oke Nmanwu to the great beyond.

But it was not Agbisi. It was Jidenma. They shook hands and embraced.

"Jasper Gee!" the fellow hailed, grinning sheepishly, clearly pleased at the encounter. "Ochinanwata."

"Jidenma! You made it?"

"Jasper Gee! Oke Nmanwu trained me up to the university level. He and Agbisi were like this." He enlaced his two index fingers.

"Are you telling me? I know. Nno."

"Oo."

"What of Jideofor?"

"He couldn't make it. You know how hustling is in South Africa."

"Nna, good to see you. Long time!"

"Jasper Gee! I heard how you dropped two boys at a go."

"My brother, na God o," Jasper said humbly. He opened the truck. "What will you drink?"

"Hero. But let me serve myself. How can my senior serve me?"

"I did not know you returned for the burial. You will assist me with the drinks."

Jasper waited for Jidenma to take a sip and relax. There was a lull in the drinks line, so the two men chatted.

"Looks like you have put up something on your land. I passed by there this morning."

"Jideofor sends trickles, and we put one brick on top of another."

"That is how to do it, one brick at a time."

In no time, a whorl of thirsty guests formed. Jasper turned his attention to them. Jidenma stayed by his side and helped dispense the drinks.

At 4 a.m., the crowd began to dwindle. Jasper sensed he could turn in to catch some shuteye before the requiem Mass slated for dawn. He thanked Jidenma, closed the bar and pocketed the keys. After the interment, guests would be fed and watered again. Under the beam of angled lights, he caught a glimpse of Rapu lolled out on an armchair in deep slumber. He pivoted, went by and shook him. No way.

"It is a sleep fuelled by up-wine," a bystander said. "He was downing the palm wine like water."

"And whisky and beer," said another. "We warned him, but he said he knew his capacity. Now see where his capacity has led him."

Jasper grimaced. He pulled his moustache pensively.

Rapu, the baby brother he had lugged around as a kid, the one he would entertain while their mother busied herself with chores, was passed out cold. When they were children and Zona had gone off to school, Jasper would attempt to lift Rapu, half-dragging him to a dry spot on the bare ground after the baby had wet himself. They went butt naked in those days, and the soldier ants had a field day biting their dusty buttocks and bare thighs. Rapu would let out a blood-curdling shriek, and Jasper would try to console him. He would pretend to locate the culprit ant and press it into the ground. *There, I have killed it,* he would tell his little brother. Then, he would distract the baby by flipping a spin top on the sand. The thing would twist and turn at high velocity, and Rapu, mesmerized by it, would stop crying.

A sigh escaped him. *We have grown now. We have each gone our own ways, strategizing for survival, forgetting past favours and past ties. Instead, we now challenge one another and grab inheritances. We are mature now to compare ourselves to our siblings, and, falling short, we gripe about it. Brothers forget when they were vulnerable, at the other's mercy, how the older protected the younger and cared for him. Those halcyon days were gone forever. If siblings could act this way, full of rancour and animus, what great hatred might there be outside, with neighbours, kinsmen, and people of other tribes who shared no ancestry with you?*

Jasper could not help the hiss that escaped him as he pulled himself out of his thoughts. What to do? Beneath the glow of the floodlight, Rapu slouched, mouth agape; a thread of saliva drooled down his jaw and onto his sleeves. A wetness darkened the cushion beneath him. At the base of the chair, a puddle of his own creation oozed.

Still smarting from their fight, Jasper was of the mind to leave Rapu there, exposed to the elements and the scorn of passers-by. He walked to the exit. At the gate, he stopped. Someone could take a picture of his brother, wet pants and all, and it would go viral in no time, and the scorpion tongues of kinswomen would soon lay into him. No, he could not leave. Despite their differences, he would not abandon Rapu in his vulnerability. Rapu was still Nne's son. They had suckled the same breasts. If anything happened, Iyom would ask Jasper, 'Where were you?' It could break her heart.

He retraced his steps. Someone offered a bowl of water, which he splashed on Rapu's head. No dice.

He drew a couple of chairs together and stretched out beside the unmoving form. Sleep lay in ambush behind his eyelids, egged on by the cool pre-dawn breeze. Jasper fought it, as well as clouds of mosquitoes buzzing about them. Around Rapu's chair, empty liquor bottles peeped at him like incorporeal eyes. They nestled against each other around an empty jeroboam of ngwo, the strong local brew.

It was not long before the neighbourhood cockerels began announcing the coming day. The sun, hidden by the greenery, splayed its rays in the blue-grey skies when Rapu's eyes twitched and opened. He sat up with a start and glared at his surroundings, uncomprehending. The owners of the compound were cleaning the aftermath of the vigil. He gawped at the empty cans and discarded bottles around him and the mounds of used paper cups and plates being swept together. He saw tables and chairs upturned. He took in the deserted bandstand. Uniformed personnel were re-arranging the venue, dragging furniture here and there. His eyes roamed till they fell on Jasper.

"You're awake."

They heaved themselves up and sleepwalked home.

~

The mourners were heading for the church when Rapu fell onto his mattress at home, still sozzled. From far away, he heard his phone ring but was powerless to answer it. The funeral service came and went; Rapu remained in limbo. In the fog of his brain, he could hear the dirge drifting across the compound walls:

Meghe uzo, onu uzo nke en'igwe
Meghe onu uzo, ka nwa nn'anyi bata.

Open the gate, the gate of heaven
Open, let our brother in.

Opaku stood still for Oke Nmanwu. Many young men, including Jidenma, dressed in palm fronds, paraded Oke Nmanwu's spacious compound, bandying large portraits of him, mourning their loss. Here was a maker of men. "We are products of his largesse," they said. Jasper was ubiquitous, talking to as many people as possible to ensure good relations with the community. Oke Nmanwu was a staunch Christian and had not dabbled into cultist practices. His money was clean, people said; it had no odour. He did not belong to any secret society, so every activity concerning his final home call was done in the open.

It was sundown when the MC's voice on the loudspeaker nudged Rapu's sleep, rousing him. His hangover morphed into a pounding headache. He struggled to sit up. *Must be that up-wine,* he thought. He had downed it without mercy. He checked his phone. Forty-six missed calls! Thirty-one were from his boy alone. Why would Stanley call him so many times? Something was wrong. Was it to know the last price of a commodity, the price below which one could not go? Not likely. He had passed that stage and could make decisions on price tags. His hands shook as he dialled Stanley's number.

"Sir, the Karu Local Government bulldozer is demolishing the plaza. Our shop is no more." Rapu could hear construction noise in the background.

"A bull-what! Our plaza, no more?" His grogginess left him. He could feel his bladder bursting. His shop, demolished? Rapu leaned against a wall and let the liquid gush down. "What of the landlord?"

"I don't know. He is not around."

"What of other shop owners in the plaza?" Rapu's stomach was in knots.

"The whole building is affected. I have been trying you since morning."

"What of our wares? Were you…?"

"I could only get a few items out, a tricycle and some parts. Looters swarmed us, took advantage."

Rapu fell back on the mattress. His shop, gone! Nothing was saved except a tricycle! He had displayed seven autorickshaws and three Jingshen motorbikes outside the shop on the eve of his departure. Were they all gone?

He leaped up, his mind racing. There was nothing he could do from Opaku. He had to get back to base as quickly as possible. He could take a rickshaw or motorbike to Opaku market square. From there, hit Awka, Nnewi, or Onitsha. Onitsha! Yes, Onitsha. Night buses to Abuja departed hourly from Upper Iweka Roundabout.

"Shut up!" he spat at Zona's brood, making a racket outside. "A burial is in progress and are you singing? Are neighbours to think we are happy that Oke Nmanwu is no more? Shut up!"

He unlatched the gate and hurried out. If all went well, by morning, he would be in Abuja. He prayed that the journey would be uneventful. Night marauders and kidnappers operated frequently and remained unchallenged on the highways.

God answered his prayers. The journey was uneventful except for bribe-seeking traffic cops. They had proliferated. Luckily, the bus driver played ball, and they progressed steadily toward the capital.

By the time he reached Karu in the early morning, the plaza was a wasteland. Scavengers were rummaging through the debris to salvage anything they thought useful. Rapu gritted his teeth at the carcass of his erstwhile bubbling shop. The upper floor, which had been undergoing roofing, had been torn down. The roofing sheets hung loose. With nothing to gird them, they gyrated in the breeze. One side of the walls had caved into a heap, forming a pyramid of concrete odds and ends. Iron rods in the mass crisscrossed each other. Twisted black rods stuck out of jagged blocks of concrete. Slabs lay sideways. Bits of wooden frames stood half-buried in the rubble. Shards of glass dazzled in the rising sun. Dust swirled up from the wreckage as foragers dug deep into the ruins with sticks, shovels, and pickaxes.

Sufficient damage had been inflicted on the building to render it unviable.

"What of the plastics seller?" Rapu asked Stanley, covering his nose from the dust.

"I would say Oga Dan was aware of the demolition," Stanley offered. "He hired a truck and evacuated his wares just as the bulldozers and caterpillars rolled in."

"And you could not evacuate any of our stuff?"

Stanley shook his head. "I took some parts and dumped them onto the vehicle for safety. Then I ran to get more. When I returned, Oga Dan had offloaded our wares."

A thought struck Rapu in the middle of his apprentice's account. "What about my safe?"

Stanley had completely forgotten about the safe embedded in one wall. Rapu ran into the debris. If he was lucky, he could recover it. And the cash he had stashed in it. Alas.

CHAPTER 41

Jasper remained in Opaku till the end of the obsequies of his former boss and mentor. After the interment on Friday, guests were entertained till late into the night. On Saturday, it was the turn of in-laws to pay the customary mourning visit. Obidie's people came with a bull and a masquerade. Oke Nmanwu had been a great in-law. He had helped to train his wife's people. He was not one to turn a needy soul away.

After his widow's people had paid their respects, other groups took their turns. Among them were the kinsmen of the spouses of the Igwilo children. They turned up with a male goat, assorted drinks, and a masked spirit. Last to come were the kinsmen of Sandra, the wife of Igwilo's son.

Throughout the funeral rites, Jasper stayed in constant touch with Amata, running commentary on the funeral and enquiring about O'Neal and Kobe. It was only on Sunday, after the outing service at the church, that he could come up for air and take leave of Obidie.

His intention was to wake with the first cockcrow and set out at dawn on Monday morning. That night, the rain the makers had been holding was let loose on the earth. It fell in long threads from the gorged sky to the saturated ground. Lightning marbled the sky, and thunder growled. The wind howled and made the trees curtsy and dance and sway. Jasper fell into a deep, dreamless sleep.

As light crept in through the window ledge, he stirred but lacked the will to rise. His bones felt heavy, and his joints ached.

He rolled from one side to the other, unable to heave up.

He felt Iyom tugging furiously at his big toe at the same time that Charity's screams reached him.

"Go and find out what is amiss."

"Is Zona not in?" he asked sleepily.

"He left yesterday. Rapu, too."

Jasper hoisted his feet out of bed and dashed outdoors. Leaves and twigs shrouded the compound, interspersed by felled fruits. It had been a heavy storm. The scent of petrichor pervaded.

Charity and her maid were outside moping at the roof of their bungalow. "My husband," she greeted Jasper. "Ochinwata. The wind blew part of our roof away. Our kitchen is a river. We have been up, cleaning."

Charity tore into the cocoyam farm. She re-emerged with a sheet of aluminum. Jasper confronted the gaping hole in disbelief. The damage was more than he could handle.

"Chisom, run and call the carpenter. Tell him what has occurred and to come at once with his tools. I am waiting."

Chisom slid off her flip-flops and took off barefoot. In no time, the fellow arrived. He clambered up his ladder and took stock of the damage.

"It is because of you that I came," he said to Jasper. "I have received three calls so far to come and repair flying roofs. The storm wreaked a lot of havoc."

"Thank you." Jasper acknowledged the preferential treatment even though he recognized the trade gimmick.

"It is always like this when the rainmaker restrains the rains for an occasion," Iyom observed from the side. She was chewing the morning stick. She spat out. "They come down with a vengeance, angry at the obstruction."

"Once you schedule an outdoor event in the rainy season, you must reckon with the rainmakers," the carpenter observed.

"Weddings one can control, but a funeral—" she left the rest unsaid.

"I heard that in Mbotu, they can keep a corpse for a year," Jasper said.

"That is overdoing it," Iyom remarked. "A corpse, without air, degenerates."

"They are great embalmers, those Mbotu people," the carpenter acknowledged from the cantilever.

Jasper handed him the torn aluminum sheet and watched as the carpenter knocked it back in place. He did not pay attention to Charity, who stood by, helpless. The beginning of a swelling was visible in her midriff. She stole glimpses of Jasper's muscles twitching involuntarily as he raised a part to the artisan. She saw the tuft of hair in the hollow of his shoulder and sneaked a view of his torso and the frizzy hair on his chest. She followed the line it made down to the birthmark below his navel and the tangle of curls descending to his groin. His pectoral muscles were taut. Compared to Jasper's spare physique, Zona's corpulence nauseated her.

"Go inside!" Nne's voice megaphoned into Charity's thoughts. "Leave the men to handle it."

~

Back in Lagos, Jasper tried to face his business squarely, but something gnawed at his intestines. His relationship with his brothers was going downhill fast. He could feel it as surely as the wedding band on his finger. The Jeep and the birth of the twins had roused a fiery jealousy in Zona. He had retaliated by blocking his brother's supply route, and on top of that, he refused to concede an inch of the family compound. Now, he had crowned it by usurping their inherited land. Jasper suspected that the genesis of the bad blood preceded the Jeep and the birth of his twin boys. Was it not this same fellow that scuttled his apprenticeship when Remi's stealing was discovered? Jasper's hand had not been in the till, so why did Zona rope him in and mete out a draconian punishment? Why? He concluded that Zona was a bad man, pure and simple. He cared nothing for family or kinsmen.

Jasper still did not know why Rapu had left in such a hurry without telling anyone. Even Iyom had not been notified. What kind of siblings are these? Rapu's land-grabbing surprised him. *You have donated your own,* he had the effrontery to say after the family meeting, *so this one is mine.* Was that how they viewed the matter? That he had donated his land? He had acquiesced to the judgement of the Umunna for peace, for equity, as Elder Okeke had counselled. That gesture had been misconstrued to mean that he had gifted Akwaeke's sons his share of Agbisi's property.

He rued these matters. Land was a frequent cause of blood-letting. Their mother was right; it was better to buy from a third party and run from sibling trouble.

The Sunday after his return, Jasper had a short siesta. When he awoke, he dressed in his jeans trousers and matching shirt.

"Where are you going?" Amata enquired as he walked into the living room. She was on the floor playing with the boys.

"Let me go and visit my brother."

"After all he did, should we not keep our distance?"

Jasper went down on all fours. The twins were almost two years old and prancing like toy soldiers. Several small teeth salivated in their mouths. O'Neal was already mouthing words. Amata had since weaned them. It was not easy raising twins. They hardly slept at the same time. As a result, his wife had lost all the extra fat she had gained in those nine months. He had teased her to get ready for their third child, whom he would name LeBron. Why stop at LeBron? Amata had deadpanned. Add Antetokounmpo. He had understood. Graduate wife, family planning. They had gotten into a routine. Jasper felt fulfilled and happy. Only his brothers irked him.

"As the younger brother, it behooves me to extend the olive branch. Nne would want that."

He looked at his feet and wiggled his toes. He thought of donning his baskets but dreaded sweating feet. The toes needed to breathe in this hot, humid Lagos weather. He opted for the leather sandals. He took his favourite baseball cap, the one that had Shaquille squiggled on it, and set it on his head. He had bought minor versions for his sons, but Amata said their heads were still too fragile for baseball caps, biko.

As he walked out the door, he saw Amata make the sign of the Cross.

~

When Jasper arrived at the Alaka Estate property, the house was quiet. He pressed the bell. Charity and the girls were still in the village, he knew. It looked like the arrangement was permanent, what with Charity running a shop there now. From what he heard, she was doing well, building up a rich clientele. Amata had been asking whether she should join Charity in the village, have her own shop, and raise the boys there so they could speak Igbo. Speak Igbo to them, he had replied. They will learn it. A child's head is empty, Agbisi used to say; whatever you put in it, he will retain. He could not deny that he had enjoyed eating fresh food all the time he spent in the village. He appreciated the serenity and calm, far from the noise and stress of the metropolis, but it was not in his plans to live apart from his wife and children like some men did, who hustled in one city while the missus and children hunkered down in another. Why marry then?

He pressed the bell again. Was there an outage? He shook the iron gate. One of the apprentices peered at him from the back, then slowly proceeded to the gate. His hands were laced with soap suds.

"Good evening, sir."

"Good evening. Omeifeukwu in?"

The lad shook his head. "He went out."

Jasper waited to be let in. But the servant stood there wrenching his hands.

"Open the gate; let me wait for him," Jasper said.

The lad scratched his head.

"O gini?"

"Oga left instructions not to open the gate if he is not in."

"What shall we call this? Do you know who is standing here?"

"Oga Jasper Gee. Please do not get angry, but that is the instruction Omeifeukwu left. I will call him to let him know you are here. I hope Master will not mind waiting in the car or in the shed across the road."

Jasper was shocked to the marrow. A chill washed over him. *Has it come to this? That a sibling cannot enter his brother's house in his absence?*

"Sorry, sir," the boy said, also embarrassed. Sibling rivalry and suspicion were common in Igboland. Each feared that the other party would outdo them or harm them or that they would visit the shaman for them and plant something where they were sure to step, thus stealing their good fortune and destroying their life. Some could kill outright. Anything to bar the sibling from overtaking them in life. People went to all lengths to continue outshining and outperforming their relations, to remain on top while the others begged for favours.

Jasper wiped his face. He felt hot as he turned and ambled to his Corolla. Shame washed over him. He sat for a while, his legs shaking frantically. The sun was waning, losing its bite, but he felt flushed. He idled the engine and switched on the AC but quickly turned it off. It was dangerous. Carjackers could materialize from nowhere and snatch your vehicle in the twinkle of an eye. He descended and strolled to the shed of the corn seller by the wayside, humming quietly as he attempted to gather his wits and forage a way out. He regretted coming. He could have been at the stadium, keeping fit, playing soccer with other sports enthusiasts. Or he could have gone on an outing with his family to Bar Beach or Apapa Amusement Park. Instead, he had opted to visit his brother to make peace, only to be treated like a leper.

The corn seller slapped a spot on her bench three times for him. He sat down and ordered some ears of corn sizzling atop the crepitating coals. A dozen native pears were lined up on the grill beside some squares of coconut. He had eaten well at lunch, but he could never say no to a corn and pear combo. He indulged and remembered to wrap some for his wife and the babysitter. He was aware that with the arrival of the twins, Amata could not stroll around the quarter as freely as she once did and treat herself to seasonal delicacies.

An hour later, Zona's Lexus cruised past, Osita Osadebey blaring from the music system. Zona, like many traders of his ilk, enjoyed highlife music, *ikwokrikwo*. The maestro's voice was reeling out the names of members of the famous Elite Merchants Club and hailing them. At some point, Zona's name was mentioned: *Chief Echezona Bespoke Okonkwo, Chairman, Managing Director, Zona Group, International Merchants, Omeifeukwu, money spinner of Opaku.* It was a huge recognition to be mentioned in the song. It showed that Zona had made it.

Jasper gave his brother a few minutes to settle in before presenting himself anew at the gate.

"Why were you waiting outside?" Zona barked, feigning anger and surprise. "Why did you not let him in, eh Chibuike? Don't you know who he is?"

The apprentice looked down at his feet.

It was all a show, Jasper knew. He played along.

"Omeifeukwu, it is okay. I was hungry for roast corn, so I opted to stop by the seller. How are you, sir?"

"We are pushing it."

"I told my wife that it has been long since I visited you. I should come and know how my big brother is doing." He followed Zona into the house.

"You did well. That is Lagos for you. Brothers live next door to each other but can stay six to twelve months and not see. Are you getting my point?"

"That is how it is."

"The people of your household?"

"They are well. Only hunger is worrying us."

"Hunger that has hope of satisfaction does not kill."

"Amen."

Zona pointed him to a seat.

The room had a musty smell. It was neat, devoid of the children's toys and clothes that characterized it when Charity held sway. Zona was fiddling with the AC remote.

"Bia, where are these boys?" he hollered. Turning to Jasper, he asked, "What shall we offer you? We have everything: wine, beer, whiskey?"

Jasper rubbed his stomach. "I am full. I ate three corns sitting outside and drank a sachet of water. Let us keep the kola for next time."

"If you say so. Don't our people say that the night has taken away the kola?"

"That is so. But that is the excuse of people who have no kola."

After a moment of silence, Jasper asked, "How is your hotel project going?"

"It is rising. Only money is what it needs. Once there is money, a project does not take time." Zona stole a glance at the visitor. Was this the reason for the visit? To continue the land dispute? Had he consulted his lawyer wife?

After the family meeting and their argument, Zona went to the new Divisional Police Officer in Opaku. He had paid handsomely for the DPO's protection and felt safe, but that did not make him let down his guard.

The brothers talked about business in general terms. Jasper needed to restock his shop again. Rumour had it that Zona was about to travel abroad on business to order goods, but he did not broach the trip with Jasper. Perhaps Akajiaku or Orimili would accommodate his needs. It was a pity that Jasper's mentor was no more. He could have turned to Igwilo in his hour of need.

Jasper raised the matter of the Elite Merchants Club. Perhaps through the club, Zona would accommodate his list.

"I am thinking of joining the Elite Merchants Club, sir."

"Is that so?"

"Yes, sir."

Zona chewed the matter. Jasper could see him literally biting his lips as he considered the proposal. He embraced himself, buried his hands in his armpits, and wiggled his squat legs. Then, unable to control the venom suppurating within him, he burst out. "Is Elite Club the only club in Lagos that every Tom, Dick and Harry wants to join it? Eh? Boy King?"

The contempt in Zona's voice reached out and pierced Jasper, who stiffened and cringed into the soft foam. His vibrating legs immobilized. The giant clock struck seven.

"Anyway, we just inaugurated new members," Zona soft-pedalled. "Are you getting my point? You are late."

The AC shuddered.

"Perhaps next year."

"If God keeps us alive."

Jasper left Zona's house without finding a resolution to the things troubling them.

"Something is wrong," he told Amata, who was digging into the corn he brought home. "We are brothers, but he has no love for me."

Amata munched away. Jasper envied her, coming from a close-knit family with siblings who got on well and did not bicker over anything. In contrast to his dysfunctional family.

"When we went home for Igwilo's funeral, I discovered that Zona had started building on one of our family lands."

"Blood of Jesus."

"Without informing his brothers. Can you imagine? When I notified Nne, she called a meeting."

"Of the Board of Directors."

Jasper smiled. Amata had a sense of humour. "Zona said one land was his and the other, Rapu's."

"None for you?"

"That I already gave my own away."

"To whom?"

"You know our custom of Ikwuchi?"

Amata nodded. It was common in many communities. In Nkwa, they called it Nkwuchi.

"One of our kinsmen, Jonas Uba Okunna, died. His widow, Akwaeke, chose Agbisi as cover. He fathered two boys with her. When Akwaeke died, Uncle Jonas's son chased the boys away empty-handed, refusing to give them even a pin from his modest estate. The boys approached Zona, but he would hear none of it. He said as long as Agbisi did not pay the bride price on Akwaeke, the boys were not our brothers."

"And so they could not inherit from Agbisi."

"The matter went before the Umunna. They decided the boys should get a share of Agbisi's estate."

Amata nodded, mouth full.

"Jonas was a poor man," Jasper continued. "He was lucky to have married Akwaeke, the most beautiful woman to tread Opaku soil. His name means wealth, yes. But all the wealth he had was in name only. In reality, he had nothing. Nothing but a humble dwelling in a corner of Opaku and his carpentry business, where he knocked together chairs and tables and the occasional coffin. Meanwhile, Agbisi, a renowned tailor, could boast several plots of land and a thriving business. So Umunna ruled to give the boys from our father's estate."

"A Solomonic judgement."

"But Zona would have none of it. We thought the matter had been laid to rest until Umunna approached me. Since Agbisi had several plots, I conceded one to the two boys, on the advice of an elder, mind you. Zona is saying that the land I conceded to them was my share of Agbisi's estate. He is already building a hotel on one of the lands, a double plot well situated on the Opaku-Nnewi road. Do not forget that the family hearth is his..."

"...as the first son. But I thought it was just the building. Does he get the whole compound? Can his brothers not build in Agbisi's compound?"

"You can see that he is a grabber. I raised the idea when I was home. He shot it down."

"What options are open to us? Is he diverging into hotel business now?"

Jasper hesitated on what question to answer. He chose the first.

"Nne is looking for a plot for us to buy. As soon as we get one, I will start something, however simple. It is only an unannounced war that catches the lame. And yes, apparently, he is venturing into the hotel business. You know our people with eating and drinking. And womanizing."

Amata tucked into the second corn and sucked at the native pear.

"Feel free to use the Jeep money," she said. "One can never go wrong with real estate."

She consumed two cobs before passing the last one to Omenma. She began to gather the stray seeds and chaff.

"This corn is delicious. Thank you. You say you bought it from the woman opposite Zona's house?"

"Yes."

He did not elaborate on how he had been forced to wait outside. There was no need to poison her mind against her brother-in-law.

"I wonder how he is managing without Charity."

Jasper did not respond. In this Lagos, one is asking how a lone man, a married bachelor as Lagosians described it, is managing when, at each point in time, ten to twenty women are ready to scoop him into their embrace. Amata tried another tack.

"Did you see the UNILAG babe Charity said has taken over her place?"

"No. He was alone in the house with his trainee boys. Charity has embraced village life. She is thriving there. I warned her that if anything happens to Zona in Lagos, Opaku will ask her questions."

"Lilu will answer Opaku," Amata retorted. She charged like a cockerel, measuring herself against her husband, arms stretched out behind her. Lilu was Charity's hometown. "A man banishes his wife to the village. Then you turn around and warn that if any harm befalls him in the city, his townspeople will hold the wife responsible. Charity's people will provide them with answers."

Jasper was agape. Such a feisty answer to an anodyne statement.

He was about to respond when Omenma's excited voice reached them. "Oniru is barring. Oniru is barring!"

The parents rushed to the dining area. O'Neal was standing with the ball. He took a sure step forward, bounced the rubber, and caught it. He smiled briefly but continued putting one foot in front of the other. A few steps from the toy basketball hoop, he flung the rubber up into the basket.

"Shaquille O'Neal!" Jasper hailed. He brought out his phone and began to film. Amata nudged the nanny.

"His name is O'Neal, not Oniru. Is he Yoruba?"

True, many Igbo tongues encountered difficulty differentiating the r and l sounds.

"If it is the same Oniru that owns half of Victoria Island, I don't mind," Jasper joked. "Let him collect our share."

Kobe was lying on his side, asleep. The babies were not identical, but it was impossible to tell them apart sometimes. For their first birthday, Amata had bought gold pendants with the initial letter of their names attached to help tell them apart. Jasper had declined to celebrate it for fear of the envy of others, opting to take them to the Ikoyi Mall instead.

Jasper bounced the ball back towards his son. Amata grabbed it midair.

"I'm part of the game, too," she said. "Omenma, you too. Women should not be bystanders to the good things of life."

Later, as the couple prepared for sleep, Amata revisited their earlier discussion.

"So Agbisi had two children with the Akwaeke."

"Tsk."

Jasper cast a brief glance at his wife. She appeared to be in a reflective mood.

"By tradition, they are Jonas's sons. But the blood coursing through their veins is my father's."

"Do I know them?"

"I don't think you have met. Or you met and were not introduced. Jidenma is around a lot. He came home for Oke Nmanwu's funeral. Jideofor is based in South Africa."

"One thing I would like to know—"

Jasper turned to face his wife. All along, he had been staring straight ahead at the ceiling, using his tongue to tease out bits of the corn husks still stuck in his teeth.

"When Akwaeke chose Agbisi, could he have refused? Like say, 'Sorry, I am married.'"

"I told you that the widow was one of the prettiest women in Opaku. They called her Omumasaru, One who does not need to bathe. Many of the kinsmen were secretly praying to be her choice."

"But Agbisi could have passed. Did Akwaeke put a revolver to his head?"

"It is the culture. Up till today, we observe it."

"So, God forbid something happens to Zona, Charity can choose you as her Nkpuchi?"

"Yes. Or Rapu."

"And you must accept?"

"Do not pull your hair over it, Stainless," he said as gently as he could muster. "Nobody is dying anytime soon."

"Another thing."

He was all ears. The ikwuchi matter seemed to bug her.

"You don't say 'I love you' at all." He relaxed, grinning.

"Women. Is it love will put food on the table?" He threw his head back and laughed. "My mates are calculating profit margin, you are talking love."

"If you are shy of saying it in public, just say one four three. I will understand."

When he calmed down, he curled a fist and improvised a mic. "Stainless. One four three. Over."

Amata was confused at first, but she caught on, "Ochinanwata. I hear you loud and clear."

They spooned and slipped into sleep, a smile on their lips.

CHAPTER 42

Upon Jasper's departure, Zona relaxed. He had thought the visit was to iron out the land matter. Or for the Taiwan order. He had no stomach for either. As far as he was concerned, the land matter was closed; the fool had given away his plot. And he could not build in the family "yard." Otherwise, his sons might claim it tomorrow, what with Charity producing females. No. As for the Taiwan order, he reckoned that Jasper was developing a big head. That was what gave him the audacity to challenge his decision about the land for the Okunna brothers. *Let him import his wares himself; after all, a lizard that climbed the oji tree is no longer a baby.* If Jasper could sign away land, he could import his own merchandise and then try to clear them from the wharf. He would soon realize how difficult it was to make a profit after all the checkpoints Customs agents erected at every step and the slipperiness of clearing agents. If one was not connected, one would not survive the ordeal. Not to talk of the short landing. What about the port rats? That would teach him. Boy King, indeed.

Zona exhaled. He pigeonholed thoughts of his family, preferring to relive the pleasant time spent with Modupe. He was a happy man. Each time he visited her, she wrung him out of every ounce of his strength. She lived on Herbert Macaulay with her mother. Everyone called the old lady Alhaja. She sold gold at the Gutter market in Oke Arin. Modupe had a three-year-old daughter for a Lagos socialite. She wanted another child but did not care for marriage. This suited Zona well. He enjoyed Modupe. She knew her onions in the love department.

Each time he went to the Simpson family house, he was treated like the governor of Lagos State. This evening had been no different. From the entrance gate, children curtsied and knelt down on the hard surface to greet him while the men stooped, gripping their ankles. One went the whole hog and lay flat on the ground. E kaabo, e kaabo, reverberated. Alhaja's tenants scurried to open doors for him. Modupe would emerge and embrace him, then would busy herself assembling refreshments—water, stout, fried meat and ponmo, or suya bought from a popular joint at Alagomeji. Zona plunged into the amala and ewedu soup, enriched with smoked sawa fish and the intestines of animals, which they called orisirisi. A side dish always contained the muscle of a cow foot or hump and other delicacies. After welcoming him, Alhaja would disappear, leaving her daughter to entertain her lover in peace. After dining, Modupe would summon the compound kids to clear the table. They were always enthusiastic, especially when they saw the mouth-watering leftovers.

Zona shuddered and clenched his groin when he remembered their first time together. He had picked on some fried kidney and liver and taken a sip of the Guinness, eager to make love to his new catch. When he came down, Modupe had hissed loudly.

Is that how you climb your wife that she born four shuldren?

He was at sea.

What of the headlamps? She asked, indicating her chest. *What of the downstream?*

What about them? He was stricken, suddenly conscious of his manhood, shrivelled and cold. The fetid smell of the room assaulted his nostrils. He had read of foreplay but was unsure what it was exactly. To him, once a man engaged gear, you pounded to the finishing line.

They are all part of it, ke, she said without flinching. *When I saw you, I thought, here is a correct man, robust, solid.* She pumped her fists in the air. *But this, this is featherweight. Bantamweight, sef.*

Bantamweight in lovemaking? He, Omeifeukwu. Zona had fumbled for his singlet and tossed it over his nether regions. All those people curtsying for him outside? For a bantamweight? He inhaled and exhaled loudly, like an air pump. Words fled from him.

Modupe rose from the bed. *That your method na selfish, one-way traffic,* she said bluntly. *I dey go piss. Rest, eat some muscle.* She pointed to the covered dish on the stool. *We go try again.*

That second time, she guided him. At a point, she had sat on him and ridden him like a Vespa, legs drawn, doubled up. He feared for his life and was wailing like a lunatic from the sensations tingling his body. If he died then, it would be a happy death.

This one, na real lovemaking, she gushed. *Give and take.*

The first thought that struck Zona was that he would try the manoeuvres on Helen but not on his wife. Charity would abuse him and wonder where he picked this new acrobatic technique from. Her loss.

He usually stayed till midnight before returning home. But Chibuike had called to say that Jasper was waiting. Even then, he would not have hurried back if not that Modupe and her mother had an all-night party to attend at Ikoyi. They had bought the aso ebi, so popular in Yoruba culture.

King Sunny Ade will be there, Modupe had crooned excitedly. *And KWAM 1.*

King Wasiu Ayinde Marshall, popularly known as KWAM 1, was a renowned Fuji specialist. In the market, he heard his melodious voice all day from his Yoruba neighbours. Ah, the rhythmic drumming. Your body moved involuntarily with it.

And Pasuma.

Pasuma?

Yes. He is also a fuji musician, Modupe said, rolling her behind, stooping and shimmying to demonstrate how they would rollick.

The blue lace material was laid out on the chair, stones flickering and twinkling. Her pink scarf and blue-pink shoes were resting on a miserable suitcase, the same one she was carrying when he gave her a lift at Benin City.

The surroundings had perplexed him. Gold sellers living almost in squalor?

This is our family house, Modupe had explained, referring to the storey building with shops and stalls surrounding it. A torn and withered awning flustered in the wind. An open bay with wide windows housed many entrepreneurs. Cables and wires crisscrossed one another. Signs covered the walls: electrical, plumbing, tailoring. At the side was an empty space. Raffia mats with images of minarets lined it, wall to wall. It looked like a mosque. A loudspeaker was propped on the cantilever.

Alhaja has over twenty buildings in Lagos. But she prefers to collect rent on them and live here.

But why? Why not enjoy the wealth? Are you getting my point? Or is the market not good?

Not good, ke? She glided one palm over the other in wonder. *Someone has over twenty properties, and you say business is not good? Alhaja goes to Dubai and Turkey, sometimes twice a month. She supplies gold trinkets to all the big women in Lagos and Ibadan. But how many beds can one lie on at a time?*

He had let the matter die but was skeptical.

Do not worry, Modupe reassured him. *We will not ask to borrow money from you.*

The wall clock struck ten.

Modupe Simpson. She had not asked him for a kobo since they started dating, had not asked about his wife or family, and had not mentioned marriage. That first time, he had expected her to fish out a condom. But no, nothing like that. And she did not support the withdrawal method either. At the critical moment, when he sensed the looming explosion, he had battled to exit and scatter his seed on the bedding, but Modupe had grabbed his cheeks and pinned him down. Her long legs were already crossed over his. He understood that he was to remain as is, where is, like a jacked vehicle. He had been so grateful for the privilege. He had licked her sweaty face, lapped it like a dog.

They had been dating for several months, and she still had not mentioned marriage. She was not interested. If it was an

Igbo lady, Zona thought, she would set sights on introducing him to her family as soon as they said hello. To his surprise, Alhaja did not interfere in his relationship with her daughter. She was always dressed in a bogus blouse and wrapper, one end of the cloth sticking out, wide sleeves of the blouse billowing as she walked. Her black, silky underskirt was always visible. She invariably wore two or more headgear: a skull cap and a scarf. Sometimes, a white shawl was thrown carelessly atop the scarf. Once, another shawl was wound around her neck so that she resembled a Tuareg. Looking at her, you would not suspect that she was a billionaire. Or that Modupe was her only child.

Where is Alhaji? he asked one day.

Who?

Your father.

Our women are lonely, Modupe answered matter-of-factly. *We are condemned to spinsterhood.*

By whom?

By family, enemies. She examined her nails. *How can one deal in gold, have money, landed property, and have marital bliss? So, out of envy, they made us live and die as spinsters.*

CHAPTER 43

Helen was not home on the day Jasper came calling at Zona's because her mother was indisposed, and she had travelled to Umuahia. Zona made sure Helen's mother lacked nothing.

Take her to the Federal Medical Centre. Or go to a private clinic. Spare no expense.

Helen had flown to Owerri, from where she chartered a cab to Umuahia. Before she departed, she told Zona how happy she felt that he cared for her in this way. He smiled and didn't say anything because all he could think of was the prospect of spending unbridled time with Modupe.

Helen had called several times, but he had learnt to abjure all other women when he was with one. After Jasper left, Zona video-phoned Umuahia.

"We are fine," Helen said, happy at last to hear from her man. "Nma must have ingested fake drugs. Thank God I got here when I did. She is stable now. We are in a private room at the FMC. Thank you. Omeifeukwu!"

"Fine babe." His voice was smug.

"My people are waiting for you to bring wine to them o."

"Let Nma get well first. Are you getting my point? We shall come in a big way. You know me, I don't do small things small."

"I trust you. Omeifeukwu!"

"Pass the phone to Nma; let me greet my in-law."

Helen beamed. "Your in-law is sleeping."

After Helen, Zona called Charity. Since that day when he had moaned another woman's name in the heat of passion, he had sobered up. Beads of sweat dotted his forehead as he recalled the moment. Mortified was the nearest he had felt. It was as if the night had stopped in its tracks. Calling another babe's name must be an indubitable sign of infidelity. He vowed to be silent in future. No matter how sweet the act, his lips would be sealed. Otherwise, one Amazon could knock okro seeds out of his mouth and change his dentition forever.

Thank God Charity had quietened down. Sending her out of Lagos defanged her. She, who used to be as fiery as a Lagos girl, coming to fisticuffs at the drop of a hat, was now spilled engine oil. His mother must have talked sense into her.

"Omeifeukwu," came the bald greeting from across the miles. "Kedu nu?"

"We are fine, sir." Charity's stomach felt heavy. She was sitting on a low kitchen stool, legs at twenty past twelve position. She picked bits of sand and placed them on her tongue.

"Nne, kwan?"

"She is well."

"Adaobi and her siblings?"

"They are fine, sleeping."

"How is business?"

"We thank God. I forgot to tell you to thank Jasper. That rainstorm last week blew our roof away. If not for Jasper, we would be sleeping under the open skies."

"Did he replace the shingles?" Zona's voice was cold.

"He called Onyeka, and they did it together. He paid the carpenter. Please thank him."

That was the straw that broke Zona. "Charity. Charity," he bayed.

Charity could sense the scold in his voice.

"It looks like how I sent you out of here to the village is not sufficient to plant wisdom between your ears. Are you getting my point? Your next bus stop and terminus will be your father's house."

Charity cringed at the spleen in his voice. "Omeifeukwu, what did...?"

"Don't Omeifeukwu me! Do you not know the way to the carpenter's house? Do you need Jasper or whomever to call a workman for you?"

"Ooo, I'm sorry."

"Sorry for yourself, idiot. You can choose Jasper to cover you when I die, not before." He hissed. "And next time something happens in my house, you inform me first. Are you getting my point? Then, if you do not know what to do, I will tell you. You have four children but nothing between your ears. All you know to do is born girls. Have sense, no. I should thank Jasper," he mimicked. "God punish you."

"I'm sorry, sir," Charity reiterated, but Zona had already ended the call.

Next, Zona dialled his mother. His intention was to reprimand her: if Charity did not have the presence of mind to call the workman to repair the roof, what of Nne? Why invite another man to his house to succour his wife? Why belittle him at every opportunity? Their mother and Jasper had been conspiring against him behind his back and now co-opting his wife into their evil schemes.

His mother answered after several rings.

"Omeifeukwu. Did they say Rapu's shop was demolished?"

Iyom had seen Charity on the phone and had heard her cries to the universe. She was expecting a call from Zona and pre-empted his planned rant.

"When? I did not hear."

"He called me."

"Was it an illegal structure? There is a lot of that in the FCT. Are you getting my point?"

"Please call him."

"I will."

"Call him and see how you can help."

"I will," Zona repeated.

"Stay well."

"Let day break."

Good, Zona murmured as he put the phone down. Good. Good. They are going down gradually. Rapu's shop was demolished. Hopefully with all the goods inside. Nothing salvaged. He will have to start afresh from square one. Ground zero. Jasper's shop is running out of stock. Good.

Zona revelled in their misfortune, forgetting he had wanted to chastise his mother. He adjusted his top gown. It was warm inside the parlour. He checked the clock. Almost eleven. He scrolled down his list of contacts until he saw Rapu.

"Omeifeukwu," Rapu greeted at the second ring.

"Kedu?"

"Not so good, sir."

Good. Good. Good. "What happened?"

"Oh, has Nne told you? I came back from Oke Nmanwu's funeral to find my shop demolished. All my goods gone, many looted. Nothing salvaged. I have never seen such a calamity."

"I'm so sorry to hear that," Zona lied. "The landlord did not have a permit or what?"

"He has absconded. No one has seen him since that day."

"So sorry." It was hard to sound sympathetic.

"Just one rickshaw that my apprentice was able to salvage."

Zona said nothing.

"I have to start afresh," Rapu complained. "Imagine. The devil is a liar'"

"Take it easy. Are you getting my point? Take it easy."

"The devil is a liar," his junior sibling said again, seeking agreement.

Zona did not oblige. "So what next?"

"I don't know." There was dejection in the younger man's voice. "I really don't know. My intention was to sell off those wares and buy more stock. As it is now, I do not have the cash."

"I thought you had another shop."

"It is as yet empty. I was about to stock it when this calamity befell me."

Good. Zona thought as he listened to his brother's jeremiad. "If you have assets, sell, get capital. Are you getting my point? Then re-stock. I will be travelling abroad soon to load some containers."

"Assets? What assets do I have?"

"You have a plot of land. Are you getting my point? You can fling it. I would be willing to buy it off you. You can use the money to order merchandise. Are you getting me?"

Charity pursed her lips, shaken. She tossed the phone (and Zona's voice) away.

"Mtcheew," she hissed, long and wet, in the direction of Lagos. Then she scratched the ruddy earth and placed a pinch on her tongue. What had she done wrong? Thank his brother for helping to fix a roof. How did that justify all the abuse?

Zona was unpredictable. In recent times, he had been more loving. For a simple thing as his brother repairing a roof, he now sounded like a burst muffler. She thought of whom to call to assuage her feelings. Her younger sister came to mind. Yes. Oby. She reached for her phone again.

CHAPTER 44

Oby could hear singing as she alighted from the bus at the Awka marketplace. She checked the time: Two minutes past twelve. It was time for lunchtime prayers at the market. Would Charity's store be open? The words of the hymn drifted through the drizzle.

My song every day, Father, draw me nearer,
Draw me nearer, nearer to Thee.

She stood behind the motley clump of prayer warriors under flimsy awnings, singing with passion, her personal needs and prayer points in mind. Her life was in turmoil and in need of an urgent miracle. At the end, she made her way to her sister's shop, with the strains of the closing hymn for company.

Za m o, Chineke za m o
Za m o, onye ker'uwa za m o

Answer me, o, God, answer me
Answer, Creator of the world, answer.

She was wet when she got to the store. The shop reeked of a powerful flowery perfume. Charity was serving two clients, two stylishly clad women adorned with loads of jewellery that clinked against each other. Oby moved the swatches and bales of fabrics and created a spot to sit and listen to the pitches.

"Meet my sister, Oby," Charity said, extending a napkin to her.

The women turned and took a good stare at Oby. The resemblance was there: same small, pointed nose, the flat bridge and small eyes, the same lip configuration with the upper fleshier than the lower, like the bonnet of a tipper.

"Is that short for Obiageli?" one asked.

"No, Obiananma: One who comes for good."

"Nno," the buyers chorused.

"Thank you, fine ladies."

Charity opened several swathes of clothes for the clients to inspect and compare. "This is Aladdin lamp design."

She picked another. "This one is crowns, silver crowns. This other is lily of the valley."

"I prefer baby pink for myself and the groom's mother," one of the women said. "My old school friends will take blue, while my women's association will wear fuchsia. What do you think?"

"I have enough of all," Charity was quick to say. "Whatever you prefer. If you want fifty of baby pink, I have it. Fifty of the blue and purple. I can package and deliver. Each packet comes with a matching blouse material. I will give you a good wholesale price since...."

"Gini wu last price?"

"Fifteen thousand for the Aladdin design, twelve for the floral. Any colour. And let me tell you, you can sell to your friends at double that price. Easily."

The fan gulped overhead. The air was stuffy.

"I would have switched on the AC, but this is low current we have today," Charity said, noticing one woman blow air into her cleavage. "It cannot carry the AC."

She increased the speed of the fan. The women whispered between themselves. Charity whispered something to Oby, and she rose.

"What is the colour code of the wedding?" Charity asked, trying to keep the transaction on its toes.

"That is what we are trying to figure out. My daughter says pink and purple."

"I can get you different shades of pink for variety. Do not take one or two. Mix it up so the event will be colourful and bubbly. My neighbour here sells head ties, assorted. We can match them for you."

"All right."

"What of the groom's mother? Have you consulted her? She may have—"

"Mtcheew. Those poor people! Honestly, I don't know what my daughter saw in that family. I have to buy my ensemble and outfit the groom's mother, too."

"It's for uniformity," Charity offered lamely.

"Uniformity, my foot! At least as the groom, wete something," the bride's mother hissed. "Drop something on the table. Our people say that when many persons piss together—"

"The result foams," the others finished for her.

Oby returned with two bottles of malt. The women cheered up as they saw the condensation forming beads on the outside. After a long swig, the transaction moved faster.

"Calculate for fifty of each," the bride's mother said in between sips. If I need more, I shall let you know. I will remit to your account, i shipuo ro m."

"Ship to you. Perfect," Charity beamed. She sat down to write out an invoice.

"You have exquisite taste, ma," Oby said to bolster the sale.

"Daalu."

"Weddings are so expensive nowadays," Oby observed, "easily one million naira."

"Listen to what she is saying," the bride's mother sniggered. "Gini wu one million? I am budgeting nothing less than three million, let me tell you. For starters, the reception hall alone costurum five hundred thousand. By the time you factor in food and drinks, DJ, and MC for the traditional and church weddings, have you not exceeded one million?"

"If the two families cooperate, it reduces the burden," Oby said. "As our people say, if we piss together, it foams."

The two friends exchanged looks. "Exactly what we said."

"My dear, it is left for the bride's family to save the occasion, let me tell you. If you wait for the groom's people, shame will kill you."

A paper was torn out. "Here it is. Seven fifty thousand plus six hundred thousand plus thirty thousand. One million, three eighty thousand."

The woman opened her bag and tossed out several bundles of notes. Charity's face lost its shine. Money! She did not like to accept cash. It was risky. But she did not want to lose this huge sale either.

"Don't you do mobile transfer?" she asked. "I would prefer that."

"But we have the cash here already," the customer insisted.

The two sides stared at each other. Oby rescued her sister when she offered to go pay in the cash immediately before the banks closed.

The sisters did not have time to celebrate the jumbo sale. As soon as Oby returned, they heard a distant shout from the direction of the main gate: *Police! IPOB!*

A harum-scarum stampede ensued. Panicky traders flung their outside wares into stalls, locked up and bolted. Buyers concluded their errands and scampered to the exits. All around, traders were yelling orders to their wards. The two sisters shuttered the doors and scrammed.

"Thank God we concluded the sale," Charity said. She crossed herself. "Every day, there is trouble in this market. If it is not a pickpocket, it is IPOB. Or a mob action, jungle justice. Yesterday, police shot a man because he was wearing IPOB colours with the image of a rising sun."

Usually, after closing the shop, Charity rode as far as the Opaku Market bus stop and waited for her mother-in-law. Iyom would take them home and close for the day. Today, there was a crowd of people trooping hurriedly out of the business areas to the bus stop. In the distance, a chorus of baritone voices chanted a war song. Heavy footfalls pounded the ground.

"ALL WE ARE SAYING, GIVE US BIAFRA!"

Usually, several vehicles would by now be vying for passengers, "chancing" one another to pick up the fare, but none was in sight, except for a fleet of Police Hilux vans. Wayfarers stood like spectators at a soccer pitch, watching out for non-existent vehicles.

What is happening today? Charity wondered. *Nne should be here by now.* She pulled her sister along. The buzz of voices stifled conversation.

"ON IPOB WE STAND!"

"MNK IS OUR LEADER!"

Across the road, armed men in riot gear stood tight-assed. Their bogus helmets and bullet-proof fatigues instilled terror. Each one held a pump action rifle in one hand, a shield in the other. Ammunition belts hung loosely around their shoulders and waists. A *cordon sanitaire* of orange cones separated the security agents from the mob, a battalion of hefty men in black.

"IPOB OR DEATH! IPOB OR DEATH!" the horde of young men chanted. The protesters had black bandanas around their foreheads, and the vanguard lifted a pole with a tri-colour flag on it. Even without reading the words written across it, Charity recognized the rising sun. Children jostled one another and ran around in anticipation of the imminent commando action.

"Go home!" Oby swatted the minors. "Go!"

"Go!" Charity urged in her turn. Some looked the age of her Adaobi. Her eyes did not leave the road. Men and women began trekking down the way to meet the commercial vehicles farther down the road, where the vehicles made a U-turn before reaching the cordoned section. The IPOBians were unrelenting:

My mother, don't you worry
My father, don't you worry
If I happen to die
In the battlefield
Never mind, we shall meet again.

Charity nudged Oby. "Let us trek down. Perhaps Nne is there."

But her mother-in-law was not there. They stood by the road and waited. The clouds were gathering again, darkening the day. A minibus approached. At their level, it swerved. The busboy hopped down with a wad of notes wedged in his palm. The few passengers inside disembarked hurriedly.

"Opaku! Opaku! Opaku!"

When the sisters were tucked in beside the driver, Oby turned to her older sibling, "Sister, how far gone are you?"

"Second trimester."

"You need an apprentice. Find a girl to assist you."

"So?"

"Climbing the stool to reach the upper shelves is dangerous. And invest in a ladder. It is more balanced."

The vehicle was filling fast. The back row was already full. The middle row lacked one fare.

"Opaku! Opaku! One chance!"

A pre-pubescent girl ran to the bus with her pan of fruits. The aroma of overripe guava immediately pervaded the bus. The vehicle rolled away.

"You are right. I will mention it to Nne to be on the lookout for a suitable person. What brings you here?"

"Trouble."

"How are your kids?"

"Fine."

"That is the most important. What of hubby?"

Oby's husband was a pastor in one of the churches in Port Harcourt, *Thunder Fire Devil Ministries.* He was known among the people as Pastor Now-Now because, they said, he could storm heaven "sharp-sharp," hold a high-level meeting with God, and obtain immediate answers to people's problems. Many, drowning in life's sea of troubles, thronged to him. At a point, he ordained himself bishop.

"He has abandoned us."

The bus gathered speed. The conductor ran alongside it, then vaulted and rode shotgun on the sliding panel of the door. His half-buttoned shirt billowed in the wind like a sail.

"What happened, Oby?"

The driver adjusted the rear-view mirror bedecked with amulets and admonished his boy, "Ol' boy, enter well. Today get as e be."

The boy lurched into the van and slid the door shut. At once, the air supply diminished, and the smell of his unwashed body spread. When he reached out for the fare, passengers clutched their noses.

Oby picked up her story. "At a point, I noticed that he was always doing vigil. Every night, he would go for prayer sessions in the church, to return at dawn. One day, I confronted him. I said that some pastors used to have vigil once or twice a month; why was his every night?"

"What was his answer?"

"That many people were suffering in these hard times, needing intercessions."

"Didn't he have prayer warriors? Must he be the one to conduct the service every night?"

"Exactly what I asked him."

"Were you having relations?" Charity interrupted. "When they are doing special prayers, they claim they have to abstain."

"Exactly. One month, two months, no intimacy. I confronted him a second time. I said, 'So husband and wife cannot meet when you are doing vigil? Are you a Catholic priest now?' Anyway, I decided to go and join in the all-night prayer."

Charity flinched. "Wait. Did you warn him that you would—"

Oby shook her head.

A tricycle was hurtling towards them. Charity stretched her neck to see if it was Iyom. The tricycle breezed past, spurting exhaust fumes like a fusillade of gunshots. It jarred the commuters. Smoky air infiltrated the bus.

It was not Iyom.

"You should not have gone, Oby. So what happened? Did you find them casting out demons?"

It was Oby's turn to adjust herself in the seat to give more space to her sister. She put up a defiant look and cleared her throat. Charity could see her sister's eyes tear up and sense that what was coming was painful.

"The church was closed. At first, I thought maybe they went to a member's house to pray, as sometimes happens. I was about to leave when I heard moans inside the church office."

Charity flipped her fingers.

"They didn't even bother to lock the door because when I tried the handle, it opened, and I saw my children's father and the choir mistress. Her mouth was on his bri-bri, and his eyes were closed."

Charity passed Oby a paper napkin. The driver cast a quick look in the sisters' direction.

"Men!" Charity exclaimed. "What shall we do to them?" She looked to the driver for support.

"Sister, it's not a laughing matter."

"Do you see my teeth? Did you make a scene?"

"Honestly, I did not. I was anxious for my kids, all alone at home. I looked at the two weasels from the top of their heads to the ground, spat, and left. Innocent came back later when he knew I would be out and packed his stuff. The followers told me that he had relocated to Lagos. With the choir mistress."

"It is well."

"Even inside the well?" She smiled feebly at her attempt to joke.

"Nothing the eye will see to make it shed blood. Calm down. Do you not see me here in the village while my husband is in Lagos? Is that normal? I hear one UNILAG girl has taken over. Have I died? Am I not the one who made sales of over one million in one day? Kee nkwucha. What did I say?"

Oby sniffed.

"Yes. Brace up. Men nowadays are not like our fathers. But for the sake of our children, we must stand in the gap."

"Opaku Square!" the driver's mate announced.

The sisters disembarked and began the final stretch home.

"Have you done a scan, sis?"

"Why? If it is a female, to abort?"

"I think you should consider birth control. Have you seen how much kindergarten school fees cost now? How do you plan to send all these kids to school? Or will they trade?"

"God forbid! They must go to school?"

"With what? Spittle?"

"But you know our men with male children or lack thereof."

"And if you get a male child now, don't you see that you will discriminate against your daughters?"

"I don't think so."

"That is what you will say. Unconsciously, by continuing to the labour room until you get a male, you are already saying that a female is not it. You are setting yourself up for hunger. I have two kids, and I know how it is pinching me."

They met many villagers running errands on foot and exchanged greetings.

"How was today's market?"

"We thank God."

"Welcome o!"

"O-o! Let day break!"

"Sometimes in the hospital, you get a male, and the nurse will swap it with a female. She has sold your male to another. Or they tell you it was a stillbirth, that they have buried it, when, in fact, it has been sold. I will follow you into the labour room this time."

Charity looked hard at her younger sister. "It is well."

"You don't know what is happening nowadays. Children are so much in demand; they have become merchandise."

"Not just children, Oby, even adults. Consider the spate of kidnappings for ransom. But are you saying that I may have given birth to boys before and that they were swapped for girls?"

"It is possible."

Okonkwo's compound came into view.

"How long ago did Innocent move out?"

As the eldest daughter of the family, Charity had responsibility for her siblings. She was the settler of quarrels, the keeper of sanities.

"Three months ago."

Charity stopped. "And you waited this long, Oby?" It was a reprimand.

Oby swallowed hard. A husband abandons his kids and wife, and it is the wife that is chastised. It was indeed a man's world. "I thought his eyes would clear, that he would come back."

"With a woman involved? She must have tied him up in the spiritual domain."

"Hmmm."

"Where is she from?"

"Mbaise."

"Ha. Have you forgotten what our people say? If you see onye Mbaise and a snake, dispose of the Mbaise person first."

"But is that not how other tribes view the Igbo people? It is plain prejudice."

"We have our custom, my dear. You will go and report to our people. They will contact his people to ask if he is still interested in the marriage. But as I said earlier, brace up. He may not return. The woman may have tied him up. Consider Iyom, my mother-in-law. She operates a commercial tricycle. If she can do it to put food on the table, you can, too."

"I am not afraid of work," Oby said, shaking her head. "But with two kids, rent, school fees? I operate a small restaurant, sis. How much can that put on the table?"

"Here we are!"

Charity pushed the giant gate. It creaked as it swung back and forth on its hinges. A racket ensued as Adaobi and her sisters made a beeline for their mother, almost pushing her down. "Mummy! Mummy!"

Charity had forgotten to buy treats for the kids. She usually bought peanuts and bananas. Today, Oby's unscheduled arrival and the last sale of the day had disorganized her schedule, to say nothing of the presence of the security agents and the standoff with the IPOBians and Iyom's absence.

Fortunately, Oby had brought food gifts. She unpacked palm kernel nuts and breadfruit seed, a delicacy, and presented them to Charity, who offered them to her daughters. A loaf of bread and tamarinds also emerged from Oby's bag, and the kids ran off to share the haul.

"I see Iyom's keke is here," Charity said. "She must have come home rather than risk the roads today."

Oby went to greet Iyom.

While they talked, Charity called Zona to tell him that her sister was visiting and would spend the night.

"No problem," he said. He sounded content, Charity noticed. Maybe the UNILAG girl was on his lap as they spoke. "How is the cloth business?"

"We are managing," Charity answered cautiously. She did not want to show that she was enjoying it or that business was good. He might take her money and shut down the store to spoil her happiness.

"You will lend me money soon to put into my hotel project," Zona said, expressing Charity's fears. "Are you getting me?"

"Ha. I was even asking whether you can inject something more into my account so I can stay above water."

"Have you not seen the hotel project I am struggling to put up?" Zona barked. "If it comes to injecting even a penny into your shop, you close it and stay home. Are you getting my point? I can still feed you and your children."

"But you gave one million to Opaku Union. When it's Char—"

"O-o-o. I should have given it to you instead."

Bats filled the air. After a few seconds, Zona continued. "You were the one crying shop, shop, shop. I open one for you now—"

"We are managing, I said." Charity did not want this conversation to drag on.

"Better. How is Nne?"

"She is well."

"Adaobi and her siblings, kwan?"

"No problem, sir."

"I see your stomach is shooting out again."

"Thanks to you."

"When are you due?"

"When God says."

"What are you dropping this time?"

"What you put inside. I want to help Iyom. We have an extra mouth to feed."

Zona realized that he had rubbed her on the wrong side. "All right," he said. "Let day break."

CHAPTER 45

"What is the world turning to?" Iyom exclaimed when Charity told her about Obiananma's ordeal. "What is this sickness with men that, when they see a woman, they forget themselves and plunge headlong into it, like a gwongworo going downhill? What sickness is this? Is it a done thing?" She spread her arms wide, looked up at the indigo sky, and grimaced. She pouted her lips like a duck's.

"I was telling her about Zona, how he sent us away because of one UNILAG girl. If not that I had the presence of mind to come to Nne."

"Brace up," Iyom said to Oby.

"Exactly what I told her."

"Brace up," Iyom continued, fixing her gaze on Oby. "Find something to do; train your children." She turned back to Charity. "I was telling your sister about Agbisi—how, from nowhere, a woman's husband died, and she said that Agbisi would be her lover. Of all the men in our community, it is Mgboye's husband that she coveted. 'Is it Mgboye who killed your husband?' I asked. 'Agbisi, a family man? What of the able-bodied young men perambulating Opaku? No, it is Agbisi.'"

Iyom flipped her thumb and middle finger to the gods. "That is how Agbisi left the children that he should have trained, went and bought a motorcycle for the widow, built her a house, my fellow woman. Money for school fees went into cloth and scarf and whatnot."

"Nne, are you still talking about that matter?" Charity cut in. "Forget it. Zona and his brothers have grown."

"They have grown, but I wanted them to go to school, to sharpen their minds. Will everybody be in the trading business? Some can be in public service. Without education, you are constrained to pursue money till you die. Government workers will work some, then rest, and get pension. Instead, Agbisi neglected his sons."

"It is well, Nne." Charity tried to divert the old woman's emotions. Agbisi and Akwaeke's issue unhinged her. "Have you eaten?"

"No. I plan to call up some okazi soup. I don't eat the wormy thing Chisom is preparing."

"You came home early today, Nne," Charity observed. "We were looking out for you on the way."

Iyom hunched her shoulders, then looked for a seat. She had been standing for long. "Since I was born, I have never seen a day like today in Opaku," she said, gathering the skirt of her long frock around her. Her legs, like a stork's, were exposed briefly.

"MASSOB, IPOB, sloganeering," Oby put in.

"Police everywhere. Every side road I took to get to the main market was blocked. I had to brave it through the town. Two times, my keke was mired in clay. Two times, benevolent people helped push it out. On getting to the hospital junction, police stopped me and asked for my particulars."

"He-e!" Charity and her sister clapped hands in amazement. "Does Nne have particulars?"

"I asked him, 'What is particular?'"

The girls laughed at how Iyom exaggerated her looks, opened her eyes wide, and stretched her neck like an ostrich's.

"It is driver's licence and vehicle papers, Nne," Oby explained.

"For a tricycle? In the village?"

"Nne, every vehicle must have documents. But it is 'parti-kola' the police want. Money for kola nut."

"People rebuked him and told him to leave an old woman alone."

"So what did you do?"

"I came home. My legs were hurting, squeezed up all day in that cramped space." Iyom hugged her knees. "And bumping in and out of those potholes." She stretched her legs out one at a time till she heard the knee unlock. Then she brought them together again and massaged her thighs.

"What of you, Charity? How was business?"

"We thank God. We have traded today's own. Let me see to the children, Nne."

Night had dawned. There was no electricity, but the moon was out in full. After dinner, Oby assembled Adaobi and her sisters and told them folktales. Charity lay on one side of the mat, replaying the day's activities in her mind. Iyom lounged beside her. The clouds drifting away commanded her attention. Chisom massaged the matriarch's joints with palm kernel oil. Its mild scent was soothing. Crickets chirped, and cicadas trilled and twinkled about them. Mosquitoes buzzed intermittently in their ears and in circles above them. The children clapped randomly to kill them.

"Ooo, these mosquitoes!" Adaobi moaned.

The guttural symphony of the frogs roared from the brushes. In the distance, a dog yelped. Chisom ran in and emerged with a mosquito coil, which she lit. Its fumes soon swirled up above them and chased away the bugs. Iyom spread one of her old clothes over the youngsters, and they snuggled close to one another. It was hygge.

"Otiii!" Oby yelled.

"Ayooo!" The children hollered in response, excited by a forthcoming tale.

"Children, there is a story I shall tell you."

"Tell us, tell us again and again; we shall listen to know if it is sweet," the children responded with gusto. Stories excited them and transported them to other realities and other lands.

The women nestled close to each other. At first, their minds cruised around their hardscrabble lives and the headwinds and crosswinds they faced. Gradually, the night breeze salved them, and they surrendered to its bucolic delights.

CHAPTER 46

It was Sunday. Zona lazed about the lounge, too drained to go to church, thinking of his bout of sentimental incontinence. Charity was expecting, Modupe was expecting, and maybe Helen too. Since her return from Umuahia, she pestered him to go meet her people.

"Soon," Zona told her, to get some peace.

She had nagged him about it until he had snapped and threatened to drive her out. "I banished my wife to the village because of you," he growled, wagging his index finger. "That is not enough? Charity does not disturb me the way you do. Are you getting my point? You have not even entered, and you nag like this. If you enter, that means war."

Helen "borrowed herself some sense" and gave him some respite.

Zona was getting tired of her. In truth, he did not want to continue the relationship. Modupe had gobsmacked him. With her, he had all the intimacy a man could ask for. He liked how she activated his senses, muscles, juices. *Oko yin dun,* she had called out the second time after tutoring him.

Okoye?

She had tapped his penis, his wilted but happy penis. *Oko. Your prick is sweet.*

And they had laughed and laughed over the matter.

My title is Omeifeukwu, Doer of Great Things, he had told her solemnly. *Call me that.* He had coached her on its pronunciation. But she could never get it right.

Omifiku, Omifuku, she repeated. And they had laughed and laughed again and again at her failed attempts to pronounce the Igbo phrase.

It baffled him that Modupe never asked for money. Even when she announced that she was expecting, which surprised him no end. Lagos girls were known as money guzzlers. To them, a man was a cash dispenser.

God will soon increase the number of your descendants, was how she put it one evening after they had cleaned up. He had turned to face her.

Increase my descendants? As how?

As in, you have scored a goal. Are you getting my point? She mimicked his trademark phrase.

A goal?

Yes o! She had rubbed her stomach.

He should have known. All this romping without a condom.

I thought you were using contraception.

Contra kini? You, Baba, you use condom?

Indeed why not? Bedding a woman of thirty, in full reproductive years, without rubber. He had been asking for it. But she was not complaining. Not worried, not asking what do we do now? In fact, it looked like she had it planned.

What was he getting himself into? he asked the rotating blades of the ceiling fan. They rolled lazily around the blue bulb attached to it. He and Modupe always met here, in the Simpson's family house. Modupe never asked to visit him or to go to short-stay inns. Each time he arrived nowadays, and it was often, she received him well, kneeling on both knees before rising to minister to him. Here was a dame who was grateful for his attention. Here was a dame who appreciated that skirts came cheap in Lagos, and if you had a man who said hello to you, you were lucky. The competition was stiff, and so far, she had asked for nothing in return. She did not ask for an upkeep allowance, pocket money, rent, or car. She was self-reliant, a rich businesswoman.

Granted, she was not pretty. Height was one of the things she had going for her. She had a pimply face and an awkward carriage. Her face was oblong, with small, alert eyes which she kohled heavily. She reminded him of the FESTAC mask. One-inch-long marks pierced each cheek horizontally. He had seen this face erupt in acne, probably during the monthlies. Her hips were something else, though. They were her major attraction. When he picked her up at Iyaro, she had been wearing a girdle, so he had not noticed them. At the end of that journey, he had dropped her at the Costain/Iponri Underpass before circling back to Alaka. He had slipped his business card into her hand.

During the week, she had paid him a visit at the shop, toting a lunch basket of amala and ewedu with titus fish, cow skin, and cow foot.

Thank you, sir, for the lift, she had said when she dropped the lunch basket to return to her shop at Gutter.

The next day, Zona had wanted his boys to return the dishes, but she said not to worry, that she would pass by and pick them up.

Do not eat lunch o. I am bringing another dish today, she announced.

He was enamoured of the delicacies. The following Sunday, when there was no market, he missed her cooking. And the woman. As he was alone in the house, he had called her and invited her over.

Are you not married? I don't want your wife to break my head," Modupe said.

She is not around.

Why not come? she had suggested instead.

What about your mother?

What about her?

He had dived into the car and gone to Yaba, all worked up and expectant. That was the first meeting with Alhaja and a retinue of neighbours, tenants, and extended family. Oko Modupe, they called him. Oko omo Alhaja. Modupe's husband. The first time he ate Modupe's yam porridge with bits of liver and herbs, he understood why Esau sold his birthright.

With Helen's return, he had to look for excuses to leave the house on Sunday. A town meeting. A village meeting. Another time, a church meeting. Today, he dressed up and sat down to burrow into his shoes. Helen insisted on accompanying him.

"To where?" he asked as he made a show of cleaning his shoes.

"To the town meeting."

"As what?"

"As wife."

He laughed uproariously, his head tilted back on the headrest. When he returned to normal, he tried to reason with her.

"See that photo over there?" It was the wedding photo of him and Charity on the wall. "These people know Charity. They don't know you. Are you getting my point? So, take it easy. When you get a photo like that, you can accompany me out, not before. Are you getting me?"

"When will they know me?" she fired back, looking at him like a traffic warden at an offender, one hand akimbo, one foot tapping the floor. "Is it not up to you to do what is expected of you so they can know me? They don't know me," she sniggered.

"Look, Helen, I am a Catholic. Are you getting my point? I am also a Knight. I cannot marry two wives."

There! He had let it out. Now, she knows where things stand.

"You did not know you were a Catholic when you befriended me?" Her voice rose to the high heavens. "Do you know how many marriages I turned down because of you?"

"We will discuss it when I return," he said, eager for Modupe's ministering and pampering. He needed time to think about what was next. *You turned down many marriages?* Her voice echoed in his head. *In your dreams.*

Later that night, when he returned home, the outline of the rectangle where his wedding photo had hung gaped at him. Below, splintered glass glistened from the outside light. A marker had been put on the smiling faces of the bride and groom, defacing them beyond recognition.

The Daily Sun
The pan-Igbo organization, Ohanaeze Nd'Igbo, has condemned the fatal shooting of an Igbo youth in a face-off between Nigerian soldiers and peaceful demonstrators in Opaku. The President-General of the group, Chief John Nwodo, appealed to the head of state to demilitarize the South-East and find a political solution to the clamour for independence. "It is the marginalization of the Igbos that is at the root of the unrest," he postulated, calling for equity and fairness in the distribution of the dividends of democracy.

CHAPTER 47

Zona was thinking. *I have a wife in the village, a live-in mistress in Lagos, and another sidekick who is pregnant.* The juggling was too much strain. He vowed to send Helen away with a handsome settlement and maintain the arrangement with Modupe. Charity appeared contented with her business in the East. On the completion of the Rangers Hotel, he hoped to gradually expand to the home front 'as per' Aku lue uno. Invest at home.

But this child, Modupe's child? Would it be his? Bear his name? Or would he have to pay Modupe's bride price for the child to be legitimately his? If not the bride price, a civil marriage? Charity would not know. But what of Helen? She would scatter his house. No, it's better to ease her out. And what of the Catholic Church? He would be excommunicated if they found out he was into multiple marriages. What a shame to attend Mass and never take the holy communion? It would be better to leave the Church completely. There were options now. He could change to the Anglican Church. They seemed to accept polygamy. Or even join a Pentecostal assembly. They were everywhere. Oby's husband had a church. Bishop Now-Now would welcome him. All it would take was a hefty envelope or seed sowing into the Building Fund. They were always building something.

What if Modupe gave birth to a boy? Would the baby be his heir? Was he the only one sleeping with her? People in the house called him Modupe's husband. And since he had been coming in the past six months, he had not met any other man or her absence. He was sure he was her only lover. But what if she also gave birth to a girl? She had said their women bore only females. He hissed. He had enough daughters.

At his next visit, he suggested that she abort the pregnancy.

"God forbid!" She flipped both indexes against the two thumbs and cast them away.

"I have enough daughters," Zona said.

"I don't."

They looked at each other; he pleadingly, she with nonchalance.

"Maybe you don't understand." She pointed to her stomach. "This is a miracle. I never, we never expected that we could have more than one child. That is why I did not mention condom to you. Our women were destined to have only one daughter. Moomie born only Alhaja. Alhaja born only me. This is a miracle."

He brought out some wads and placed them on the table. "Please go and do a scan. If female, remove it. Please. I don't want any more females."

She took the money and shoved it back into his briefcase. "Keep your money, Mister. I am telling you a second pregnancy is a miracle, you are talking about removing it. Laye laye. Never!"

When Alhaja learnt of Zona's stance, she told her daughter to cut all ties with the *omo Ibo,* never to see him again.

At her next antenatal visit, Modupe requested a scan, not to know the baby's gender, but to ascertain that it was thriving.

"The fetus is viable," the doctor said, handing her a photo. "The way it is presented, we can see the genitals. It is male. Congrats!"

She broke the news to her mother first. Alhaja fell to her knees and praised Allah, and then she danced around the compound, screaming, "The curse is broken! The curse is broken! Allah be praised! The curse is broken."

Not only a second grandchild but a male!

Next, Modupe summoned Zona. He had stayed away for some time, sulking. But he missed Modupe. He missed how she made him feel like royalty and ministered to him without any demands or nagging. He missed the delicious meals. His brain associated her with good times, with the delights of the flesh. He raced to Herbert Macaulay.

"And na boy, sef."

"What did you say?" He was incredulous.

"I say na man. Baba bomboi!" she teased him.

A son. At last, a son!

"Modupe Simpson!"

"Omifiku."

"Modupe!"

"Baba Bomboi."

He had wanted to abort a boy! A male child! After all these years! He fell on his knees by her bedside and began croaking one of the market fellowship hymns. He vowed to take care of mother and child, his son.

Still, she never asked for money, unlike Helen, who asked for money from morning till night. Even Charity appeared to be self-sufficient now. He paid the children's school fees and sent chop money. That was it. No extras. But Helen? *Gimme gimme gimme. Money money money.* Money orbited every conversation.

He would name the boy after his father, Joachim. Yes, Joachim; middle name, Ezenwa, head of all the children. Jasper fathered sons before him but called them strange names. His son will bear Agbisi's name.

Another thought struck him. Why name his son after that wicked tomcat? After the scandal he tainted Iyom and her kids with? He was already a lad when Agbisi started frequenting Akwaeke. He knew because his father would leave in the late evening and not return till the next day. He knew because sometimes, when Iyom went to the farm, Akwaeke would sneak in, and Agbisi would banish him and his brothers out in the yard. What of the times Agbisi sent him with presents to the widow? Swatches of fabric, bags, slippers? What of the yams and domestic animals he gave Zona to carry to the widow? He used to obey because it was inconceivable to say no to one's father. Even when Jonas's son warned him to never set foot again in their house or risk losing all his teeth. Even when Iyom picked a quarrel with Agbisi. He could still remember her shrill voice: *Agbisi, Agbisi, you have three sons, Agbisi. Train your children. Do not waste your resources on the widow. Agbisi, send your sons to school.* But the lure of Akwaeke's honeypot must have been too over-powering.

Zona was in Primary Six at the Opaku Central School. He had passed into the famous Okongwu Secondary School, Nnewi. All of Iyom's pleas to Agbisi to send his boys to school fell on deaf ears. *They will learn a trade,* he had maintained. Out of Iyom's meagre savings, she was able to enrol her first son in school and pay for the first year. Echezona was brilliant and excelled in school, but Iyom's resources soon ran out. She persevered, selling off jewelry and her prized clothes till he reached Form Four. Echezona would not return to Form Five even though he had come first in the session's exams.

Agbisi, please, in the name of God, train your boys, Iyom had pleaded to deaf ears. *At least the first son. Train Echezona to Senior Secondary.* But Agbisi had diverted his resources from the burgeoning tailoring business to Akwaeke. He bought her a Vespa and mowed down her mud house. In its place, he supervised the erection of a cement house, plucked out the withered thatched roofing, and substituted it with modern shingles. The widow's sons were in primary school when Zona scratched from Okongwu and was sent to do apprenticeship in motor spare parts with Chief Moneke, president of the Igbo Union in Kano.

Suddenly, it occurred to him that he was the true son of his father. What he was doing with Modupe, was it not what Agbisi did with Akwaeke? He had all but abandoned his responsibilities to his wife and children and had become obsessed with a mistress. Now he knew how Agbisi felt with Akwaeke, understood the tenacity, the unflinching attention. People accused Akwaeke of fetishizing Agbisi and of feeding him a love potion. Had Modupe mixed something for him? He could not tell. All those dishes she brought to his shop and the ones he downed at Herbert Macaulay. The only sure elixir she was guilty of feeding him was the one she sat on. That and her ministrations fueled his love, combusted his desire, and powered these "away matches" like a diesel engine.

"Well, let the baby be born first, and we will see," he concluded. "Are you getting my point? Look after yourself. If you need anything—"

"I am getting your point." They laughed.

He placed a wad of notes on the ottoman. A man must look after his woman, even if she was well-to-do, he told himself. If she was poor, she would use the money to feed well, smell sweet, and decorate herself for general maintenance costs, as women called it. If she could afford it, well, then the money was landing charges.

"Eat well, look after my boy." He wagged his finger at her playfully.

Modupe was elated, thanking God that he had come around, though nothing on earth would have made her do what he had contemplated.

She teased him. "E-e. Because na male, 'Look after my boy.' If na girl, 'Remove it!' O ga!"

He put on his clothes, drew her nearer, and planted a noisy, prolonged kiss on her forehead. Without underwear, she dressed up to see him to the car. As she walked, her wrapper dived into the line dividing her rear cheeks. They zig-zagged like the faulty tyres of a Mack truck. Her headlamps gyrated. He liked to watch her.

"O daaro!" Alhaja shouted from the alcove. "Good night o, Shief!"

"Good night, Alhaja," he greeted in return, inclining a little.

It was the signal the whole yard was waiting for. It erupted in a flurry of greetings.

"O daaro, sir."

"O daaro, oko Modupe.'

"O daaro," Zona waved.

"You will speak Yoruba by force," his mistress smiled, unabashed.

"For your sake, I will learn it."

He was in seventh heaven and felt like the Oba of Lagos.

"Thank you, sir." She curtsied. "Omifuku."

~

One day, Zona was in the shop when Modupe came calling. She had the usual basket with a mini cooler inside, covered with lace linens and napkins.

"I brought you Sallah meat from Alhaja."

She was dressed in a long, floral flowing robe with lace trimmings. A hijab covered her thatch. Lots of kinky and noisy jewellery adorned her neck and wrists. A pair of gold hoops descended from her ear lobes. She exuded a strong oud perfume.

The past weekend had been Eid-El-Kabir.

Zona lifted the antimacassar. "All these for me?" He led her inside the small office. They embraced.

Modupe opened the dishes. Apart from the amala and soup, a whole plate was filled with roasted mutton.

"Wow!" he gushed, inhaling the aroma of fried onions, Nsukka pepper, and curry. "Thank Alhaja for me."

"She will hear."

He pulled Modupe close and caressed her midriff. "How is my boy?"

"Your boy is kicking fine."

She did not wait around. "I have to return to the shop," she said. He grabbed her wrist. He locked the door, aiming for a little loving, but she twisted free.

"Look after my boy."

Zona plunged into the meat. There was a mix of cuts—innards, flesh, rib, skin, all deliciously spiced. Satiated, he passed the rest to his salivating apprentices. Then he stretched.

He folded the copy of the *Daily Sun* he was holding. IPOB news filled the pages. The government was unshaken in decimating them, fishing them out and mowing them down. What of kidnappers and bandits and Boko Haram terrorists? Kid gloves there. He needed to walk the market, feel its pulse, and get some air. His goods were on the high seas. He was thinking of another trip to China, this time to procure the fixtures for his hotel. It would be cheaper, straight from the factory. Middlemen inflated prices. He had a catalogue and was earmarking the pieces. Every item of furniture, from the sanitary wares to the kitchen and restaurant equipment, would be ordered directly from the factory in Shenzhen. *Ship through Kano,* a Customs officer had whispered to him, *and pay no duty.*

"I'm stepping out," he said to the head apprentice.

The weather was balmy. A thin cloud covered the azure sky. A mild breeze blew from the Atlantic, circulating different whiffs in the air, sometimes of food, other times of gunk. The afternoon was ebbing away leisurely. The market was as boisterous as ever. Throngs of people hurried in all directions; colourful umbrellas of telecom providers flapped above mobile phone entrepreneurs. Zona clutched his nose. The carcass of a rat, bloated almost to the size of a kitten, lay amid discarded corn husks and plastic sachets and the ubiquitous black mayonnaise underfoot. Music sellers blared different tracks to attract buyers. *Is every music not on YouTube now? Why buy CDs?* He sidestepped a cripple on the path, brandishing a bowl for alms. A hawker with several belts harnessed to his shoulder proposed a number to him. He declined. He hardly wore corporate attires because of his ballooning midsection, preferring the loose local outfits with capacious tops and draw-stringed bottoms.

Jasper's shop was along the way. He went by and was surprised to see it shuttered. Itinerant sellers had set up shop in front of its appurtenances. Two female hawkers dozed on the bare ground, their trays of wares beside them.

"Omeifeukwu!" the locals hailed when he came into view.

He waved. "What is happening with Jasper Gee?" he asked, pointing to his brother's shop. Perhaps he had run out of stock again.

"His apprentice is indisposed," someone answered. "Jasper took him for treatment."

Good. Good. Good. "Since when?"

"Two days now, sir."

"Oh. I did not hear. I will call him."

He had no intention of calling. Each to his own. Shop closed, no revenue. *Good.* A Jeep to run, male twins to feed, and no income. Good. A sick apprentice meant medical expenses. Good. Good. Good. He remembered Amata's dowry dotting the village house, with nowhere to install any of it, and his Schadenfreude increased. *Yet he is gunning for land to build,* with his shop closed and with depleting stock. *Good good good.* Boy King, indeed.

~

Before closing time, Orimili Nnewi sent his boy to get a set of Nissan shock absorbers from Jasper. It was the boy who reported that Jasper's shop was closed. The chief called Jasper immediately.

"Orimili," Jasper greeted.

"Your shop i-s closed. I sent my boy to get some part for a cus-tomer."

"Thank you, sir. My apprentice fell ill. We are at the Medical Centre."

"Since when?"

"Tabato, sir." Three days ago.

"How is it do-doing him?"

"He says his whole body is aching, and he cannot stand for long. Shivering."

"Is it malaria?"

"No, sir. The clinic ran a test. Came back negative."

"Typhoid?"

"Negative Widal test too, sir. I have never seen this kain thing."

"Send hi-m home," Orimili said curtly.

"Sir?"

"S-send him home imme-diately. Let him continue treatment at home. Do you hear what I am s-saying?"

"Yes, sir."

"If anything happens to him in Lagos, God forbid, you will be accused of using him for money rituals. Send him ho-home."

"Orimili."

"That means the shop will be closed for one week," Jasper told Amata that evening.

They were discussing Orimili's advice to send Ebuka to Opaku.

"I can start going to the shop again," Amata said. "The boys are big enough."

"But Omenma is too small to mind two active toddlers," Jasper protested.

He could not think properly. Ebuka's health niggled at his mind. Every entrepreneur craved healthy apprentices, not one that sprang health challenges. As an apprentice, you were there to grow your master's business, to help him expand, not to be a drain on his resources. You were expected to build the funds from which he would draw to set you up. For two days, Jasper had not opened the shop. To boot, he was expending money to nurse Ebuka back to health.

"We can all go. The boys can play or sleep at the back. People do it all the time."

She was right. Uncountable children accompanied their parents to the market. They played with other kids around family stalls and sheds and dozed under tables. Some ran errands. Many sold in the temporary absence of the adults. Jasper said nothing. He massaged his temple and pulled at his moustache.

"We will take food and drinks."

Jasper was calculating his losses. Now, he would add the cost of another junket to the East. The doctors at the Federal Medical Centre had said Ebuka would be fine with time, but Orimili's advice had merit. It is better to let Ebuka's parents see him alive and nurse him back to health. He remembered Ebuka's father, Elder Okeke's admonition: *If anything happened to Ebuka, his mother would not survive it.* Worse would be if he was accused of using Ebuka for rituals.

He looked at Amata. Since she had the babies, she had been home. She looked the better for it, resting and watching over the house, far from the hustle and bustle of Lagos life and the humid weather that made one perspire like an over-heating radiator. Between Ebuka and him, they had managed the shop.

"You could close early. Latest five pm, you leave the market."

She nodded consensus.

He began to throw the ball into the rim of the toy basketball hoop. His twins watched with excitement. They were on the floor, propped up against the sofa, the cups' snouts firmly in their mouths, their eyes darting from their father's hands to the floor to the net.

The next day, Jasper drove his apprentice to the East in his wife's Camry. Numerous roadblocks, extortion posts, actually, slowed them, but he controlled his temper, tipping a crumpled note into the palms of the uniformed sleeves to save time. From experience, he knew that all the vehicle papers could never be complete. Some road blockers had been known to ask for the emergency triangle, a fire extinguisher, and a waste basket. Last Christmas, car owners told of how they had been asked to tender the receipts of the customs duty paid on their vehicles. Many abandoned their family on the roadside to rush back to their stations for the document.

"Tell me what concerns traffic police with customs duty," he grumbled to Ebuka, reclining beside him. "It's extortion, pure and simple. And hard-heartedness to make our people suffer. Mark my words, one day will come when our people will fight back, clear these people from our space."

They reached Opaku late evening. Jasper drove straight to Elder Okeke's compound.

"I will take him to the clinic near the marketplace," he told Ebuka's father, "To continue treatment there."

Ebuka's mother jumped into the car, but her husband ordered her out. He accompanied Jasper to the clinic, where Ebuka was admitted. Jasper paid all the charges.

"I do not know, but every two years or so, a strange illness strikes Ebuka," Elder Okeke said casually on their way out of the facility. He was in the middle of sending a thumb of snuff into his nostril. He paused to hook the crook of his walking stick into his wrist. "His body shuts down. After a while, it will re-open for business, and life goes on." He sent the snuff up, sniffed repeatedly, then clapped his hands to shake off remnants. "We are aware of it."

Jasper's lips chewed one another.

"Thank you for the care you lavish on him."

It was late at night when Jasper knocked on his mother's gate. He was surprised to find Rapu at home. They exchanged greetings. Jasper explained his mission home.

"You did well," Iyom said when he finished. "Orimili is a wise man."

The following morning, after the brothers had downed a mound of cassava fufu and okro soup, Rapu revealed his plans to travel to South Africa.

"Since my shop was demolished, I have not been myself." He bent his head, unwilling to look up, knowing that there was a silent sibling rivalry and he fell behind.

"I thought you had another shop," Jasper asked politely, but he saw Rapu frown. He must be feeling frustrated, Jasper thought, lagging behind in this silent competition among brothers.

"Yes. But I was yet to stock it. I lost over ninety percent of my wares and savings in the demolition."

"It can't be easy." Jasper empathized. "We are on our own. If we make it, all well and good, but when we lose, we are alone in bearing the cross. No insurance, no mitigation of the risks. You dust yourself and move on."

"Only one keke was saved," Rapu continued. "Or so Stanley claimed. I drove it for commercial service, to get chop money. But the police extortion was strangulating me. Transporters work for the police. They eat all our profit from the constant demand for bribes. With the bad roads, breakdowns, fuel consumption, in the long run, one does not break even."

"I know. Over here in the East, it is worse. Once you cross The Niger Bridge, you meet a roadblock every hundred meters. And it is money they want. Nothing else. We are an occupied territory."

They paused, each brother occupied with his own thoughts. Eventually, Rapu spoke. "I want to go try my luck in Joburg. My house rent will soon be due. I do not have it. I paid two years' rent up front for the plaza shop. The landlord absconded with it."

"Do you know your way around South Africa?"

"I met someone in Abuja who is based there. I will connect with him."

"We hear terrible things about that place, how they do not like our people. That we are taking over their businesses, their women."

"We cannot, because of death, shun war," Rapu quoted soberly.

After a while, Jasper asked, "What of your apprentice? What will become of him?"

"I don't know yet. I'm still reflecting."

"He could manage the new shop. Whatever he is able to—"

The agreement between Master and Apprentice was sacrosanct, not to be breached capriciously, except by the unscrupulous.

"Stanley is a womanizer," Rapu blurted out, unable to calm his galloping nerves. "He will run the shop aground. I have been trying to control him. If I'm not there, he is certain to go overboard."

Jasper cringed. "An apprentice, a womanizer? What shall we call this? Is he not living with you?"

"No. I have only a one-room apartment."

"How do you control him then? Twenty-four hours a day, you should know the whereabouts of your apprentice. Even if it means him sleeping on the corridor or veranda. That is part of the training. With what money does he womanize? Do you pay him salary?"

"I am sure he has been robbing me."

Jasper reflected further on the matter. Apprentice living large, chasing skirt? When he served Oke Nmanwu, he did not know any girl's name, talk less of befriending one. In Oke Nmanwu's service, you accounted for every minute of the day. Church service, errands, apprentices went together.

"An apprentice, a womanizer?" Iyom echoed. "Is that what he went to Abuja to do? If he impregnates a girl, what do you do?"

"But he has served you for several years," Jasper maintained. "He is entitled to some settlement if you are going away. For equity's sake."

"I don't know. I will compensate him somehow. I have not decided yet."

Iyom interrupted their talk. "Jasper, I hear that Donatus is looking to sell their land by the Central School. Go for it. I am going to the market. Let me see if I can make some money out of people returning from the morning market."

"Thank you, Nne," Jasper replied. "I will go and see Donatus in the evening. As for going to the market to carry passengers, I think it is too dangerous, Nne. You have no licence, and the roads are terrible. If something happens… God forbid! And your leg problem."

Iyom had recounted her experience with the traffic police for the tricycle's documents and her own driver's licence.

"How will I eat?" his mother asked, alarmed.

"I will see if my in-law can supply you drinks to sell here," Jasper said, thinking on his feet. He cast a quick look around the compound. There was ample space for a table-top enterprise. "He is a major distributor. You can switch to selling drinks. It is better than the keke, biko."

"What will happen to my keke?"

"You can get someone to drive it and make daily returns to you. Or you sell it."

"I can't sell it. Charity is expecting. We may need it in an emergency."

"After her delivery, you sell it, though Omeifeukwu can afford to buy his wife a jalopy."

"Jasper Gee!" the matriarch cried. "You always think of your mother. Thank you. May God bless you more."

"Amen."

Rapu recoiled.

CHAPTER 48

After lunch, Rapu sneaked to the local witch doctor. Otogirigiri sat cross-legged among his paraphernalia. As the client advanced on the squiggly path to his shrine, he kept his eyes on a basket of water before him, thinking, *This must be a yahoo-yahoo job.* Internet fraudsters were a shaman's best customers. *Do something for me so that when I make a pitch to white folks, they will believe me and send the cash.*

If so, Otogirigiri would need a human tongue, which he would coat with charms and get the customer to ingest. It rendered the words of the fraudster sweet across the airwaves and able to convince his potential victims in Australia and Canada, New Zealand, America, and Brazil to make the Western Union transfer. It raked in a percentage for the shaman, too.

Or was it an abductor? Recently, a parade of child abductors had come calling, looking for toddler-enticing charms. He had such a potion, already pre-mixed in biscuits. Once a toddler ate it, he or she would follow you to the ends of the earth, no looking back. Yes, he decided. This customer looked like an abductor: young, dashing. A ladies' man lacking the cash to fuel his lifestyle. An aeroplane landed in the basket of water with a splash. Otogirigiri ducked.

"It is about my parcel of land," the client said, backing the red covering on the door. "I want to safeguard it against trespass."

If Otogirigiri recognized his townsman, he did not let on. Parcel of land.

"Is it in contention?"

"Envy and grabbing exist among siblings. I want to safeguard what is mine."

"Naturally."

So, it was a land matter. One of Agbisi's sons. Was he disputing a parcel of land with another or wanted the fellow dead? No, just a simple safeguard. They set out to view the land.

Money exchanged hands.

Later that evening, Otogirigiri went back to the land and, amid incantations and ululations, concocted his potion. He attached a red cloth to a clay pot and hung the fetish on a birch at the edge of the plot for all to see.

"Any trespasser who steps into this land even to pluck a fruit will not see the morrow," Otogirigiri swore. He flung his goatskin bag behind him and tucked in his loin cloth.

Rapu nodded in complete agreement.

On the way out of the bush, Otogirigiri asked, "I see you in an aeroplane."

Rapu was taken aback.

"I'm planning to travel." He paused. Might as well divulge the destination. "To South Africa."

They stopped. Big bags drooped from the medicine man's eyes. Tufts of snuff-stained hair protruded from his nostrils.

"Have you done insurance for abroad hustle, for foreign currency?"

Rapu had never heard of that.

"You want to go and hustle abroad without protection? My people perish for lack of knowledge. My man, do what your mates are doing. It is war out there. Don't go to battle naked, without ammunition."

"You are right."

"It would require a ram."

"I will think about it."

On his way home, Rapu waved a tricycle down.

One passenger was already seated at the other end of the bench. Midway, he alighted. Rapu spread out in the whole back seat. He sensed the driver stealing a glance at him in the rear-view.

"Nno, sir," the fellow began by way of breaking the ice. His eyes darted between the mirror and the road until he established eye contact with Rapu. Welcome. "I see you do not recognize me."

"No," Rapu confessed. Opaku grew in leaps and bounds, with new families springing up and the frontiers of the town extending in all directions.

"Josiah," the man said simply.

No bell rang in Rapu's head. He hung his arms on the backrest of the seat and stared at the half road.

"Stanley's uncle," the driver explained. He was excited, intent on identifying himself. "I am a younger brother to Stanley's father."

Ah. Josiah Sure-banker. The gambler.

"Oho! Ndeewo, sir," Rapu enthused. He would have preferred to be left alone with his thoughts. Where to get the ram and how much. But the operator was not done.

"Thank you for looking out for Stanley and his family."

"Oo. Thank God," Rapu said. *How am I looking out for Stanley and his family? He serves me, and I feed and clothe him like all apprentices.*

Josiah patted the handlebars of the vehicle. He turned to face Rapu. "Thank you for this. It is what is feeding me and my family—my wife and my five children. Thank you."

Rapu sat up like one stung by a bee. He brought his arms down, leaned forward, and examined the vehicle, looking for the mark he imprinted on his wares. There it was on the dashboard.

"Eze got one, too," Josiah said.

"Eze?"

"Ezekiel. Stanley's brother. Thank you, sir."

Just then, a tricycle came hurtling from the opposite direction. On seeing Josiah's vehicle, it tooted. The two operators waved to each other, wide smiles exposing rotting teeth like a paint chart.

"Ezekiel," Josiah said, pointing to the receding, wobbly box. "Thank you. May God replenish your pocket."

That night, Rapu did not sleep. He turned and twisted, creaking his bed. At one point, Iyom called out to him.

"Is something the matter? If it is the demolition, leave it to God. Remember your name. Rapuluchukwu. He will reshuffle things in your favour."

Rapu was boiling with hatred for his mother. Was she not the cause of his losses at that demolition? She had dissuaded him from befriending Oluchi, whose brother operated a store in the plaza. He knew Oluchi's brother would have salvaged his goods if he had befriended her. Instead, Iyom had discouraged him from "toasting" her.

"You are the cause, Nne!" he hurled from across the wall, unable to stomach the pain. "You are the cause of my travails!"

Iyom scrambled up from her bed, fearful of her last son. Involuntarily, she cupped her shoulder, where he had hit her. But she was unable to let the accusation pass.

"How am I the cause?" she shouted back. "Was I there? Did I tell the local government to demolish your shop? You and Zona, every time something goes wrong, it is Mgboye."

Rapu left the room, knowing if he stayed there a minute more, he could hit his mother again, which could be fatal this time. He could hear her hasten to bolt the door and the sound of her dragging something heavy, probably Agbisi's disused Singer, to barricade it.

That night, he barely slept. He saw himself piggybacking Stanley, Josiah, and Ezekiel. At dawn, he returned to the witch-doctor. Otogirigiri peered into his body of water. Is he coming for the abroad hustling medicine? He threw the cowries and stirred the basket of water. Revenge formed on the water.

The curtain was yanked aside.

"Someone has defrauded me," Rapu said between clenched lips. "I want to punish him."

"Naturally."

His eyes were the colour of the cloth on Otogirigiri's miniature door.

CHAPTER 49

Amata found it difficult to manage the shop with the twins in tow. The first day after her husband took his apprentice home, she got them ready for the outing, smelling nice and cuddly. She packed lunch and their toilet bag in the car and then returned to the flat for the thermos and her brood. It was then that she smelled the tell-tale odour.

"Mummy, let us change him at the shop," Omenma suggested, keen for a vehicle ride. Amata looked at the whimpering boy, uncomfortable in the mess.

"No," she said. "It won't take long."

She lay O'Neal down and deftly pulled the trainer pants. Trash, wipe, Vaseline, talc, trainers. She was foisting him into his onesie when Kobe puked and let out a staccato of farts. It was already past seven. Amata looked out at the long stretch of immobile cars lined on the road, honking frenziedly. It would take them nothing less than three hours to snarl into Idumota. And the sky was darkening.

"We will stay home," she told her girl. "I can't stress myself."

She put on Teletubbies on the screen and crashed on the sofa, eager to check her emails. Her phone rang. It was Anthonia Akpan, a customer whose details she had registered.

"I need to service my Forerunner. Can you send your boy with the parts?"

"Sure," Amata replied, wondering how to swing the sale without Ebuka. "We charge two thousand for delivery in Lagos.

But if you can pick it up, there is no extra charge."

"Add an injector cleaner and power-steering oil."

She slid from the sofa and raised her arms into the air. "Hip! Hip! Hip!"

"Hurray!" three young voices answered, though they knew not why.

She texted Jasper's account number to the customer. The twins were clambering over her, ignoring the TV. She settled them on the floor and proposed toys to them. Then she went into Ebuka's room, where they stocked spares. She identified the items that had been ordered and packaged them. Jasper soon called to confirm the remittance. She had made a sale from home. An hour later, a logistics guy on a motorbike passed by and picked up the goods for Ms. Akpan.

CHAPTER 50

Jideofor called Jasper to say that he had seen Rapu in the Hillbrow area of Johannesburg. Jasper dialled Omeifeukwu. When Zona heard, his mind went straight to Rapu's parcel of land adjacent to his hotel project.

"Let him go," he said. His mind was already in overdrive. Rangers Hotel needed extra space for a car park and an event place. He had bought the land next to his, but Rapu's would complete the picture. It would provide another entry point to the facility. He began to plan a trip home to execute his scheme. The earlier, the better. It was also time to pay another courtesy visit to the police boss.

When he got home that night from the shop, Helen had a surprise for him. She was brooding. Again. He checked his phone: 6:37 p.m. It was not late.

"O gini kwa?" he asked, a tad impatiently. What is it this time? She was unpredictable and made him apprehensive each time he neared home. He determined to send her packing. A mistress should be cheerful and bright. This one sulked half of the time. Worse than a wife.

"One man came here. I refused to let him in."

"One man. Did he say his name?"

"Anatogu."

"Chief Anatogu?"

"Something like that."

"Chief Anatogu, Omenuko?" It was a big title: Benevolent even in times of economic distress. Charity's father.

Helen said nothing.

"And you refused to open?"

"Since I did not know him."

Zona went to the nearest seat. He lowered himself into it.

"What happened?" He was nervous. Omenuko was his in-law, a revered relationship in Igboland.

"When he rang the bell, I thought it was the girl I had sent to buy me bread. When I saw them—"

"Them? How many?" He tapped his feet.

"They were three. The Anatogu man, one woman and another man."

Zona glowered at her.

"I blocked the door, said they could not enter, that you were not in. They asked after Charity. I told them that no one of that name lived here."

When the blow landed on Helen's head, it knocked her over a dining chair and against the table. Her ears rang. Her eyes swelled. Her mind went to the last beating she had suffered. From this same man's wife.

"That was my father-in-law. Are you getting my point? Do you put food in your nostrils? I opened a shop for you, yet laziness will keep you at home, eating and looking for trouble."

He caught his breath. This was the opportunity he was looking for. He keened over her. "Go and pack your stuff and leave my house! This minute! Are you getting my point? This minute."

~

Helen shrank back in fear. She held one part of her face and crawled to the room, keeping a good eye out for any sudden movement from Zona. She had never seen him this angry. Was it her fault? Was she to open the door to strangers that she did not know? *I will pack an overnight bag,* she thought, *and go to Bisi until he calms down.*

Zona was standing in the parlour with a drink in his hand when she emerged from the room.

"Omeifeukwu. I'm sorry." The voice was coquettish, babyish. She wore a hangdog look.

"Sorry for yourself." He flung a wad of notes in her direction. "I don't want to see you here again. Are you getting me? Out!" He opened the door and held it for her.

"I'm sorry, Omeifeukwu. I did not—"

"Get out! First, you broke my wedding photo. I endured it. That is what gave you the audacity to disrespect my in-laws."

She wanted to appeal further, perhaps go on her knees. He moved towards her menacingly. She grabbed the bundle of notes and trudged into the night. Zona followed on her heels.

"Where are these boys?!" he asked the night. "Lock that gate! And do not let that tramp set foot here again. Are you getting my point?"

"What of my things?" Helen cried from afar.

The door slapped shut.

CHAPTER 51

Iyom peered through the window carved out of the perimeter wall that enabled her to sell from the comfort and safety of her compound. Jasper, true to his word, had negotiated some weekly allocation of crates from his father-in-law. The pick-up truck brought beer, soft drinks, and malt. The drinks moved fast. Iyom usually bought a block of ice from down the road and chilled some loose bottles in a cooler. Charity added sachets of water. Iyom's drink business had rolled off. In charcoal, above the window, Adaobi had scribbled "Nne's Trading Company Ltd."

One Saturday, three weeks after Rapu disappeared into thin air, Adaobi followed her mother to the shop. Iyom sat by her kiosk, waiting for customers. Alaoma and Eloduchi sat beside her, bent double over a grinding stone. Iyom was cracking palm kernels for all three. Birdsong filled the air. E-e-e, bleated the ewe with child. Chisom strapped the last baby to her back as she spread the laundry.

"If she is asleep, lay her down," Iyom called out. "Don't break your back."

"She has not slept deep," came the reply. "If I put her down now, she will cry."

The lone laundry line was filled. Chisom hung the washing on shrubs and tree branches.

"Don't forget feed for the goats."

"Once the baby sleeps, I will go."

"Nne," Eloduchi began, slurping on the nuts.

"No talk with food in your mouth," Iyom admonished.

Eloduchi chewed fast, eager to off-load what was on her mind. Iyom passed her a sachet of water.

The gate creaked open. Iyom pivoted. Three men stood there. She could not place the faces. Someone had not latched the gate.

"Who is it?" she called out. "Who are you after?"

"We are looking for Rapuluchukwu Okonkwo," one of the men stepped forward to answer. He was rotating a hat in his hands.

"Who is looking for him?"

"We are."

Iyom rose and splayed the palm nuts to her granddaughters. She tied her wrapper firmly and started off towards the men, at a loss what this could portend. They looked dour, like stale soup. Jasper had called to say that Rapu was now in South Africa and that Jideofor had run into him. *Ooo,* Iyom had remarked. *As long as he is fine. A man must hustle.*

She dragged a bench forward. The men's faces were tight, creased. She diverted her gaze. What could be wrong? Their leader, the one who spoke, wore an olive-coloured kaftan ensemble. The second fellow was in faded jeans and a white singlet. The third wore a fading jumper and trousers made from local fabric.

"Is it for good?" She thought that whatever it was, she would claim that no male was at home and that they should postpone the matter till her sons returned. Whatever the matter.

"We are looking for Rapu," the leader said again.

She pointed them to the bench.

"This is not matter for a seat," the second man said aggressively.

"Whatever it is, please sit." Iyom pleaded. She sensed trouble. Her heart thumped.

The elder invited his delegation to accept. They lowered themselves into the wood.

"Chisom, bring three sachets of—!"

"Iyom, do not worry. We are on an important mission."

"Where is Rapu?" the belligerent one barked. "Where. Is. Rapu?"

"This is his house," Iyom acknowledged. "But he is not in." The palm kernel had dried her throat. She swallowed. "Anything? Is there a message?"

"We want to ask if this is the boy we articled to him as an apprentice."

At the mention of apprentice, comprehension dawned on the old woman. Josiah. Stanley's people. Josiah, sure-banker Josiah, who had gambled away the settlement money from his master.

The fellow beckoned to a lad in the middle of a blue tricycle parked outside the gate. The boy came down and stood in front of Iyom. His flaky skin was pink with buttons, pus-filled scabs, patches, and cracks, like ageing skin. When Stanley was apprenticed to Rapu, Iyom remembered a dark-skinned, energetic youngster. She opened her mouth wide and furrowed her brow.

"Stanley? What happened? Is he sick?"

"That is the question we came to ask your son. This is not the boy we gave him to train. Yes, it is Stanley. At the same time, it is not our Stanley."

Iyom shook her head. She turned to the lad. "Stanley, what happened?"

"Northeast brothel."

Northeast? Brothel? Northeast brothel? It made no sense.

"That is what he has been repeating," the uncle said. "Nonsense that we do not understand."

"Northeast brothel demolished the plaza," the apprentice continued.

"Mtcheew," the leader hissed.

The ewe was tottering towards the gate. Without taking her eyes off the visitors, Iyom admonished Chisom to close the gate.

"He is not talking sense," Josiah said. "For the past week, it has been like this. And we did not hear from Rapu. That is why we said let us come and ask questions."

Iyom was dumbfounded. She gazed from one man to another, her right hand holding her jaw in place.

"You did well. I know that Rapu's shop in a plaza was demolished. But brothel?" She turned to Stanley. "Were you running a brothel?"

"Northeast brothel."

The elder shook his head, then cleared his throat. "We want our son back," he said matter-of-factly. "If we wronged Rapu or our son wronged him, let him tell us, and we shall make restitution. But we want Stanley back the way he was when your son took him on."

"Northeast brothel demolished the plaza. Tricycle demolished the plaza. Northeast brothe—"

The men shushed him. The middleman bent down, shook his head wistfully, and hissed.

They shifted up to make space for Stanley, who squeezed himself onto the bench. All eyes were on the woman for the way forward.

Iyom was confused. What had her last son concocted and run away from? The alacrity with which he absconded to South Africa was suspicious. She had ascribed it to youth. As young men, they could not stay idle, but no one could conceal a pregnancy for long. When a hen farts, it takes flight, thinking that Ani, Earth is privy to it. That was why she had insisted on education. But Agbisi would not hear. This restlessness, an educated person did not suffer it. He would land a job and settle into a routine. Now, consider this mess. All eyes were on her. She needed to think fast, measure her words.

"I am sorry about this development," she began, tiptoeing around the matter. "As you can see, I am all alone with the children." She opened her palms and then pointed to the toddlers and Chisom. "It was just last week that Jasper called, telling me that Rapu had been seen in South Africa. I said, oo. A man must hustle. If that is where his chi proposed to him after the demolition of his business, all well and good."

"Plaza demolition the tricycle."

"You all know Omeifeukwu, Chief Echezona Okonkwo, trading in Lagos. And Jasper, of Jasper Gee Trading Company, also in Lagos."

"Ochinanwata. We know him."

"They are Rapu's big brothers. I shall inform them of your visit. Let them ask their brother what happened and chart the way out of this situation."

She cast another look at the rube and looked to the hat-wielding man. "Have you taken him for treatment?"

"Where have we not gone?" the spokesman queried. "We have been to the government hospital. They could not help us. We have taken him to several deliverance mountains, but no progress. That is why we said maybe Rapu can help us. He passed the smelling shit, so he will have to pack it out."

Iyom nodded pensively. Yes, if Rapu was the cause of the malady, it behooved him to find a solution.

"Otherwise, we shall tell him that—" one of the men contributed, unable to hold the anger any further.

"No, no, no," the elder nudged his companion. "One thing at a time. Let us structure our response. We agreed we would present the matter to the Okonkwos, not so?" He did not wait for confirmation. "Not because we do not know what to do or how to retaliate."

"Is Stanley the first boy to do apprentice?" the wild one interjected. "Is Rapu the first master? Why should our case be different? If something is amiss, we have our custom of settling disputes." He looked to his mates for corroboration. "If not for some Opaku kinsfolk who saw him mumbling and ambling aimlessly in the market. They contributed money to bring him home."

"You did well to come and ask questions," Iyom said again in an unctuous voice. "That is the way of kinsmen. I will convey your message to Rapu's brothers. They will find a solution. Please, my lords. I plead with you."

CHAPTER 52

As soon as Chief Anatogu reached home, he dialled his daughter's number. Charity was the first child of her parents. They had a soft spot for her.

"ChaChaCha!"

"Omenuko."

Her father related his encounter in Lagos, how they had been invited to a meeting of Ohaneze Nd'Igbo, Lagos Branch. He had taken Charity's mother along to brief the Igbo elites on the Women's August Meeting. After the morning session, they decided to surprise their daughter. They met a lady who refused them entry into Zona's house, saying no Charity lived there.

"I was shocked to my marrow," Omenuko concluded. "ChaChaCha, when did this happen?"

"Npa, we have been in Opaku for some time now, the children and me."

"What happened? Was there a quarrel?"

"It is because I have been bearing females. When my co-wife bore twin boys, Omeifeukwu's face turned against me."

"Is it not what he deposited inside you that you will render?" Charity recognized her mother's voice.

"Odibeze," she greeted.

"My daughter."

"We are fine, Npa. We have settled well here with my mother-in-law. Adaobi and Alaoma attend school. Omeifeukwu opened a shop for me. Do not worry, Npa." She rubbed her stomach.

"Do not tell me that!" Chief Anatogu sputtered. "My fellow man treats my daughter like a sucked-up orange, and you tell me not to worry? Look at Obiananma. Her husband, the so-called man of God, has eloped with another woman, leaving my daughter to fend for two kids. Now this. And you tell me not to worry."

"I do not know what our men are becoming," Charity heard her mother remark in the background.

"Are they Igbo?" From across the miles, Charity could hear the spite in her father's voice. "Igbo men do not behave like this. To us, the family is supreme and sacred. Our young boys now—" he hesitated. "Nowadays, they commit impunity!"

"It's all right, Npa," Charity said again. "I will give birth any time now," she added.

"What number is this?"

"Five, sir. Another girl."

"That should do it, Cha. Do not go that road again. Do you hear what your father is saying?"

"Yes, Npa."

"A female is an asset. Train these ones. Children are very expensive to rear nowadays. It is not like before, when we had farms and barns. God knows what He is doing when He sends females our way. You hear?"

"Yes, sir."

"It will go well for you, my daughter. ChaChaCha."

"Omenuko."

"Let day break."

"Nma, good night."

~

So this Helen has moved into my home and is even now calling the shots. And denying my parents entry. It is well. Charity adjusted her head-tie and contemplated whether to close the shop and go home or wait to see if luck would shine on her and some big customers would come in to purchase fabrics. On another thought, she decided to close up to avoid the evening stampede.

A few steps to the hearth, she felt her water break. She located her trousseau.

"Chisom, go and call Nne."

"Is it labour?" the young girl panicked.

"I think so. Look after the house while Nne takes me to the clinic."

Iyom helped Charity into the tricycle and jumped in, clearly flustered, and it showed in her driving. She bumped into the rugged road at full throttle, not minding the potholes and craters. Charity was thrown up and about. She cradled her belly with one hand and, with the other, held on to the rod dividing the two compartments. When her head hit the roof of the vehicle, she could no longer keep quiet.

"Nne, you are driving like 007. Easy. Let me not deliver on the road."

Luckily, Eliza, their kinswoman, was on duty at the hospital. She checked Charity in and asked Iyom to leave.

"It will not be before daybreak. You can come back then."

"I want to stay," the old woman said stubbornly. "I want to enter the delivery room with her."

"Not necessary, Nne," Charity said, mustering a smile. Her heart went out to the old woman. Oby had planned to accompany her to the labour room, but like a thief, labour sometimes came unannounced.

"Suppose you born male and they sell it?"

Eliza spoke up. "Has she delivered here before, Nne? If that is what they do in Lagos, we do not do that here. And do not forget, Charity is my co-wife. Go on home. She is in safe hands."

"Nne, remember Chisom is alone with the kids. Biko, go and stay with them," Charity pleaded between cramps. She and Obiananma had done the scan and knew the baby to be female. *It is well,* she had said, resigning her fate to God.

Reluctantly, Iyom acquiesced and left.

Eliza pulled a chair to Charity's side. "Listen, Charity. Did you do a scan?"

She nodded. "A female."

"What number now?"

"Five."

"No male, yet?"

Charity shook her head. "And my father said not to go this way again."

"Any caesarean?"

She nodded. "One."

"Listen. We have three other women here in labour. Do you want to go home with a male child? You are my person. I can do that for you."

Charity was already shaking her head. How? Nurse another woman's child? How could she be separated from her own flesh and blood?

"No sentiments here, Charity. Think well. Zona has already sent you out of his Lagos house, not so?"

She made a dentilingual sound.

"It is just a matter of time before he brings someone else in."

"Ha. A UNILAG girl has already moved in."

"Listen. Once that one has a male for him, *Nunc dimitis* for you. So, think well. We can give you a male. You can safeguard your marriage."

"What of my own child?"

"Exchange is no robbery," the midwife quipped. "Your girl goes to the other woman. I am doing this for you. We charge a lot for this service. It's up to you, but you must decide fast so I know how to set things up. You are my person, and that is why I want to help you protect your marriage. It will be between you and me, and we will—" Here, Eliza pinched her two lips together to indicate secrecy.

"My people know I am expecting a girl."

"Scans can lie. Listen. It is not etched in stone. Sometimes, the scan says A, but B materializes. That is not a problem at all. Think about it. I shall be back, but remember, time is ticking."

"It is well."

The smell of disinfectant and drugs nauseated Charity. She heard infant cries mingle with the wailing of women. *Shut up!* A shrill voice rebuked the wailers. *When you were lifting your legs up, you were enjoying it. Don't deafen our ears here.* She watched the staff scurry in and out of the ward, laden with supplies and pans, dragging poles hooked to sachets of saline. Outside, she saw anxious families on stoops and corridors, alert for news. Many came with their sleep gear. They were not allowed into the wards, so they spread outside the corridors like campers.

Charity was facing a dilemma, and her mind was in overdrive. *I know that Helen has moved into my husband's house,* she reasoned. *She must be pregnant. If she brings forth a male, I am finished. I will just be answering missus in name only. I have an opportunity to get a male child and secure my position in my husband's heart and the Okonkwo hearth. God has aligned things for me to deliver in Opaku Maternity Centre, where my co-wife is matron. Is this not an answer to my prayer? If I decline this opportunity, I will have myself to blame. I must grab this lifeline with two hands. I must.*

A contraction hit her. She whined and writhed in agony till it passed. Her thoughts went to the child she was about to bring into this world. She had already named her Enuma—Heaven Knows. What would become of her Enuma? Who would get her? Who would raise her? What if a medicine man bought her and spilled her innocent blood for rituals? Could she keep Enuma and still get a son in addition? Did Amata not give birth to twins? Everything was possible. A stab pierced her abdomen. She bit her lower lip, turned this way and that, and shook her legs to ride it through.

Several spasms later, Eliza reappeared to check on her. When their eyes met, Charity nodded.

"That's the way to go, my dear. Four hundred thousand."

CHAPTER 53

On Zona's next visit to the Simpsons, he was greeted by a very old woman staring into space. She was half-clad, and her long and flat breasts, shrivelled and lined, rested on her wrinkled stomach.

"Granny," Modupe said.

"Your grandmother is still alive?"

"Who kill am?"

He fumbled. "I mean, I did not know. It's the first time I'm seeing her. Are you getting my point? How old is she?"

"Alhaja is in her mid-sixties. We celebrated her 65th birthday party two years ago, at the primary school there. Closed all the roads around here. So Moomie must be eighty plus."

On hearing her name, the old woman turned. She had white woolly hair sprouting on crêpe skin around a braided red skull cap.

Modupe curtsied. "E nle, ma."

The old woman showed her toothless gums amidst swathes of spittle. She pointed a withered finger at the man.

"Oko Modupe?"

The mistress nudged Zona to greet.

"E-nle, Ma," Zona parroted. His mouth was dry. The woman, wonder of wonders, inclined slightly towards him.

"Welcome," she mumbled and stretched her thin lips in a monkey grimace. She rubbed her stomach and nodded.

His mind went to his last fight with Charity. She had called him a wizard. *You are the wizard. When normal people are home, you are perambulating, fleeing your house.* How did she put it? A fugitive. She had called him a fugitive from home.

The wiry woman in an oversized skirt, half of her underskirt showing, was babbling things the businessman could make nothing of. Modupe elbowed him again, and they moved on.

"She is greeting you for the pregnancy. Everyone is excited that it is a male. I told you about the curse that is about to be broken."

"What of your grandpa?" he asked. He did not want to be surprised again by relatives from space. Any grandpa would be at least a century old.

"No grandpa as such," his mistress answered. "I told you our women are condemned to the unmarried life. But grandpa is in Benin. Remember when you first gave me a lift?"

"Yes. You said you were on a business trip. A gold digger."

"Dealer. Granny is a goldsmith."

"He must be a hundred years old?"

"Easily. He and Moomie did not marry, though."

"Why is he based in Benin?"

"He is Bini. Originally from Ife, but he settled in Benin and—"

My God! Zona flipped. *What have I got myself into?*

"Alhaja is Ijebu."

"Is Alhaja Moomie's only child?"

"Yes. Just as I am Alhaja's only child. I told you. They made us born only females who will not marry. I told you. Remember?"

Who, in the lap of intimacy, remembered anything?

"But you will reverse the curse."

"Curse? What curse?"

"The curse of 'borning' only females. With my boy," she caressed her protruding belly, "the curse will be broken. I thought I would have only Aduke."

"Aduke?"

"My daughter. The girl I bore for Doherty."

"Doherty?"

"Abeg come and be going. You are tired."

But he was not tired, just dazed and unable to process any

more of the information pouring out like smoke from a faulty muffler. What had he got himself into? When she approached him in Benin, he had thought she was a simple Lagos girl. He had befriended her, thinking of a quick fling. Now, here she was, carrying his baby, and it turned out she was not Lagosian but Bini and Ijebu and had a curse hanging over her head, which he, an Igbo man from Opaku, Chief Echezona Bespoke Okonkwo, Omeifeukwu, no less, would break. He exhaled, helpless and defeated. Others will fart and get away with it; his fart morphs into human manure.

Zona found the whole thing galling. He sat awhile in the car before turning the ignition. Only one thing grounded him: Modupe was having a boy. If not for his heir in her belly, he would have made himself very scarce. The thought of relocating to Abuja entered his mind. People easily dropped out of sight in the Federal Capital Territory, much like a drop of top-up oil. But when he thought of his unborn son, he knew he would go the whole hog.

The following weekend, when Zona visited Opaku, Charity was hanging baby things on the line. He peered through the wall's fancy blocks. He tapped on the steering. Charity hurried out to welcome him. Zona's jaw dropped. She was flat-stomached.

"What happened?"

"I have delivered. A girl," she hastened to add.

"I see. And no one saw it fit to tell me."

"Nno."

He descended. "When?"

"Last Uka Nkwo." Last Nkwo market day that fell on a Sunday. That was ten days ago. Another girl, he said to himself. Thank God Modupe was having a boy.

"How are you people?"

"We are well. Adaobi! Alaoma! Eloduchi! Where are you? Come and greet Daddy. How is business?"

He ignored her. Five girls in a row. He grimaced and rolled his mouth into a cloaca, like someone who perceived a bad smell. "So you delivered ten days ago in my house, and no one deemed it fit to inform me."

Iyom emerged from the copse.

"Omeifeukwu. Welcome." She smiled. "Thank God for journey mercy. I hear the roads are knotty."

Zona ignored her. He opened the trunk. "Call your girls to off-load the foodstuff," he said to his wife.

The smile on Iyom's lips and excitement at seeing her son reversed.

Alaoma and Eloduchi carried in two loaves of bread. Chisom did the heavy lifting, taking several tubers of yam, plantain, and pineapples. Odibeze, Charity's mother, emerged, carrying the newborn. She greeted Zona and went back in, saying the sun was too grilling on the infant.

Iyom offered Zona the kiosk bench, then briefed him on how Stanley's people had come to lay a complaint.

"Shall I send for them?" she asked. "When you have rested? Tell them that you are home?"

"Nne," Zona stapled his hands and cleared his throat. "The lizard that climbed the orji tree is no longer a baby. Are you getting my point? Rapu is of age. The head that disturbs a hornet's nest is the one that will be stung, not Echezona's head."

With that, he rose. It was time to inspect his hotel project. However, he needed to ease himself first. He went to the side of his dwelling and emptied his bladder against the wall.

"Shall I ask Jasper then?"

"You can ask whoever you want," Zona retorted in a petulant voice, wiping his hands with a rumpled tissue. "All I know is that I am the first son, and no one can take that from me."

"Then do what first sons do!"

"When it is trouble, you remember Echezona. But when it is prayer and blessing, it is Jasper."

"I pray for all my children."

"Now you are turning my wife against me. Otherwise, how can my wife born and no one tells me? And you are here. Or is it not my child? Maybe it is not my child."

"Nne, it is enough," Charity threw in. "It is enough. Omeifeukwu, go to where you are headed."

"Every time you come home, it is to make trouble," Iyom added. "Every time. Is it a done thing? One cannot sit with you and have a dialogue. It is one accusation after another." She turned away.

"Keep behaving like this, and I will throw you out one day," Zona shouted after her.

Iyom stopped. She turned her head like someone with a strained neck. "Throw me out? Of my husband's house?"

"Your husband is dead."

"Omeifeukwu, it was I who said not to call you when I delivered Enuma," Charity said.

"Oh, you have named her, too."

"Yes, Enuma. When I delivered Makua in Lagos under your nose, did you name her? You abandoned us in the hospital. This is the reason I said you shouldn't be bothered. Not Nne's fault. She is the one who drove me to the maternity in the middle of the night. This is not how to repay her."

Anger mounted in Zona. His hand formed a fist, and he made to hit Charity when he remembered he was in the village. Women were getting more powerful. If he so much as laid a finger on her, the womenfolk would compose a song ridiculing him. If the Elite Merchants heard, he would not see the end of it for a long time. He murmured something, stepped into his car, and reversed out of the gate. Then he stopped, got out and strode towards Charity, his bulbous index finger wiggling in her direction.

"It looks like how I sent you out of my house in Lagos is not enough. I shall send you back to Omenuko before you call the shots in my house. Are you getting me?"

"O o send me back. How many places will Helen occupy? Or do you think I don't know how she denied my parents entry into your house? Send me back. Is my face burnt? If you do not send me back, shame on you." She booed him, put her palm to her lips and howled.

Odibeze appeared and dragged her daughter in. "Enough."

Zona was not surprised that Charity knew about the altercation between Helen and Omenuko. *Of course, her father would have reported the matter to her. But she is not current.* He entered his car and sped away. *Just because I shouted Helen in my ecstasy. She does not know that Helen is out of the picture. Something greater than Helen is here, my dear.*

A big sign proclaimed Rangers International Hotel. The hotel was coming up as planned. A Tomlinson cement mixer was whining away and churning out fresh slurry. Artisans dotted the scaffold, knocking, hitting, pounding. Women with infants on their backs nimbly manoeuvred head pans. The CEO beamed with pleasure. He went to the side of the road and undid his pants. It occurred to him that he was pissing too frequently. He sighed and cast a careful look around the property to assess developments in the neighbourhood. The adjoining plot that he had purchased gave the building space an impression of prestige. Now, if he annexed Rapu's parcel at the back, the hotel would look expansive. An exit gate could be created, with additional parking, and maybe an event centre.

He strolled to the back to view his project from Rapu's plot and estimate the work that needed to be done there. As soon as he rounded the corner, he saw the frightful fetish dangling from a branch, oozing a foul odour. He backed off.

"No-go area," the foreman said behind him.

"I was thinking of buying it off the owner; create a private entrance."

"Leave well alone, sir. I hear Donatus is flinging his plot."

"I heard so, too, but it is the one by the school."

"He needs money. If the price is right, he can keep that plot and sell this one to you. You enlarge your coast."

Zona continued along the bush path. He surveyed the terrain and saw the trappings of a bungalow on his half-brothers' acre. Cassava leaves and yam tendrils vibrated on well-carved-out mounds and ridges.

He spat out, stepped aside and dialled Donatus. "Ọmeifeukwu on the line," he said when Donatus answered. "I am interested in your plot."

"Ha. Omeifeukwu. I am already talking with Jasper about it. We have almost conc—"

"Almost cannot kill a bird. How much?"

~

Zona returned directly to Lagos from the site. He was away in Guangdong to buy furnishings for his hotel when his phone vibrated.

"Shief," the shrill voice said.

"Hello," he said doubtfully. It sounded like Alhaja. Then he remembered that Modupe was due. "Hello, hello, hello!"

"Ello."

"E nl-e Ma," he crooned in a velvet voice, inclining slightly to the elder across the seas.

The line went dead.

He panicked. With quivering fingers, he dialled back. What was it with Modupe? Like everyone in her compound, she had been worried about the curse and had not wanted him to travel. Alhaja had advised that they have sex every day to bring on labour. After market, every evening, he had passed by Herbert Macaulay for the pleasurable duty. Had Dupe delivered? Or had the curse set in? *We are condemned to born only females?* she had said. Would the curse allow her to deliver a male? His heir? He trembled and clenched his groin lest his pipes burst in public.

CHAPTER 54

It was a trying time for Jasper and Amata. Without anyone to ambush customers out front, business tanked. The young CEO was constrained to stay in his shop and await patrons. Some independent lookouts directed a few customers his way. He paid them a commission. At one point, he thought of asking Amata to resume at the shop. Omenma could manage at home with the twins. But Amata vetoed the idea. An emergency could arise, she cautioned. The toddlers were a handful for an adult. They could easily overwhelm Omenma. And what about abductors? Male neighbours spying for a chance to ravish the little girl. No, she would never leave the twins alone with a minor.

One arbitrary day, Amata packed up her brood and accompanied Jasper to the shop. It was hectic, but it allowed her time with Jasper and the opportunity to introduce Omenma to the business.

The heavy morning rain caused a humongous traffic. It petered to a drizzle just before midday, and a cowering sun finally came out, late for its daily appointment. It shimmered on the roofs and reflected in the poodles of water on the broken alley between the warrens of stalls. Store owners drained out rain water from awnings. Business was slow. Only a guy who traded in alloy wheels and car accessories was making brisk sales. Young boys congregated there, caressing wheels with the faces of sliced tomatoes and citruses. Colourful Louis Vuitton knock-off steering wheel covers were snapped up fast.

"This is why we should set up the e-commerce aspect," Amata opined. "Customers can call us from wherever, and we will supply the parts to them."

"It is not as easy as that," her husband replied, crossing his long legs. "Do not forget that it is best for the buyer to come with the damaged part. Otherwise, you will be running up and down with wrong parts."

"They can take a photo of it and send it through WhatsApp," Amata maintained, convinced of the superiority of her argument. "Please give it a thought."

She nudged Omenma. "There is no reason you should not learn this business. Look around. Women are doing it."

Jasper was not comfortable with the idea of Omenma being introduced to the market. He pointed to the army of young men hustling in the market. "Look, it is like dropping a grain of corn among poultry. I cannot keep an eye on her and on my goods," he warned.

"Omenma can keep an eye on herself," Amata said, loud enough for the girl to hear. "If a woman allows herself to be deceived, she is to blame." She pulled her ward's ear. "Are you hearing?"

"Ee."

"It is not as easy as that," interjected the local gossip sitting on a stool opposite the shop, resting while she waited for someone. "At the age of puberty, adolescence is packed with hormones. It can be very crushing for our youth. Girls needing extra policing."

Amata had to strain her ears to hear. "I have warned her but will keep an eye on her. After all, she is someone's child."

"Yes. Keeping a strict eye on her. Men of today are not letting females alone. They are buzzing around them like flies over a heaping of excreta."

The tedium of life in commerce was numbing. A few patrons sauntered in with damaged parts. Oil and fuel filters exchanged hands. Brake pads and lining were sold. A fellow came for some headlamp bulbs and two pins. *Not much,* Jasper thought, *but slow and steady, and we'll get there.* A wheel drum, a fuel pump sold.

At midday, the market fellowship erupted.

You alone are worthy, Lord,
To be praised and adored.
You've been faithful, Lord,
From the ages past.
That is why Your name is forever more.

Passers by gifted money to the twins when they saw O'Neal and Kobe dressed in matching outfits.

"Taiye, Kehinde. Ki Olorun wo won papo," they prayed. May God keep both twins.

"Isee. Thank you," Amata answered.

"She called them Taiye, Kehinde," Omenma observed.

"That's what the Yoruba name twins," her mistress explained. They sat on the doorstep, playing with the boys. More money came their way.

"Cook beans for them o," one elderly woman advised Amata. "Twins like beans, the watery kind."

"Yes, ma."

"May God provide for them."

"Isee."

Omenma continued going to the market with Jasper and Amata. She minded the toddlers while Amata went to the bus stop to scout for customers. Jasper stayed at the shop. Fortunately, Orimili usually sent his boys to get parts from Jasper Gee. Some days, those were the only sales they made, and Jasper was grateful for the patronage. Obidie, Oke Nmanwu's widow, had started coming to oversee her late husband's business, and her boys sometimes directed business Jasper's way. A condenser was sold here and a compressor there. Best of all, the widow incorporated Jasper Gee's orders into her imports from China.

"Do we stock Chinese car parts?" Amata asked one languid afternoon.

"No. Europe. Japan. Korea."

"Then why buy parts from China? They can't be original."

"Originals are costly. China is a good imitation, more affordable."

"Do we carry originals?"

"Some major importers stock them for high net-worth customers. But it is better to get a second-hand original from Ladipo Market. A customer who seeks an original part here may end up paying exorbitant for a Chinese clone."

"China clones everything."

"Even vehicles. I have seen a Chinese-cloned Toyota bus, complete, from top to bottom."

One day, the Lagos Island Town Council tax collectors passed by, checking tax receipts. Traders were expected to go to the Head Office of their own volition and pay tax after self-evaluation. Jasper showed his receipts.

"Daddy, what if one is not up-to-date?" Omenma asked when the officials had left.

"They seal up your shop. Before it is unsealed, you will pay a fine, and the Tax Office will determine how much tax you will pay. Better to evaluate yourself, be up-to-date, run away from trouble."

"No wonder Lagos is rich. Their internally generated revenue is high," Amata said. "Imagine all these markets teeming with traders."

"Lagos is the commercial capital of West Africa. With our population, the ocean and the ports are in a class of their own."

"Other States are trying to imitate them, but Lagos's revenue is sky-high."

"They are overdoing it," a neighbour said. "Take Anambra State. The way they are going about it is too stringent and arbitrary. Small businesses will fold up."

The rowdiness rose another notch when a bell ringer emerged, announcing the end of the world. The racket roused Omenma and jolted the twins. They peered out with bulging eyes.

"Repent, the world is coming to an end."

"I thought it was the oklika seller," Omenma said to Amata.

"It is the same kind of bell the second-hand clothes sellers use," Amata agreed.

"Buy plantain!" the voice of a hawker wove into the evangelist's.

"Romans 3:23 says that all have sinned and come short of the glory of God. But all is not lost, brethren. Hebrews 4:16, 'Let us therefore come boldly unto the throne of grace that we may obtain mercy.'"

He swung the bell again vigorously and vanished into the throng.

As the evangelist disappeared, who did they see in the shop but Jidenma, lugging a bulging jute bag?

"Ochinanwata."

Jasper was surprised. "Are my eyes playing me tricks?"

"No, it's me."

"What brings you here?"

"Nna, na hustle o! Jideofor sent me these T-shirts to fling. I have distributed them to some boys. One guy is coming for this bale."

He came into the shop as he spoke. Jasper introduced the adults. "My wife, Amata. My kinsman, Jidenma Okunna."

They embraced as village folks do. The younger fellow turned to Jasper. "You call me kinsman, but I am your brother. Agbisi was our father. Any other talk is an understatement."

"Nno," Amata smiled. "Jasper has told me about you."

"Oo, great woman!" Turning to Jasper, he hailed, "Jasper Gee! Ochinanwata."

The twins were sitting on the makeshift bed behind the counter. O'Neal lifted his hands to be carried. Jasper seized the opportunity to pass him a ball.

"Dunk! O'Neal, dunk!"

He crouched, waiting for his son to pass him the ball. Amata intervened. "He wants to be carried," she said to the visitor.

Jidenma stooped and lifted the boys, one after the other, above his head. They chuckled. "Do it again."

He rifled through his pocket and extended some notes to Amata.

"For the twins. This is my first time seeing them. You just dropped two boys at a go. Jasper Gee!"

"Nna, it is the Lord's doing," Jasper said. He pointed to a stool. "Sit down. Are you in a rush?"

"It's hustle we are hustling. I applied for government employment. Nothing yet. Instead of sitting down and moping, I said let me hustle. Can I wait for the fellow here? This bag is heavy, and you know these area boys."

"Certainly," Jasper said. "In Lagos, the fear of area boys is the beginning of wisdom. You can leave the bag here. Just open it and let us see if my size is there. Amata, is our water exhausted?"

Amata served the visitor a sachet of water, and Jidenma assuaged his thirst while tipping the bag over. Assorted packets of brightly coloured shirts spilled out. They were neatly and squarely folded in transparent nylon.

"All sizes are there," the visitor said. He bent down and selected a couple for Jasper. He added another for Amata and a small size for the babysitter. Omenma was overjoyed. It was her first brand-new wear.

"I can't stay long," Jidenma said. He cranked up and checked his mobile phone. "I have to take the night bus to Abuja to sell another consignment. Prices are higher in the capital than in the East. In Onitsha, they price these shirts like pepper."

"Everyone is a trader in Onitsha. They want rock bottom prices."

The two half-brothers discussed various things. At Jasper's questioning, Jidenma revealed how he was surviving. "I do market runs, accost buyers for traders. Anything but stay home."

"If you stay home when every adult is away, you will be the suspect if anything gets stolen in the yard."

"Jideofor said Rapu didn't look too good," Jidenma said when Rapu came up. He whisked out his phone and shared Rapu's number with Jasper.

"Rapu is my brother, but sometimes, I do not understand him."

"I hear his apprentice's family has an axe to grind with him."

"In fact, Nne called me to meet with them."

"Don't go," Jidenma warned.

"No?"

"Are you the Lamb of God that wipes away people's sins? Let Rapu sort himself out. Do not dabble in another person's mess. Look at these soldiers here." He pointed to the twins. "They should be your priority now."

"I see what you mean," Jasper said. He had had enough of Rapu for a lifetime. "It is Nne tugging at me to come and settle the matter."

"Let Omeifeukwu handle it. He is the firstborn."

"Nne said he was home last week but declined to meet Stanley's people."

"Steer clear. Whenever Rapu returns, he will answer Stanley's people."

Amata dished lunch for her husband and his brother. Jidenma relished the home-cooked bitter-leaf soup and fufu. The aroma of ogiri pervaded the shop and escaped its confines.

"And with stockfish to boot," the visitor cooed. "Wow! Jasper, you are a lucky man. My wife, thank you."

They licked their encrusted fingers and belched noisily. It was from Jidenma that Amata learnt of Enuma's birth. *Fifth girl,* Amata thought. *Poor Charity.*

Soon, the retailer Jidenma was waiting for arrived. They strewed the goods in front of Jasper Gee.

"Rock bottom prices!" Jidenma yelled. "Best T-shirt. Five, five hundred naira each! Three for one thousand. Who wants it?" He clanged a bell. People gathered over the wares.

"Mind your wallet!" Jasper warned his wife. He leaned over the counter and watched.

"Oh, yes! Oh yes!" bellowed Jidenma. "Best T-shirt from RSA here! Five, five hundred naira! Unisex T-shirts! Who wants it?"

In no time, the merchandise sold out. As breezily as he came, the peripatetic hustler vanished.

"You resemble each other," Amata observed to her husband. "Just the moustache is different. While yours is like the handlebars of a bike, his looks like the bristles of a toothbrush."

They guffawed.

"We have the same father," Jasper conceded. "You heard him. Any other thing is an understatement."

At four o'clock, Jasper thought they should pack up. He did not want to wait till the frenzied closing of the market. Amata and Omenma began assembling the children's stuff.

Suddenly, raised voices travelled over the hubbub of the market.

"Get out! Leave my shop!" It was a deep, baritone voice.

Fights and brawls were in the DNA of the market. A soprano voice answered, "Your mother is sick, and you ignore her."

"Get out! Witch!" a guttural voice hurled.

"Who has stepped on Uche's toes?" Jasper asked.

"Prostitute! Go and ask your boyfriends to help."

Amata flinched. Such a senior man to use gutter language at a woman in broad daylight. She crawled under the counter and peeped out. The woman so addressed stepped back, crossed her arms in front of her and stared with insouciance at her abuser. She was middle-aged and wore a long Ankara skirt-and-blouse ensemble. Her well-manicured toes peeped out of shiny slippers. Silver tufts of hair dotted the threshold of a scarf. As so often happened, a mixed bag of people gathered to watch the exchange, the youngsters praying for an escalation to kill the incipient boredom.

"Woman, what is it?" someone asked.

It was an elder eager to broker peace. One guy tried to rein Uchenna in, but he shouldered the fellow aside and charged.

"His mother, our mother, is ill." The fake Versace beach bag in her hands swung wildly as she gesticulated. "We have been calling him. I decided to come and find out what the problem ...."

"You are the problem," the enraged trader shouted her down. "I demand respect from the family as the first son. No. You soil yourselves, marry riff-raff, fuck every Tom, Dick and Harry. When I talk, no one listens. But when you need money, you remember Uche." He bent down to pick an object to launch. Three able-bodied guys jumped on him.

"Nna, take it easy," they pleaded.

Jasper shook his head sorrowfully. Family squabbles. We all come from homesteads with leaking roofs, he reflected, thinking of his own siblings. He recalled the punch their mother had taken from Rapu and Zona's hostile attitude. First son trouble was everywhere, owing primarily to financial hardship. Once a man had cash flow issues, he was a wounded lion. Money is a man's beauty.

"Something baffles me," Amata whispered. "Why is it that once there is a shouting match between two individuals, the man hits below the belt, calls the woman a prostitute and assigns lovers to her? What has that got to do with the sick parent? Is it to disgrace her?"

"Only an *efulefu*, a useless man, will engage in this type of behaviour," Jasper answered. He gathered the fan belts, pulled in one of the wooden doors, and slid the bolt.

Uchenna was unrelenting, implacable. He lurched forward, spewing spittle and invectives, "I will waste you!"

From a safe distance, the sister launched her own verbal missile, fully charged, "Uchenna, I na eli nsi!"

It hung in the air like a funnel of smoke, lingered, swirling, until understanding descended: *Uchenna, you eat feces!*

Uchenna searched for a weapon, anything. He saw a muffler nearby, grabbed it, and charged. The owner of the part sat calmly, observing the drama.

"That muffler is fifteen thousand naira," he warned in an icy voice. "I no take sorry."

Uchenna reconsidered. He dropped the muffler. When he looked up, his sister had melted into the market. He tootled back to his shop, swearing and pointing to the sky. The crowd, dissatisfied at the alacrity with which the budding fight had ended, reluctantly dispersed.

Amata felt abused. Young apprentices had witnessed the exchange, including Omenma and Uche's boy, fifteen-year-old Casimir. The market was not a place to raise children. Or was it just the testosterone-charged spare parts section? No, it could not be. Men dealt in every merchandise possible—cosmetics, fashion, foodstuff. No sector was exclusive to women. Was it frustration, then? Many traders were selling identical items. Sometimes, sellers outnumbered buyers. Many displayed goods every day, hung around, waiting for buyers that never came, and pleaded with passers-by to patronize them and break the jinx. At the end of the day, many went home disgruntled, poorer than they had come. They returned the next day for a repeat performance. It could unhinge the strongest of men.

After dinner, Amata called her sister-in-law.

"Charlingo! Congrats."

"Who told you?"

"Jidenma stopped by our shop today."

"Yes o! I have tried. Like the proverbial lizard that dropped from a tree and nodded several times, if people will not praise me, I will praise myself."

"My dear, a female is also valuable."

"I pray my next will be a boy."

"Blood of Jesus. You will go again?"

"Do I have a choice?"

Poor Charity, Amata commiserated. The quest for a male child was an odyssey. She thanked God for her good fortune in that department. Next, she dialled her sister.

"Engineer Luz Umeh, Congrats! You have graduated. You are awaiting your call-up papers for the National Youth Service posting. Doh, doh, doh, come and help me out with your nephews for a while." Please, please, please.

Two days later, Louisa arrived Lagos. From that day, Amata left Omenma and her twins in her sister's care and accompanied Jasper to Idumota.

When Charity closed her phone, her mind went back to her labour room experience. She had acquiesced to the switcheroo to save her marriage. As soon as she had decided, a calmness enveloped her. Shortly afterwards, Enuma slipped out. But the switch was not to be. No male baby was born that night in the maternity hospital. Eliza had to induce two women who came for a routine check-up. Seven deliveries, seven girls.

Early morning, Eliza had come shaking her head. "Nothing so far, my sister."

Iyom visited in the evening, which effectively put an end to the swapping scheme. *That's my fate,* Charity said, a sonless wife.

CHAPTER 55

Elder Okeke called Jasper to announce Ebuka's full recovery.

"He will leave Opaku tomorrow," the elder said. "He is not doing anything for us here."

Jasper counted the hours to Ebuka's return. His spirits lifted just thinking that things would soon revert to normal, and for the first time in weeks, he relaxed. With Ebuka around to manage the store, he could afford to travel to the village and see Stanley's family. He had no idea what the issue was. Was it a tiff between master and apprentice? Woman issue? *Stanley is a womanizer,* he recalled Rapu saying. If so, why not let him go? An apprentice had no income. With what money was he chasing skirts? Or did master and boy covet the same woman? Or was it a case of stealing? Or insubordination? These were the main causes of strife in the master-servant relationship. He decided to find out the nature of the bone of contention.

"How is Johannesburg?" he asked on hearing his sibling's voice. He thought of his own botched travel plans. "Have you settled down?"

"Settled? Things are not as I thought. My contact disappointed me."

"How so?"

"When I arrived Joburg, I messaged him. He told me he was in Cape Town and asked me to take a train and meet him there, a twenty-seven-hour journey."

"Twenty-what!"

"Yes, but I opted for the bus, kwela-kwela, they call it. This country is developed. People say it's like London and America."

"So?"

"I met my contact hawking sweets and chocolate at the train station. Imagine. I slept three nights at the station with him and his mates. It was one Igbo guy there who told me about some Opaku indigene. It turned out to be Jideofor."

"Yes, his brother was here recently. He gave me your number."

"I'm back in Joburg with him, marking time."

"If things are not moving, you can come back. One cannot, because of shame, swallow sputum."

"I am incubating one or two projects. If they don't work out, I shall return. These people do not like us. Our people are into all sorts. The temptation is strong to join them."

Jasper cleared his throat. Enough of the small talk. Rapu also girded up. *Here it is, Stanley.*

"Did you settle your apprentice?"

Silence.

"...because his people went to see Nne. Stanley was behaving like a sick—"

Silence.

"Nne said he looked mental."

"Stanley got what he deserved," Rapu declared. "He was bilking me, spending my money on girls. I warned him."

"Is that why they say he is mentioning brothel, Centre-West brothel, or something like that?"

"He even sneaked my tricycles out to his brothers. Lied that they were looted in the demolition."

"But we have Umunna," Jasper reminded his brother. He was getting exasperated. "If you have issues with your apprentice, you table it before our kinsmen. You do not resort to jungle justice."

"He had it coming," Rapu declared again. "He got his due."

"You were at the Opaku town hall meeting we had during the last mass return. Do not resort to self-help in your quarrels with your brother. Do not involve the khaki people. Let Umunna mediate."

"My battery is about to die," Rapu warned.

As if on cue, the gadget beeped three times and went off.

~

Rapu exhaled in relief. Jasper's was the last voice he had expected to hear. The call literally dropped from the sky. From across the continent, he could feel Jasper's accusatory voice jabbing at him, judging him without hearing his own side. So Otogirigiri's charm had taken effect on the deceitful Stanley.

I am the wronged party in this matter, he proclaimed loudly to the walls, poking his chest. *Stanley defrauduru m. He was an apprentice from hell. Instead of gathering with me and growing my business, he dug a hole in my pocket and siphoned away my sweat. He is paying for it.*

He plugged his phone into the socket, then stretched his tired legs in the cramped rooming house he was squatting in. True, Umunna warned kinsmen against resorting to personal help in settling scores, but personal help was quicker and immediate, while Umunna took time to convene, hear both sides and ask questions, leaving the guilty party to enjoy the sweat of the wronged party and the wronged party to stew in anger. No. He had no patience for that slow-grinding process. It is best to hit the enemy hard, decisively; that would teach him to hustle like his mates. There is no shortcut. Imagine! After one suffers to gather the coins over time, one riffraff appears to reap where he did not sow. *I spent seven years slaving away for my own master, seven good years. Only for a rogue apprentice to—to—*

His head throbbed just thinking of Stanley, and his neck ached. It was because of Stanley that he had left the comfort of home to hustle in a foreign land where he knew not his left from his right, where cars drove on the left side of the road, and the steering wheel was on the right. He knew the tricycle business, but here he was in a country without commercial tricycles. True, the women's backsides were extra-large, but he lacked the means to indulge.

Rapu felt his shirt pocket for the ram's horn from Otogirigiri's rituals for abroad hustling. His mind travelled back to the banks of the Opaku stream, and a shiver glided down his spine. The day was just opening its bleary eyes when he and two other clients gathered on the shore. Each of them had brought a ram. Otogirigiri had asked each man to disrobe.

Now, straddle your animal and hold it by the horns.

They had complied.

Now lift up its front legs!

The others had done as they were told, but Rapu's phallus was long. It dangled down and chafed the animal, arousing it.

Give him a rope to immobilize his manhood, Otogirigiri had instructed one of his acolytes.

Rapu had paused to bind his penis to his thigh, and in that split second, the animal had bolted.

Your enemies are at work, the medicine man had pontificated, *but they will not succeed.*

The disciples had pursued the lamb and brought it back. Wielding a sharp machete, Otogirigiri had sliced off the quadruped's forelimbs.

I am slicing off the hands holding you hostage. I have loosened your bonds. Travel abroad. Foreign currency will flow to you like this water.

And he had scattered some notes on the stream, the colour of fresh engine oil.

CHAPTER 56

After the call, it dawned on Jasper that Rapu was the harbinger of Stanley's ruination. He had a mind to let things be, as Jidenma advised and wait for Rapu's return. He passed the smelling feces; let him be the one to clear it out. But how to appease Nne? She often called, asking to organize a meeting with Stanley's people.

"They can retaliate," Iyom said. "And we can't tell how. The heart of man is desperately wicked. Let us save that boy. If anything should happen to him, God forbid, our family will pay dearly. You know our people."

He decided to consult his older brother, to put heads together. Their mother would want that.

When Zona returned from his foreign trip, Jasper went to his shop.

"Go to Opaku," Zona ordered. "Plead with Stanley's people to wait till Rapu's return to table the matter before our kinsmen. Any decision taken by the collective would be binding on Rapu."

Jasper decided that once Ebuka returned, he would leave. This time, he would take the luxury bus to Onitsha and, from there, hail a cab to Opaku. He was driving his vehicles too much. To service them after each long-distance trip drilled a hole in his pocket. The wear and tear from the bad roads was beginning to tell on them. Oil was dripping from his Corolla, and its tyres were losing traction. Moreover, the police checkpoints extorting car owners every inch of the way increased the toll on his finances.

Perhaps he could also seize the opportunity to visit Cy in Côte d'Ivoire. If Ebuka manned the store and Louisa was around to keep her sister company, what was to stop him? It was now or never. He scrolled down his phone contacts. He would sound Cy out and arrange a quick trip to "disvirgin" his passport.

"Hello. Cy Mukeke! My man, Voilà."

"Oga, it's not Cy."

"Oh, Sorry. Is it a wrong number? I am seeing Cy on my screen."

"Oga Jasper Gee! Ochinanwata!"

"Who is on the line?"

"It's Cy's brother, sir. Polycarp."

"PolyPoly. Kedu?"

"Oga, it's bad news o."

"O gini?"

"Cy's in MACA, sir."

"MACA?" It did not ring a bell.

"Maison d'Arrêt et de Correction d'Abidjan."

"Meaning?"

"Maximum Security Prison, sir. *Na* Abidjan."

His handset thunked on the floor. Cy…He retrieved it. … in prison? "What happened?"

"He go Brazil for business. On return, they nab him at the airport."

"Afia ntu?"

"Yes, sir."

"E sentenciala ya?"

"Twenty years, sir."

"My God!"

"The worst part is that our father just passed on."

"Don't say that again!"

"And Cy is the first son."

"My God!"

He put off his phone, subdued. Cy in jail. Twenty years. Powder business. Why dabble in contraband, knowing the risks involved, knowing that his old man was old and could join his ancestors any moment?

It was a huge fear entertained by Igbo patriarchs with sons hustling all over the world: to die in the forced absence of the first son. To join the forefathers without whispering with his heir.

Jasper flipped his thumb against the middle finger, went into the room and collapsed on the bed. His heart was racing, his jaw clenching.

"Cy Mukeke, my friend," he wailed. "What shall we call this? My friend Cy. What shall we call this?"

He remembered their last meeting at Idumota when he advised Cy that slow and steady won the race. But boys were in a hurry to get rich, drive an SUV, and build mansions. He could still recall Cy's answer: *Lagos babes don't understand slow and steady.* What will the babes understand now, Cy? And Jasper gnashed his teeth. He did some introspection and thanked God for Amata. She was the one who held him back from embarking on the trip to Cy. *Do you know what he is into?* she had asked the last time. *You can only vouch for yourself.*

Suppose he had been with Cy when the unthinkable happened? Suppose he was roped into the investigation? Jailed?

And he loved Amata more. A man's wife, while spurring him to greater heights, must also know when to restrain him from himself.

When Jasper emerged from the bedroom, Amata and her sister were in the dining room, busy with the twins. He had never known his wife to be so talkative. He lay on the couch in the living room and eavesdropped on the sisters. With their sonorous voices, they were two birds twitting. He could see that they enjoyed each other's company and wished he could say as much for the Okonkwo brothers.

With Zona and Rapu, it was competition and suspicion, one trouble after another. What were they disputing? Every day, betrayals, back-hand dealings. Zona had gone behind and scuttled his land deal with Donatus, making a mouth-watering offer the seller could not refuse. He had let it go. There would be other plots up for sale, Iyom had counselled. Every day, sharpening knives. He listened to the sisters. The sound of their voices soothed his shattered spirit. He summoned his phone and searched for the NBA website. Milwaukee Bucks were playing the Golden State Warriors.

~

"So when are you tying the knot with Ugo?" Amata asked Luz.

"Ugo is past tense. Omenma, bring the baby's cup."

"Blood of Jesus. You broke up with Ugo? What happened?"

"It's a long story," Luz said. She felt the temperature of the beverage. "This cup, for O'Neal or Kobe?"

"Anyone. The way you were saying Ugo, Ugo, Ugo, I thought he was the best thing that happened since nkwobi. And was he not a pharmacist or…?"

"He was studying medicine."

"They don't look for work after graduation. They can set up their practice from the get-go."

"He was an abortionist," Luz said simply. "That's how he was paying his school fees. I did not know all the while until I paid him a surprise visit one day and caught him in the act. Anyway, I'm dating Emeka now. He is a lawyer."

"Lawyers are two for a penny, you know. Including yours truly."

"I know, but they still have opportunities. And they don't do D&C."

"What are you waiting for then?"

"M-o-n-e-y."

"That's the problem with graduates. No cash. Before they get a job, if at all, then save for rent, wedding, family—"

"The best suitor is a graduate who hustles. Get a degree, but be an entrepreneur."

"So how does he survive now, Emeka?"

"Mercenary."

"Mercenary, kwa?"

"Impersonates candidates and takes common entrance exams for them. He is paid handsomely."

Amata shook her head. "What a country!" She picked up toys and gathered the juvenile crockery.

Luz began cooing a lullaby to the fractious child.

"Remember Onwa's promise," Amata cautioned her sister.

"Every day, Emeka disturbs me for intimacy. Every day."

"I hope you have not given in."

"And lose my Jeep?"

"Good. Though if you ask me, I don't understand all the hype about sex. Nothing to write home about."

"Ha."

"It's not sweet," Amata said. "Period."

"Maybe you people are not doing it well."

"Where are these twins from, if I may ask?"

"I mean—"

"Hark! an expert."

"The internet is there. You can always consult it."

"He has slept," Omenma announced before Amata could reply her sister.

"Let me cally him in. O'Niru too sreep."

"Are you saying that marriage is not sweet?" Louisa asked immediately Omenma carried O'Neal into the bedroom. She lifted Kobe.

"In my view, with the little I have seen, it depends on the man. If you marry a choleric man, you will not enjoy the marriage. Like one man in the market, the smallest thing ignites him. The last time his sister came from home to tell him about their sick mother, he flared up, calling her names and saying she sleeps around. A sister."

"He would not be a joy to live with."

"If he treats his sister like that, a person who suckled the same breasts as him, how will he treat a wife, a total stranger he spent money to marry? Same with my in-laws. One has banished his wife to the village because she gives birth to only females."

"Husband and wife are complete strangers who move in together."

"Yet in Igboland, we say that they have become siblings."

"Cat and mouse siblings. Kobe, sleep! Omenma, please come and rock Kobe to sleep."

Amata began a lullaby, but the children's minder interrupted her. "Mummy, I know one song that Kobe rikes."

"Okay. Sing it for him."

Omenma cleared her throat and began:

The lat and cockloach inside the car
The lat is the dliver
The cockloach is the passenger smoking ciga.

The sisters laughed, but Kobe smiled and squirmed in excitement.

"Rat, Omenma, not lat. Driver, not dliver. Cockroach, not cockloach. Take Kobe inside and continue to sing for him."

"Sister, Omenma should go to school."

"I know. I've been thinking about enrolling her, but I am afraid of this Lagos."

"As how?"

"Sexual predators. I had a tailor down the road, a local man, nothing fancy. One morning, I went to his workshop to collect a blouse. You know what I saw? Schoolgirls in front of a laptop, watching a blue movie."

"I hope you reprimanded them."

"My dear, I was too disgusted. I grabbed my cloth and never patronized him after that."

"He was grooming them."

"Exactly. When Omenma came to live with us, I said I can't let her out like that. Not in this Lagos. There are wolves everywhere."

"He has slept!" Omenma came back to announce.

The women heaved a sigh of relief and stretched.

"Are they not too big for the cup?" Louisa asked. "They are going to three now."

"Soon. They need protein to grow tall and strong. You see that basketball over there? Anyway, my advice to you is do not succumb to Emeka. What if, after you succumb, he tells you his parents are against the union? That they don't want him to marry from Nkwa? Or marry a Catholic, that they are Pentecostal? What then? Once the hymen is gone, it's irretrievable. And the Jeep too. Oh, has Jasper eaten? See me neglecting my husband."

"Daddy has eaten," Omenma answered. "He is sreeping on the sofa."

"Oh! Thank God. Luz, let us turn in. Ebuka is arriving tomorrow. He will follow Jasper to the market. We will stay home and have a blast. Let day break."

Jasper remained on the sofa while the women retired to their different bedrooms. The news of Cy's incarceration riled him. While he lay on the sofa trying to make sense of how Cy could have gotten into such a mess, he eavesdropped on the conversation between his wife and Louisa. He was shocked to hear Amata say that sex was not sweet. As much as he tried to listen in on their remaining gist, his mind stayed put on his wife's concern. Jasper understood that one of the ways to get a woman quickly unhappy in marriage was not to be able to knock her out in bed.

He surfed the web and realized that he had been approaching intimacy like a Formula One race. As an apprentice, his mates had bantered about love, but he had paid scant attention, not having a girlfriend. Now he understood there was no whistle, no sprint, no race, no four-wheeler. Rather, it was a bicycle for two, each pedalling together until the couple breasted the tape.

When he joined his wife in the room, he knew she would be expecting the usual hop, skip and jump. He surprised her. Afterwards, Amata lay ensconced in his side, luxuriating in the aftereffect.

CHAPTER 57

Two days after his father's call, Ebuka was still nowhere to be found.

Amata called Pa Okeke. "When is Ebuka coming, sir?"

"Wonderful!" the Elder exclaimed. "He left tabato." Three days ago.

"Blood of Jesus."

Jasper grabbed the phone from his wife. His heart was already pounding. He conferred with Ebuka's father. Ebuka had left Opaku at first cockcrow to catch a bus to Onitsha. From there, he was to board an early bus to Lagos. If all went well, he should have reached Lagos at sundown the same day. Clearly, something was amiss.

The next day, news of what transpired at Onitsha started filtering in at Idumota. The security agents had carried out an operation and mopped up criminal elements at Enugu, Aba, Umuahia, Awka, and Owerri. Some said it was the dreaded Operation Python Dance. Others swore it was the Special Anti-Robbery Squad. At Onitsha, another dawn raid at Upper Iweka Motor Park rounded up a coterie of stragglers accused of IPOB affinity. They were passengers waiting for their buses to fill up, witnesses said. The soldiers shoved them into trucks and drove away.

Python Dance, Jasper mouthed. If not for the loss of lives it occasioned, the government had funny names for their campaigns. He had heard of Crocodile Smile. And Monkey Palaver. What of Baboon Blood? One day, it was the SARS. The next, the army is on the lookout for IPOB. Is every Igbo man a member of IPOB?

He had first heard about the group at the town meeting but knew nothing else about them: where they met or their chain of command. Yet every Igbo man was an IPOB suspect. It appeared that simply being Igbo was a crime in Nigeria. All these ethnically motivated raids were really attacks aimed at ethnic cleansing, to decimate Igbo menfolk. *It does not suffice that they discriminate against us and deny us empowerment jobs and loans.* Now, they increase hostility and violence towards people who ask for nothing but peace to hustle, create wealth, and raise their families.

One mind told Jasper that Ebuka was in trouble. He was young. He was male. He was able-bodied. He was Igbo.

"It is not something to discuss over the telephone," Jasper told his wife. He folded his RSA t-shirt into a duffel. "I need to go myself, make enquiries, and also see about Stanley."

"But your kinsman advised you to let Rapu handle his shit."

"I'm just trying to kill two birds with a stone, my dear." He patted her on the shoulder. "If I am home for Ebuka, I might as well seize the opportunity to calm Stanley's people and buy time."

Amata was downcast.

"I won't be long. You have your sister to keep you company. Forget about going to the shop. I should be back by the weekend."

Returning by the weekend was being too optimistic, but that was the only way to calm his wife. It warmed his heart to see her concern for him.

"One four three."

She smiled.

SARS. They had a post at Awkuzu. Another at Neni. He would have to visit the two, if necessary, to find Ebuka and then bail him out if it was not too late. Sometimes, those rounded up were led to the bush and shot point blank.

It would cost money. Money, Money, Money. Everything costs money. They tell you that bail is free. Ha. But why arrest someone who has done nothing wrong? Standing in a motor park to board a bus was not a crime.

Jasper lay awake until late, thinking about his upcoming trip.

The next morning, he and Amata stood outside the flat saying their goodbyes when a scrawny fellow strode up. At first, they thought him a madman, one of those town-dwellers on the margins of sanity. If he was carrying a jute bag, he would pass for one of the many scavengers who scoured Lagos's rat-infested neighbourhood dumpsters in search of valuables and edibles.

"Morning, Sir. Mummy, good morning."

"Ebuka!" the couple exclaimed.

He explained that their bus had been attacked at Ore by bandits wielding AK-47 rifles. Passengers had scampered in all directions. He had dashed into the bush and followed another wayfarer through the wilds to Lagos.

"The roads are bad, sir," he concluded, taking I n Jasper's travelling bag. "Kidnappers, ritualists, police brutality."

Amata's stomach churned. "Ebuka is here," she said with pleading eyes. "You don't have to go."

Jasper drew her aside. "Remember Stanley's people. I won't be away for long."

He left instructions for Ebuka about the shop. He slugged his gear over his shoulder, set his Shaquille cap and embraced Amata. He was wearing the black shirt Jidenma had gifted him, the one with yellow spikes like a flash of lightning on the left breast.

"This is the fifth bus, sir," the ticket master said.

Jasper paid for a seat and walked round the bus, gauging its reliability. He kicked the tyres. Sturdy.

"Free seating!" the bus mate announced to passengers mounting the Volvo Marcopolo. Jasper rued the safest spot to occupy. The front rows were out of the question in case of a head-on. The last three at the rear were also vetoed in the event a tailgater's brakes failed. The safest were the middle rows. Even then, he knew not to opt for the driver's side because of the danger presented by on-coming vehicles. A window seat on the right flank had its attractions. You could control the airflow and buy snacks from the hawkers that besought travellers. But killer herdsmen and kidnappers also erupted from the right side, firing indiscriminately. The passengers there were usually the first line of attack.

My best bet is an aisle seat, near the rear door. He located one such and sidled into it.

"Switch off your phones!" the driver's mate yelled down the aisle. It was a precaution against spies who fed info to criminals about the bus's trajectory.

Jasper hurriedly called his wife. "I am taking Ekeson Transport. We are leaving Jibowu now. Passengers have been told to shut down their phones. I will check in at rest points. One four three."

The journey went without incident. At Ore, when they stopped for a bathroom break, Jasper dialled home as promised. *So far, so good.* Amata beamed.

"I will call again when I reach Opaku. One four three."

~

Three hours later, Iyom dialled Amata. She had been trying to get Jasper to no avail.

"Rapu's apprentice has died."

"Blood of Jesus."

"Tell your husband not to come home until we know what his people are planning."

But it was too late. As the Marcopolo hurtled eastward, Jasper, in his safe aisle seat, curled like a cable, snoozed, unaware of the snake in the rafters that had slithered down and was, even now, baring its fangs.

CHAPTER 58

"Hello. Omeifeukwu, sir."

"My wife," Zona answered, startled by the call from Jasper's wife. He hoped his brother was in some kind of trouble. "Hope nothing."

"Jasper travelled home by bus this morning. Nne called to say that Stanley has died, that trouble may be brewing."

"Hmmm."

"I have been calling him, sir, but you know how passengers are required to put off their phones."

"Oh, he went by public transport?"

"Yes, sir. Ekeson."

"So, what do you want me to do?"

"Nne says you know the Police Area Commander. Can you notify him to caution Stanley's people to maintain the peace?"

Zona felt diminished. Something happens and Nne does not inform him, Omeifeukwu. But when there is trouble, she remembers him.

"Who am I?" he exclaimed. "I'll tell you: I am a nobody."

"What do we do? Jasper doesn't know that—"

But Zona had signed off. He was furious with his mother for sidestepping the head of the family and reaching out to Jasper. Now, when there is a whiff of danger, they remember Zona. Tsk. He put away his phone and reached for his newspaper.

Another thought crossed his mind. He reached for his phone. On the third ring, a voice answered. "Ezekiel on the line."

When he finished talking with Stanley's brother, he called the District Police Officer. "An IPOB troublemaker is coming to ferment trouble as we speak."

~

Later in the night, an agitated Iyom called her first son, and as he had been doing lately, he did not answer his mother's calls.

Iyom called Jasper's wife back.

"Has he arrived?" Amata was close to tears with worry.

"Has he reached you?" Iyom asked at the same time.

Louisa stood behind her sister. She, too, was a bag of nerves. Something was wrong, terribly wrong. Jasper should have reached Opaku by now. She placed a hand on the small of Amata's back. She could feel her sister's panic as if by osmosis.

"Maybe they had a breakdown. It often happens. These bus drivers don't service their vehicles."

Amata clutched at this ray of hope. She sought out her chaplet.

"I pray so. Nne, go lie down. I will call as soon as I hear from him."

Amata knew the old woman would not sleep a wink, and her heart went out to her. They loved the same man. She dialled Jasper's number again. It rang for a while, then a computerized voice came on: *The number you are calling is currently switched off. Please try again later.*

Throughout the night, Amata tried Jasper. Whenever she woke during the night, she checked for missed calls. None. She sighed heavily. *Blood of Jesus,* she prayed into the darkness; *please let him reach safely. Please let no harm come to the father of my children. Please, God.*

She fell on her knees, clutching her chaplet, squishing it round and round her palms. It snapped, scattering the beads in her hands. Still, she caressed them feverishly, and they felt like liquid, like blood, roiling in her palms. She was there until the Imam yodelled for dawn prayers. Louisa came in and sat by her.

A cup of tea was in her hand. At Lou's inquiring gaze, Amata shook her head. "So unlike him."

"Drink this."

"Could he have been kidnapped?"

Louisa circled the cup with the spoon. Amata declined the beverage, preferring to fast for good news.

That whole morning, Amata was on the phone, calling family and friends. No one had news of Jasper.

At noon, Louisa reached out to their parents.

"What bus did you say he took?" Onwa asked.

"Ekeson."

Onwa drove down to the Onitsha terminus of the transport company. He counted eleven military checkpoints on the fifteen-kilometre journey.

"All our buses from Lagos have come in, Chief," the station manager declared.

"Can I peruse your manifest?"

The manifest was brought. The Station Manager scrolled through the lists. On the fifth, Onwa saw the name: Jasper Okonkwo. He pointed to it. "There he is."

"I told you, Chief. All our buses came in as scheduled."

"What must have happened? That man is my son-in-law."

"If anything has happened, it must be between here and Opaku," the transporter said. He closed his ledgers and stood up.

A pensive and confused Onwa made his way out. From Onitsha to Opaku was a straightforward fare: one could hail a taxi from the Upper Iweka overpass to Obosi, on to Oba. At Oba, either veer left into Ojoto and on to Opaku or continue down to Ozubulu and enter Opaku from there. Either way was an hour's journey. What could have happened?

Outside the station, a dwarf busboy accosted him. He was wiping his hands on a dirty cloth, and had been eavesdropping around the manager's counter.

"O nwelu oyi nwanyi?" Does he have a girlfriend?

It was a possibility, Onwa thought and smacked himself for not thinking along that line. A married man could have proclivities that led him to play away matches once in a while. He also had several peccadilloes under his belt. He reflected on this. Jasper did not strike him as a ladies' man. He shook his head and strode to his vehicle. The fellow followed.

"I suspect SARS or IPOB."

Onwa stopped.

"They are the people disappearing our boys," the gnomic man repeated. "SARS and IPOB."

"How so?"

"IPOB recruits you by force. SARS hunt IPOB."

CHAPTER 59

Another sigh escaped Amata as she sat, clad in black, with the womenfolk. Eliza was shaving her curls, the long hair she had nurtured for ages. Copious whorls of it fell about her shoulders and chest. Louisa gathered them.

In the background, the church group intoned the Litany of the Dead.

O Compassionate Lord Jesus.
Grant him rest, oh Lord.

Devastated was how she felt. The events were hazy, but her mind replayed them without bidding. Three days after her husband's journey, still no news of him. Her father had sent a vehicle to bring her, Louisa, the twins, and Omenma back to Nkwa, saying, *Whatever it is, we will weather it together.*

He must have died, the locals said. To disappear like that? With a young wife? And two sons? It is not usual. He must have met a reversal of fortunes, opined Dr. Ofoma, the senior public servant. Jasper had said he would go to SARS stations to make enquiries about Ebuka's whereabouts, but he could not have because Ebuka returned that same morning before he left for Opaku.

Amata had mixed feelings. She was just eager to get on with her life. But how? At thirty, with two young sons? And without a man's protective armour. She dreaded the last aspect of the rites when the head of Jasper's kinsmen would address her: *Amata, your husband is no more. Who out of his brothers do you choose to "cover" you?*

Ikwuchi. Agbisi had done same to Akwaeke. They had discussed it, she and Jasper. It dawned on her anew. Jasper was no more. Blood of Jesus.

May the soul of Jasper and the souls of the faithful departed...

Through the mercy of God rest in peace. Amen.

She got up and surveyed the compound. Unsure of what would become of her, she flung herself on the ground and began wailing, a long, deep-throated cry.

"Eh! Jasper. Gone? Ochinanwata, tell me what I did to you to bring me out like this and abandon me in the middle of nowhere."

The women lifted her up. They joined her in her wailing, the widows among them crying the loudest as their own memories flooded back.

Jasper, late? Amata shuddered as sympathisers surrounded her. Louisa stood by her, rubbing her shoulders, salving her.

"It is enough, woman," the clansmen exhorted her. "Dry your eyes. You have two boys to cater for now. Gird up. Kee nkwucha."

"Death does not know how to kill," a sympathizer hissed. "Jasper, so young, so soft-spoken, ... and his mother is still alive!"

When the funeral date had been fixed, Zona's wife had come, pleading with her not to choose Omeifeukwu. She had come with gifts: two heads of cloth, Super Wax, a scarf, the trending fashion.

Jasper's two brothers sat with their different age grades, making small talk and waiting.

~

From where he sat, Rapu threw glances at his brother's widow. How comely she was! He thought of her dowry. The expensive household equipment still stood untouched in the interstices of the family house. Already, she had twin boys for Jasper. He would adopt them if she chose him. They were the same blood.

The trip to South Africa had not worked out. Too much internecine war among the Igbos there; people snitched on one another, ambushed kinsmen and betrayed trust. He had scurried to use the return stub of his ticket before it lapsed.

~

Amata was thinking of her encounter with the parish priest about the Ikwuchi custom. It was not difficult for the Church to find fault and raise a ruckus that could tar one's image, make one the laughingstock or gossip fodder of the women's associations, sometimes to the extent of ex-communication.

Are you sure Jasper is dead? the padre had asked.

He has been silent for over two months, Father.

But he could be alive. Remember the prodigal son.

No, he could not be, she wanted to say. Not Jasper. Be alive and incommunicado? No. He has met with a horrible fate.

With no sign of life? she asked the priest.

It happens. He could be in trouble and not have a way to communicate.

It is his people who decided.

What if he comes back?

Silence.

Are his brothers not married already?

One is not, Father.

Is that the one you will choose?

Probably, Father.

Probably?

I don't know, Father.

Give to Caesar what is Caesar's, and to God what is God's, the priest quoted from the Gospel of Mark.

Who is Caesar here, Father?

You have to figure it out yourself, Mrs. Okonkwo.

"Why will you choose Rapu, a sapling?" her sorority friends asked, mouths agape. "Our people say he who must eat frog should choose the one with eggs. Omeifeukwu is already well-established. Don't you want an easy life? How will you raise these boys? Now that you have the opportunity to release the throttle—"

"Charity is my friend. We belong to the same societies. And the Church does not accept polygamy."

Rapu's intended had also come for the funeral ceremony, a Gabourey Sidibe lookalike. She was family now, wasn't she? Did she know about *Ikwuchi*? She must, since she hailed from a nearby village. The whole of Igboland practised it.

"Sister, ndo," she said to Amata with a side embrace.

"Thank you, Nonye. Daalu."

Was she also subtly pleading for space? *Please do not choose Rapu. Go for the well-to-do brother.* Was that what Nonye was telegraphing?

She slapped a crawly insect on her neck, crushed it and flicked it away. And allowed her mind to slip again into the past.

Rapu, true, on return from South Africa, had visited. *Any news? Have you heard from him?* She shook her head at all the questions.

To disappear like that? Did you quarrel?

Was it not the shit you passed that he was going to clear? She wanted to scream at him.

How long now?

Three months now.

I brought some garri and plantain for you. Hope the boys are doing well.

They are trying their best. They miss their father. But they are surviving.

On another occasion, he had asked, *How long has it been now?*

Five months.

And still no news?

She shook her head.

Umunna checked mortuaries, hospitals, and police detention centres?

Yes. Nothing.

Ha. Okay, let me run along. Here, this is twenty thousand naira chop money.

Thank you, sir. O'Neal, Kobe, say thank you to Uncle.

And the twins would interrupt their basketball game to mumble, *Uncle, thank you.*

~

Amata will choose me. I am the older. There is a pecking order. I, first, Zona assured himself. Since Jasper's disappearance, he had been providing for her, sending foodstuff and pocket money, and rendering advice on family issues. He began supplying motor parts on credit to Jasper's shop.

If Amata chose him, as he believed she would, he would bring in the outside son Modupe had given him. Zona thought of the boy and smiled involuntarily. He had named him Odumegwu. Awesome. Yes, the arrival of a son after so many attempts was a thing of awe. Modupe Simpson, first round, a boy. Did she feed him a philtre to invigorate the elusive Y chromosome? Charity was too quarrelsome. Her X chromosomes rode roughshod over his Y, but Dupe's X had deferred to his.

When the elders announced their decision to bid a customary farewell to Jasper, he called Amata.

"How are you, dear?"

"Fine, sir. Omeifeukwu."

"Umunna have fixed a date."

Amata sniffed. She was always respectful to Zona, always calling him "sir," which sounded distant, Zona felt. It would soon change. When they became intimate, she would loosen up.

"The soldiers?"

"They are fine, sir."

"You know if you need anything, not to hesitate."

"Yes, sir."

Zona's eyes crinkled with pleasure. The braggart was out of the way forever. He would inherit his widow, "knack" her, and pump his seed into her. He would be the only man alive to climb her, not like all these his other women, who had succumbed to the wiles of many a man before him. Amata would choose him. He sent her a text:

> *Dear, I will care for you. I am willing to pamper you the way a beauty queen should be pampered. Please, give me a chance.*

Would she respond? She did, after an interminable hour: *Thank you, sir. I appreciate.*

Still distant and non-committal. What if she did not select him? No way, he thought. She would not choose Rapu with a fledgling business. Would she go outside the nuclear family and take a cousin or uncle? It had been known to happen. His mind scanned the confraternity of uncles and cousins. None was as strong as he, financially. Didn't women say, No finance, no romance? He would be Amata's first choice.

Zona's intention was to upgrade Amata's flat to a duplex on the other side of town. Charity's predilections for violence would not deter him. *It is tradition,* he would tell her. *Look, it is Umunna that decided, not Zona. And it is the widow who chooses, and one cannot refuse. Custom. Agbisi did it with Akwaeke. Ask Iyom. And if it was me gone, you would not hesitate to pick Jasper, the way you were flitting over him like flies on a roadkill.*

Charity would have no choice but to accept. Without a male child, who was she to complain? With five girls that will marry and move away, was his lineage not facing extinction? Thanks to Modupe, he had an heir. Amata would produce more for him.

He could not imagine his kid brother winning the lottery of Amata's heart because Rapu was already negotiating a girl's hand. Zona had accompanied him to knock on Nonye's door. Rapu should content himself with her. Or would he pursue two things at the same time, like the proverbial dog that attempted to answer two calls simultaneously and ended up losing its voice completely?

~

Rapu's age group chatted nearby. They had heard about the misadventure with his apprentice and how Stanley's family had taken their pound of flesh and Umunna had closed the matter. Stanley died. Jasper died. Case closed.

"Jasper's wife may choose you," a mate said to Rapu.

"Choose a sapling? With Omeifeukwu on the table? You know women. No euro, no eros."

They looked towards the entrance of the family house. Jasper's cairn was a rectangular mound. It lay next to Agbisi's, marked by wilting wreaths and stones atop the loose soil. On the other side of it, the clansmen exchanged banter.

Rapu, a struggling trader, did not, for one minute, suspect that he would win the ballot in a duel with Echezona, a high net-worth mogul, whose hand was strong and who could maintain two women easily as well as a school of children. He had shops all over Lagos and was grooming a host of apprentices. How many blocks of real estate did he not command? In Festac, Ijesha, Isolo? And building something now at Lekki. Not to mention his Rangers Hotel.

~

Nine months later, the elders met again.

"This absence is not empty-handed," they said. "Is he dead? How can someone be silent like that and cut off all contacts? Does he not know he has a family? This thing is not empty-handed. Wife, you say he was coming to Opaku?"

"Yes, sir. He was to come for Ebuka and Stanley. In the morning, as he was leaving, Ebuka walked in. So he said he would come and meet Stanley's people."

"You say you have checked Facebook and all the 'sosho' media?"

"Yes, sir."

Did they drug him? Sell him into slavery? Use him for rituals? Jasper, who was running a successful business here, did he up and disappear like exhaust smoke? It is not empty-handed. Something greater than nte entered nte's trap.

"I hear that they kill off the person and collect his organs," the town crier said, nursing a drink.

"Yes, but it is for those crossing the desert, going to Europe. The missus said he was coming to the East. Or do they harvest organs in Nigeria now?"

"Anything is possible in Nigeria, my brother."

"Wife, you may go. We will whisper together, and revert."

The elders of the clan met again and decided that not knowing was too much stress and uncertainty. It had never happened before. Zephaniah, son of Oti, was incarcerated in Malaysia. He sent word. Ephraim, his brother, was held in Tihar, New Delhi. Umunna received word of it. Nothing from Jasper. He is no longer on this side of the grass, they concluded. Better to do the funeral rites and let him rest in peace, wherever he is.

They gathered for the ceremony. It was a sad event, but Amata persevered. The shock caused her menstrual period to do a vanishing act again. Still, the women advised her to wear sanitary napkins to bed. *So Jasper's spirit will not come in your sleep and have relations with you. The pad will discourage him.*

She nodded. They did not know Jasper. Blood did not deter him.

Iyom was struck dumb by the turn of events. She, who used to banter on and on like an idling engine, became silent like spilled motor oil. All she did was sigh and hiss and shake her head. She aged overnight and walked with a cane now. Once, peering at his image in his wedding photo, she let slip that she did not believe her Jasper was gone. A child one carried nine months in the womb will pass on, and his mother will not feel it? But she went along with the clansmen. As a woman, you did not have the final say. You acquiesced to the elders and kept your thoughts to yourself. Something, however, died within her.

Amata's people's sorrow was beyond description. Onwa and Odoziaku mourned the mishap that had befallen their jewel. They rallied round Amata and stationed Louisa permanently with her. *Do not leave her side,* they entreated.

On their own, they made enquiries at the Police and Army headquarters. *We are looking for our in-law, Jasper Okonkwo, alias Ochinanwata, MD, Jasper Gee, of Umueri village, Opaku Autonomous Community. He left Lagos for the East by road, leaving behind a young wife and two children. Kindly contact your posts for any information about him.*

Amata sniffed, remembering. Louisa's hand squeezed strength into her. She rationalized her situation and concluded that she did not want to divide the family. For one, how sure was anyone that Jasper would not return? How sure that he was not held somewhere and would one day walk in to find what?

Someone submitted that he had travelled abroad, that it had been a nagging hunger in him to see outside. Initially, Amata had entertained that thought, as well. But their passports were in the bedside drawer. Could one travel outside Nigeria without the green booklet? No. Harm had come upon her beloved husband. He was in a land of no return. Otherwise, nothing would have kept him away from his wife, from his O'Neal and Kobe. And the LeBron and Antetokounmpo they were planning. She felt her life losing control, going out of whack, like a MACK truck wobbling downhill without brakes.

"Sis," Louisa whispered to her. "Consider that you have a say. Suppose Umunna imposed a choice on you, bundled you to one party? Here, for a change, they are giving the woman an opportunity to decide who to cover her. This is the second time they are asking you. This is a buffet of grooms. Pick one."

Deep down, she wanted Rapu because he was single and unencumbered. But he was still battling to stay above water. And now, with the setback he had suffered, it would be an uphill task to provide for her and the twins. Add to that his penchant for fetishism. She made a dentilingual sound. People expected her to respect Echezona and pick him, but what of his wife? Charity was like a sister. How could they now share a man? And the Church? Too complicated. She would be excommunicated and unable to belong to any church societies. All these thoughts twirled in her head.

If she chose Rapu, Zona would feel slighted. His benevolence to her would dry up; he was capable of that. And she would be plunging a knife further into the family brotherhood. In short, it was better not to choose any of Jasper's siblings.

Then came the question for real: Amata, who, among our kinsmen, do you choose to cover you?"

She swooned and crumbled. *Blood of Jesus. I am a widow! A widoooow!*

The women revived her. And the elder, Ishienyi, posed the question again. "Who among Ochinanwata's brethren do you choose to cover you?"

"None," she said aloud to the assembly.

"You do not want any of Jasper's brothers?"

Amata shook her head, her eyes fixed on the ground.

"You will stay like that?"

"Tsk."

"On your own?"

Silence.

"What of outside the immediate family? His cousins? Uncles? Kith and kin?"

Again, she shook her head.

"Church dismiss," someone quipped.

"It is the shock," another someone said.

"Poor girl," the family head commiserated.

CHAPTER 60

Amata returned to Lagos, back to the business. She still had Ebuka. After five years of apprenticeship, he was due to be freed. Where would she see the money to set him up? She hoped that sales would improve. But what sales? Competition was rife. Every day, freedmen entered the sector. True, many migrated and set up in other parts of Nigeria: Kaura Namoda, Zungeru and Karshi, but a handful remained south to swamp the market. Sure, the Jeep's money was still banked, but it was for the twins' education. Now more than ever, she needed to set money aside for their future.

Zona sent an SMS. *Tough woman, why reject us? Are we not good enough for you? I thought you would accept me and let me spoil you a little. Please rethink. I am waiting.*

He could not wait to make love to Jasper's wife. Modupe had tutored him. He knew his bearings now. He sent foodstuff and gifts to Amata, accompanied by a bulging envelope.

Rapu was hopeful. He had thought that there would be no contest, that Zona would win hands-down. However, when Amata declined to choose, hope surged; were the two brothers so equally matched that a decision was hard? Perhaps the widow needed more time to reflect, to consider what she could gain by pitching her tent with one or the other. If Amata chose him, his life would be set out for him, made, even. He would ditch Nonye, and settle down in Jasper's house, fuck his wife and take over the business. His tricycles and motorbike trade would swallow

Jasper's spare parts shop. He would save on the bride price, a wedding ceremony, the in-laws and all the nuptial activities that guzzled money. In competing with Zona, Rapu had not dared to hope. Now, after revisiting their situations, it dawned on him that Amata might pick him. He was single; he had no encumbrances. He weighed his manhood.

He engaged Otogirigiri again to shuffle things in his favour, to make the sought-after Amata fall for him.

"Consume three turds; three, of female human feces," the witch doctor prescribed. "And your brother's widow is yours."

On his return to the capital, he sent her an SMS: *Hope you had a safe journey back. I understand how you may be feeling. Take your time and reflect. I know it is not easy. I care.* He transferred some money to her account.

How astute of her! the women of the village said behind Amata's back. Choose one and shut one valve. Choose no one, and continue to chop from the two. Ha. Wise girl, Amata. Right from the night Jasper brought her from Nkwa, her eyes blinking like hazard lights, they had suspected that this was a shrewd woman.

Amata re-embraced her routine. But she was beginning to miss the company of the opposite sex. Many men eyed her and spoke to her in innuendoes. She knew what they wanted. They saw a woman sexually starved and needing the male muscle. But she was shy and could not come out openly to yield. She had no experience in flirting. Jasper had been her only love.

There was Chief Okwo, also known as Ogalanya, Rich Man. He supplied her Honda parts.

Pay when able, no rush, he said when he presented her with his last invoice for eight million naira.

That benevolence gave him the excuse to call her often and ostensibly ask about the business. He always ended with: *If you need anything, anything at all, fine woman, let me know.*

Could he fund Ebuka's freedom? Pay one year's rent for a shop for him and supply him the start-up goods? Remove that headache from her?

The Chairman of the Market Association passed by frequently to check on her. Her shop was always the first port of call for his boys for any parts customers wanted. He had boys on the streets, scouting for customers. He had instructed them to direct some her way.

What of Akajiaku, the major importer who bought several containers at a go and retailed them to the traders? He was a classy man, always impeccably dressed. When he went "English," he would wear Savile Row suits. If he went native, it would be a spry fabric for his ensemble, with a fancy cap placed jauntily to hide a receding hairline. He wore mules made of snakeskin, zany things. He passed by her shop periodically and fawned over her, always with a gift—a Michael Kors purse, a bottle of Miss Dior perfume, or a piece of jewellery that he bought at the duty-free shops of world capitals. He would always ask about Jasper as a cover-up, his eyes imploring.

Any news from my friend?

Amata would shake her head.

You don't say! Some people endowed with ample buttocks don't know how to sit. To abandon a fine baby like you in the market and disappear. If there is anything I can do for you. Anything at all.

Akajiaku!

Her church members' husbands were also eyeing her. Their wives, suspicious and anxious to protect their turf, watched with full headlamp eyes whenever Amata was around. They stopped inviting her to their homes. Their paths only crossed at society functions. Behind her, the women analyzed the graph of her life, how it had plummeted, from Jeep and Camry and twin boys to a missing husband.

The Chairman of the Market Association passed by [illegible] quently to check on her. Her shop was always the first port of call for his lads for any pieces of jewellery wanted. He had boys on the streets scouting for customers. He had instructed them to direct some her way.

When Akalaku, the major importer, who bought several containers at a go and [illegible] them to the [illegible]? He was a classy man, always impeccably dressed. When he wore [illegible] he would wear Savile Row suits; [illegible] it would be [illegible] for his [illegible] with a [illegible] and [illegible] to [illegible] matching [illegible]. He wore [illegible] made of snakeskin [illegible] things. He passed by her shop occasionally and showered over her always with a gift — a Michael Kors purse, a bottle of Miss Dior perfume or a piece of jewellery that he bought at the duty free shops of world capitals. He would always ask about Jasper as a [illegible] his [illegible] importer.

'Any news from my friend?'

Amara would shake her head.

'You don't say? Some people are blessed [illegible] *Jasper* [illegible] *a fine baby like you* [illegible] *if [illegible]* [illegible]'

'*Kedu?*'

After church, [illegible] husbands were also eyeing her. Their wives, [illegible] to protect their turf, [illegible] when Amara was around. They snapped anything [illegible] to their [illegible] functions [illegible] the woman [illegible] of her life [illegible] losing husband.

CHAPTER 61

One day, Alloy Malaysia invited Amata to the opening of his Plaza at Dolphin Estate. Alloy, a big-time clearing agent, was the PRO of the Elite Merchants Club and cleared the containers of many Igbo importers. Amata attended the function. The Club members filled the emporium. Amata recognized Dona Agupusi of Blue Anchor Clearing Agency and Rhedmac's Goddy Ezeemo. The guests ate and danced and exchanged pleasantries, ribbing each other mercilessly across the hall. The big men wore prestigious aliases like togas: Ide, Okemiri, Akunwata, Nkenkenyi, Owelle. Titles flew across the hall like missiles, and the popular greeting of three strikes with the arm in one direction and the last in the opposite was re-enacted at frequent intervals. Some clenched their staff of office, a foot-long stick carved of bone or ivory; others gripped fly whisks or round leather fans. They donned an assortment of wears: the ubiquitous velvet red cap, Abiriba hat, ishiagu fabric in various hues and designs, French suits, and the occasional T-shirts and half-shoes. Johnny Walker, Hennessy and Remy Martin were dispatched with alacrity. A smorgasbord of Igbo delicacies delighted palates at intervals. It was a splashy event.

As daylight dimmed, Amata worried about her geriatric jalopy. She bade farewell to those around her and slipped out, conscious not to cause a stir. Her fears were confirmed when her car would not start. A guest standing by helped her push it into the plaza premises.

"Tomorrow, bring a mechanic and sort it out," he said, flicking dust from his shirt. "Care for a lift?"

"Where are you kidnapping my customer to?" a man asked benignly from the shadows.

It was her bank manager. He offered to take Amata home, and a friendship was kindled. At first, Amata felt shy, but the banker insisted, tugging at her drawstrings till all her defences crumpled, and she gave in. Her in-laws supplied all her sustenance needs, while the banker provided clandestine comfort between the sheets in short-stay inns. This went on for almost a year.

One sweltering day, after the midday worship in the market, Amata swooned and collapsed. It was unprecedented. Neighbours rallied around and revived her. Ebuka alerted Omeifeukwu, who rushed her to the hospital.

"I shall be back," Zona told Amata as she was being wheeled in. "Let me close the shops. You know these boys."

When Zona dashed back to the market, his head apprentice calculated the day's revenue. It was a little over three hundred thousand. He lodged it in the safe.

"Lock up and go home," he told Chibuike. "Who is sleeping in the shop tonight?"

Chibuike pointed to a recent apprentice. "Keep your eyes and ears open," Zona warned the boy. "Are you getting my point? Be on the lookout for area urchins and arsonists."

He hurried to Amata's store. As he approached, he saw the blinking neon lights: Jasper Gee's Trading Company. *So she has not changed the shop's name. We buried the man, but his shop still reflects his name. Like his sons, he is carrying on.*

"Where is the day's take?"

"No sales today, sir," Ebuka answered. "How is Mummy?"

"Fine. You are the one due for freedom?"

"Yes, sir."

"Have you seen a vacant shop?"

"Yes, sir."

"Where?"

"Opaku, Sir."

"You want to base at Opaku?"

"Yes, sir, by the mechanic village there."

Made sense. Zona leaned on the counter and transferred five hundred thousand naira to the boy. He was impatient to return to the hospital. He had been waiting for this opportunity to get closer to the widow, to get her beholden to him, to choose him.

"This pays your rent for one year. You can stock it from my warehouse. Sell and settle."

"Our agreement says one hundred thousand naira goods, sir. This sum covers it."

"In that case, use it to organize your freedom. Do not disturb your madam."

"Thank you, sir. Omeifeukwu. But—"

"O gini kwa?" What again?

"Who will stay with Mummy?"

Omeifeukwu was astonished. Apprentices were two a kobo. "Are apprentices hard to get in Igboland?"

"Mummy wants a female."

A female in a market bursting with men? "Is it not to drop a cockroach among hens? Are you getting my point?"

"She said that women need to be empowered, sir, that they can also learn the trade and become importers."

"Amata said that?"

"Yes, sir. I have a sister who just finished Teacher Training.""

"Send for her, then, and put her through before you graduate."

Zona checked his watch and turned to go. "Close the shop. I am going back to the hospital."

"Yes, sir."

The radius between him and Idumota lengthened. The cacophony of the market receded, replaced by the incessant drones of vehicles, beeping of horns, and screeching of rubber on asphalt. The lagoon breeze was stuffy and warm.

Women need to be empowered. He had five daughters. And a secret son from a Yoruba woman. Modupe had "helped" Charity bear a male child for him. *Born more sons for me, Modupe,* he had pleaded. On sons hang all the laws and the prophets. But Modupe had demurred. *One son is fine. You have broken the curse. Thank you.*

Hold it. One son did not cut it. It was too risky. He needed backup to secure his legacy. He would look elsewhere again. Many young girls roamed the streets, searching for a place to perch. So far, he wowed them in his Rangers Hotel. But he needed a permanent girl, a mistress, like a car needed a spare tyre. If Amata chose him, his swivel eyes for skirts would cease. He descended the ramp at Costain and veered into Apapa Road. He felt light-headed. He dialled Modupe.

"How is my son?"

She giggled. "Your son is fine, Omifuku."

"When will you start going to the market again?"

"I have started. I have weaned Hakim."

She could never pronounce Joachim.

"You are ready for another belly," he teased.

She giggled again. "Omifuku! Baba bomboi!"

He smiled. Modupe had that effect on him with her blithe ways.

Joachim. He recalled the naming of his son. Modupe had insisted that the ceremony take place in his house. *That is how people will know you are the father.*

At dawn, seven days after the birth, a parade of women in veils and burqas and men clad in flowing gowns of the rainbow colours had waddled into his house. Moomie and Alhaja were there, as were so many aunts and sorority members and bead-wielding imams. Arabian scent mingled with musty smells. Murmurings of Masha Allah and Bismillah were expressed. And Allahu Akbar. God be praised, it had not lasted too long. His apprentices had attended as witnesses to spread the news: Zona now boasted a son. He had invited a few Lagos-based kinsmen. Through them, Opaku would also hear. His bloodline was secure.

What names do you give your son? the declining Imam had asked, displaying orange-tinged teeth.

Joachim Odumegwu Ikenna Ezenwa Okonkwo. It was a mouthful for the fellow.

Kini?

He had repeated the boy's names seven times: Joachim Odumegwu Ikenna Ezenwa Okonkwo.

So shall it be, the Imam had quickly acquiesced, unable to attempt the tongue-twisting names. And he had watched as the baby's lips were dabbed in turns with salt, honey, and palm oil. *May your life be sweet and tasty.*

Amin.

King Sunny Ade had entertained at the all-night ceremony that followed at the Simpson family house.

Ezenwa was apt; he was the prime child, the exalted.

Zona swung into the hospital gates.

He parked and hurried into the lobby. It occurred to him that he should have bought a hot meal for the patient. He thought of heading out again but sensed that she may have been discharged. He had been gone for over four hours. At the desk, he met a stalk of a guy in a white lab coat and slumber cap, a Jack Ma lookalike.

"Mr. Okonkwo?"

"Chief Okonkwo."

"Please take a seat."

The white coat led him to a bench. He placed a hand on Zona's shoulder.

"So sorry."

Zona sprang up.

"We lost the baby. We tried our best."

"Baby?"

"Stillbirth. I'm so sorry."

Zona stared dumbly at the fellow. Baby?

The doctor exhaled loudly. "We tried our best. Please come back tomorrow. The patient is under sedation."

The medico's pager beeped. He patted Zona tenderly again and marched out of sight, blabbering into the gadget.

Baby? Amata?

He stood up, his legs like those of a child standing for the first time. He lurched forward and tottered. He sat back down. The weight of the cap pressed on his head. He removed it and wiped his face with it. He clenched and unclenched his bladder. Baby? Amata? After what seemed like an hour, he rose again and, with a tightened groin, sauntered to the Gents.

EPILOGUE

The head of the Umunna was on his feet. News had reached them that Amata, late Jasper's wife, had given birth to a stillborn in Lagos. For whom? they asked. She denied it and said it was a mistaken identity. The elders did not know whom to believe. Zona maintained what the doctor had told him. Did you see the baby? No.

Not me, Amata swore. Okonkwo is a popular Igbo name. True.

The elders put their heads together. *The same woman who rejected her husband's brothers is entertaining an outsider? We cannot be docile while a goat eats palm fronds off our heads. Our custom demands that we let her go.*

"No. We cannot let her go," a voice of reason intervened. "She is raising two Opaku sons. Let us call her again, one last time and ask her to choose who will cover her from her husband's clan. If she spurns us a third time, we let her return to her family. When Jasper's sons reach adulthood, they will seek out their paternity. But to bear the illustrious Okonkwo name and be opening her legs to outsiders? No."

They summoned Amata again.

The next weekend, the widow arrived at Opaku with Louisa in tow. Odoziaku took custody of her grandchildren.

The elders gathered under the shade of the mango and bread-fruit trees. The sky was overcast, but the clouds were swimming away frantically. Amata walked in and recollected briefly at the rectangular patch. It was time to build a slab over his grave. If not, rushes would sprout like they had on Agbisi's tomb.

She went to pay her respects to Iyom. Jasper's mother had withered. She sat in her bed, looking scrawny, rubbing her kneecaps, sorrowing for her son.

"Amata, my child." Her voice, barely audible, quaked.

"Nne o."

They held each other and shed silent tears. Behind Iyom, Amata saw one of Agbisi's old Singer foot sewing machines. It wedged her dowry of cooker and freezer. A patchwork of spiderwebs crisscrossed them. They were still gathering dust, yet to be opened. Anyone she chose today would inherit it all. She unpacked gifts for the old woman: a small pharmacy of blood tonic, vitamins, and painkillers.

"You were a good wife to my son," the older woman said in a whisper. "I am happy he had you, though for too short. Many envied him because of you."

"He was good to me, Nne. Jasper was a good husband."

"I know. We cannot question why God gives power to the devil. Look after his sons. And bring them once in a while to soothe me. When I see them, I see Jasper."

"You have no problem there, Nne."

"He was the stick I leaned on, my shade from life's darts. That I ate or had clothes on my back was Jasper." She patted the cloth around her waist. "This Star wrapper was from him. Without him, my life is like food without salt." A tear dropped, and her voice quivered.

"It is all right, Nne. Firm your heart." She clasped Iyom's shoulder.

Iyom dislodged the snivel from her nose with the ends of her cloth. She seized the opportunity to wipe the tears from her eyes. She drew her daughter-in-law closer and cleared her throat.

"Amata, I know why our husbands have summoned you again. This is the third and final time they will seek Ikwuchi for you. It is our custom. I did not opt for it in my time because Agbisi widowed me late in life. But you are young."

Her voice descended another notch. "I will not tell you whom to choose, but remember that it was because of Rapu that Jasper lost his life. I do not know what basket he wove on his apprentice and fled. When Stanley died, his people avenged him. Jasper was the scapegoat. The same Rapu fought with your late husband here in this yard."

She massaged her shoulder blade in remembrance of the episode. Amata stared ahead. A column of *agbisi* ants was marching from a crack in the wall to the window ledge.

"The punch he threw at Jasper when I tried to mediate landed here. As for Echezona, he is my first son. An abysmal first son, if I am to say. I am not proud of how he handled family issues. If he had gone to Stanley's people to pacify them when he was home, as I begged, Jasper would not have needed to return and fallen into the trap they set. I begged Echezona, 'Go and meet the police chief. You know him. Go and meet him and bail your brother out.' He did not. Zona has always been greedy, to the extent of taking over the double plot that belonged to Agbisi's sons. He has a hotel on it now. A first son must have consideration for his siblings. Zona wanted to be the only cock crowing in this yard. That is all I have to tell you."

"Daalu, Nne."

"It was the wrong son that died," the old woman concluded. "Let it be. We cannot question God."

"Amata!" Louisa's voice was frantic.

"Over here."

"You are stayed for," Luz quoted from *Hamlet*.

Amata rolled her eyes. "Let me ease myself, and I will be with them."

The afternoon was aging fast. *KroKroKro,* the crow cried overhead. Amata went behind the barn. A mound of dry leaves and sundry garbage was burning there. It emitted an acrid smell. She bunched up her long skirt and spread her legs, all the while ruminating on Nne's words. There was an aspect she did not understand. The bride price that Jasper paid, what would happen to it? Would Onwa return it? As she turned to join the meeting of the kinsmen, she met one of them going behind the house, unclasping his belt.

"My wife," he greeted.

That raspy voice was familiar.

"I have something to whisper to you," he added.

She tarried.

Smoker, she thought. Who among her husbands smoked? When he emerged from the farm, he introduced himself.

"You town people never remember village folk, do you?" He stamped vestiges of piss off his feet. "Nwagbo. Paul Nwagbo. Charity brought you to my—"

"Paulinco!"

"Himself. Paul International."

They entwined in a loose embrace. He lowered his voice.

"Listen to what I am about to say. Not many people are aware of it. Agbisi, your father-in-law, fathered Akwaeke's children."

Amata made to walk. "I know. Jasper told me."

"No, he could not have told you because he did not know. Our kinsman, Jonas, was shooting blanks. You understand?" He patted his groin. "He arranged for Agbisi to father children with his wife. All the children borne by Akwaeke—all three—were fathered by Agbisi. That is why, when Jonas joined our ancestors, his widow did not think twice about choosing Agbisi to cover her. Because they were already sitting by the fire when the harmattan winds blew. You understand?"

She nodded.

"What the Umunna is asking you to do is not new. Ask your father. You have the same custom in Nkwa."

"What of the bride price that Jasper paid?" the widow asked. "Will Nkwa return it?"

"It was not only Ochinanwata that paid your bride price," Paul explained. He spat out a blob of phlegm and used the end of his shirt to dab at his lips. "One person does not pay the bride price. All the kinsmen contribute to it. A wife belongs to the kinsmen, not only to her husband. So when you choose another kinsman, the need for another bride price will not arise."

Amata nodded. The matter was clear to her now. She thanked Paul.

"Mummy, they are calling you." It was her erstwhile apprentice, now Managing Director, Ebuka Motor Parts Company.

"On my way." She turned towards the assembly. "One final thing, Paul. How did Akwaeke die?"

In all the family gossip, she had not heard how the love affair ended. She knew that with time, Jasper would have told her. But time, they had not had. Paul looked like the community's memory.

"Echi eteka," he answered simply. He fished about in his pocket. "In her farm."

Echi eteka was the name of a venomous snake. It literally meant *Tomorrow is too far.* Its victims did not see the morrow.

"Agbisi died a short while after her." He tapped the Marlboro and extricated one stick. "He pined for her, wasted away." He placed the cigarette in his mouth. A lighter was in his palm. He lit the stick, sucked on it.

"Ama!" Louisa yelled. "You are keeping everyone waiting."

Louisa was standing with a guy who was looking up the tree, poking a fruit with a long pole. Half of his face was hidden behind a thicket of hair. His beard, sideburns, and moustache merged like Fidel Castro's.

Louisa said, "Come and meet Jideofor."

They shook hands. "You must be Jidenma's brother."

"*Gbam*. Kedu?"

"So-so."

"I'm sorry about Jasper Gee. He was a unicorn."

"Thank you. You people and facial hair. Jasper had a moustache like the handlebars of a bike. Your brother's own stands at attention like the bristles of a toothbrush. What shall we call your own?"

"Ikemba," he answered without hesitation. Those nearby laughed. It was a reference to the Biafran warlord.

"Amata!"

Jideofor joined his kinsmen. Zona and Rapu were already seated, as were many others. They came because this would be the final time the widow, Amata, would be asked to make a choice. They were each expectant, but if she spurned them again today, it would be over. She would figuratively return to Nkwa and continue her life. If and when another suitor came for her, Nkwa would return Opaku's bride price.

The oldest man in the clan rose. His crown was all salt, the part not covered by a red felt fez. He was tying a cloth that reached his ankles under a black ishiagu top. His kinsmen bade him sit, but he remained standing.

"Opaku, kwenu."

"Yaa."

"I want to stand to address our wife here." He fluttered his fingers at Amata and paused to nibble at the alligator pepper in his hand. It sharpened his vocal chords.

"Amata, our wife. A big thing happened to you. You lost your husband at a tender age. A big blow. But it was the way that Chukwu ordained it. You are not the first to suffer such a calamity. Neither will you be the last, though we do not pray for such. We have buried Ochinanwata. But he left two brothers behind that can cover you, provide for you. If you were widowed at a ripe age, beyond childbearing, we would let you be. But you are young. And made of flesh." He turned to his kinsmen. "Do I speak your mind?"

"Ishienyi!"

"Your husband's people have mandated me to ask you to pack and go back to your father's house. There, you can entertain any man you fancy, far from the Okonkwo patrimony. We cannot have you bear our revered name and bring unknown blood into our family. No one can take the place of Ochinanwata, a worthy son of Opaku. But we cannot jettison our custom and behave like men without penis balls."

The audience nodded. "That is how it is," they said, in kola nut-stained teeth and gums.

"Ishienyi aba n'ite," Nwagbo hailed him in full. Elephant's head cannot fit in a pot.

"That is why we ask you again and for the last time: Out of your kinsmen, who do you choose to cover you?"

All eyes were on Amata. Would she choose someone this time? Or would she remain obstinate?

There was no escape, Amata knew. With the banker, she had dropped the ball. In her bereavement, her menses had ceased again, had blindsided her. She had carried the pregnancy to full term without any inkling of her condition. She had confided in the midwife, who had asked why she came to the labour room without a baby bag and why she had not attended their antenatal clinic.

I am as stupefied as you are. Believe me. I had no idea.

When Amata delivered the baby, and it was a stillbirth, she did not know if to be sad or happy that what would have been a shame to her and her family had been averted. She made up her mind not to allow another man close to her until she was ready to remarry.

However, she missed the male muscle. That night, the last night with Jasper, had been the best. He had been more concerned for her pleasure. And then he had vanished. She suspected that an enemy had done him in, probably Stanley's people, to avenge Stanley's death. They must have waylaid him on the way and handed him over to the dreaded SARS. Jasper languished in the detention centre, no, concentration camp, for months without a way to contact his people.

Iyom's pleas to Zona to meet with the Commissioner of Police and bail out his brother had fallen on deaf ears. *I'm on it, I'm on it,* Zona harped on. Until it was too late. Until Jasper had succumbed to the tortures and deprivations the camp was known for. By the time Opaku knew his whereabouts, it was in the notorious Awkuzu River that they found his remains. Jidenma recognized the polo T-shirt with yellow lightning spikes. The renowned Mbotu embalmers were floored. There was no lying-in-state. They had not let her see his corpse.

Someone handed her a mug of up-wine.

Amata returned from the past and its horrors. She sipped and gulped some.

Good sign, the women said. *Last time, she did not accept the drink.*

Now, to take it to the man of her choice.

The widow tried to speak. Every neck in the audience craned to hear her. She sniffed and cleared her throat.

"Take it to your choice," an elder said. "No need for words. Go!"

The women, standing outside the circumference of men, shone their eyes on the widow. Charity was shuddering like a car, her lastborn tied to her back. *Don't go to Zona, please God,* she prayed. Oby stood by her sister's side. *God, let her not choose Omeifeukwu.*

Amata cradled the goblet and rose, incandescent in the evening sun. The palm wine imbued her upper lip with a thin white moustache. She remembered the night of her marriage when Jasper had brought her back here—the dancing, the merry-making. She had felt uneasy, a premonition of evil lurking in the shadows. Today, she had no such feeling. The future looked sanguine. Overhead, on a twig, a winged soloist serenaded the ceremony.

She steadied her hands and walked gingerly through the seated crowd. She was careful not to spill the liquid billowing in the cup as she moved. She took another sip to reduce the spilling.

"Ha. Will she quaff it all and return the mug?" someone quipped.

Amata advanced.

The arc of her progress went by Zona. As the widow approached, he cranked up. His eyes came alive. He transferred his leather fan to the left hand, freeing the right for the trophy. Amata genuflected before him, ever so lightly, and continued. The collective arched their eyebrows and exchanged looks. Charity and Obiananma embraced.

Rapu's neighbour nudged him. *She bypassed Omeifeukwu. She is coming to you.* He straightened up. Otogirigiri has done it. He puffed his chest and sucked in his budding beer belly, ready to extend his arm and welcome the prize. Two steps from him, Amata swerved right. The gathering let out a loud oh.

Step by step, she progressed. Then doubts set in. What if he was not available? What if he had someone? Was not interested? What if he refused to accept the mug? What then? It had not occurred to her. She should have asked Nwagbo, *Can the chosen kinsman decline? Or was he obligated to accept?* She remembered asking Jasper when they discussed the matter, *Could Agbisi have refused when Akwaeke chose him?* And he had answered that Akwaeke was the village beauty; every man coveted her. If he accepts, I will relinquish the shop to him and dust up my wig and gown.

Amata swanned to the graduate, who hustled, knelt down, and raised the mug to him. Jidenma's eyes opened wide in surprise. He inclined, grabbed the chalice with two hands, tilted back and gulped down the drink. They both had the white moustache now. His still resembled the bristles of a toothbrush.

THE END

ACKNOWLEDGEMENTS

Coffee shops have, from time immemorial, provided a conducive environment for writers to craft their narratives. The tent poles of *Sons of the East* were pitched at the Starbucks Café, South Keys, Ottawa, Canada. Thank you, Starbucks.

I offer my sincere gratitude to the extraordinary people without whom this book would not have materialized at this time. First and foremost, my dear mother, Ogbuefi Maria Akabogu, who, at ninety-eight years old, remembered to inquire about the progress of "that book you're writing" and whose recollections of some Igbo customs, informed parts of this story. Mama, you are the *sine qua non.*

The University of Alberta, Edmonton, as your 2021-2022 Writer-in-Residence, I had ample time and resources to flesh out this story. A special thanks to the team at the Department of English and Film Studies for going over and above the call of duty and making me feel at home: Cecily Devereux, Mike O'Driscoll, Christine Wiesenthal, Marilyn Dumont, Uche & Chioma Umezurike, Christine Stewart, Dianne Johnson and Jumoke Verissimo.

My sincere gratitude to Bibi Ukonu at Griots Lounge Publishing. 'Tayo Keyede, I am indebted to you for serving as the third eye and for knowing viscerally what this writer wishes to say. Thank you, Peter Midgley, for the excellent eye when you edited the early draft of this story. Fred Martins, for the cover design, thank you. I doff my hat to May Akabogu for incisive comments and for graciously sharing her literary resources.

I appreciate my amazing fellow writers, who provided priceless critique and moral support: Unoma Azuah, Chinyere Obi-Obasi, Sir Victor Anoliefo, Odafe Atogun, Abubakar Adam Ibrahim, Nduka Otiono, Khainga O'Okwemba. To my book club members, Nnenna Okoronkwo, Salamatu Sule and Wemimo Azeez, infinite thanks.

My gratitude extends to my loving family, Nesochi Chinwuba and Arinze Okai, for countless hours of unrequited personal assistant work. Afy Chinwuba, Zulu Okai and Zik Okoye, your inspiration was indispensable. Sam Chinwuba, your experience as an attorney to our Igbo moguls in the import-export business enriched this narrative. Daalu.

To Chiefs Angus Nwoye (Nwachinemelu), Felix Maduka (Anyanba), Tim Ikedue (Okemiri) and Ben Ojinime, Igbo tycoons in Abidjan, and their devoted 'Lolos', who provided insights into the business world, merci beaucoup.

To my readers, thank you for keeping the faith.